WALKABOUT

The triumphant novel of love and adventure on the harsh Australian frontier, and the men and women who battled natural disasters and human betrayal to make their dreams come true...

Alexandra Kerrick: She and her husband had conquered the mighty Outback with courage and perserverance. But their legacy meant nothing when the heir to the riches of Tibooburra Station vanished.

Jeremy: Deserted by his mother, denied by his father, he grew to manhood searching the vast frontier for a reason to live—and discovered that he had left it behind.

Jarboe Charlie: The Aborigine tracker taught Jeremy to forge his future from the savage land, but not even he could prepare the youth for the dangers of society.

Fiona: Beautiful but penniless, she wanted nothing more from life than the passionate fulfillment she found in Jeremy's arms.

Aldous Creevey: Twisted with hatred, he vowed to destroy the Kerricks and all they held dear by revealing a secret that had long lain buried in the untamed wilderness.

Other *Leisure* books by Aaron Fletcher:
OUTBACK
OUTBACK STATION
WALLABY TRACK
OUTBACK LEGACY

WALK ABOUT

AARON FLETCHER

LEISURE BOOKS ▐ NEW YORK CITY

A LEISURE BOOK®

August 2000

Published by

Dorchester Publishing Co., Inc.
276 Fifth Avenue
New York, NY 10001

Cover Art by Pino

ISBN 0-8439-4755-1

Printed in the United States of America.

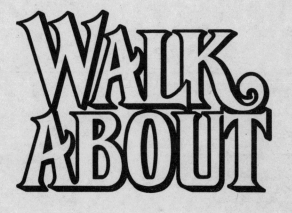

PART I

PART I

Chapter One

"Jeremy, come here, please."

Gripped by fear, the boy ignored his mother's voice. He sat on a limb in an ironbark tree in his back garden, his refuge in times of distress. The events which had unfolded over the past weeks seemed to be drawing to a conclusion; something dreadful was about to happen.

No one had told him the reasons for what had happened, and he had avoided asking. He had tried to disregard what was taking place, merely wanting his secure, orderly world to remain unchanged. But that morning, his mother had kept him home from school, and she had put out his Sunday clothes for him to wear.

"Jeremy, I know you can hear me," Clara Tavish called. "Now come here, my dear."

Reluctantly, the boy climbed down from the tree and stepped toward his mother in the kitchen doorway. Among the things that had happened, the one that had troubled him most was how she had changed until only her loving smile was the same as always. Doctor Oliver

Willis had come to the house with increasing frequency to see her, but she had still become ever more pallid and thin, her eyes often red from crying.

They were once again red from crying as she bent over him, brushing bits of tree bark off his clothes. "Promise me that you'll be a staunch little man, my love," she said softly.

That was what she always said when he had to keep from crying, and it made his fear swell within him. Steeling himself against some unknown ordeal, Jeremy managed a nod in reply. Then his mother took his hand and led him through the house toward the parlor.

Their footsteps echoed hollowly in the house, the furnishings having been taken away. The boy's half-brother and two half-sisters—all much older than he—had moved out and taken some things, then people had bought other items. He had begun running home from school each day, fearing that nothing would be left of his home when he got there.

In the parlor was a middle-aged couple whose expensive clothing marked them as having position and wealth. Jeremy knew the woman, who had visited twice before that he could recall, and brought him toys and sweets. Her white hair seemed out of place, because her attractive face had no hint of wrinkles. She had been very affectionate toward him when she had visited before, and she smiled now as he stepped into the room.

The man with her was a stranger to Jeremy. His white hair was matched by wrinkles and other signs of middle age, but he had the bearing of a youthfully vigorous man. He was tall and muscular, with strong, rugged features that relaxed in a smile as he gazed at Jeremy.

"Jeremy," Clara said, "I'm sure you remember your grandmother, Mistress Alexandra Kerrick. As I've told you, she and her husband live far away in the outback, and he came to Sydney with her this time. He is Mr. David Kerrick, your grandfather."

The boy bowed, muttering a greeting. The relationships his mother had mentioned meant nothing to him, because his only bonds of kinship and love were with her, and to a lesser degree with his half-brother and half-sisters. He knew he was different. In the schoolyard, boys had pointed it out bluntly by calling him a bastard.

Alexandra stepped closer to Jeremy, bending over him. The tulle trim on her wide hat brushed his head as she hugged and kissed him, and the scent of her perfume stirred his vague recollections of the several times she had visited when he had been too young to remember clearly. "It's always such a joy to see you, my dear," she told him. "And each time I do, I'm astonished by how you've grown." She turned to her husband. "Jeremy's very large and husky for his eight years, isn't he, David?"

"Indeed he is," the man agreed. "He's a fine, handsome lad."

Jeremy tried to smile, but he was uneasy about them and wondered why they were there. Then, as he noticed what was beside the front door, his fear exploded into panic. He wanted to run to the ironbark tree in the garden and climb to the top of it, but he was unable to move. A bundle containing his clothes and other things was beside the door. Like the furnishings, he was being taken away. His mother was giving him to the man and woman.

Alexandra saw his reaction, her eyes conveying sympathy as she touched his face gently. Then she turned to his mother. "Clara, I know your torment must be more than any mortal should have to bear," she said. "I earnestly wish that I had some way to lighten that burden."

"You have, Mistress Kerrick," Clara assured her. "My other children aren't situated to see to Jeremy, and I intended to write to you about him. This has worked out much better than I had hoped."

"David and I thought we were coming to Sydney on business, but I realize now that God's hand was guiding us. I would have come post haste in any event, if you had written. Attending to Jeremy will be a pleasure, not a duty. Isn't there anything else we can do?"

"No, my only concern is my children, and now their future is bright. As you know, Sir Morton established my other children in good positions, and now Jeremy will have all the advantages you can give him. I haven't tried to explain it to the boy, which has been weak of me."

"No, it wasn't weakness, Clara. You've shown great courage in this situation. At the appropriate time, I'll explain everything to Jeremy. As for what Morton did, it was the minimum fulfillment of an obligation."

"Many wouldn't have done it, though, Mistress Kerrick. My mind is at peace about Benjamin, Agnes, and Daphne, and I'm most grateful to Sir Morton. Well, I see no need to delay...."

Her voice faded, ending the conversation, and Alexandra turned to her husband with a nod toward the bundle beside the door. The tall man stepped to the door and beckoned to someone waiting outside. A moment later, a coachman came in for the bundle and carried it out.

As Jeremy turned to his mother to beg her to keep him, she bent over him and took him in her arms. "Please don't give me away, Mother," he pleaded. "Please keep me with you."

"I can't keep you with me, my love," she whispered brokenly, squeezing him tightly and kissing him. "In time, you'll understand why."

"Please, Mother..."

"I can't, my love, I can't," she told him, her voice breaking with a sob. "Remember that you promised to be a staunch little man, so you mustn't cry. Be a good boy, and obey your grandparents."

Her tears were damp against his face as she kissed him again. He tried to cling to her when she released him, but she took his arms from around her neck, kissing his hands. Then David Kerrick effortlessly lifted the boy on one arm and stepped toward the door with him.

Jeremy looked over the man's shoulder, reaching out toward his mother in a silent gesture of despair. She and Alexandra hugged each other, both of them weeping, then the boy had his last glimpse of his mother as he was carried outside. Alexandra came out, her footsteps uncertain as she wiped at her eyes with her handkerchief, and the door closed behind her.

A carriage waited at the end of the path. Taking his wife's arm with his free hand, David guided her down the path and helped her into the vehicle. He stepped inside and sat on the seat across from her, placing Jeremy beside him; then the carriage moved away from the house and down the street. Jeremy was stunned, too bewildered to cry. What was happening seemed unreal to him, a nightmare from which he would presently awaken.

Alexandra controlled her weeping, drying her tears with her handkerchief. She and her husband sadly discussed the situation in terms that Jeremy was unable to understand, but it seemed to him that matters would have been perfect if they had merely been left as they were before. David turned to Jeremy, patting his shoulder gently with a large brown hand.

"We know you're frightened and confused, lad," he said, "and it would be strange if you weren't. But within a short time, you'll be very happy. I know that you'll like living at Tibooburra Station."

The boy nodded and mumbled a reply to be polite, but he silently disagreed with what the man had said. David turned back to Alexandra, talking with her about plans to return to the station within a few days. Tears formed in Jeremy's eyes, and he blinked them away, remembering his promise to his mother not to cry. But it was difficult for him to keep the tears at bay with the turmoil of despair churning within him.

As the carriage turned a corner, Jeremy looked out and saw that they had left Wynyard, the district of neat, modest homes where he had always lived. Through gaps between trees and buildings, he glimpsed Sydney Cove and its forest of masts. The carriage went down Hunter Street and through the center of the city, moving slowly in the heavy traffic. The foot pavements were crowded with recent arrivals who were on their way to the gold fields, carrying packs with shovels and picks tied to them.

The carriage turned onto Macquarie Street, making its way to the Wooloo district of the city. It was a fashionable area of large, luxurious mansions that overlooked Hyde Park and the Royal Botanic Gardens that were set back from the shoreline at Farm Cove. Jeremy realized that the carriage was going to the house that belonged to his father, another term of relationship that meant nothing to him. While he had been in the city one day with Agnes and Daphne, they had pointed out Sir Morton Kerrick to him.

After that, he had glimpsed the man every few months, always at a distance—except for one time. On that occasion, he had been on an errand for his mother near the center of the city and had seen his father coming down the street. He had stopped and smiled in greeting, wondering if his father would come to a cricket game at the school, like other fathers. The man had brushed past, either not noticing him or not knowing who he was.

The bustle and odors of the city were left behind as the carriage moved down a broad, quiet avenue flanked by stone walls and shaded by the lacy foliage of towering pepper trees. Turning in at a gate, the carriage went up a drive through landscaped grounds toward an imposing, three-story Victorian house that bristled with gables, turrets, and gingerbread trim. At the front of the house, the drive led into a circular courtyard.

As the carriage stopped, a stern, heavyset woman came out of the house and down the steps, her dark, severely plain dress and the keys on her belt identifying her as a housekeeper. A maid who followed her took the bundle of clothes as David and Alexandra exchanged a few words. Then David stepped back into the carriage, which moved away again as Alexandra took Jeremy's hand and led him up the steps behind the housekeeper and maid.

Inside the tall double doors was a broad, lofty entrance with a gleaming hardwood floor and an ornate staircase at one side. As she led the way toward the stairs, the housekeeper commented that a guest room had been prepared. "I'm very pleased that you thought to have that done, Mistress Roe," Alexandra replied. "Is Mistress Deirdre in?"

"Yes, madam. She returned a short time ago, and she's in her room."

"Ask her to come to Master Jeremy's room, if you would. I'd like her to stay with him until dinnertime."

"Very well, madam."

The elegant, luxurious surroundings and the servants with their formal manner were very strange to Jeremy, making him ill at ease. However, he felt less uncomfortable upon hearing that Deirdre was there. Deirdre was a photographist, greatly admired by his mother and half-sisters. For as long as he could remember, she had been a frequent visitor at his house and had always brought toys and sweets for him.

The housekeeper led the way into an upstairs room that appeared half the size of his whole house to Jeremy. The furniture in the spacious, airy room had the dark, satiny gleam of highly polished walnut. The maid and housekeeper put his things into drawers and then went back out, and a few minutes later, Deirdre came into the room.

Tall and slender, she was in her mid-twenties and resembled her mother, with brown hair and deep blue eyes. In grand Victorian style, she wore a dress made of lavender brocade, with patterns of lace on the bodice, cuffs, and high collar. She smiled radiantly, her eyes sparkling. "Jeremy, dear!" she exclaimed in pleasure. "I've been looking forward to seeing you."

"G'day, Aunt Deirdre," he replied, her affectionate, exuberant manner drawing a wan smile from him, despite his feelings.

She put her arms around him, hugging and kissing him. "I know you're very sad now," she told him. "But the worst of it will pass within a few days, and then presently you'll be much happier."

"Yes, mo'm," Jeremy muttered, not wanting to contradict her.

"Deirdre," Alexandra said, "if you'll stay with Jeremy,

I'd like to attend to some errands. He shouldn't be by himself until he becomes more accustomed to his new situation."

"No, he shouldn't," Deirdre agreed. "I'll be more than glad to stay with him, Mother." She turned to Jeremy, pointing toward an occasional table and chairs under a window. "Sit down there, Jeremy. I'll get some things from my room that I think you'll find interesting."

The two women left the room as Jeremy went to the table and sat down. From what they said, everyone evidently believed he would eventually adjust to the upheaval in his life, but he felt that his turmoil was too great to ever overcome. It all seemed so unnecessary to him. He could have simply stayed with his mother, even if most of the furniture was gone. Tears filled his eyes as he gazed forlornly out the window, and he wiped them away, remembering his promise to his mother.

Deirdre came back in, carrying a box with several smaller ones stacked on it. When she opened the large box, Jeremy saw that it contained a stereoscope, a device for viewing slides, and sets of slides were in the smaller boxes. One of his half-sisters had a stereoscope and a few slides, and on occasion, she had let him look at them.

"These slides were made from pictures that I took," Deirdre explained, opening the boxes. "I take the pictures on glass plates, then send them to a company in London. They make slides from the plates and sell them, and I get part of the money. Here, look at this set first."

In his sorrowful yearning to be back with his mother, Jeremy had no interest in the stereoscope, but he obediently took it and began placing the slides in it. The first set consisted of scenes of Aborigines in various poses and activities around low bark dwellings. As he peered at each of the slides, Deirdre told him about her journey to the Darling River far to the west of Sydney to photograph the people.

The next set was more scenes of Aborigines, then there were several sets that were views of camps in the gold fields. They showed men panning for gold, cooking in front of their tents, and grinning triumphantly as they displayed nuggets. After that, there were pictures of sheep stations, farms, vineyards, and various cities in Australia. Deirdre talked about each of the places, relating incidents that had occurred there.

The boy listened absently and looked at the slides, his grief dominating his thoughts. At the very center of the day's shattering events was a fact that seemed impossible. It was inconceivable to him that his mother would give him away—yet she had, and he was unable to think of any explanation for why she would do something so strange and cruel to him.

The hours dragged past, and when the light began fading, Deirdre lit the oil lamp on the table with a friction match. A short time later, there was a knock on the door, and a maid stepped in. "Dinner will be served shortly, Mistress Deirdre," she announced, bobbing in a curtsy. "Madam wishes for Master Jeremy to dine with the family instead of having a children's table in the kitchen anteroom."

Deirdre thanked the maid, putting slides back into the boxes. After she stacked them, Jeremy followed her out and down the hall as she returned them to her room. Stepping back out into the hall, she straightened Jeremy's collar and coat, then took his hand and led him to the staircase. As they went downstairs, Jeremy saw that his grandparents and father were coming out of the front parlor and crossing the entry to the dining room.

In his mid-thirties, Morton Kerrick was of average stature and inclined to be portly. He was bookish-looking, with sallow features from rarely being outdoors. His most distinctive characteristic was the unusual pale shade of blue of his eyes, the same color as Jeremy's.

Alexandra and David smiled at Jeremy, but Morton continued toward the dining room until his mother spoke to him with a note of impatience in her voice: "Morton, don't you intend to greet your son?"

"Yes, of course," he replied, appearing unsure of what to say. His pale blue eyes seemed very cold and aloof as he turned to Jeremy. "Well, are you getting settled in satisfactorily, then?" he asked.

"Yes, sir," the boy responded automatically.

Morton nodded, pursing his lips. "I'm pleased to hear it." He pondered what else to say, then: "Naturally, you have my sympathy over what has happened. I might add that I'm favorably impressed because you're not sniveling about it. It does no good to whine, does it? What? Eh?"

"No, sir," Jeremy replied timidly as Morton prompted him, the man's meaning unclear and his attitude disconcerting.

"That's quite right. Your mother wisely decided that her—"

"Morton," Alexandra interrupted, "I haven't discussed the facts with Jeremy. And do bear in mind that he's eight years old. Your manner is more fitting for conversation with an adult, and a stranger at that."

"I know how old he is," Morton replied, turning to her. "But I'm not what one would call experienced in dealing with children."

"That much is clear," Alexandra remarked, and pointed to the dining room. "Let's dismiss it and go have dinner, shall we?"

Morton shrugged and nodded, stepping toward the room. Alexandra and David smiled at Jeremy, and Deirdre patted his shoulder affectionately as they followed Morton. The boy felt even more ill at ease in the unfamiliar, luxurious surroundings because of his father's attitude toward him.

In the dining room, the table was large enough to seat scores, making the five places set at one end of it seem almost lost on its gleaming expanse. Morton sat at the head, his mother and father to his right. Jeremy sat next to Deirdre on the other side of the table, surveying the lavish array of costly silver, china, and crystal with awe and confusion.

Deirdre unobtrusively showed Jeremy which utensils to use as the maid served the various courses of the meal, but he had no appetite. He was also fearful of breaking one of the expensive dishes, or of turning something over on the shiny table. Longing to be back with his mother at the small, simple table in their home, he barely tasted the soup, then the salad, and then the fish course. Morton ate with gusto that revealed the reason for his portliness as he and the others talked about various subjects.

The discussion meant nothing to Jeremy, but he listened absently as he waited for the meal to be finished. At first, the conversation concerned a sheep station adjacent to the one owned by his grandparents. They referred to it as Wayamba Station, and the owners were a family named Garrity. Silver ore had been found on the border of the station at a place called Broken Hill.

"If Pat Garrity were still alive," David mused, "there might have been bloodshed at Broken Hill. He had a special fondness for that place. As it is, there's been trouble enough. Elizabeth Garrity had her stockmen build a fence to close off Broken Hill from the station."

"I don't understand why," Morton commented. "The mine at Broken Hill is being developed by a consortium. There aren't crowds of prospectors fossicking about, as there are at other places."

"Elizabeth simply doesn't want them to set foot on Wayamba Station," Alexandra explained. "She prefers isolation and has an extreme dislike for the inroads of civilization into the outback."

"I've never understood how Colin's wife came to be in charge at Wayamba Station," Morton said. "I would have thought that either he or his sister Sheila would take over the station when their father died."

"It's a matter of disposition," David replied. "Neither Colin nor Sheila has the qualities it takes to manage a station, and they would be the first to acknowledge that. Elizabeth does, which Pat Garrity recognized. He saw to it that she learned what she needed to know when the time came for her to take charge, and I must say that she runs things superbly."

The discussion continued as the maid brought in a rib

roast on a platter, then it turned to other things over the main course, all of them as remote to Jeremy as the talk about the sheep station. Then the meal ended, bringing him a sense of relief. He felt as though he had successfully completed an ordeal, having broken or overturned nothing.

The family left the dining room, Deirdre going to the parlor with her brother and father, and Alexandra accompanied Jeremy to his room. With the crystal chandelier in the entry behind them, their shadows flowed ahead of them up the ornate staircase. As they reached the upstairs hall, Alexandra remarked that Jeremy had eaten very little at dinner.

"I beg pardon, mo'm," he replied automatically.

"No, no, there's no need to apologize," she told him quickly. "I simply don't want you to be hungry, my dear. You'll undoubtedly have a better appetite when you're more accustomed to your surroundings. I'll wait here in the hall while you get into bed, then I'll come to tuck you in."

The boy opened the tall, heavy door and entered the room. It was filled with dark shadows, the lamp on the table turned low. Completely unlike his small, comfortable room at home, it was vast, somber, and hostile. Jeremy found his nightshirt in a drawer, undressed, and put it on. Then he climbed into the bed, which was so huge he almost felt lost in it.

Alexandra tapped on the door and came in, crossing the room to the bed. Jeremy's nightshirt, a hand-me-down from Benjamin, was much too large for him. The opening at the collar left part of his shoulders and chest exposed, and he saw his grandmother look at the birthmark on his shoulder as she adjusted the covers. Her hand was warm and gentle on his face as she bent over to kiss him, but it was not his mother's hand. She picked up the lamp from the table and left. The room fell into darkness.

Along with the darkness, sorrow closed in on Jeremy. He felt completely bereft, separated from his mother and put into a strange, uncomfortable place. His father evidently disliked him, and while the others were kind, they were only acquaintances at best. He was unable to keep his promise to his mother any longer, and tears streamed down his cheeks as he sobbed bitterly, his torment of grief finally pouring out of him.

In addition to his anguish, he remained totally perplexed over why the upheaval had happened. For his mother to give him away to others clashed with everything that he knew and felt about her, but she had done just that. Then, as he thought about it, an explanation suddenly occurred to him. His tears ceased as he pondered.

On innumerable occasions, he had heard his mother express her earnest desire for her children to have good situations in life. Just before he had been taken away, his mother had commented about the advantages that the Kerricks could provide for him. She had apparently decided that she had done all she could for him, and she had turned to the Kerricks as his relatives to advance his fortunes in life.

His mother had made a mistake, and what he had to do in order to correct it was obvious. He had to convince her that staying with her would be best for him, even if they were penniless. That promised to be easy enough, because his mother had always been willing to give full consideration to his wishes.

As the solution to the problem unfolded in his mind, Jeremy's sorrow faded. He had no memory of becoming drowsy, but it was suddenly morning, and a maid was coming into the room. She wished him a cheery good morning, filled the pitcher on the washstand with hot water, and left. Jeremy climbed out of bed and stepped to the washstand, thinking about how to slip away from the house so he could go and talk with his mother.

Looking at the pitcher and bowl on the washstand, he hesitated. They appeared to be made of finer china than his mother's best dishes, which she had sold to someone a week or two before, and breaking one of them would be a disaster. The boy cautiously placed the bowl on the floor, then carefully lifted the pitcher off the washstand and poured the water into the bowl. Then he knelt beside the bowl, washing his face and hands.

His hands were still damp when he replaced the bowl on the washstand, and he almost dropped it. Gasping in consternation, he gripped it tightly and splashed water down the front of his nightshirt. He slid the bowl onto the washstand, sighing in relief, and used the hand towel to daub up drops of water he had spilled on the shiny floor.

As he finished dressing, there was a tap on the door and Alexandra came in. She smiled warmly, exchanging greetings with him, then he went out and downstairs with her. Hunger pangs stirred in his stomach, and when they reached the dining room, he saw that it was less formal and intimidating than the night before. The food was served in dishes on the buffet, and the others were filling plates and taking them to the table.

The silver serving dishes contained thick slices of cured ham, eggs, toasted rounds of bread, and sliced fruit dusted with sugar and cinnamon, a meal that would have been a rare treat at Jeremy's home. Alexandra filled a plate and cup for him, and put them at his place beside Deirdre's. The beverage was coffee, which had an unusual but pleasant taste, and the ham and eggs were delicious.

As he ate, he accidently got a spot of grease on the snowy napkin he had placed on his lap, copying Deirdre. He furtively folded it under, hoping no one would notice. The others talked about their plans for that morning, revealing a way in which he might be able to leave without being seen. Deirdre was going to the daguerreotype studio where she worked, David had business in the city, and Morton and Alexandra intended to visit a house that had been her home many years before. If he could stay at the house, Jeremy knew that he could simply leave when they were gone.

"I'm sure I'll be able to get free again this afternoon,"

Deirdre said. "There haven't been all that many customers of late, and Mr. Robinson is always very understanding about my absences to take trips and such. So it's agreed that we'll meet back here for tiffin?" The others nodded and commented in assent, and she turned to Jeremy. "Would you like to come to the studio with me? I believe you'd find it interesting."

"No, mo'm," he replied. "I beg pardon, but I'd rather stay here."

A momentary silence fell, Deirdre looking across the table at her mother for guidance. Alexandra shook her head, smiling regretfully. "I think it would be much better for you to have company for the present, my dear," she told him gently. "And what would you do here all by yourself?"

"I'd look around in the stables, mo'm," Jeremy blurted, saying the first thing that came to mind.

David smiled at the boy affectionately, pleased by the remark. "Are you fond of horses, then, m'lad?" he asked.

"Yes, sir," Jeremy replied, grateful for the support that the excuse had drawn from his grandfather. "I like them very much, sir."

"Well, you'll see plenty of them at Tibooburra Station," David told him, then turned to Alexandra. "Love, I see nothing wrong with the lad's staying here and looking at the horses."

Silence fell again, and Alexandra looked at Jeremy. He realized that while his father's eyes were cold and keen, his grandmother's could be much more penetrating. Although they were tender and loving, they seemed to bore into him, searching for his thoughts. She studied him for a long moment, then reluctantly nodded. "Very well," she said. "Do be cautious around the stalls, my dear, because some of the horses are quite spirited."

"Yes, mo'm," Jeremy replied, suppressing his sigh of relief.

As the others filed out and went to get coats, hats, and gloves, Jeremy found his way through the house and out the back door. He went down the path to the courtyard in front of the stables, where a groom and coachman had just finished harnessing a team to a carriage. It moved down the drive toward the front of the house to take Morton and Alexandra away.

The groom and a stableboy led two horses hitched to buggies out of the stables, and a moment later, Deirdre and David came down the path from the house. They smiled at Jeremy, Deirdre repeating her mother's warning to be careful around the horses. Then they stepped into the buggies, and the small vehicles moved briskly down the drive. When they reached the street, Jeremy went back up the path to the house.

In the hallway, he met a maid who stopped and asked if he wanted anything. Jeremy shook his head, telling her that he was going to his room, and went on down the hall toward the stairs. When her footsteps faded behind him, he turned back to a side entrance that opened onto the drive. He quietly went out, then ran down the drive toward the street.

Once he was out of the sedate Wooloo district, Jeremy was merely one among the many on the crowded streets, and he relaxed somewhat. Eager to talk with his mother, he hurried through the congestion, dodging carriages and drays as he crossed streets. The traffic diminished as he approached the Wynyard district, then he finally reached his street. He ran down it, but when his house came into view, he slowed.

A year before, a neighbor had given him a kitten that had died. It had almost looked asleep, but there had been a subtle difference, some vital quality missing. His house looked like that now. Chilling fear replacing his excitement, Jeremy began running again.

His fear was confirmed as he dashed up the path and into the house. It was completely empty, not a piece of furniture or any other belongings left. The echoes of his voice seemed to mock him as he went through the bare rooms, calling for his mother. Perplexed and dismayed, Jeremy stepped out the kitchen door and into the back garden.

At the adjacent house, he saw the woman hanging up laundry, and he crossed the garden toward the fence. "Mistress Griffin!" he called. "Do you know where my mother is?"

The woman turned, surprised to see him, as well as at his question. "Why, don't you know, Jeremy?" she replied. "Your mother is on her way back to Scotland, dear. Her ship left early this morning."

Jeremy was stunned at first, so shocked by what the woman had said that he could only gaze at her numbly. Then he thought about what she had told him, together with related facts, and drew a conclusion that was more than an upheaval. It shattered the very foundations of his life.

His mother had often reminisced longingly about Scotland, still missing her homeland after many years in Australia. He concluded that her yearning had become so intense during the past weeks that it had made her ill, and she had begun preparations to return to Scotland. Having Benjamin, Agnes, and Daphne move out of the house and into lodgings had been the first step. Then she had disposed of their belongings.

The last step had been to dispose of him, giving him to the Kerricks. Although she had known that he would be eagerly willing to go anywhere in order to stay with her, she had chosen to leave him behind. The one who had been the embodiment of love to him had abandoned him.

The pain of rejection was a searing agony, a rending wound in a vulnerable place where he had never needed defenses. He turned and ran, his torment fueling a compelling urge to flee and escape from what had happened. The woman called out to him, but he barely heard her. He ran back through the house, down the path, and then along the street.

Tears blurred the scene around him as he fled aimlessly from one street to another. Presently, he was on a crowded street, people shouting as he bumped into them, and drivers cursing as horses swerved away. He wiped his tears away so he could avoid others. His legs were weary and his lungs burned as he panted breathlessly, but he had to continue running.

Chapter Two

"I suppose the house looks smaller to you," Morton remarked. "I've been told that's how people usually feel when they return to places where they lived many years before."

A flood of memories that were made more intense by bittersweet nostalgia raced through Alexandra's mind as she glanced around inside the wide entry. Then she turned to Morton. "Provided they lived there as children, don't you think?" she countered. "And also left there as children. I was nineteen when I left here, and I've been back since then."

"How does it look to you, then?"

"Much the same as when my father owned it." Alexandra stepped to the parlor doorway and then to the dining room, looking at the furniture draped with dust covers. "I see that it's well-furnished."

"Yes, I keep furniture in all the properties that I let out on lease," Morton told her. "The extra rental I can obtain more than pays for the furnishings, and the properties lease more quickly."

Alexandra went down the hall and out the back door, Morton following her. She looked at the garden and recalled when she had planted flower beds there long before. Those flower beds had been replaced by others, but the garden looked very pleasant on the balmy autumn day in March of 1854.

As she and Morton stepped out into the garden, a stout, grizzled old man in workman's clothes came around the corner from the carriage drive. He lifted his cap, grinning cheerfully. "G'day, mo'm, Sir Morton," he said. "I was on my way to your house down the street, Sir Morton, and I saw your carriage here. If this lady is thinking about leasing this house, I might be able to answer some questions she might have."

"No, this is my mother," Morton replied. "Her father owned this house and her family lived here at one time, and she wanted to see it. Mother, this is Hodgkins, the caretaker for a number of my properties."

Alexandra exchanged greetings with the man, then asked him about his name. "Years ago, there was a man with the same name who worked as a gardener at the MacArthur estate, Camden Park. Are you related?"

"Aye, that was my older brother, Tom," the man told her. "My name's Sam Hodgkins. Tom passed away twenty-six years ago this past spring, and we laid him to rest in the churchyard at Parramatta. He lived at Camden Park, and I've lived here all of my life, but we visited back and forth. Your family used to live in this house, Mistress Kerrick?"

"Yes, the name was Hammond, and my father was an attorney. That was more years ago than it seems when looking back upon them. Time does slip away from one, doesn't it, Mr. Hodgkins?"

Sam smiled wryly as he emphatically agreed with her. Alexandra continued talking with him, discussing events of years before in Sydney. While conversing with older people in the city, she always wondered if they would recall the newspaper stories in September of 1821, when she had been kidnapped by bushrangers. If anyone could, she knew it would be this old man, who would have also learned of the incident by word of mouth. He would have been told about it by his brother, because Tom Hodgkins at Camden Park had been the last one she had seen before being kidnapped.

Like all the others, however, Sam revealed no sign of remembering anything about it. She was relieved, preferring her kidnapping to remain in the past, because her children knew nothing about it. But she was not surprised. Over the course of three decades, memories faded, and the incident had been relegated to forgotten pieces of paper buried in musty archives.

More than that, she was widely known as an owner of Tibooburra Station. To people at large, she was known only as that, and everything else associated with her was lost in the dominating reputation of the station. It and Wayamba Station were legendary, known throughout Australia as the giant stations that were the western anchor of civilization in New South Wales.

Sam mentioned the station, talking about a cousin of his who had been there. "Jake was a teamster until he died fifteen years ago," the old man continued. "He made one trip out there with a group of a dozen drays that delivered supplies and brought back wool, but he never went again. He said it was the far end of creation, and he didn't like the outback."

"Many people don't," Alexandra replied. "We've hired several stockmen who had to leave because they couldn't endure it. That isn't only due to the isolation, though. The outback is a different sort of land in ways that some find unsettling. We aren't as isolated as we once were, because our supplies are delivered and our wool clips are taken away by riverboat now. They come up the Darling River to Wilcannia, which is just across the river from the eastern border of Tibooburra and Wayamba stations."

The old man nodded, commenting that it was a distinct

change from when his cousin had gone there. He continued talking with Alexandra a few minutes longer, then started to make his farewells and leave. Morton asked him to stay, saying he wanted to talk with the old man. "There are several things I'd like done at the stables," Morton explained, pointing with his cane. "Let's walk back there, and I'll show you what they are." He turned to Alexandra. "Would you like to go with us, Mother?"

"No, I'll be in the house when you finish, Morton. It was a pleasure to meet you and talk with you, Mr. Hodgkins."

Sam replied courteously, lifting his cap, then he and Morton walked away toward the stables as Alexandra went back inside. She stepped down the hall toward the front of the house, looking in the rooms. Now that she was alone, her footsteps the only sound breaking the stillness in the house, her memories of when she had lived there decades before were more clear. But talking with Sam Hodgkins had also resurrected her bitterly painful recollections of the ordeal when she had been kidnapped.

A number of things always reminded her of the incident, particularly the places she had been taken as a prisoner of the bushrangers. One was on the road west of Parramatta, where it crossed the Nepean River. On the south side of the road was a dark, thick forest that had somehow remained untouched while the surrounding area had been turned into pastures and crop fields during the last thirty years. The bushrangers had left her tied in the trees there while they pillaged farms in the vicinity.

Over the years, however, her repugnant memories of that place had become mixed with pleasant associations. David had told her that when he had been a convict assigned to the compound at Parramatta, he had spent his Sundays camped in that forest, dreaming of establishing a sheep station in the outback. Morton's brother, Jonathan, had said that was where his wife, Catherine, had agreed to marry him. They had gone there with a lunch and a bottle of Camden Park wine, an outing that had changed their lives as well as Alexandra's. They and their three daughters lived at Tibooburra Station and were a constant source of joy for her.

Alexandra climbed the staircase and went into the room that had been hers. The furniture under the dust covers was entirely different from that of years before, but the room still seemed very familiar to her. She stepped to the window, which faced onto the back garden and stables.

At the stables, Morton was pointing with his cane as he talked to the caretaker. Alexandra reflected that he had apparently never wondered why he bore no resemblance at all to David and Jonathan. She was thankful for his lack of curiosity about it, because only she and David knew that Morton's natural father had been one of the bushrangers who had kidnapped her, a man named Enos Hinton. That had been the origin of Morton's pale blue eyes and a birthmark on his shoulder, characteristics he had passed on to Jeremy.

For years, she had feared that Morton would have Enos Hinton's criminal traits, because he had been a difficult child. That concern had faded in time, when she had realized that it was simply his personality. He was distant toward people and very slow to form relationships, because the one thing he feared most was trusting someone and then being betrayed. She had managed to win his full confidence and love as a boy, and that strong, close bond had remained between them through the years.

More recently, and particularly during this visit, she had become worried about him again. He had grown more peevish and self-centered than before, indicating that he was unhappy. It was affecting his health, because he was eating too much, vainly trying to feed some inner need. One reason she had asked him to bring her to the house was so she could talk with him in private to find out what was bothering him. When she saw the caretaker leave and Morton returning to the house, she went back downstairs.

Alexandra took the dust cover off a couch in the parlor, and a moment later, Morton came down the hall and into the room. "Let's sit and talk, Morton," she suggested. "We've some time to spare."

"Gladly," he replied. "I always enjoy our quiet chats, Mother."

As they sat down, Alexandra asked him about his business affairs, and he began telling her of the most recent developments. She knew that it was a measure of his absolute trust in her, because he had always been very secretive. His first criterion in hiring employees was loyalty rather than efficiency, and children of present or former employees were always hired before others.

Morton was one of the wealthiest men in the colony. In addition to being the sole owner of a gold mine on the Murray River, he was a principal shareholder in banks and a marine insurance firm. Finally, at the end of their long conversation, he mentioned that he had recently invested a substantial sum of money in a number of large cotton mills in England.

"I do wish they had been wool mills," Alexandra remarked jokingly. "We don't grow cotton at Tibooburra Station, you know." She reached over and took his hand, changing the subject. "Are you happy, Morton?"

At first he started to dismiss the question with a laugh, which was understandable. He possessed a title and great wealth, he was on good terms with officials from the governor down, and social invitations were a constant demand upon his time. Then he hesitated, looking out the window.

"I often feel that everything I do, I've done countless times before," he mused, searching for words. "There seems to be very little point in bothering with it." His voice faded, then he sighed and shrugged. "It's difficult to explain, Mother."

Alexandra felt relieved, identifying the problem as boredom and immediately knowing the solution. "Even so, I believe I understand, Morton," she told him. "For years, your father and I struggled to build up the station, and a few years ago, we bought the land between it and the Darling River. Once we've finished paying for that, it'll be done. It's like climbing a ladder, with nowhere to go after reaching the top rung."

Morton squeezed her hand affectionately, smiling in admiration. "That's it precisely, Mother. You're very wise, you know."

"No, if I were wise, I'd have avoided pitfalls that were very nearly my undoing. I'm merely experienced, Morton."

"Call it what you will, you've been my guiding light since I was a boy. It was through following your advice that I was knighted, and your counsel has brought me many other successes. You've felt this way, then?"

"No, because I have another ladder, one with an infinite number of rungs. I have my family, which includes you, my dear." She smiled, patting his hand. "You need the same, Morton—a family."

Morton pondered for a moment, then slowly nodded. "Yes, that's true, Mother," he agreed. "I've never given the matter any serious consideration, but I've always assumed that I would eventually have a family."

"You've never met a woman who has directed your thoughts into those channels," Alexandra told him, laughing, then she sobered. "But it would be a mistake to search for a wife, Morton. With your wealth and position, you would certainly find one, and probably the wrong one. You're still a young man, and you'll meet the right woman. For the present, content yourself in the knowledge that this feeling of purposelessness will pass."

"Yes, you're right, as usual," he said. "I already feel more content after talking with you." He took out his watch and opened it. "The others will return to the house soon, because it is almost time for tiffin. We can continue talking in the carriage."

They replaced the dust cover on the couch, then left the parlor and crossed the entry to the front door. Morton locked it behind them, and as they went down the steps to the carriage, Alexandra commented on how well the house had been maintained. "Yes, I don't allow my properties to fall into disrepair," Morton replied, helping her into the carriage. "Benjamin Tavish attends to that. In fact, he sees to everything connected with my real estate holdings and transactions. He's very efficient and dedicated."

"I'm extremely pleased that he's doing so well. While I was going about the city yesterday, I saw the dress and millinery shop that you financed for Agnes and Daphne. It seems to be a well-appointed shop and in a good location, and it should draw ample customers for them."

Morton agreed, expressing confidence that the shop would be successful. As the carriage moved down the street, Alexandra continued discussing the Tavish family with him. His association with them dated back many years, to when Clara Tavish, a widow in financial straits, had become his mistress in order to provide for her children. Alexandra had persuaded him to end the affair and to make arrangements that would support Clara and her children. However, after that had been done, Clara had discovered that she was pregnant, and Jeremy was the lasting result of the liaison.

Alexandra looked out the window, deeply depressed as she thought about Clara. "I daresay poor Clara is in desperately poor spirits just now," she remarked sadly. "She's had more than her share of misfortune."

"Yes, it's a terrible situation," Morton said gravely. "Other doctors agreed with Doctor Willis that the only treatment for cancer is laudanum to dull the pain while awaiting death. But I believe Clara made the best decision, given the circumstances. Her sister in Edinburgh will look after her until the end, and she always wanted to be buried among her ancestors. Most important to her, of course, is that her decision will save her children months of constant grief while watching her die by stages."

"Indeed, her first thought has always been her children. The journey will be dreadfully lonely for her, though."

WALKABOUT 35

"Undoubtedly, but it'll be as comfortable as possible. As I mentioned before, I had Benjamin make the bookings, with no expense spared. Everything that could be done has been done for her."

Alexandra sighed, looking out the window again. "I must explain the situation to Jeremy as soon as possible," she mused. "The poor tyke shouldn't be kept in the dark about all this confusion." She turned back to Morton. "Do try to unbend more toward him, my dear. I realize that you aren't accustomed to dealing with children, and the state of affairs is uncomfortable for for you. However, the lad probably thinks that you dislike him. We'll be leaving very shortly, and you mustn't part with him on those terms. He's your son, so do make an effort to be more congenial with him, Morton."

Nodding patiently, Morton replied that he would try. A few minutes later, the carriage drew up at the house, and the housekeeper met them as they went inside. She took Morton's hat and cane, telling him that the head clerk at his offices had sent some urgent papers for him to examine. "The apprentice who brought them is waiting in your study, Sir Morton," she added, then she turned to Alexandra: "Mr. Kerrick is at the stables, madam."

Morton stepped into his study, and Alexandra went down the hall through the house, presuming that David was with Jeremy. When she stepped out the back door, however, she saw that David was sitting alone on a bench in front of the stables. He stood up as she went down the path toward him.

Even when they had been apart only a short time, his warm, loving smile always conveyed keen pleasure at seeing her again. She smiled in response, then glanced around. "Where is Jeremy, David?"

"A maid told me that he's in his room," he replied.

"The boy shouldn't be alone," Alexandra told him, starting to turn away. "I'll go get him, and we'll keep him company for now."

"No, wait," David said. "I bought a cart pony for him. Let's wait until it's here before you fetch him out."

Alexandra smiled, keenly pleased. "That was very thoughtful of you, David. The poor lad needs something to raise his spirits, and that should do it if anything can. Where is the pony?"

"I took it to a saddlery to have a saddle and bridle fit to it. Ruel Blake stayed there while I went to attend to other things. He'll be here with it presently."

Alexandra nodded. Ruel Blake was one of the stockmen who had accompanied them from the station. "Has Deirdre returned yet?"

"No, but she should be back soon. Here, let's sit down, love."

"Jeremy has a birthmark, you know," she commented as they sat on the bench. "It's almost exactly like Morton's."

David turned, looking into her eyes. "You're not letting that old worry bother you again, are you, love?" he asked gently. "If Morton's nature isn't exactly what we'd prefer, that's simply the way he happened to turn out, and not because it came from any source. He's your son, and he's also my son. Everything else should be completely forgotten."

"No, I was only making a passing remark," she replied. "I put that worry to rest long ago. But I haven't forgotten what happened, because I'll be eternally grateful for how understanding you've always been."

"I'd expect you to be just as understanding if a cutpurse jumped out of an alley and hit me on the head with a club," David told her. "Being the victim of a criminal is a misfortune that can happen to anyone."

The subject was dropped, and they began talking about other things in their usual natural, easy flow of companionable conversation. Their love had become richly mellow over the years, but at the same time it retained a fresh, new quality. It gave each moment that Alexandra spent with David a special meaning to her, and made each day poignantly enjoyable.

They broke off talking and crossed the courtyard in front of the stables to meet Ruel Blake as he rode up the carriage drive, leading a dappled cart pony. Ruel was a barrel-chested, bearded man in his late forties, wearing rugged, durable stockman's garb. He dismounted, lifting his hat to Alexandra, and led the pony closer for her to look at it.

A moment later, Deirdre came up the drive in her buggy. She stepped out of it, asking about the pony, and exclaimed in pleasure when David told her that it was for Jeremy. "It's a beautiful pony, and I'm sure it'll cheer him up, ' she said. "Where is he?"

"In his room," Alexandra replied. "We've been waiting for the pony to arrive before we brought him out. Please go and get him, if you would."

Deirdre smiled in anticipation of the boy's reaction, walking up the path toward the house. Alexandra stroked the pony's muzzle and looked at it as David talked with Ruel. An employee at the station for many years, Ruel was one of the senior stockmen. He was in charge of the other stockmen and the jackaroos who had come on the trip to attend to the wagons and horses, and David talked with him about preparations to leave.

A woman shouted inside the house, an unusual intrusion upon the dignified quiet enforced in the household by the stern housekeeper. Then other voices rang out, maids calling Jeremy's name as they moved from room to room. Alexandra exchanged an alarmed glance with David, then they hurried up the path toward the house, Ruel following them.

Deirdre burst out of the back door, her face pale with concern. "He's not in his room, Mother!" she exclaimed anxiously. "Nor anywhere else in the house. A maid saw him and spoke with him, but that was hours ago."

Alexandra tried to convince herself that he had to be nearby, but she remembered his attitude at the breakfast table. He had been evasive, his eyes avoiding hers. It had made her uneasy then, and now the memory of it created an upswell of chilling apprehension within her. Morton stepped out the back door, asking what was wrong, and Deirdre explained.

He was unconcerned, seeing no reason for alarm. "The boy's merely wandered off," he commented. "I'm sure he'll return presently."

"Morton, I'm dreadfully worried," Alexandra said, interrupting David as he started to reply irately. "He undoubtedly went to the house in Wynyard, looking for his mother, and he must be terribly distraught now. We must look for him immediately. He is your son, Morton."

Morton hesitated, resentful over David's attitude, then nodded. "Very well, Mother. It's possible, I suppose, that the boy went to Benjamin or his sisters. Benjamin is at my offices, of course."

"Deirdre, you go there in your buggy," Alexandra said, turning to her. "If Benjamin hasn't seen Jeremy, go ask Agnes and Daphne about him. The rest of us will go to the house in Wynyard."

By the time Alexandra finished talking, Deirdre was running toward her buggy. Ruel followed Alexandra and David as they hurried toward the carriage in front of the stables, and the stockman ran to his horse. Morton stepped into the house for his hat and cane, then walked quickly down the path.

Deirdre's buggy charged down the drive, and the slower carriage began moving with its door hanging open as Morton ran the last few paces. He jumped in, slamming the door, and the coachman cracked his whip as the vehicle lurched forward.

When the heavy carriage swerved onto the pavement, the buggy was racing down the street far ahead of it. Alexandra saw the buggy turn off as Deirdre took a shortcut to Morton's offices. A few minutes later, the carriage slowed as it reached the business district and the heavy midday traffic.

Ruel rode ahead of the carriage, shouting to clear a path, but progress was still tediously slow, with drays, wagons, vendors' carts, and other vehicles clogging the streets. The traffic began thinning out as the center of the city was left behind, and the carriage moved at a faster pace.

When it finally reached the house, Alexandra threw the door open and jumped out before it stopped moving. She ran up the path and inside, the others following her. Searching the house took only a few minutes, and even though she had harbored little hope of finding Jeremy there, Alexandra was still deeply disappointed when they saw no sign of the boy.

She walked back down the path with the men, talking about what to do next. "The neighbors may know something helpful," she speculated, "but we'll probably end up having to search the city."

"Yes, that's true," David agreed. "We'll need more help to do that. Ruel, we'll ask about the boy around here, and you go get the other stockmen and the jackaroos. Get back here with them as fast as you can."

The stockman nodded and touched his hat, stepping quickly to his horse. As he rode away, Alexandra hurried toward the adjacent house up the street, as David went in the other direction, and Morton and the coachman crossed to the houses on the other side of the street. Alexandra ran up the path and knocked on the door, and a woman wearing a broadcloth housedress and mobcap opened it.

The woman recognized Alexandra from her visits with the Tavish family, greeting her by name. "My name's Amelia Griffin," she added, then her smile faded into an expression of concern. "Oh, you're probably looking for little Jeremy, aren't you, Mistress Kerrick."

"Yes, you've seen him today, then?"

"Aye, he was here about three hours or more ago, I'd say. The poor lad was looking for his mother, he was. I told him that she was on her way to Scotland. But I didn't say anything about her illness, because I didn't know if I should." She hesitated. "Or perhaps I shouldn't have told him anything at all about her. Did I do wrong, Mistress Kerrick?"

Alexandra shook her head, considering only herself to

blame for not having kept someone with Jeremy. "No, I can't fault what you did. Did you happen to notice in which direction he went when he left here?"

"No, I didn't, Mistress Kerrick. He left here like a hare with hounds on its heels, and I didn't see which way he went."

"Do you have any idea of where he may have gone? For example, do you know of boys who were friends of his, or places he liked to go?"

The woman pondered, then shook her head regretfully as she said that she was unable to think of anything that might be helpful. Alexandra thanked her, stepping back down the path. As she walked down the street, the men were also returning. They had learned nothing from those they had talked with, and Alexandra related what the woman had told her.

While Alexandra was talking with the men, Deirdre's buggy came up the street at a fast pace, Benjamin Tavish in it with her. It drew up at the curb, and as they stepped out, Deirdre said that neither Benjamin nor his sisters had seen Jeremy. Alexandra's heart sank, the possibility becoming more remote that the boy could be found quickly.

Collecting her thoughts, Alexandra talked with Benjamin to find out if he knew anything about Jeremy that would narrow the search. A tall, well-built man of nineteen, Benjamin was handsome and had a pleasing personality that matched his clean-cut good looks. In addition to being acutely worried about Jeremy, he was anxious to please Alexandra, and he struggled to think of facts about the boy that would be helpful.

After a moment, however, Alexandra realized that Benjamin knew very little about Jeremy's activities. The only conclusion she could draw from talking with Bejamin was one that filled her with an anguish of pity for the boy—Jeremy had been close to his mother and no one else. Now she was gone, leaving him behind, and he had no idea of why she had deserted him.

A distant patter of hoofbeats grew to a rumble, then a

roar. Then it turned into a thunderous pounding as the stockmen and jackaroos swept around a curve in the street and charged down it at a headlong run, a cloud of dust swirling up behind them. Dogs barked madly and people dashed out of houses to look as the fifteen riders raced down the street.

Along with a deafening commotion, they brought the atmosphere of the distant outback to the city street. Their horses were powerful, shaggy beasts, completely unlike the sleek animals hitched to the buggy and carriage. Their faces were bronzed by the sun and they wore distinctive stockman's clothing, their wide hat brims turned up on one side. Most of all, their furious pace and attitude conveyed that they came from a land of no half measures, where everything was done with unbridled verve and determination.

They reined up, dust billowing and their horses wild-eyed and panting heavily. David stepped out into the street and talked to them, describing Jeremy and telling them to search around the docks and the parks in the city. "Are there any questions?" he asked when he finished.

"Where will you be, Mr. Kerrick?" Ruel asked.

"I'll be searching as well," David replied. "If you find him, take him to Morton's house. If you don't find him by dark, come to the house and we'll discuss what to do next. Are there any more questions?" The men and youths shook their heads, and David motioned them on their way as he stepped back. "Very well, be about it, then."

The riders divided into two groups as Ruel pointed, snapping orders. Then they wheeled their horses around and the groups rode away in opposite directions at a pounding run. As the noise faded and the dust settled, Deirdre and Benjamin stepped back to her buggy. "We'll go to the school, Father," she said. "We'll talk to the teachers and boys who know him, and perhaps they can suggest likely places where he might be."

"That's a very good idea," David replied. "We'll go to the Royal Botanic Gardens and look around there, so meet us there when you're finished at the school." He turned to Alexandra, smiling reassuringly. "Now don't worry about the boy, love," he told her. "If we don't find him by nightfall, I'll have a notice put in the newspapers and offer a reward. One way or another, we'll find that lad, and we'll find him soon."

Alexandra forced a smile as she stepped toward the carriage, deeply depressed by ominous foreboding. At the breakfast table that morning, her instincts had warned her to have someone stay with Jeremy at all times. Now her instincts were telling her that David was absolutely wrong, and he was being far too optimistic about finding Jeremy.

Chapter Three

As he began waking, Jeremy tried to cling to sleep, its blankness an escape from the tormenting anguish that rushed in to replace it. But it ebbed away as the penetrating cold woke him and brought him to full consciousness. Tears filled his eyes to overflowing and crushing despair gripping him. He sobbed as he shivered from the cold.

The ground was damp where he lay in a brushy pasture, and the autumn dawn had an icy chill. He heard men talking and stirring beside the road a hundred yards away, where they had camped for the night. Presently, there was a smell of smoke as they built up fires to prepare breakfast.

The sun rose, its warm rays taking the chill from the air. As he gradually stopped shivering, Jeremy heard the men on the road set out down it, singing and whistling cheerfully. Drying his tears, he sat up.

Parramatta, a large town some fifteen miles west of Sydney, was a short distance away. At dusk the previous evening, he had passed through it. The men who had spent the night beside the road were gone, and others were coming through the town and down the road. Virtually all on foot, they were prospectors on their way to the gold fields.

The driving compulsion to flee still tugged at Jeremy. He felt uneasy about being all alone, but his only alternative was to be with his grandparents. While they had been kind to him, he had been intensely uncomfortable in the large house. More important, they were associated with what his mother had done to him, the agony he was trying to flee.

As he stood up and crossed the pasture to a brook, questions rose in his mind about his eventual destination, how he would obtain food, and other practical matters. Then he forced the thoughts aside. Thinking about the future stirred harrowing reminders of the past, and he concentrated on immediate concerns.

One of those was being identified as a runaway, which would result in his being returned to his grandparents. After drinking at the brook, he washed his face and made himself presentable. Then he pulled his cap down to conceal his face as much as possible and stepped back into the road.

At first he felt conspicuous among the others on the road, then he saw that no one looked at him with undue attention, least of all the prospectors. They were avidly intent upon reaching their destination, walking rapidly and passing him. A few farmers in carts and other travelers were mixed among the prospectors, but they also barely glanced at Jeremy.

One man was different from all the others. He wore ragged stockman's clothes and a hat, and carried his belongings in a canvas dilly bag instead of a pack; a rolled blanket was slung over his shoulder. Studying him, Jeremy recalled what he had heard about swagmen. They were footloose wanderers of the tracks in the outback, carrying their belongings—their swag—with them. By tradition, they were given enough rations at each station to reach the next one down the track. The man was evidently a swagman who had found it necessary to come east for some reason, because he glared about him in dissatisfaction and walked quickly, apparently hurrying back to the solitude of the outback.

The odor of smoke lingered over ashes where prospectors had camped beside the road, along with the scent of the food they had prepared for breakfast. The smell reminded Jeremy that he had eaten nothing since the previous morning, but the physical discomfort of his hunger was minor compared to the raw pain of grief that kept surging from the back of his mind. He tried to ignore both of them, looking around and studying his surroundings.

The farthest he had ever been from Sydney before was Parramatta, and the scene around him was completely new and different. It was entirely rural, large farms set back on each side of the road, with people gathering in crops from fields and stock grazing in pastures. The openness of the region was pleasant and somehow inviting, strongly appealing to him.

That impression was increased manyfold when he reached the peak of a long incline in the road. He had heard about the land west of Prospect Hill, the slope he had just climbed, but that had given him no indication of its visual impact. The landscape opened out into a vast panorama, the rolling terrain falling away into the wide, lush valley of the Nepean River. Back from the other side of the river, a jumble of foothills climbed up to the Blue Mountains, the peaks rising into the sky in a backdrop for the scene.

The view touched Jeremy in an ineffable, fundamental way. Although he had never seen it before, he felt a closer affinity with it than with the streets of Sydney. Its very enormity answered some deep, yearning need that he had never realized he had. The feeling was strange, but comforting. It embodied a promise that the broad expanse of land would offer an escape from the wrenching shock that had shattered his life.

The sun climbed into the sky, the day becoming warm. Jeremy took off his coat and carried it; his hunger increased and he became thirsty. At midday, he came to a brook that crossed the road, where others were stopping to drink and fill metal water flasks. Jeremy drank and walked on, trying not to look at those munching cheese and ship biscuit.

The hours of the afternoon passed, and Jeremy became weak with hunger and very thirsty again. In the late afternoon, he studied the area around the Nepean River as he approached it. The village of Penrith was at the end of a lane that led up the river from the north side of the road. On the south side was an expanse of thick forest beside the river that had remained in a primitive state in its surroundings of pastures and crop fields.

The possibility of obtaining food in the village was outweighed by the danger of being identified as a runaway, and he was even more thirsty than hungry. He turned off the road into the trees, going through them toward the river. The change was abrupt, the busy road at one moment, and in the next, he was all alone in a deep, thick forest.

Sunlight filtered through the dense foliage overhead, becoming green twilight among the huge trees. Bark dangling from shaggybarks made them look as if they had been savagely attacked by some fierce animal that lurked in the forest, and the pale trunks of ghost gums were eerie in the soft light. He smelled smoke as he stepped around a tree in his path, then he was suddenly facing an Aborigine man camped on the other side of the tree.

Wearing stockman's clothes, a wide hat, and boots, he was an older man, with white hair, mustache, and bushy beard. He was also large, some six feet tall with a heavy-set build. His dark features were deeply scarred from smallpox, adding to a distinctly forbidding appearance. He sat by the campfire among his belongings, his black eyes narrow and suspicious as he stared fixedly at Jeremy.

The boy started to apologize for intruding, but he was

almost speechless with surprise and fright. "G'day," he stuttered, touching his cap.

"G'day," the man growled in a deep voice, his attitude contradicting the spirit as well as the meaning of the greeting.

Jeremy walked past the camp, and as soon as he had a screen of foliage behind him, he began running. The encounter had made him keenly aware that he was all alone in what could be a very hostile world. He slowed to a walk again, the trees opening out at the edge of the river.

The water was delicious as Jeremy drank thirstily, but it intensified his hunger. He was also weary, because his sleep the night before on the damp ground in the pasture had been anything but restful. The sun was warm on the river bank, and the deep grass looked soft and inviting. He lay down, and a moment later, he was fast asleep.

When he woke and opened his eyes, he was looking out over the river, its surface gleaming in the rich colors of sunset. Then, suddenly conscious of someone else near, he turned his head. The Aborigine man was standing a few feet away, gazing at him inscrutably. Jeremy quickly sat up and eyed the man warily, ready to spring to his feet and run.

"Are you hungry?" the man demanded brusquely.

Jeremy hesitated, then nodded eagerly. "Yes, sir."

The man silently beckoned, then turned away. Jeremy climbed to his feet and followed the man through the forest. An appetizing scent of meat being cooked wafted with the smoke of the fire through the trees.

At the camp, a chicken was roasting on a spit over the fire, and potatoes were baking in the coals. Flames leaped up as drippings from the chicken hissed in the fire, and the smell made Jeremy ravenous. His mouth watering, he seated himself as the man sat down beside the fire.

The man turned the chicken, a shower of drippings spilling down and making the fire blaze up, then he began turning the potatoes with a forked stick. "My name's Jarboe Charlie," he said tersely. "What's yours?"

"Jeremy," the boy replied, wondering about the man's unusual name. "Why did your parents call you Jarboe Charlie?"

The man was silent for a moment, then answered grudgingly: "They didn't," he replied curtly. "My real name is Jirburdarli, but it's hard for white fellows to say or remember a name like that."

The boy nodded, studying the man without openly staring. He had a bearing much like that of a constable—a pronounced readiness and ability to deal with trouble from others. That menacing self-assurance, together with his large size, made him seem sinister.

Jarboe was also taciturn, far more inclined to silence than to conversation. Jeremy had met old seamen around the docks in Sydney who were the same, and who detested chatter. He had found that if he remained silent, showing that he had no intention of plaguing them with pointless jabbering, presently they would talk. Even though he felt as though he were bursting with words, he restrained himself from speaking.

After a moment, Jarboe spoke: "Others have camped here before," he remarked, breaking up sticks and tossing them onto the fire.

"How do you know?" Jeremy asked.

"Those rocks were there when I got here," Jarboe replied, pointing to the circle of stones around the fire. "From the look of them, they've been there for many years." He glanced around at the bark that had fallen off the large eucalypt near the fire, then picked up a stick and probed at the bark. "And somebody left something when they camped here."

"What is it?" Jeremy asked, craning his neck.

Jarboe uncovered a bottle buried in the bark and picked it up, examining it. "It's a wine bottle, the kind that Camden Park bottled their wine in a few years ago. White fellows are forever throwing away useful things. This would make a good water bottle."

"A metal flask is better," Jeremy suggested, pointing to

the flask among Jarboe's belongings. "One made of glass is easy to break."

"Not if it has leather around it," Jarboe told him. "Wrapped in leather and with a shoulder strap on it, this would be a good water bottle. That's the kind people used before they had metal ones." He put the bottle aside and turned the chicken again, noting the boy's hungry stare at it. "What are you doing wandering about by yourself, Jeremy?"

"I'm a swagman," the boy blurted, unable to think of any other reply.

Jarboe blinked in surprise, then pursed his lips to keep from laughing as he added more wood to the fire. Sunset was fading into twilight, and the flames cast a flickering glow among the tree trunks in the gathering dusk. After a moment, he resumed talking about the bottle. "It probably meant little to the one who had it first," he said. "But if it had been important to him, it would still have something of his spirit in it."

"What do you mean?"

"Belongings that are important to you have something of your spirit in them, and it stays. The elders among Aborigines exchange things like that, and it keeps them in contact with each other over long distances."

"They know what each other is doing or something?"

"Mayhap, but I don't know. The elders don't talk about their secrets except to each other, but I remember some odd things."

Jarboe continued, relating an incident from when he had been a youth with his tribe. The elder in charge of a group within the tribe had possessed a piece of carved stone given to him by another elder. It had broken one day, and the group had set out toward the group led by the other elder. Upon reaching the others, they learned that the elder in charge of it had died on the same day that the carved stone had broken.

Darkness had fallen when Jarboe finished, and the glow of the flames highlighted his dark, bearded face with its stern lines and deep pockmarks. On the edge of the firelight, ghost gums were grey forms that seemed to move as the flames leaped up and then subsided. In that setting, it was easy for Jeremy to accept the story as ungarnished fact.

"So if that bottle was important to the one who first had it," Jarboe added, "or if something important happened while he was drinking the wine, it'll have something of his spirit in it."

Jeremy nodded, his full attention on the chicken once again. The skin was a crisp golden brown, with darker streaks where drippings had dried in the heat from the fire. Jarboe opened his canvas dilly bag and rummaged through the fire-blackened utensils in it. One was a billycan, a tall, slender pint container that was used to brew and drink tea. He put it back into the bag, ruefully commenting that he had no tea or flour.

"And I have only a bit of salt left," he continued wryly. "Before long, I'll have to find some work and earn a few shillings so I can buy myself a good supply of rations."

The food being cooked seemed more than sufficient to Jeremy, and his hungry anticipation grew when Jarboe took the chicken from over the fire. The man slid it off the spit into a small kettle, then he scraped the potatoes out of the hot coals. Using a tin plate and a clean slab of bark as a plate for Jeremy, Jarboe carved off portions of the chicken and divided the potatoes, sprinkling measured pinches of salt over them.

The food was still hot, but Jeremy ignored the stinging in his mouth as he began devouring his portion. Under the crisp skin, the chicken was succulent and flavorful, and the potatoes were baked to a soft consistency inside their hard crust. The food seemed the most delicious that Jeremy had ever eaten as he gulped it down. Jarboe ate more deliberately, talking about the food, and he mentioned that it was his share from a farmer.

"A farmer gave it to you?" Jeremy asked through a mouthful.

"Aye, only he didn't know it," Jarboe replied. "And he

doesn't know how the roofs on his sheds got repaired last night. I did that as a fair return for a fair share of tucker."

The boy wondered if it still amounted to stealing, then dismissed it. "This certainly tastes good," he remarked, taking another bite.

Jarboe's black eyes twinkled in amusement as he nodded. "It does, and I'm sure that you know about fair sharing. In the outback, anyone who stops in at a sheep station is freely given enough rations to get to the next one down the track. Being a swagman, you'll know all about that."

"That's right," Jeremy agreed quickly. "That's how it's done."

Jarboe chuckled and nodded, tossing a chicken bone into the fire. He finished eating and fastened a lid onto the kettle containing the remainder of the chicken, then put it into his dilly bag. Then he searched in his coat pockets. "I always like my dudeen after I eat," he commented.

The word was a slang term for a clay pipe, and he took it and tobacco out of his pockets. His tobacco was in the form referred to as a fig, the tobacco leaf cured and compacted into the color, shape, and size of the dried fruit. He shaved thin slices off the fig with his knife, packing them into the pipe, then lit it with a twig from the fire.

As the man puffed on his pipe contemplatively, Jeremy gnawed the last shreds of meat from bones and tossed them into the fire. After he finished eating, the warmth of the fire, the large meal, and fatigue combined to make him irresistibly sleepy. His eyelids were too heavy for him to keep open, and he was already falling asleep as he lay down.

It was late at night and the fire had burned down when he woke, Jarboe shaking his shoulder. "It's time for me to go," the man said, gathering up his belongings. "Do you want the rest of this chicken?"

"No, thank you," Jeremy replied, sitting up. "I'm still very full. Would you like for me to carry any of those things?"

The man frowned, his dark, scarred face looking fierce in the dim light of the low flames, and Jeremy realized that Jarboe had intended to leave by himself. His earlier reserve had returned, and he shook his head, his attitude one of deferring the matter until later. "No, throw some dirt on the fire," he ordered curtly.

Jeremy tossed dirt on the embers as Jarboe put the wine bottle and other things into his dilly bag. The man slung the ropes on the bag and his blanket over his shoulder, along with the strap on his water flask, then Jeremy followed him through the trees in the thin moonlight filtering down into the forest. Near the road, Jarboe picked a path between smoldering fires where prospectors were camped, and they stepped out onto the road.

Turning west, they crossed the wooden bridge over the river and continued on down the road. For an hour or longer, they walked in silence. Jarboe appeared to regret his indecision over leaving by himself, his moody quiet indicating annoyance. Jeremy wanted to stay with the man, but being regarded as an intruder clashed with his pride, making him resentful.

The man spoke first, commenting about needing a share of vegetables. "So that's why you wanted to travel so late at night," Jeremy remarked. "That's the best time to get a share of vegetables, isn't it?"

"Aye, and I don't like to travel on roads and tracks that are crowded," Jarboe replied. "The fewer people there are, the better for me."

Jeremy wondered why Jarboe was so concerned with avoiding others. The man had a distinctly solitary nature, but he also had an appearance and demeanor that would make others more than willing to give him all the privacy he wanted. Then the boy dismissed that train of thought. The silence between them broken, Jarboe continued talking with Jeremy as they walked down the road in the moonlight.

After they turned off at a narrow road that led past farms, another subject came up that left Jeremy with unanswered questions about Jarboe. The chill of the au-

tumn night had settled, and the boy made a comment
about it as he shivered. "Aye, it's a bit nippy," the man
agreed. "But this isn't a mark on how cold it is now in
Hobart."

"Have you just come from Van Diemen's Land, then?"
Jeremy asked.

"Never mind that," Jarboe said quickly, his tone gruff
and regretful over referring to Hobart, then he became
more amiable as he continued, "When we get the share
of vegetables, we'll find a place to camp and build a fire.
That'll soon take the chill out of our bones, won't it?"

Jeremy nodded and replied, puzzled over Jarboe's abrupt dismissal of his question. It appeared that the man
had some secret that he wanted to keep hidden from
everyone, even those who could be of no possible threat
to him. A moment later, Jarboe walked more slowly,
studying a farm at one side, and quietly pointed out features that made it suitable for their purposes. The fields
were partially dug up, the vegetables still in the process
of being gathered. More important, the house was at a
distance from the road and from a footpath that led down
the side of the crop fields.

They turned onto the footpath, Jarboe taking a cloth
bag from his dilly bag and stuffing it into his coat pocket.
Then he put down his dilly bag, blanket, and water flask
beside the fence at the edge of the crop fields. "Keep an
eye on the house, Jeremy," he said quietly. "Whistle if
you see a light there or hear anyone moving about."

Jeremy nodded, whispering a reply. Jarboe climbed
over the rail fence with light, agile movements that be-
lied the age revealed by his white hair and beard, then
he disappeared among the shadows cast by the thin light
of the waning moon. The boy watched the house, the soft
noises made by insects and distant calls of night birds
the only sound in the quiet night.

As the minutes passed, Jeremy wondered if he would
be able to stay with Jarboe. He was a strange, forbidding
man, but he was also a focus of stability among the utter
chaos that Jeremy's life had become. Jarboe clearly

wanted to be alone, and it seemed likely that he would leave by himself the next day. That possibility was an ominous one, and Jeremy dreaded the prospect of further turmoil and being left adrift again.

The wait seemed interminable, but finally Jarboe emerged from the shadows and climbed nimbly back over the fence with the cloth bag, which bulged with vegetables. "This is a fair share, no more or less," he said quietly, putting the bag into his dilly bag. "Any less wouldn't be fair, and any more would be stealing." He slung the dilly bag over his shoulder, then gathered up his other things. "Let's go, Jeremy."

"What took so long?" Jeremy asked as they stepped back toward the road.

"Giving a fair return for the fair share of tucker," Jarboe replied. "Cows had got through the fence around the hayrick, so I repaired the fence and stacked the hay back up. We'll go back to the main road and up it for a little way, then we'll find a place to camp."

Jeremy commented in satisfaction, looking forward to a warm fire, but Jarboe's reference to the distance turned out to be what the boy considered a vast understatement. When they returned to the main road, they turned west again. Then they crossed the Emu Plains, went through the foothills, and continued on up the road as it wound into the mountains.

Walking up the road became a grueling torture for Jeremy. His legs ached with fatigue from climbing the steep slopes, and the wind was icily cold at the higher altitude. However, he was tormented by fear that if he was unable to match Jarboe's pace, the man would definitely leave by himself the next day. That fear was like a stinging lash, driving Jeremy to find the strength to keep up with the man as mile after mile passed.

Dawn was only a few hours away when they reached a brook and walked back into the forest beside it. Jarboe kindled a fire with his flint and steel, and Jeremy sat down beside it, shaking with cold and almost exhausted. The man continued moving about, collecting longer sticks and slabs of bark. He pushed the sticks into the ground in a line a few feet from the fire, inclining them toward it, then covered them with the bark. The makeshift shelter retained the heat, the space between it and the fire becoming as cozy as a room warmed by a fireplace.

Jarboe untied the rope around the ends of his blanket and unrolled it. It was covered with an oilskin coat to keep it dry, and extra clothes were rolled up inside it. He handed the coat to Jeremy. "Here, put this around you and it'll keep you a bit warmer."

Jeremy thanked him and, wrapping the long coat around himself, lay down. The oil-soaked muslin protected him from the damp chill of the ground, and it also provided a much more vital comfort. With the thin fabric around him, somehow he felt less vulnerable to the onslaughts that had turned his life into an ordeal of anguish, and he immediately fell asleep.

He woke slowly, feeling very warm and comfortable. As he opened his eyes, he saw that Jarboe's blanket was around him as well as the oilskins. The man was sitting beside the fire and stirring the small kettle; an appetizing aroma rose from it, blending with the smoke from the fire.

Jarboe turned as the boy sat up and stretched. "You had a good sog, didn't you," he remarked amiably. "This is about ready to eat."

Jeremy put the blanket and oilskins aside, stood up, and stepped to the brook. Over the chattering of birds, he heard prospectors singing on the road a hundred yards away. As he knelt beside the brook to wash, the boy noticed a straight, narrow opening in the foliage. Looking at it more closely, he saw that it was an overgrown trail.

The water in the mountain brook was frigidly cold, and Jeremy shivered as he hurried back to the fire. Jarboe had just finished tying his blanket and oilskins into a roll again. He put it down and took his tin plate out of his dilly bag, then began filling it with stew from the kettle. The stew was thick and meaty, made from the remainder of the chicken from the night before, along with potatoes, onions, and carrots.

Jeremy was worried about whether Jarboe intended to leave by himself, but he was too apprehensive to ask. He was also ravenously hungry, and his mouth watered as he watched Jarboe divide the stew between the plate and kettle. The man handed Jeremy the plate and spoon, then took another spoon out of his dilly bag and began eating from the kettle.

As they ate, Jeremy mentioned the trail he had seen, and Jarboe nodded in approval. "You have good eyes, Jeremy," he remarked. "That's an old Aborigine trading trail, and most white fellows wouldn't notice it. When I first came to Sydney, it was with a trading party."

"How long ago was that?" Jeremy asked.

Jarboe chewed reflectively, gazing into the distance. "It was well over forty years ago," he said reminiscently. "I'm from the Aranda tribe, out near the center of the continent. It took us about a year to get here, what with hunting food along the way. Three of the trading party stayed, and the rest went back. I'm not sure what happened to the other two who stayed."

"What did you do in Sydney?"

"A bit of this and a bit of that," Jarboe replied, his tone discouraging any further questions on that particular subject.

Observing the warning in the man's voice, Jeremy quickly turned to a neutral topic: "Are there many of those trading trails?"

Jarboe nodded emphatically, replying that they were numerous. He continued, referring to the fact that the Blue Mountains were part of a landform called the Great Divide, which stretched nearly the length of the continent. According to conventional wisdom, it was impassable along part of its length, but Jarboe explained that there were Aborigine trails at frequent intervals at all but the most difficult points across the Divide.

When they finished eating, Jarboe took out his pipe and tobacco. Jeremy gathered up the dishes and took them to the brook to wash them, eager to demonstrate his willingness to do his part of the tasks. He carried them back and put them into Jarboe's dilly bag as the man puffed on his pipe in musing silence. Then the conversation resumed, and Jeremy's heart sank as Jarboe said that he had to travel on to the west by himself.

"It's not because I want to," Jarboe added, "because I don't. You're a good mate to travel and camp with, and I've never thought that about many. But I intend to go on a walkabout before long, and go back to the place where I was born. I'm not staying here."

"I could go with you," Jeremy suggested anxiously.

Jarboe shook his head firmly. "No, no. Like I told you, my tribe is out near the center of the continent. There are also other reasons why we can't stay together. For an Aborigine man and a white fellow boy to be mates and travel about together is unusual. It might draw attention, and I don't like to do that. I'd rather not be noticed at all."

"Why?"

"Never mind that," Jarboe said curtly, dismissing the subject. "I just don't like to, and that's enough said. But you're a boy who draws attention. It's not your fault and it doesn't make you unhandsome, but you have eyes like a bunyip's. Your eyes could stare a hole through a gum tree."

"What's a bunyip?"

"It's supposed to be a spirit that hides in creeks and billabongs, and jumps out at people who come to get a drink. Mayhap stories about bunyips are just like tales that swagmen tell. I don't know, but I do know that anyone who sees your eyes will remember them for a while."

"I can keep my cap pulled down."

"Aye, but there are many other things. I have an idea that some people are mightily worried about you just now. It's easy to tell that you've been raised well and looked after. Does your ma know what you're doing?"

Jeremy turned away, grief welling up within him from being forced into talking about the agonizingly painful subject. "She doesn't care," he said, controlling his voice. "She gave me away and went to Scotland. She could have taken me with her, but she didn't."

The explanation stopped Jarboe cold, the determination on his face changing to pity. He almost reached out to Jeremy in sympathy, then tugged on his hat brim instead. "Well, I'm sorry to hear that, Jeremy," he muttered. "It does look as though she could have taken you with her, doesn't it? What did your pa have to say about her giving you away?"

"He didn't care, because he doesn't like me. I'm a bastard."

Jarboe cleared his throat uncomfortably, scratching his beard. "Aye, well, there are much worse things," he said reassuringly. "As far as that's concerned, my ma and pa weren't churched by white fellows' customs. That amounts to something of the same sort, I suppose."

"Do you mean that you're a bastard too, Jarboe?"

The man had strong reservations about the term, his dark features becoming grim as he frowned. "Any who've called me that have had ample cause to remember the occasion," he growled, "and none ever ventured to do it a second time. But using white fellows' customs as a measure, it might not be entirely off the mark." He shrugged, changing the subject: "Who did your ma give you to? It must have been to other relatives."

"It was to my grandparents. I barely know them. I don't want to live with them."

Jarboe sighed in dissatisfaction, gesturing helplessly. "Sometimes we must do things whether we want to or not," he said curtly. "Now I don't like this any more than you, but there's naught that can be done about it. I can't take you with me, but I'm sure that your grandparents will look after you well. You can go back down the road to Penrith, and anyone there will be more than willing to help you get back to your people."

The man's attitude ended the discussion, and panic swelled within Jeremy. He wanted to explain his feelings and plead with Jarboe, but his pride intervened, bringing a steely determination not to beg. "No, but I'll make do in one way or another," he said quietly.

"Then that's your choice," Jarboe snapped impatiently, "and you can do as you wish. I've given you my advice, and if you choose to ignore it, that's up to you." He put his pipe in his pocket as he stood, picking up his blanket, dilly bag, and water flask. "It isn't as though you don't have a home, is it?" he fumed. "And I've learned enough from you to know that it's a good home. Unless you're as daft as a kookaburra, you'll go there."

"No, I'm a swagman."

"If you're a swagman, then I'm a Merino ewe!" Jarboe retorted irately. He drew in a deep breath and released it in a sigh, his anger fading. "I'd truly like to take you with me, Jeremy, but I can't," he said remorsefully. "I'd like nothing better than for us to be mates, but I can't."

"I understand. Goodbye, Jarboe."

Jarboe sighed again, then muttered a farewell and walked rapidly toward the trail beside the brook. As the man disappeared down the trail, Jeremy's disappointment was a crushing burden. It occurred to him that Jarboe might relent and return, and he listened for footsteps.

As the minutes passed, the possibility that Jarboe would change his mind faded. Jeremy propped his elbows on his knees and buried his face in his hands, writhing inwardly with anguish. While he had been with Jarboe, his grief over what his mother had done had been more subdued, other things claiming his attention. Now it returned with renewed force.

The cheerful singing of prospectors on the road carried through the trees, clashing with Jeremy's sorrow. He reflected that they had reason to be lighthearted, because they were self-sufficient adults. The events of the day had proven to him how desperate his situation was when alone, and how fortunate he had been to meet Jarboe. That good fortune having vanished, Jeremy struggled to keep from bursting into tears of despair.

Then, hearing heavy footsteps, Jeremy spun around

and saw Jarboe coming back up the trail. He was breathing heavily, as though he had been running, and a furious scowl on his bearded, pockmarked face made him look threatening. "I thought I'd find you here!" he barked. "What are you doing still sitting here? Didn't I tell you to go to your grandparents?"

Jeremy's surge of joy changed to resentment and refusal to be intimidated. "You also told me to do as I wish!" he shot back.

The man glared at Jeremy, but he appeared more disgruntled at himself than anything else. "Aye, mayhap I did at that," he admitted, and beckoned as he started to turn away. "Come on, then. You can go with me."

"Do you want me to go with you?" Jeremy demanded.

Jarboe turned back, his eyes narrow as he glared. Then his anger faded and he nodded in resignation. "Aye, I shouldn't, but I do. So come on, and pull that cap down to hide those bunyip eyes."

The boy tugged his cap down as he stood up and stepped to the man. They began walking down the trail in silence, an expression of rueful acceptance of the situation on Jarboe's scarred face. After a few minutes, he glanced down at Jeremy, who smiled, and he smiled in response.

"Where are we going?" Jeremy asked.

"Bathurst. I don't like towns, but you need some swag if you're going to be a swagman. You also need some proper clothes, boots, and a hat, because that suit and those shoes won't do for walking the tracks."

"How will we get them?"

"Bathurst is a big town, and many wealthy people live there. They hang out blankets and clothes on laundry day, and they put boots out on back steps when they've been freshly blacked. There are billys, tin plates, and such about. It shouldn't be too hard to find you a share."

"But only a fair share," Jeremy added. "Any more than that would be stealing, wouldn't it?"

"Aye, that's right," Jarboe agreed, chuckling. "We wouldn't want to steal anything from anyone."

Chapter Four

"G'day," the boy called across the crop field, replying to Jeremy's greeting. "I haven't seen you before. You don't live hereabouts, do you?"

"Live hereabouts?" Jeremy echoed, laughing. "No, I live everywhere, as well as nowhere at all. I'm a swagman."

The freckle-faced farm boy, some twelve years old, looked both intrigued and skeptical. He crossed the plowed field to the fence at the edge of the road, the doubt fading from his expression as he studied Jeremy. Along with an oversized stockman's hat and heavy boots, Jeremy wore a canvas coat and rumpled dungaree clothes that were somewhat too large, and a rolled blanket and canvas dilly bag hung from ropes over his shoulder.

"Aye, I suppose you are a swagman," the boy acknowledged enviously. "I wish I could roam about wherever I wished instead of working on this farm at the beck and call of my pa. My name's Freddie Cargill."

Jeremy was gratified by the boy's reaction, but he also

disliked making others jealous of him. "Being a swagman is more work than you might think," he said. "There's more to it than just roaming about." He pointed across the road, where Jarboe had sat down in the shade of a tree on the warm afternoon. "That's my mate, Jarboe Charlie, and my name's Jeremy."

Freddie exchanged an affable nod with Jarboe, then turned back to Jeremy. "Most swagmen are farther west than this, and the main track hereabouts is to the east. What are you and your mate doing here?"

"We're not overly fond of the main tracks," Jeremy replied, "and we'll go out toward the west before long." He looked at the field, where Freddie had been bagging potatoes. "We could use some potatoes."

"Come and get all you want," Freddie invited, eagerly generous. "There's onions over in that next patch. You can take some of them too."

Jeremy dropped his blanket and dilly bag, and glanced at the farmhouse as he climbed over the fence. "Will your father mind?"

"Don't worry about him. My pa and the rest of my family are at the Phelps farm, the next one down the track."

Jeremy nodded, crossing the field with Freddie. It had been plowed to unearth the potatoes, which were clustered in the furrows on the far side of the field. Near the road, the potatoes had been gathered and bagged, and the bulging jute bags were scattered at intervals beside the furrows. Two pair of thick stockings made Jeremy's oversized boots fit well enough for walking the tracks, but they slipped on his feet in the plowed field. He trudged heavily through the soft dirt, talking with Freddie.

The farm boy asked where Jeremy had been during his travels, and Jeremy replied vaguely. While he had no wish to boast, he was also reluctant to admit that his travels on the tracks were limited to the four days since he and Jarboe had left Bathurst. Freddie then broached a subject that remained very painful for Jeremy. "Did your ma and pa just let you go your own way?" he asked. "Or did you run away from home?"

The questions reminded Jeremy of what had happened, bringing a keen pang of sorrow. His grief always returned during quiet, introspective moments, but for the most part it was suppressed by activity and the changing scene around him that claimed his full attention. He shrugged off his sadness, replying, "I don't have a mother and father." He was satisfied that he was being truthful in spirit, if not literally.

Freddie gazed at Jeremy sympathetically, apparently intending to explore the matter in more detail. Jeremy quickly changed the subject and commented that bagging potatoes must be hard work. This led to a long conversation, and Freddie appeared grateful to have a willing listener as he complained about his work at the farm.

Jeremy picked up an empty jute bag from a stack among the furrows, then he and Freddie went to the adjoining field, where onions had been plowed up. Freddie helped gather up onions and put them in the bag, telling Jeremy that there had been a hired man to help with the work at the farm, but the man had suddenly left one night a few weeks before.

"He went to fossick for gold," Freddie continued as they returned to the potato field. "Many hired men do, so Pa had paid him in advance to keep him here. Pa opined that he went to Eureka, because a new gold strike had been made there. It's only about a day's ride away, over to the east of the main track, so Pa went looking for him to get the money back."

"Did he find the man?"

Freddie shook his head. "No, Pa said it was a waste of time to look amongst the hundreds milling about in all directions. Many were foreigners who couldn't answer a question in English, so Pa came on back." He pointed to a furrow. "There are plenty of big potatoes in that furrow."

They stepped to the furrow and began putting potatoes

into the bag, Freddie talking about another event that
had made more work for him. He told Jeremy that the
Phelps family, the owners of the adjacent farm, had gone
to Bathurst to attend the funeral of a relative. During
their absence, Freddie's family attended to essential
chores at their farm.

"Why did the whole family leave?" Jeremy asked.

"Pa said that the one who died must have left money,"
Freddie replied, "and they all went so they could get a
full portion of it. It's made more than ample work for
us, though. Pa takes my ma and my sister and brother
over there twice a day to do the chores."

Jeremy glanced at the road, worried that the family
would return soon, and the elder Cargill would undoubtedly be far less generous than his son. He hoisted the
heavy bag and carried it toward the fence, continuing
his conversation with Freddie. "That does make much
more work for you," he commented, "but it will end when
the Phelps family gets back."

"Aye, that's true," Freddie agreed. "They're supposed
to be back three days from today, and I hope it's not any
longer than that."

As the boys came up to the fence, Jarboe crossed the
road and reached over to take the bag from Jeremy. He
lifted it to his shoulder, thanking Freddie. "You're more
than welcome," the boy said, "and that's a few less for
me to bag." He turned to Jeremy, smiling wistfully. "If
you ever come back this way, stop in to see me."

"Yes, I certainly will," Jeremy replied sincerely, liking
the boy. He climbed over the fence and picked up his
blanket and dilly bag, then waved as he and Jarboe set
out down the track. "Goodbye, Freddie."

The boy waved in reply, then kicked at clumps of dirt
as he glumly went back across the field to resume working. Jarboe moved the bag on his shoulder, judging its
weight, and nodded in satisfaction. "You're a handy traveling mate, Jeremy," he remarked. "I daresay that lad
wouldn't have given me one potato, much less this hefty
lot."

"I could have got more, but I feared that his father would come back at any time," Jeremy said. He related what Freddie had told him about the absence of the Phelps family from their farm. "And they're not due back until three days from now," he added as he finished.

Jarboe smiled, keenly pleased. "We'll find a place nearby to camp, and wait until dark. From the size of the farms around here, we won't have to worry about any noise that we might make. It'll be out of earshot of other farms, even if there's a dog at the farm that barks at us."

Jeremy nodded in agreement. They were in the western edge of the foothills, the Blue Mountains filling the horizon to the east. It was a region of large farms and runs where sheep and cattle were fattened for market. The pastures belonging to the Cargill farm were on the right side of the track, and on the other was a brushy cattle run, with no house on the property. A short distance ahead, the track curved to the left.

As they went around the curve, Jeremy saw that a tree-lined creek was the boundary between the Cargill and Phelps farms, and it led back to a wooded ridge a mile away. At the bridge across the stream, Jeremy and Jarboe turned off the track and went up the creek toward the ridge. The land gradually sloped up to the forest, the creek splashing and babbling over stones.

When they reached the forest, they chose a place near the creek to camp. Leaving their swag at the camp, they went down through the trees to the edge of the forest above the Phelps farm. At the center of the large pastures, crop fields, and orchards, barns and other outbuildings were set back from the sprawling farmhouse. The Cargills and their two teen-aged children moved about the buildings at their tasks.

Jeremy and Jarboe made themselves comfortable under a tree, the man chewing on the stem of his empty pipe. The Cargills finished their work and left in a wagon, the vehicle going down a lane to the track, then disappearing around the curve on the other side of the creek.

Some two hours remained before sunset, and Jeremy and Jarboe waited for darkness.

The ridge was a high point in the surrounding terrain, providing an unobstructed view of the land west of the foothills. It was an immense, rolling plain, with creeks wandering among the farms and stands of open forest. It seemed boundless, stretching to the horizon. However, as he looked at it, Jeremy knew that the full extent of what he could see was only a tiny area compared to the vast expanses of the outback.

"You like the open spaces, don't you, mate?" Jarboe remarked.

Jeremy glanced at Jarboe, realizing that the man had been studying him reflectively. During the past few days, the man's scarred, stern features had become warmly familiar to him instead of forbidding, and now they were creased in a musing, affectionate smile. "Yes, I'm looking forward to going into the outback. I'll like it there."

"Aye, you will," Jarboe agreed. "Many don't, and I wasn't sure about you at first, but I am now. Well, we need to get some money to buy a few necessities, then I'll be ready to go on my walkabout."

"That's when people go back to the place where they were born?"

Jarboe took his pipe out of his mouth, shaking his head. "No, it's not the same for everyone. It's when people go to the place where they belong. For me, that's where I was born. It could be a different place for other people, mayhap a place they've never even seen."

"I don't know what you mean."

Jarboe chewed his pipestem again, pondering for a moment. "It's when people go to a place that's a part of them," he said slowly, searching for words. "And where they're a part of the place. The one place where they belong in every way." He shrugged again, shaking his head. "I don't know any words that would explain it better than that."

Jeremy weighed what Jarboe had said, and searched for an apt, concise term among those he had learned at school. "Would it be the place that's their heritage?" he suggested.

Jarboe stroked his beard reflectively, then smiled and nodded. "Aye, that's it," he replied. "A walkabout is when people go to the place that's their heritage. I daresay some never find it, though."

"It could be that mine is in the outback," Jeremy said. "When I go there, I might be going on my own walkabout."

"Aye, that's true," Jarboe agreed. "Considering how much you want to go there, the outback might be where you belong. It could very well be that your heritage is out there somewhere, Jeremy."

They fell silent, Jeremy gazing over the land to the west again as the sun sank lower in the sky. At sunset, he and Jarboe returned to their camp to get the things they would need at the farm. Rummaging in his dilly bag, Jarboe took out his knife and a short crowbar for prying open doors, then they went back down through the trees as dusk settled.

Full darkness fell and the moon rose as they continued on down the slope to the farm. The fence that separated the pastures from the crop fields was made of rails, quarter sections of logs with their ends stacked together in a zigzag pattern. At a low spot in the ground that remained marshy after rain, the fence was sagging, the rails having rotted over the years.

"This is overdue being repaired," Jarboe said. "It won't be long until the cattle push through and get into the crop fields, and mayhap stray off the farm and get lost. If we can find the wherewithal to repair it, that'll be more than ample return for a share of tucker."

They climbed over the fence, and as they went down a path through the crop fields toward the outbuildings, a dog at the front of the house heard them and began barking. Jarboe went to a tool shed, taking out his crowbar. "Why don't you go and try to pacify the dog, Jeremy," he suggested, prying at the lock hasp on the shed.

"No one will hear it, but it's only doing its duty, and there's no reason to keep it worried about us."

Jeremy went around the house, to where the dog was tethered on a rope in front of the steps. At first the dog snarled and snapped at him viciously, but it gradually subsided to suspicious growls as the boy spoke soothingly and slowly came nearer. The animal sniffed his outstretched hand, wagging its tail tentatively, and Jeremy stroked its head.

The dog had overturned its water bowl while leaping about and barking, and Jeremy refilled it from a rain barrel at the corner of the house. The boy petted the dog a few minutes longer, then went back around the house. He found Jarboe at a pile of seasoned logs behind the barn. The man had brought steel wedges, a mallet, a hammer, and other tools from the shed, and was moving one of the logs out into the moonlight.

During the next three hours, Jeremy and Jarboe worked at a hard, concentrated pace, splitting rails and replacing some forty feet of the fence. Jarboe derived satisfaction from passing on skills and knowledge to Jeremy, who enjoyed learning from the man. While they worked, Jarboe demonstrated how to place the wedges in the logs to split them smoothly, and the best way to assemble the fence so it would be strong and durable.

When they finished and walked back down the path toward the outbuildings, Jeremy speculated about the reaction of farmers when they discovered repairs that had been made on their property. "They must doubt their own senses at first," he said, laughing. "Then they probably don't mention it to anyone else for fear of being thought either a liar or daft."

"They probably don't," Jarboe agreed, chuckling. "Doing it this way saves us from answering questions about ourselves, though. We also give fair return for a fair share of what we need, and it would be a better world if everyone would do the same."

"We didn't do it where we got my share of clothes," Jeremy pointed out.

"That's different," Jarboe replied firmly. "That was the same as getting a share of rations from a sheep station, where a fair return isn't necessary because those where we got your share of clothes were rich people. Farmers get what they have through their own labor, but stations and rich people get it from the labor of others. The fair return would have to be made to those who actually did the work, and we don't have any way of doing that."

After he thought about it for a moment, the reasoning seemed logical enough to Jeremy. Jarboe replaced the tools they had used in the shed and peered closely at the hasp in the dim light as he pushed the nails back into the same holes in the wood. Then he tapped it with his crowbar, setting the nails firmly and leaving no evidence that they had been removed.

At the smokehouse, Jarboe slid the tip of his crowbar under the lock hasp on the door and worked the nails out of the wood. He stepped inside and brought out a flitch of gammon from which pieces had been cut. Jeremy held the cut end as Jarboe sliced off a portion, then the man returned the slab of cured bacon to its hook inside the smokehouse.

After Jarboe replaced the hasp, they stepped to the henhouse. The chickens clucked and stirred as the man moved from one nest to the next inside the long, low building, then emerged with eggs in a cloth bag. Jeremy carried the gammon as they went back toward their camp, its savory aroma reminding him that his last meal had been early in the day.

At the camp, Jarboe kindled a fire and sliced part of the bacon into a pan while Jeremy peeled and washed potatoes and an onion beside the creek. Jarboe chopped them up into another pan and put it on the hot coals, pouring drippings from the bacon into it. When the bacon was fried, he divided it between their tin plates and cracked eggs into the drippings.

The appetizing scent rising from the pans in the cool night air made Jeremy ravenous, and when the food was finally cooked, he ate hungrily. The thick rashers of gammon, a rare treat, were crisp and delicious. The fried potatoes and onions had a hearty flavor from the bacon drippings, and the eggs were a perfect accompaniment to the rest of the food.

When they finished eating, Jeremy washed the pans and plates in the creek, then stacked them beside the fire to dry. As he unrolled his blanket and pulled it around him against the evening chill, he commented on how delicious the meal had been. Jarboe agreed, but added that it would have been even better with a billy of hot tea to accompany it.

"But we don't have any tea," he continued, "and we're almost out of salt." Taking out his pipe and tobacco, he morosely eyed the fig, which had been reduced to a small, dark lump. "I'm almost out of tobacco, and I can't do without my dudeen after I eat," he grumbled. "We must find some work and earn a few shillings to buy the things we need."

The statement was one he had often made, but more as a wish than as a definite plan. Jeremy knew that if he mentioned that a hired man was needed at the Cargill farm, Jarboe would reply that the farmer would ask too many questions about them. The boy also knew that Jarboe would turn down a suggestion of finding work in a town, because he avoided them whenever possible. For some reason, he was extremely cautious about meeting others, and even on the tracks, he eyed other travelers warily before passing them.

During the past days, Jeremy had pieced together a few facts about Jarboe from comments he had made. He had lived in New South Wales for many years, and then in Van Diemen's Land, the large island off the south-eastern coast. Over the years, he had worked part of the time at jobs where he had learned carpentry, farming, and other trades. But what he had worked at most of the time, as well as why he was wary of people, remained a mystery.

Jeremy became sleepy, and he lay down in his blanket beside the fire. For a few minutes, he talked drowsily with Jarboe as the man smoked his pipe, and the boy related what Freddie had told him about the hired man who had slipped away in the night to go and search for gold.

"Aye, that often happens," Jarboe observed. "Ever since gold was found here, it's been hard to keep workers on any job for any wage. Did the lad's pa find the man and get the money back from him?"

"No, there were too many people about. He also said that many of them were foreigners and couldn't speak English."

Jarboe nodded thoughtfully, puffing on his pipe. "Aye, many of them would be foreigners," he muttered to himself. "Of late, more and more foreigners have been coming to the gold fields here."

Curious about Jarboe's interest in that fact, Jeremy asked why it was important. The man replied vaguely, saying it had reminded him of something, and he continued pondering as he puffed on his pipe. Then the boy closed his eyes, settled himself comfortably, and fell asleep.

The next day, it became evident that the presence of a large number of foreigners in Eureka was of considerable importance to Jarboe. He woke Jeremy early, telling him they were going to the mining town, and after a quick breakfast, they set out down the track at a much faster pace then on previous days. Jeremy asked Jarboe what had prompted his sudden decision to go to Eureka, and the man merely replied that it was to find work so they could earn money and buy the supplies they needed.

Jeremy knew that more was involved, and the only evident reason was that Jarboe was less wary of foreigners than of Australians. That made little sense to the boy, but it also seemed illogical to him that the large, muscular man would be cautious about other people at all.

During late afternoon, they came to the main track in the surrounding area, which followed the course of the Turon River. It was as crowded as the road west of Sydney had been, scores of prospectors going in both directions and traveling between mining towns that were scattered through the region. Characteristically, Jarboe was reluctant to venture onto the crowded track during daylight hours, and he led the way up to a wooded slope in a sheep run that overlooked the track and the river.

There was a bridge a few hundred yards up the river, and at the other end of it a narrow track led on back into the wooded foothills. Studying the bridge and the track, Jarboe speculated that it was the route to Eureka. Jeremy agreed with him, the track matching the general description that Freddie had given on the location of the mining town.

At sunset, the prospectors on the track began making camp beside it and the river. After full darkness fell, Jarboe and Jeremy went back down the slope and turned onto the main track, the campfires lighting their way to the bridge. They crossed the bridge and set out down the narrow track.

When they passed a campfire, Jarboe asked the two men sitting beside it if the track was the one to Eureka. The prospectors, speaking with American accents, replied that it was. As he and Jeremy continued on down the track, Jarboe commented about the men's accents. It was a conversational remark, but Jeremy detected a note of satisfaction in the man's voice.

Several miles on down the track, they went back into the trees a few yards and camped for the night. Shortly after dawn the next morning, they set out down the track again. Most of the prospectors were also heading eastward, only a few coming back from Eureka to try their luck elsewhere. Jarboe kept his hat pulled low, peering at all of them warily.

At mid-morning, an explosion rang out to the east, causing echoes that bounced between the hills. Jarboe commented that blasting powder was being used, and as the conversation continued, Jeremy found that the man had some familiarity with prospecting. He told the boy that most prospectors panned for nuggets and gold dust, but blasting powder was used to prepare mine ore to be processed to extract the gold.

The next explosion was much closer, its echoes rippling back and forth for a longer time. An hour later, Eureka came into view when the track reached the head of a wide valley. The town was perched on the hill at the north side, and the entire valley was an expanse of churned earth that was pocked with innumerable holes, with hundreds of men swarming around them.

Jarboe turned off the track, leading the way around the valley toward the source of the explosions in an area that had been fenced off at the far end of the valley. A cookhouse, small barracks, and other buildings stood at one side. Inside the fence, some twenty men were working around a large outcropping of rock, part of which had been demolished.

The men inside the fence suddenly scattered, taking cover. One end of the rock outcropping disappeared into dust and flying bits of stone as a loud explosion rang out, making the ground shudder. The echoes bounced between the surrounding hills as the dust drifted away. The men returned to the rock shelf, a few more feet of it broken into rubble.

Two men were working at a small, low building that was set apart from the others, carrying out kegs and what looked to Jeremy like coils of thin rope. He asked Jarboe what they were, and the man replied that they were kegs of blasting powder and rolls of fuse. Jarboe walked slowly, studying the men, then stepped toward them at his normal pace.

The men were removing bungs from the kegs, inserting the end of fuses, then pushing the bungs back into place to hold the fuses. Jarboe greeted them, commenting on the loud explosion. "It should have been loud," one of them replied. "That shoot was fourteen small kegs of powder."

"Is there any pick and shovel work to be had here?" Jarboe asked.

The man shook his head. "No, we've just begun preparing this site. Jobs are going begging in town, though."

Jarboe thanked the man, turning away. Past the buildings and fenced area, Jarboe studied the prospectors. Some who were within earshot conversed in foreign languages, and Jeremy noted that it pleased Jarboe. They went on around the end of the valley and into the town.

It consisted of some five broken streets of buildings, and it was completely unlike any place Jeremy had ever seen. The buildings were made of fresh, unpainted lumber, which gave the town a flimsy, temporary appearance. Most of all, it was a bedlam of activity. The busiest day that Jeremy had ever seen at the docks in Sydney seemed calm compared to the frenzy in this town. The streets were jammed with vehicles and everyone was rushing to and fro.

Among the crowd of grimy, bearded prospectors were narrow-eyed men in dapper, flashy suits and women wearing heavy cosmetics, gaudy dresses, and feathered hats. Most of the businesses were barrooms, with loud music and raucous laughter blasting from their doorways. Uniformed constables were here and there in the mass of people, and one was dragging two drunken prospectors toward the jail. It was a structure built of heavy timbers, with bars on its windows. Adjacent to it was a bordello, a two-story, windowless building that had a red lantern hanging over its front door.

Another constable was leading four manacled men, and Jarboe frowned as he looked at them. He told Jeremy that the men had probably been arrested for digging without licenses, and he saw no reason why prospectors should even be required to have licenses. Then his frown faded as a livery stable near the end of the street drew his full attention.

A portly, middle-aged man at the wide front doors of the stable was seeing to customers. He was clearly flustered, trying to do too many things at the same time. He had been cleaning the stable, and while renting out two horses, he was taking back others that were being returned. The stable was large, with some thirty stalls. The rear doors were open onto a yard where buggies were parked, and there was a small house adjacent to the stable.

When the customers left, Jarboe stepped toward the man and asked if he needed workers. "Aye, indeed I do," the man replied quickly. "Either that, or grow another pair of hands. My name's Fred Harrison."

Jarboe introduced himself, then pointed to Jeremy. "The lad has been attending school in Sydney, and I'm a friend of his family. His pa asked me to bring him home to the station, and I've run short on funds. So I'd like to have work, but I'm not looking for a permanent job."

Fred nodded in satisfaction. "That matches what I need, because my son usually works with me. He went to Sydney to get married, and he'll be back with his bride before long. Come on, I'll show you what has to be done, and you and the boy can start to work now."

As they stepped into the wide, lofty center of the stable, Jeremy was relieved by Fred's attitude. The man was completely incurious about him, interested only in the work he wanted done. "I can see to customers," Fred said, "but it's been several days since the stalls have been cleaned. The coach company stops here for passengers, and I stable horses for them. If they knew the state of my stalls right now, I'd lose my contract."

"We'll see to that first, then," Jarboe told him. "But if it's been several days since they've been cleaned, we won't finish today."

"I don't expect you to. The coach stops here only once a week, and it'll be a few days before the next one. The pay is seven shillings a day, along with meals. Hand your plates and billys in the back door of the house, and my wife will fill them. And you can bed down in the harness room."

Jarboe nodded in agreement with the terms, and Jeremy followed him to the rear of the stable. They put their swag in a corner of the large, cluttered harness room, then Jeremy helped Jarboe collect a wheelbarrow, shovels, and other tools. Then they took off their coats, rolled up their sleeves, and set to work cleaning the stalls.

Sweat streamed down Jarboe's dark, pockmarked face and into his beard as he worked with the same concentrated energy as he put into repairing things on farms at night. Jeremy had formed the habit of copying him, throwing himself into work. It made the hours fly, and the glow of sunset was shining through the wide doors by the time several stalls were clean and the compost pile in the yard behind the stable was somewhat larger.

Fred was pleased with the amount of work that had been done, smiling in satisfaction as he took out his purse. "I'll call that a day's work," he said, counting out seven shillings into Jarboe's hand. "It's as much or more than I've ever seen a hired man do in a day."

Jarboe nodded in thanks, pocketing the money. "I believe in giving fair return for wages or anything else. I noticed a side of good saddle leather in the harness room, and I'd like to buy a piece of it."

"Use as much of it as you want," Fred replied. "My wife has dinner cooked, so take your billys and plates to the back door. I'll close up here presently, because I don't expect many more customers today."

Jeremy and Jarboe went to the harness room for their plates and billys, then took them to the kitchen door of the house beside the stable. Margaret Harrison, a matronly, middle-aged woman, filled the billys with tea and piled the plates high with generous amounts of peas, rice, and roasted mutton. Jeremy had his usual healthy appetite, and he took bites of his food as he and Jarboe carried their dinner to a bench behind the stable.

After eating, they went up the street to a general store. In the gathering dusk, the street was even more crowded and much noisier than during the day. Jarboe warily scanned the crowd on the street, then peered at those in in the store before he and Jeremy entered it. At the counter, he bought sweets for Jeremy and several figs of tobacco for himself.

When they left the store, they avoided the crowd by

going behind the store and then down the back street that led past the yard at the rear of the stable. In the harness room, Jarboe lit a lantern, then filled his pipe and lit it as Jeremy unrolled his blanket on a pile of hay. The boy lay down, settling himself comfortably on the soft hay.

Jarboe took a slab of leather down from a nail in the wall, then opened his dilly bag and took out the wine bottle he had found in the forest where he and Jeremy had met. Puffing on his pipe, he began cutting a piece of leather to fit the bottle. Jeremy lay and watched the large, bearded man working over the leather in the yellow glow of the lantern.

"Why do you always look people over so much, Jarboe?" he boy asked.

Jarboe sat up, taking his pipe from his mouth and turning to Jeremy. "What do you mean, mate?" he asked amiably.

"You always look at the people around you really closely, and before you go up to someone, you study them."

Jarboe shrugged. "Well, it's good to know who's around you, Jeremy."

The boy nodded, knowing the evasive reply was the only answer he would get. Jarboe puffed on his pipe and resumed cutting the leather as Jeremy watched. The boy hoped that whatever the man's reason was for being so watchful about others, it would never cause trouble. However, the fact that Jarboe was secretive about it seemed to suggest that it could.

Chapter Five

The detonation of blasting powder in the valley woke Jeremy at daybreak the next morning, beginning another busy day. After frumenty and tea for breakfast, he and Jarboe resumed cleaning the stalls. They stopped for a midday meal of bread and cheese, then finished the stalls and began replacing the straw on the floor in the wide center of the stable. At the end of the day, they had completed the last of the overdue cleaning.

When they carried their dinner to the bench behind the stable, Jarboe stepped inside and brought out the wine bottle and leather cover. He had soaked the leather in water during the day, and as he ate, he fastened it around the bottle. Lacing a rawhide thong through holes he had punched in the edges of the leather, he drew it together in a tight seam.

After he finished eating, Jeremy stepped inside the harness room and brought out a scrap of leather the size of his palm. He made a sling, using Jarboe's knife to punch holes in opposite sides of the leather, and attached two rawhide thongs to it. At the ends of the thongs, he tied loops to fit over his forefinger, then gathered up small stones.

With a stone in the sling, Jeremy began spinning it and looked around in the fading light for a target. Aiming at a scrap of wood in the compost pile, he let one loop slip off his finger. The stone thumped into the compost a foot above the wood. The boy adjusted the loop so it would slip off his finger more easily, then tried again. The second stone slammed into the wood with a loud crack, shattering it.

Jarboe smiled, attaching a shoulder strap to the bottle through slots in the leather cover. "You're a good shot with a sling," he remarked.

"Good enough that I got into trouble a few times," Jeremy replied, laughing. "It's getting too dark to see anything."

"Aye, it is," Jarboe agreed. He took out a wooden stopper he had whittled and pushed it into the bottle. "But I'm finished with this now. There's you a water bottle, mate. When that leather dries out completely, it'll be good and tight around the bottle."

Jeremy took the bottle, smiling happily. "You did it for me?"

"Who'd you think I was doing it for?" Jarboe chuckled. "Of course it's for you. That's good leather, so the bottle should last you for a while."

Delighted with the bottle, Jeremy followed Jarboe inside to the harness room. The boy groped about in the darkness for his dilly bag, starting to put the bottle away. Then he changed his mind and kept it beside him as he lay down on his blanket. Sleep evaded Jeremy as he thought about his conversation with Jarboe when the man had first found the bottle, and the boy wondered if it might contain something of someone else's spirit.

Jeremy touched the damp leather, certain that the bottle was a link between himself and some unknown person. Although it had been discarded, he treasured it so much that he felt it must have had at least some important associations with the one who had first owned it. Settling himself comfortably with his hand on the bottle, he fell asleep.

Beginning the next day, the work was less exhausting than before, and they labored at a steady pace that filled the hours punctuated by explosions in the valley. After the daily cleaning in the stalls and the center of the stable was completed, Jeremy filled the water buckets in the stalls and put hay in the feed bins while Jarboe brushed and groomed the horses.

After the daily work was finished, Jarboe combined other tasks with a process of passing on skills to Jeremy. The boy was frightened of the more spirited horses until Jarboe taught him how to control them. A few of the horses had loose shoes, and Jarboe showed Jeremy how to replace the nails and tighten the shoes on the horses' hooves.

With their wages, Jeremy and Jarboe began accumulating supplies of tea, flour, salt, and other necessities, and storing them in the harness room. Jeremy observed that when they went to the general store, Jarboe gradually became less watchful about the people around him. He began helping Fred at the front of the stable when several customers arrived at the same time, then he started going to a barroom for a glass of rum on some evenings, usually returning to the stable after Jeremy was asleep.

On the day the coach was due, it arrived late. It drew up in front of the stable in the middle of the afternoon, a single team of weary, lathered horses hitched to it and the other team tethered behind. The grizzled driver climbed down from the box, complaining bitterly about the horses. "Two of them threw shoes," he growled angrily, talking to Fred. "I hope you have horses with good shoes on them."

"That's all I have here," Fred assured him. "My new groom has seen to every horseshoe in my stable."

The driver grunted and turned to the passengers, three men and a woman who were stepping out of the coach. "The restaurant is right up the street," he told them.

"Don't take any longer than thirty minutes to eat, because I have to make up some lost time." He turned back to Fred. "I'm carrying mail and such, as usual. I'll deliver it to the general store and be back in a few minutes to help with the horses."

"Why don't you go have something to eat?" Fred suggested. "The boy here can see to the mail, and we'll take care of the horses."

Jarboe and Fred stepped to the horses as the driver nodded and reached up to a compartment under his seat. He took out a mail bag and a stack of newspapers tied with string, handed them to Jeremy, and followed the passengers. Jeremy carried the bag and newspapers through the stable, going toward the back street to avoid the crowd on the one in front. As he went out the rear doors, he glanced at the newspapers. Then he froze, fear gripping him as he gazed at the top newspaper in the stack.

On the front page was a large notice offering a reward of five hundred guineas for information leading to locating him. It included a complete description, with a particular mention of his pale blue eyes. At the end of the notice was a request to direct all correspondence to Mistress Alexandra Kerrick at Tibooburra Station, Wilcannia postal office.

Almost without thinking, Jeremy flung the newspapers on the compost pile. He buried them with the pitchfork stuck in the compost, then he hurried down the back street with the mail bag. Then he frantically tried to think of what he would say when the store owner asked about the newspapers.

The problem failed to materialize, as the mail bag created a stir of excitement among customers in the store. They crowded around to find out if they had mail as Jeremy handed it to the store owner. The man said nothing, opening the bag to look through the mail, and Jeremy hastily left.

Returning to the stable, Jeremy realized that his reprieve was likely to be short-lived. More people arrived in Eureka every day, any one of whom could have read the newspaper elsewhere. His only certain escape was into the outback, when Jarboe went on his walkabout.

He thought about confiding in Jarboe, then dismissed it. During their conversations, he had avoided mentioning his family name, and Jarboe had evidently never thought to ask about it. He was certain that Jarboe would never be tempted by the reward, not for an instant. However, the man had a strong sense of right and wrong, and he might consider it his responsibility to notify the Kerricks of the whereabouts of their grandson.

A few minutes after Jeremy returned to the stable, the coach driver came back with the passengers. The boy waited with bated breath for any mention of the newspapers, then sighed in relief when the coach left. Jarboe kindled a fire in the forge at the rear of the stable and Jeremy pumped the bellows, heating iron to make new shoes for the two horses that had cast them. Fred brought the horses that needed to be shod, then stood at one side and watched as Jarboe and Jeremy worked over the forge and anvil.

Then the store owner came into the stable, talking to Fred. "What happened to the Sydney newspapers today?" he demanded. "Didn't the coach driver bring any? I've had a score of customers wanting to buy one."

"I didn't see any newspapers," Fred replied. He turned to Jarboe, who shrugged and shook his head. Then he looked at Jeremy, and the boy quailed inwardly as he shrugged. "It appears he didn't bring any," Fred told the store owner. "Or perhaps he forgot to leave them."

"Well, they won't forget to charge me for them," the man growled, turning away. "But they'll have a long wait to get paid."

The store owner left the stable, still grumbling. Fred laughed, amused by the man's annoyance, and Jarboe chuckled. Jeremy put a piece of iron he had been forming on the anvil back into the force and pumped the bellows furiously to conceal his reaction.

It was almost sunset when the horses were shod, and

Fred began preparations to close for the day. Jeremy and Jarboe finished up final tasks for the day, then took their plates and billys to get dinner. After they ate, Jarboe left to go to a barroom for a glass of rum, and Jeremy tried to think of excuses he could use to get the man to leave on his walkabout.

Nothing came to mind, and Jeremy vented his feelings by casting stones at pieces of wood in the compost pile with his sling. The wood shattered into splinters as the stones slammed into it. When darkness fell, the boy went inside to the harness room and lay down on his blanket. His anxiety kept him awake for a time before he finally fell asleep.

When he woke the next morning, Jeremy immediately had an even more urgent concern. There was no sign of Jarboe, and his blanket was still rolled up the way he had left it the previous morning. Jeremy leaped up and ran out into the stable, looking around the large, dim building. Seeing nothing of Jarboe there, the boy rushed outside, searching frantically for the man.

As the boy looked around behind the stable, Fred stepped out of the back door of his house. "Your mate got himself put into the lockup," he said. "He sent word to me about it by a man late last night."

"What happened?" Jeremy gasped.

"There was a ruction at the taproom where he went last night," Fred explained. "Several constables went there to arrest some fossickers who had been digging without licenses. Jarboe tried to stop the constables from taking the men. When he did that, a bunch of other fossickers joined in to help him, and the constables arrested the lot of them."

"When will he get out, Mr. Harrison?"

Fred sighed and shook his head. "Not for a few days, and I'm unsettled as to what to do about the work." He shrugged, turning back to the door. "Get your breakfast and then do what you can about the work in the stable, Jeremy, and I'll think about what to do."

The boy went back inside to the harness room for his

plate and billy, racked by anxiety. Being separated from Jarboe, even if only temporarily, made the boy feel lost and alone.

Having no appetite, Jeremy ate his breakfast to quench the hollow feeling in his stomach, then set to work. His immediate concern was to keep Fred from hiring a man to replace Jarboe, and the boy drove himself at a frantic pace. After rushing to carry water and hay to the stalls, he began cleaning them. He strained at the wheelbarrow, pushing it to the compost pile to empty it, then ran to each stall he had cleaned with fresh straw.

At midday, the boy was tired, but Fred seemed satisfied with the condition of the stable. Jeremy asked if he could leave for a few minutes to go and talk with Jarboe, and the man nodded agreeably. The boy went to the back door of the house for his midday meal of bread and cheese, then gulped it down as he made his way up the crowded street to the jail.

The low, dark building with its barred windows looked somber and intimidating to the boy. He cautiously opened the door and stepped into a grimy office where several constables were sitting about, laughing and talking. One of them turned to Jeremy, frowning impatiently. "What do you want here?" the man growled.

Unnerved by the atmosphere and the man's attitude, Jeremy gulped nervously. "I'd like to talk with Jarboe Charlie, sir," he replied timidly.

"Well, you can't!" the man barked. "Now begone with you!"

Jeremy hastily backed out the door and closed it as the constables laughed raucously. For a moment, the burden of problems piling one upon another seemed too much for the boy to bear, and tears sprang to his eyes. Then his feeling of helpless sorrow was overcome by burning resentment toward the constables and determination to talk with Jarboe.

The boy stepped into the narrow alley between the jail and the adjacent bordello. The only window at the side of the jail was farther back, with a wooden shutter instead of glass pane behind the bars, and the shutter was open. Over the hubbub of bawdy laughter and revelry coming from the windowless bordello, the boy heard men talking inside the jail.

Gathering himself, Jeremy leaped up and grasped the bars, then pulled himself up to the window. Inside was a single large cell with some twenty men in it. Jarboe was talking with a dozen others, and just as Jeremy saw him, he noticed the boy at the window. "Jeremy, lad!" he exclaimed in pleasure and relief, stepping toward the window. "I've been worried about how you were getting on, mate. Are you all right?"

"Yes. When will you get out, Jarboe?"

The man sighed ruefully, shaking his head. "Not until a magistrate gets nere, which will be a few days. Can you manage until then?"

"I suppose I can," Jeremy replied uncertainly. "Perhaps I can think of a way to get you out of here sooner, Jarboe."

The suggestion created silent amusement among those around Jarboe, the men suppressing their mirth to avoid offending the boy. But a man who was standing by himself across the cell and had a sour, ill-tempered expression reacted differently. "How would some scavvy boy do that?" he grumbled sarcastically. "It'll be a long wait to see that happen."

Jarboe's scarred face suddenly became vicious as he turned on the man. "You watch your bloody tongue when you speak about this lad!" he snarled. "If you don't, I'll rip it out by the bloody roots!"

The man paled, fear replacing the scorn on his face, and he turned away. Those around Jarboe also came to Jeremy's defense, treating his remark seriously. "You give it some thought, lad," one man encouraged him. "Think of a way that we can all get out without paying a fine."

"Aye, you do that," another man added, the others commenting in agreement. "If you can get us out, we'll be greatly obliged to you."

Jarboe smiled and reached through the bars to pat Jeremy's arm affectionately. "Don't worry about things, mate," he said. "Whatever happens, it'll only be a few days, and I have the funds to pay a fine."

Jeremy nodded unhappily, his arms tired from clinging to the bars. "I'll come back and talk to you again as soon as I can, Jarboe."

"I'll look forward to it, mate. Don't try to do too much at the stable. Keep yourself occupied so you won't worry, and let the rest go."

The boy dropped to the ground and turned toward the street. The prospects of being able to free Jarboe appeared very poor. Going in through the office to open the cell door was out of the question, and other ways seemed equally impossible. The building was exceptionally strong, and opening a hole in the wall of the cell would take many hours of very noisy labor.

As the boy stepped dejectedly toward the street, the ground trembled from another explosion in the valley. Jeremy looked at the jail again, wondering about the possibility of obtaining a share of the blasting powder and using it to make a hole in the jail wall. He recalled that the man at the mining site had said that fourteen kegs had been used in one explosion.

Jeremy started to return to the window and ask Jarboe's opinion about using the blasting powder. Then it occurred to him that he had been gone from the stable as long as he dared, because for the present he had to keep Fred satisfied that the work was being done. Pondering the idea of using the blasting powder, Jeremy hurried toward the stable.

He continued thinking about it through the afternoon, working at the same furious pace as that morning. An added advantage of freeing Jarboe occurred to him, making any possibility of accomplishing it more appealing. As a jailbreaker, Jarboe would want to flee from Eureka immediately.

At the end of the day, Fred was satisfied with what Jeremy had done. "Perhaps we can bide our time until

Jarboe is out of jail," he said. "But my wife mentioned that if it takes very long for him to get out, your family might be worried about you. Will they?"

"No, sir. They know I'll be all right as long as I'm with Jarboe, and there was no set time for us to reach the farm."

Fred nodded and started to move away, then turned back. "Farm?" he echoed. "Jarboe said that your family owns a station."

"They do," Jeremy stuttered hastily, flustered by his mistake. "It's a station, but they also do some farming there."

Fred pursed his lips, studying Jeremy with a musing frown. Then he silently nodded, seeming dissatisfied with the answer as he turned away and began preparations to close the stable for the day. Jeremy stepped toward the harness room to get his plate and billy, mentally castigating himself for speaking without thinking and making Fred suspicious.

While he was eating his dinner, Jeremy reconsidered his plans. He had intended to go to the jail to talk with Jarboe about using the blasting powder, but the conversation with Fred had made him uneasy about any delay. In addition, while he was sure he could get a share of the blasting powder without being caught, Jarboe might consider it too risky.

When dusk gathered, Jeremy carried his and Jarboe's swag out and placed it on the bench, ready for them to grab up and leave quickly. He opened Jarboe's dilly bag, taking out the man's knife, flint and steel, and small crowbar. Full darkness had fallen when he finished, and the boy hurried down the back street toward the edge of town.

As he made his way around to the south side of the valley, Jeremy avoided the prospectors who were swarming up the path toward the town, and he tried to decide how large a share of the blasting powder he would need. The jail wall was less substantial than the rock the men were demolishing, indicating something less than fourteen kegs. In addition, he was faced with the practical problem of carrying the kegs to the jail.

At the mining site, light shone through the windows of the barracks and cookhouse, and Jeremy heard men talking inside them. The other buildings were dark forms in the weak moonlight filtering through high, thin clouds. The boy crept through the shadows to the small building where blasting powder and fuse were stored, then took out the crowbar.

It had seemed effortless when Jarboe had removed lock hasps, but the thick metal plate resisted stubbornly. Then it began lifting away from the doorjamb, the nails sliding out of the wood with a squeaking noise that seemed deafening to Jeremy. The door finally opened, and he slipped inside.

The interior was a cluttered, confusing jumble in the impenetrable darkness. Finding a wooden box of fuse, he shoved a coil of it into his coat pocket. Kegs were stacked all about, but he feared upsetting a stack with a crash that would bring men running from all directions.

As he cautiously moved around, he found one keg by itself, and it was larger than the ones the men had been working over. Deciding to start with it and return for more, he hoisted the heavy keg and quietly carried it outside. He lifted the hasp and pushed in the nails far enough to hold it, then picked up the keg again and went back through the shadows.

While lugging the keg around the end of the valley, Jeremy revised downward the share of blasting powder he intended to get. Even though the night was cold, sweat streamed down his face, and he had to stop occasionally and sit on the keg to rest. He realized that the single keg was all he would be able to carry to the jail, but he believed it would at least loosen the timbers in the jail wall sufficiently for the men to push them aside.

Entering the town, he wearily carried the keg down a dark street that led toward the rear of the jail. When he was near the jail, he was guided by noise from the bordello, women's shrill laughter blending with the hoarse, drunken guffaws of men. Jeremy stumbled into the alley between it and the jail, panting and sighing in relief as he set the keg down.

After prying out the bung with Jarboe's knife, Jeremy slid the end of the fuse into the hole and pressed the bung back in. Halfway between the window and the rear of the building, the wall overhung the foundation a few inches, making a place where the keg fit neatly. Jeremy unwound the fuse and stretched it away from the keg, then took out the flint and steel.

He struck the flint and steel together over the end of the fuse, sparks raining down on it. It flared, making a spot of bright, white light in the dark alley as it hissed and sputtered, burning toward the keg. Jeremy put the flint and steel in his pocket as he stepped toward the window.

The boy leaped up and grabbed the bars, then pulled himself up to the window. The shutter was closed against the chill of the night, and Jeremy held on with one hand as he reached through the bars and tapped on the shutter. "Jarboe!" he called in a loud whisper. "Jarboe!"

A moment passed with no reaction from inside the cell. Jeremy looked down at the fuse as it burned steadily toward the keg, then rapped the shutter harder. "Jarboe!" he called more loudly. "Jarboe, open the shutter!"

Over the bedlam of revelry from the bordello, the boy heard men's sleepy voices on the other side of the shutter. Then it opened. "What are you doing up and about, Jeremy?" Jarboe asked from the thick darkness of the cell. "You should be fast asleep at this hour, mate."

"No, I'm going to get you out now, Jarboe," the boy told you. "You and the others in there be ready to run so they can't catch you again."

Other men stirred around Jarboe, exchanging quiet, amused comments about Jeremy and what he had said. Jarboe chuckled, sounding puzzled. "Aye, very well," he said. "But how are you going to do it, mate?"

"By making a hole in the wall," Jeremy replied. "I got a share of the blasting powder from that place across the valley. One of the large kegs was all I could carry, but it should knock the timbers in the wall loose so you can shove them out of the way. Or it might be enough to make a hole large enough to get out." He looked at the fuse again and turned back. "We'll know very soon now, because most of the fuse has burned down."

Silence fell inside the cell, the only sound that from the bordello. Jeremy glanced at the fuse once more and saw that it was very short. "Well, you and the others get ready," the boy said when Jarboe made no response. "I'd better go now, because the keg will blow up in a moment." He started to release the bars, then hesitated: "And perhaps you and the others should move away from the wall, Jarboe," he added as an afterthought.

The man said something in a voice that sounded strange to Jeremy as he slid to the ground and hurried out of the alley, but the fuse was too short for him to linger. He stepped around the rear corner of the bordello and sat down, and over the noise from inside, he heard Jarboe and others in the cell shouting. The boy presumed they were waking everyone in preparation to flee, but being so loud about it seemed unwise to him and certain to alert the constables in the office. Then the keg detonated.

At that instant, Jeremy realized that he had vastly underestimated the explosive force of the blasting powder, which was devastating. As the deafening roar rang out and the ground heaved, the alley between the buildings was filled with a boiling cloud of red flames that lit up the night. The rear wall of the bordello lurched, slamming into Jeremy's back, and it knocked him flying out into the street behind the buildings.

Debris rained down around the boy as he climbed to his feet, his knees weak and his head reeling. Then he turned and gazed in awe through the smoke and dust at the scene of destruction. The jail had been knocked off its foundations and was canted to one side. Most of the wall was gone, it and the edge of the roof reduced to rubble in the alley.

The blast had also ripped away part of the more flimsy

wall of the bordello, exposing tiny rooms on both floors. In the glare of flames leaping up from shattered oil lamps, naked men and women were stumbling to their feet in a clutter of overturned furniture and splintered wood. The wall had supported the second floor, which sagged toward the alley. The things sliding out of those rooms included men and women in beds, shrieking in consternation and flailing about as they plummeted into the alley.

People began shouting and racing down the street toward the jail as Jeremy ran into the alley. He scrambled over the debris toward the gaping side of the jail, the blazing fires casting a dim glow through eddying smoke and dust. The boy saw that the prisoners had gathered against the far wall and appeared unharmed but dazed, staggering about aimlessly.

Jeremy leaped onto the slanted, broken floor of the cell, picking out Jarboe's tall, burly form, in the light from the fires. He took the man's arm and pulled him toward the alley. "Come on, Jarboe!" he shouted. "We must get out of here and run! Come on, Jarboe!"

The man gazed at Jeremy blankly, but followed with shuffling, limping steps as the boy tugged his arm. They climbed over the rubble in the alley, going toward the back street. A crowd was collecting at the other end of the alley in a growing commotion of laughter at the naked men and women and at the constables stumbling out of the wrecked jail in bewilderment.

As he and Jeremy went down the dark street, Jarboe recovered his wits. He limped and walked ahead with his usual determined stride, leading the way between two buildings and across the main street to the livery stable. A few minutes later, they had their swag from the bench behind the stable and were hurrying on down the street toward the track.

The last buildings fell behind, along with the glow of flames and the noise of the crowd. Jarboe had said nothing since leaving the jail, and he remained silent as he limped down the track in the darkness. Jeremy was too apprehensive to speak, afraid the man was furiously angry.

At a distance from the town, Jarboe stopped at a creek beside the track. He knelt awkwardly, favoring his sore leg, and splashed water on his face. "Jeremy, mate," he said quietly.

The man's voice sounded normal rather than angry, and Jeremy felt cautiously relieved. "Yes, Jarboe?" he replied quickly.

Jarboe splashed water on his face again, then sighed as he climbed to his feet. "Mates always talk things over before either of them commences to do anything, Jeremy. From now on, I'd like for us to do that. All in all, I'd have rather got out of jail by paying a fine."

The boy hesitated, weighing whether or not to explain why he had proceeded without consulting Jarboe, then decided to leave it until later. "Very well, Jarboe. I hope no one in the cell was hurt."

The man shook his head and started to reply, then suddenly burst into gales of laughter. "No, no one was more than knocked about a bit," he replied mirthfully. "But I wager it'll be a long while before any of them tells a lad to get them out of a lockup again. Come on, let's go, mate."

Jarboe continued laughing heartily as they went on down the track, and the boy smiled in satisfaction. Now that the man was in a jovial mood, everything had worked out just as Jeremy had wanted. They were leaving Eureka behind, along with the problems that had been closing in on him.

However, he realized that others elsewhere might have read the reward notice, and it was possible that he and Jarboe would meet some of them. That was a nagging worry in the back of his mind, preventing his satisfaction at the moment from being absolutely perfect.

Chapter Six

"That man's an old lag if I ever saw one," Jarboe said quietly.

Jeremy peered through the brush at the stockman, who sat on a slope and watched his sheep, his horse grazing nearby. The expression that Jarboe had used referred to an emancipist, a former convict, and Jarboe had sounded disgruntled. He had intended to ask the stockman for a few pounds of mutton, but the possibility that the man was an emancipist was evidently an obstacle to that, which puzzled Jeremy.

From a distance of over a hundred yards, the man's features were difficult for Jeremy to distinguish clearly. "I suppose he could be," the boy said, then shrugged. "What difference does that make, Jarboe?"

"I just don't like to bother with old lags," the man replied. "Let's get back to the track, and mayhap we'll see another flock today. If not, we can use another small slice of the salt pork for dinner tonight."

Following the man through the brush, Jeremy wondered what the real reason was behind Jarboe's evasive answer. Then the boy dismissed it as they reached the track, having accepted the fact that there were some things in Jarboe's past that the man preferred to keep to himself.

They resumed walking down the track, which stretched like a ribbon across rolling hills blanketed by tussocks of coarse spinifex grass and mallee brush. Stands of shaggybarks, ghost gums, and other eucalypts were scattered among the low growth. Here and there on the hillsides were grass trees that looked like assemblages of mismatched parts, with long spikes growing from large, grassy tufts at the ends of bare, gnarled limbs.

From the crests of hills that the track crossed, the unchanging terrain reached the horizon in all directions, the Blue Mountains now far behind. At long intervals, tracks branched off to the sides, leading back to the home paddocks of sheep stations. They and the occasional flocks of sheep were the only evidence that the region was inhabited, and Jeremy expected to see nothing more for weeks to come. The only town on the track was Menindee, some four hundred miles to the west, where the track ended at the Darling River.

As they walked down the track, they scanned the nearby hills for another flock of sheep. They had very little salt pork left in their supplies, and over the past few days, Jeremy had suggested that a mallee fowl or other small animal would do as well as mutton. "I could get one with my sling," he added.

"We don't need it," Jarboe told the boy. "We have tucker, and taking a share from the land is the same as taking a share from a farm. You shouldn't take anything you don't need. Always remember that, mate."

"Yes, I will. In any event, I don't see any animals just now."

"Then you aren't looking properly. Don't look for an animal, because they won't stand out in the open for you. Look for an eye or an ear. Look for a movement, or a shape to a bush that doesn't belong there. If you'll look properly, you'll see a 'roo right now."

After gazing around, the boy saw a kangaroo's ears and the top of its head as it watched them from tall spinifex two hundred hards away, and he pointed it out. "Aye, but it took you too long by far to find it," Jarboe said. "You were looking everywhere, not just in the right places."

"What do you mean?"

"The only time 'roos will be amongst trees is when they're sleeping, and they won't eat mallee if they can find spinifex. When you look for animals, you must think like them and then look where they'll be."

"Yes, I see. That's true for all animals, isn't it?"

"Aye, even sheep and cattle. I've seen stockmen searching for sheep when a flock has been scattered, and they've been looking high and low in places where sheep would never go. People put their minds to ruling over animals, not studying them. If you'll study animals and their habits, you'll do a much better job of dealing with them."

Jeremy nodded in understanding and the conversation continued, the man telling him about the habits of various animals. The past weeks had been an education for the boy, as Jarboe pointed out and explained details about the terrain, foliage, and wildlife. In their specifics, the discussions had been largely on how to survive off the land, but their overall implication had been philosophical. Jarboe had taught Jeremy to view himself as only one part of the complex of animals and plants, and to live in harmony with his surroundings rather than to attempt to dominate them.

The sky was covered with thick clouds on the cold, early winter day, and the light began fading early in the afternoon. From the crest of a hill, Jeremy saw a thick grove of river gums ahead, trees that usually grew in the vicinity of water. He pointed out the trees to Jarboe, and the man nodded, saying they would stop there and camp for the night.

When they were closer to the river gums, Jeremy saw

that they were clustered around a billabong, an oxbow lake remaining from a creek that flowed only during rainy weather. He and Jarboe turned off the track at the billabong and chose a place to camp, then shared the tasks.

Jarboe gathered dry, seasoned limbs for firewood, while Jeremy carried pans and the billys to the billabong. During the first days of their journey westward, bush flies had been a nuisance, particularly near water. They had largely disappeared with colder weather, and only a few buzzed around the boy as he filled the utensils at the edge of the water.

The fire was blazing when Jeremy stepped back through the trees. He placed the billys in the edge of the fire, and he and Jarboe put on pans of rice and peas to cook. Then the man cut two thin slices of salt pork into another pan, and Jeremy mixed a pan of damper, unleavened stockman's bread made from flour, salt, and water.

While the meal was cooking, darkness fell and brought the penetrating chill of evening. Jarboe pushed long sticks into the ground and Jeremy covered them with slabs of bark, making a reflector, and they sat between it and the fire. They talked about the journey, Jeremy commenting on how long it had been since they had seen other travelers.

"We'll probably see a few swagmen on down the track," Jarboe speculated, stirring the pans. "This track is busy mostly during the spring, when wagons bring supplies from Bathurst and take the wool clips back out. From about halfway down the track, the wagons come from Menindee and take the wool back there, and it's sent down the river on riverboats."

"Will we stop in Menindee, Jarboe?"

The man pursed his lips, turning the damper in the pan, then shrugged. "It would be good to work for a few days and get the money to buy some things we'll need for the journey on to the west," he replied noncommittally. "When we get there, we'll decide what to do."

The reservations in Jarboe's attitude matched Jeremy's feelings, because he was sure that the Sydney newspapers were sent to Menindee. Then his full attention turned to the food as it finished cooking, his appetite as robust as usual. Jarboe took the billys off the fire and sprinkled measures of tea into them, then filled his and Jeremy's plates.

After they ate, Jarboe took out his pipe and filled it as they drank their tea. Jeremy finished his tea and lay down in his blanket, talking with Jarboe as the man smoked his pipe and sipped the last of his tea. The boy asked exactly where the outback began, and Jarboe told him that there was no set boundary or general agreement about it.

"Most people say it's west of Bathurst," he continued, "but others would place it elsewhere. It's a matter of opinion, Jeremy."

"I believe we've been in the outback for a time now," Jeremy remarked. "I like it very much here, so I feel like I'm in the outback now."

"Then you are," Jarboe replied, smiling. "I once heard a fellow say something about it that sounded odd, but it makes more sense than arguing over a map. He said that reaching the outback is a bit like meeting a woman you want to spend the rest of your life with. It's something you know without having to think about it. If you think you're there, then you are."

Jeremy yawned sleepily and wondered about a matter that the man's remarks had indirectly touched upon. "Did you ever have a wife?" he asked.

Jarboe sobered as he puffed on his pipe, silent for a moment, then he slowly nodded. "Aye, I did, but only for a short while. She died of smallpox, the same sickness that made all of these holes in my face."

"Couldn't you find another one?"

"Aye, I could have," the man said musingly. "But I couldn't find the same feeling within myself that I had for the first one, so I didn't bother with another one. Also, I couldn't put the first one out of my mind. The fact is, I still can't put her out of my mind."

The man's voice had become quiet and reflective, as though he was talking to himself. He continued in the same tone, speaking about a young woman who had died over forty years before, and Jeremy listened drowsily. The boy was unaware of starting to fall asleep, but he suddenly woke and it was early morning, and Jarboe was stoking up the fire.

The same thing often happened during their conversations at night, and Jarboe accepted it as a matter of course. Now he smiled as Jeremy sat up in his blanket and stretched. Jeremy took the billys to the billabong and washed his hands and face. He returned to the fire, and after a breakfast of tea and leftovers, he and Jarboe set out down the track again.

It was another dull, overcast winter morning that accentuated the uniform grey of the mallee and eucalypt foliage, but to Jeremy it was the beginning of another cheerful day filled with the promise of interesting developments. He and Jarboe looked for sheep near the track as they talked, the man continuing to point out things and teach Jeremy bush lore.

Near midday, Jeremy was the first one to see a flock of sheep in a valley to the south of the track, and Jarboe nodded in approval. They turned off the track, the man picking a path that provided concealment in brush and trees as they made their way toward the valley. When the stockman came into view on a slope above the sheep, his horse and dogs near him, Jarboe stopped. Jeremy waited while Jarboe studied the man from a distance, and when he was finally satisfied with what he saw, they moved forward again.

The stockman was a rangy, bearded man in his forties. He was cordial but taciturn, obviously more accustomed to solitude than to the company of others. Jarboe introduced himself and Jeremy, giving the same reason for the boy's presence that he had told to Fred Harrison in Eureka.

The explanation was wasted on the stockman, who was

uninterested. "I'm Tom Humphries," he said tersely. "You've come a good way."

"Aye, it would do to break in a pair of boots," Jarboe replied. "We're almost out of salt pork, and I'd rather not ask for rations at a home paddock when that's all we need. I thought we might get some mutton from you."

Tom pointed to his flock, which numbered several thousand sheep. "I'm not short on mutton," he remarked dryly. "There's a carcass at my camp on the other side of the hill. Cut a quarter from it, or however much else you'd like. The weather's cool enough to keep it fresh for you."

"Aye, it is," Jarboe agreed. "I'll take a share of the mutton, then, and I'm grateful for it. G'day to you."

Tom nodded and replied in farewell. Jarboe and Jeremy crossed the hill, where they found a bark hut, a smoldering fire in front of it, and a sheep fold made of poles and rope a short distance away. Cooking utensils were stacked beside the fire, and a whole mutton hung in a tree near the hut, a canvas cover on it to protect it from flies.

Jarboe removed the canvas from the mutton and took out his knife. He cut off one of the large, fat hindquarters, smiling in satisfaction, and put it in a cloth bag. After replacing the canvas, he slung the bag over his shoulder, then he and Jeremy set out back toward the track.

When they camped that evening, a thick, juicy cut of mutton that had roasted over the fire was the centerpiece of their dinner. As they ate, Jeremy commented that neither mutton nor salt pork would be available where they were going. "Aye, tucker is more plentiful here," Jarboe admitted. "But bush tucker is good, and it's ample if you know where to find it. Also, it's more healthful that what some stockmen eat."

"What do you mean?"

"Well, some stockmen live on meat, dried peas, rice, damper, and such. After a while, they'll get scurvy if they don't have some pickles, preserves, or something of the sort. That's why you and I have a few quandongs when we find them, because they'll also ward off scurvy."

Jeremy nodded. The subject had come up before, and he liked quandongs. "How do your people make a fire, Jarboe?"

"They carry fire with them in a firestick," the man replied. "They use the dried stalk of a plant for a firestick." He pointed into the darkness, toward the marshy edge of the billabong where they had camped. "A plant like those reeds. I'll gather some directly and show you how it's done."

After they finished eating, Jarboe stepped away from the fire into the darkness and returned with a handful of dried reeds. He explained that an ember would smolder for hours in the pith inside the reed if it was waved about occasionally to keep the ember hot. "In my tribe and several others," he added, "the people live in groups of twenty or so and join together now and again for tribal meetings. In each group, it's usually a young woman who carries the firestick as they travel about."

As he talked, Jarboe put the tip of a reed into the fire to ignite the pith within it, but the entire reed burned hotly. He tossed it into the fire, commenting that it must be too dry, and picked up another one. It was either too green or wet, not burning at all. After he tried several more, he managed to get the pith smoldering in one of them, but the ember died out after a moment even though he waved the reed about.

"These must be the wrong kind of plant," he grumbled, wadding up the rest of the reeds and throwing them into the fire. "In any event, like I told you, it's usually a woman who takes care of the firestick."

The conversation turned to other things, Jarboe filling his pipe and lighting it, but he was quieter than at other times. More than disgruntled, he seemed troubled because he had been unable to make a firestick with a reed. Over the past weeks, he had reacted the same way when he had been unable to recall something about a plant or animal under discussion. He apparently wanted to believe that he had remained unchanged by his way of life for over forty years, that he could step back into what he had left behind long before, and evidence to the contrary disturbed him.

His reaction was similar the next day, when he and Jeremy were shunned by a small band of Aborigines. They consisted of five adults and four children, two who still had the bright blond hair that would darken when they were older. Jarboe called out and waved to them as they filed up a hill at one side of the track, but they ignored him and disappeared over the hill.

"Unfriendly lot," Jarboe muttered in disappointment. "Well, it would have been hard for me to talk to them unless they speak English. That didn't seem likely, because they didn't appear to live at the home paddock of a station, where they might learn a little English."

"Their language is different from your tribe's?" Jeremy asked.

"Aye, it is," Jarboe replied. "There are any number of tribes, Jeremy, each with its own language. Those with territory next to each other can usually talk back and forth a bit, but no more than that."

He told Jeremy that the differences between tribes extended to many activities besides language. Customs varied from one tribe to another, as did weapons, clothing, and the implements of everyday life. However, as far as he knew, the beliefs on the origins of all living things were the same or very similar among all of the tribes.

The subject having been broached, Jarboe began explaining the Aborigine beliefs of creation to Jeremy. The world had been created at a period that the man referred to as Dreamtime, which bore no relation to real time as measured in seasons or years. During the Dreamtime, the primal creators emerged from the earth and moved across the land, singing all of the various types of plants and animals into existence. They then departed back into the earth, and the locations at which they had emerged and disappeared turned into the rivers, billabongs, valleys, mountains, and other landforms.

In its details, the concept was complicated and lengthy. Jarboe told Jeremy about it in a piecemeal fashion over a period of several days, in between their discussions on other things. He explained that in a sense, the primal creators had never departed. They remained as a force to intervene when needed by their creations, and as laws that governed behavior. The paths they had traveled, known as Songtrails, covered all of Australia. Tribal elders sometimes traveled part of a Songtrail, singing the same chant as the creators and repeating acts of creation, or Dreamings.

During the time that Jarboe was telling Jeremy about the concept, the weather turned colder and rain fell intermittently. He finished on a rainy evening, while they were eating dinner in a bark hut they had assembled in front of their roaring fire. Jeremy questioned Jarboe on several points that were unclear to him, then asked what purpose was served when elders traveled part of a Songtrail and repeated a Dreaming.

"I don't know," Jarboe told the boy. "Like I've said, the elders keep their secrets among themselves. I daresay, though, that it's much the same thing as when white fellows go to church."

"That's for worship. Are the elders worshipping the creators?"

Jarboe put his empty plate aside and pondered, taking out his pipe and tobacco. "They probably are, in a way," he mused. "But what they're doing might be closer to the plays about the birth of Christ that white fellows have in church at Christmas. Having those plays is more or less repeating something that happened so as to think of it anew, isn't it?"

Jeremy nodded in agreement, the question answered to his satisfaction. Finished eating, he put his plate aside and reached for his billy. As he took a drink of tea, another point occurred to him. "What happens if a farmer plows up part of a Songtrail and plants crops there, Jarboe?" he asked. "Or if a fossicker digs up part of one while searching for gold?"

The man shook his head somberly, cutting thin slices off his tobacco fig and putting them in his pipe. "Well, there's trouble, isn't there?" he replied gravely. "Not understanding each other's ways has been the cause of most of the trouble between Aborigines and white fellows."

Jeremy suddenly felt extremely ill at ease, because he had never thought of Jarboe as being different from himself in any significant way except that the man was an adult. Now, even though he tried to reject the thought, he became keenly aware that they were of two different races. It was the most intensely uncomfortable moment that the boy had ever experienced. He regarded Jarboe with deep affection, and he wanted no barriers between them.

"I'm very sorry that trouble happened, Jarboe," he said awkwardly.

"So am I, mate," the man replied, puffing on his pipe. Then he suddenly smiled. "But that has bloody naught to do with you and me, does it?"

The man's warm smile made the boy's discomfort fade, and he smiled. "No, nothing at all," he replied emphatically. "It couldn't have anything to do with us, because we're mates."

Jarboe nodded, changing the subject, and he laughed as he began relating what he had heard about one of the most famous of local explorers, Charles Sturt. Believing there must be an inland sea at the center of Australia, he had taken a boat and sailors with him on a journey there some ten years before. The boat had been abandoned in the gibbers desert at the center of the continent, and upon returning from the arid, desolate region, the sailors had sworn they would never again venture away from the oceans.

The change of subject and Jarboe's laughter dispelled Jeremy's lingering uneasiness, and he was even glad that the issue which had caused his disquiet had arisen. Through discussing and then dismissing it in an atmosphere of perfect harmony with Jarboe, his friendship with the man had been cemented still more closely than before. Feeling very content, the boy wrapped his blanket around himself and lay down as he continued talking with Jarboe while the patter of rain on the bark hut lulled him to sleep.

The rain continued through the night and into the next day in a slow, steady downfall that shrouded the nearby hills and copses of trees in a misty curtain. Jeremy and Jarboe slogged down the muddy track, the rainwater trickling from their hat brims and down their oilskins. Jarboe speculated that the Lachlan River, which he believed they would reach within two or three days, would probably be flooded from the recent rains.

The conversation turned to other things, then Jarboe broke off in mid-sentence. A man emerged from the rain, coming up the track toward them. After studying the man for a moment, Jarboe relaxed.

The traveler was a swagman, a small, bandy-legged man with a gray beard. He was bundled in a coat made of sheepskins with the fleece turned inside, and he had a cheery good nature. Calling out in greeting as he approached, he said his name was Gideon Harris. Jarboe introduced himself and Jeremy, then asked about the condition of the Lachlan River.

"It's running a banker," Gideon said. "I went upstream and made a bit of a raft to put my swag on, then swam and pushed it across. I ended up only a short distance downstream from the track. If the raft hasn't washed away, you could use it and save yourself some bother."

"Aye, that's true," Jarboe agreed. "When we get to the river, we'll look for the raft. How far is it from here?"

"You're about a day and a half or two days away," Gideon replied. He scratched his beard, his manner becoming hesitant. "I know it's asking too much out on the tracks, but do you have any tobacco to spare? None of the stations where I've stopped for the past while have been able to give me any, and it's been weeks since I've smoked my dudeen."

Jarboe nodded, having spent much of the earnings from the livery stable in Eureka on tobacco, and opened his dilly bag. When he handed Gideon a fig, the man suggested they cut it in two, but Jarboe insisted that the swagman take all of it. Gideon thanked him gratefully, then Jarboe and Jeremy exchanged farewells with the man and continued on down the track.

Along with the rain, the temperature had fallen, and Jeremy envied the swagman his warm, waterproof sheepskin coat. The boy's thin oilskins were less than perfectly waterproof, allowing icy rainwater to seep through, and they were no protection at all against the cold. However, he had long since resolved never to complain about discomforts and hardships, and he made no mention of the swagman's coat.

Near dusk, they stopped in a grove of trees and camped. The rain had diminished to a soft, thin downfall when they set out again the next morning, and the visibility was better than during the heavier rain the previous day. Jeremy could see more of the landscape, and he noticed that all of the streams flowed westward, because the terrain sloped gently to the west. He mentioned it to Jarboe, who replied that they had reached the large expanse of land that was drained by the Lachlan River.

When they camped that evening, Jeremy heard a distant rumble after the birds fell silent at nightfall, and Jarboe told him it was the sound made by the flooded river. The following morning, they went on down the track to the next rise, then saw the river from the crest of the hill. The Lachlan was a relatively small stream during dry weather, but heavy rains in its drainage area and on up to its headwaters had flooded it far out of its banks, turning it into a foaming, muddy torrent that filled a valley some four hundred yards wide.

The deep reverberation of the enormous volume of water gushing downstream was like an unbroken drumming of distant thunder. Where the track disappeared into the edge of it, the water swirled around the mallee, spinifex, and other foliage. Farther out, only the taller growth in spots where the ground was higher stood above the water. At the submerged banks of the river, the tips of tall trees were visible, swaying in the swirling currents.

The broad stretch of floodwater looked perilous to Jeremy as they went on down the track. Then Jarboe pointed out the raft the swagman had told them about. Made of driftwood, it was lodged against trees about fifty yards from the edge of the water. Jeremy commented that the raft must have floated away from where the swagman left it. Jarboe shook his head, replying that the river had risen that much higher since the swagman crossed it.

"It's still rising," he added, "and heavy rain might still be falling upstream. We'd better get across while we can, mate."

It seemed dangerous to Jeremy, but he nodded, trusting Jarboe's judgment. "We'll need to build a raft, then," he pointed out.

Jarboe gazed out over the water for a moment and then shook his head as he took off his oilskin coat. "No, that would take too long, and we can wade out to that one." He spread the coat on the ground and put his swag on it, then stood on one foot as he began taking off his boots. "Keep your pants, shirt, and socks on, and put everything else on that coat, Jeremy. I'll tie it into a bundle and carry it, and you follow me. We can reach the raft without getting into water that'll be over your head."

"It'll be cold, though," Jeremy observed, doing as Jarboe had said. "And shirt, pants, and socks won't be of much help against it."

"No, but they'll be of some help," Jarboe replied. "Getting into water that's very cold can be risky, because it can sap your strength so much that it'll knock you out like a club over the head. Even wet clothes will hold some warmth to your body and protect you to an extent. When we get to the other side, we can put on our extra clothes and dry these."

Reaching the other side of the river seemed an increasingly uncertain proposition to Jeremy, and he failed to share Jarboe's confidence that they could wade out to the raft without the water rising over his head. It looked too deep to him, but he said nothing as he shivered in his shirt sleeves, the cold mud soaking through his stockings. Jarboe folded the oilskin coat over their belongings and tied it with rope. Then he hoisted the large bundle to his shoulder and Jeremy followed him into the water.

The water was so cold that it was intensely painful, taking the boy's breath away. The frigid chill penetrated to his bones, but he had to struggle to keep up with Jarboe, which warded off numbness. The man pushed rapidly through the water, taking a zigzag course toward the raft. The water rose to his wide back and Jeremy's chest, then subsided back down to the boy's waist and Jarboe's hips as the man changed directions.

"Tell me what I'm using for landmarks to find shallow water, Jeremy," Jarboe called over his shoulder. "Then I'll tell you why."

The boy knew the real purpose of Jarboe's remarks, because the man had said that thinking about other things made discomfort easier to bear. Jeremy forced himself to concentrate on the path that Jarboe was taking through the water, analyzing it. After the man changed directions two more times, Jeremy saw that he was following one particular species of tree.

Shaking uncontrollably with cold, Jeremy spoke in a weak, quavering voice. "You're going from one paperbark tree to another," he said.

"Good lad!" Jarboe replied. "Aye, this river floods from time to time, and uproots many trees. Paperbark trees have shallow roots, so any that are standing where the river floods must be on ground that's a bit higher. The raft is only a short distance farther, and we'll be there in a moment."

Every second seemed unendurably long to Jeremy. His teeth were chattering and his body shaking, and even Jarboe was shivering. Then they finally reached the raft. The man placed the bundle on it and started to lift Jeremy onto it, but the boy stubbornly refused, determined to help. Jarboe nodded in approval, pushing the raft away from the trees.

The raft drifted downstream, and Jarboe swam behind it as he guided it between trees and out into the river. Jeremy clung to the raft and thrashed his legs, doing what he could to help. Farther out in the river, the raft began moving downstream more rapidly. It barely missed the tops of trees as it picked up speed, then it reached the open water.

The expanse of roiling, muddy water seemed enormous to Jeremy, with brush, trees, and other debris spinning around the raft as it careened downstream in the swift current. The boy's legs were almost lifeless, but fear of the swirling floodwaters fueled his strength to move them and nudge the raft toward the other side of the river. Jarboe glanced upstream in alarm, kicking furiously hard, and Jeremy turned to look.

A huge tree was bearing down on them, weighing tons and moving more rapidly in the current than the raft. Its towering mass of roots was plowing through the water like the bow of a ship, and the long, thick branches spreading out from its broad trunk were sweeping other debris under the water. Jarboe turned the raft to an angle that was partly downstream and across the current as he continued kicking hard, trying to evade the tree.

Jeremy thrashed his legs and did what he could to help. Above the rumble of the river, he heard the tree approaching, its branches swishing and the water gurgling around the roots and trunk. The sound grew ominously loud as the roots and trunk passed behind him. A thicket of wet foliage swept over him, the tips of branches dragging against him and scattering leaves on the raft. Then the tree floated on downstream.

Where the river curved, the floodwaters met a line of low hills, and eddies in the current carried the raft into a backwater between two hills. It was littered with debris, and a dozen drowned sheep, a kangaroo, and a variety of small animals floated among the uprooted saplings and brush. Jarboe touched the bottom with his feet and shoved the raft into the brush on the side of the hill. Jeremy tried to stands but his legs collapsed under him.

Jarboe lifted the boy and carried him up the hill to a sheltered niche among large boulders, then hurried back down the hill. His teeth chattering and his body jerking in spasms from the cold, Jeremy barely had the strength to pull his knees up against his chest and wrap his arms around them, trying to warm himself. A moment later, Jarboe returned with the bundle.

The man took out Jeremy's blanket and wrapped it around the boy, then stepped to a nearby eucalypt and dug into the bark it had shed. After gathering an armful of slabs that were still dry, he carried them back to the boulders. His hands shaking with cold, it took him several tries to ignite sparks in tinder with his flint and steel. He finally coaxed a flame to life and piled the dry bark on the fire as it blazed up.

Shivering with cold, Jarboe changed into his other clothes. The heat of the fire penetrated Jeremy's blanket and wet clothes, making his skin tingle painfully at first as his numbness faded. As he sat up in his blanket, he noticed that the rain had stopped and he commented on it.

"Aye, we'll have a few dry days now," Jarboe said, glancing up at the sky. "And cold, windy ones, or I'll miss my guess. But we'll soon have the wherewithal to keep warm, mate. The skins from those drowned sheep in the water down there will make a good coat for each of us."

"How will we cure the skins?" Jeremy asked.

"With the inside bark from peppermint tress," Jarboe replied. "That'll cure them quickly, and also give them a good smell. I'll get some tallow from the sheep to rub on the skins and make them waterproof, and the leg tendons from that 'roo down there will make good thread to sew the coats." He opened his dilly bag and took out his knife. "We'll stop here for a day or two while we scrape the skins and put bark on them. You stay there beside the fire and keep warm, and I'll go skin the sheep."

As the man went down the hill, Jeremy shakily climbed to his feet and changed into his dry clothes. The boy had never before felt so drained of energy, but pride prevented him from sitting beside the fire while Jarboe worked. He spread out his and Jarboe's wet clothes on a boulder to dry, then went to the scattered trees on the hill and collected firewood.

The cold wind that Jarboe had predicted was already beginning, its chill penetrating Jeremy's dungaree clothes and canvas coat. The space among the boulders was cozy, containing the heat of the fire, and each time he carried back an armful of wood, the boy paused to warm himself. When he had gathered a large stack of firewood, Jeremy took the billys around the hill to fill them at a rivulet that trickled down the slope.

The water in the billys was just starting to boil when Jarboe came back up the hill with a large bundle of sheep-skins. As the man spread the skins out on boulders to dry, Jeremy set the billys off the hot coals and sprinkled pinches of tea into them.

Jarboe sat down beside the fire, taking his billy with a nod of satisfaction. "Hot tea will go down good just now," he remarked, and glanced at the firewood. "I see you've been busy, mate."

"So have you," Jeremy pointed out.

Jarboe laughed, taking out his pipe and tobacco. "Aye, well, cold has to go through quite a lot of fat on me before it can get to my bones and gristle. Even so, I was cold, so you took that river crossing in good form. I've never known anyone who could have done better."

"Will we have many more rivers to cross?" Jeremy asked.

"No, only the Darling River at Menindee," Jarboe replied, filling his pipe. "We'll be able to cross it on a ferry or some sort of boat, because many people go back and forth across the river there."

"People from sheep stations west of the river?"

"Some are from the stations, but most of them are people going back and forth to a mining operation at a place called Broken Hill. Workers and supplies come up the river from Adelaide to Menindee, then go to Broken Hill by wagon. It's a more or less constant traffic."

"Do they go on the same track that we'll use?"

Jarboe shook his head, lighting his pipe. "No, we'll go straight west, on the track through the sheep stations. Broken Hill is to the northwest." He took a drink of tea and puffed on his pipe as he resumed describing the region. "Broken Hill is on the south boundary of a sheep station called Wayamba Station. It's so big that crossing it on a horse takes days. To the north of it is another one the same size, called Tibooburra Station. Between the two of them, they graze a goodly portion of all the sheep in New South Wales. And half of the tales that swagmen tell are about the people who own those stations, the Garrity family and the Kerrick family."

Jarboe took another drink of tea and continued talking about the sheep stations, Jeremy listening to him absently. The conversation had turned the boy's thoughts to the Kerrick family, and to his grandmother in particular. He had fond memories of her, because she had always been kind and affectionate toward him. However, she had known about and concealed his mother's intentions from him, and her involvement with the upheaval that had shattered his life made his feelings about her mixed.

At that moment, Alexandra Kerrick was thinking about Jeremy. Ever since the day that the boy had disappeared in Sydney, he had never been far from her thoughts.

The rain had stopped for the first time in almost two weeks, and Alexandra was riding across the broad, open valley that was the home paddock of Tibooburra Station. As her horse cantered slowly up the track leading out of the valley toward the south paddocks, the cold wind had a damp, earthy scent from the rain. All across the vast miles of the station, the soil had been watered to grow fresh graze for the tens of thousands of sheep.

It was a season she enjoyed, but now her thoughts were only of Jeremy. Wondering where he was and what he was doing, she worried that he might be cold, hungry, lonely, and perhaps in danger. The letters in response to the reward notice in the newspapers had been disappointing. Some had been transparent lies in an attempt to claim the reward, while others had been from well-meaning people who had obviously seen a boy other than Jeremy. Only one or two had been from people who might have actually seen him, but even those had been no more than a tantalizing possibility.

At the top of the rise on the south side of the valley, Alexandra reined up and gazed over the home paddock. It was a view that she never grew tired of admiring. The tree-lined Tibooburra Creek stretched down the center of the valley, curving behind a knoll-like hill that rose abruptly from the level terrain. At one side of the hill were the shearing shed and its pens, along with the warehouses, barracks, cookhouse, and other structures in the complex of station buildings. On the other side of the hill, gardens, fruit orchards, and cottages for married stockmen spread along the creek, with an Aborigine village farther down the stream.

In a level expanse halfway up the hill, a massive, three-story stone house was set in landscaped surroundings. It was the heart of the giant sheep station, and to Alexandra it symbolized her life's work. Decades before, she and her husband had lived in a bark hut where the house now stood, building up the sheep station in the remote wilderness.

Her satisfaction was marred as she looked at the house, because a Kerrick who should be living there was missing. She had always loved Jeremy and yearned to have him near her. When she had visited the Tavish home on her trips to Sydney, she had longed to bring him back with her. Her respect for motherhood and the knowledge that Clara adored her son had kept her from asking for him, and now she wondered if that had been a mistake. Over the years, she could have won his confidence and love, and he would now be where he belonged.

As she started to ride back down the track, Alexandra heard a horse approaching from out of Dingo Paddock. She waited, and a moment later, the rider came into view. He was Eulie Bodenham, the son of an Aborigine woman and a well-born English eccentric. In his forties, he had been an employee at the station since his boyhood. A few days before, he had been sent to see if any of the south paddocks were flooding from the rain.

The man rode up to Alexandra, touching his hat as he grinned cheerily and greeted her. "Good day, Eulie," she said. "How are the paddocks?"

"Wet enough, mo'm, but the stockmen don't need any help," he replied. "The worst are Boar and Gidgee Paddocks, where creeks are running bankers, but all of the sheep are safe." He took an oilskin bag from inside his sheepskin coat and handed it to her. "While I was down there, I went over to Wilcannia and picked up the mail from the postal office."

"Thank you very much, Eulie," Alexandra said, keenly pleased. "The river isn't too badly flooded to cross, then."

Eulie shook his head as they rode down the track together. "No, mo'm. It's not too bad at Wilcannia, but I heard that it's out of its banks down at Menindee. I was told that very few riverboats are venturing upstream from Adelaide, and if the river gets any higher, they'll stop altogether."

Alexandra nodded and continued talking with the stockman, but her thoughts were on the bag of mail. She earnestly hoped it contained information that would lead to finding Jeremy, or at least news of his whereabouts. However, her experience with other mail she had received about the boy warned her not to let her anticipation build too high.

The stockman rode up the hill with Alexandra, then led her horse away. As she went up the walk toward the steps, she heard her three granddaughters laughing and playing in the gardens behind the house. Justine, the eldest, was almost nine and would soon leave to attend Sydenham Academy in Sydney, and Anastasia and Eudora were seven and six years old. She loved them devotedly, but she was also privately disappointed. Even as very young children, it was obvious that none of them would ever have the slightest interest in the sheep station, and they would probably choose to live in Sydney.

As she started to go inside, Alexandra saw Catherine, her daughter-in-law, in the station cemetery at the edge of the gardens beside the house. Alexandra went back down the steps and along the path that led through the gardens. A white picket fence enclosed the cemetery, where there were a dozen graves with headstones of native granite. Creighton and Martha Hammond were buried there, along with Daniel Corbett, Kunmanara, Adolarious Bodenham, other employees, and two swagmen who had died at the station.

Catherine was plucking weeds off the tiny grave of Infant Kerrick, her stillborn son. An attractive woman in her thirties with black hair and green eyes, she and Alexandra had a very warm relationship, and the sorrow on her face was replaced by a smile as she turned. "I'm almost through here," she said when Alexandra showed her the mail. "It's time for the girls to go inside, so I'll bring them in and join you in a few minutes."

"Very well. I'll ask a maid to make tea for us."

Catherine smiled and nodded, then turned to the grave again. Alexandra went back up the path toward the house, thinking about Catherine's constant attention to the small grave. Several times each week, she cleared weeds off it and mourned over it. Alexandra could well understand the shock and sorrow of carrying a baby for nine months and then having it born dead. However, the stillbirth had happened almost two years before, and it seemed to her that Catherine's grief had become morbid and excessive.

The downstairs maid, Emma Bodenham, took Alexandra's coat and hat as she went inside. Alexandra asked her to make tea, then went into the parlor and sat down at the desk, opening the oilskin bag. Thumbing through the letters, she put aside several that were addressed to employees. Others concerned the business affairs of the station, leaving one letter.

It was from a woman named Margaret Harrison in

Eureka, whose husband owned a livery stable. It stated
that Jeremy had been there with an Aborigine man
named Jarboe Charlie, and they had worked at the stable
for several days. Another paragraph described the circumstances that had resulted in the man's being in jail,
then stated that he and the boy had disappeared on the
night that the jail had been demolished by an explosion.

There were other details, convincing Alexandra that
the boy was indeed Jeremy. She recalled a recent article
in the Sydney newspaper about the destruction of the
jail, which the authorities had attributed to prospectors
who had released friends in the jail. David had been
amused, commenting that the prospectors had evidently
been more determined to free their friends than prudent
in how they had gone about it.

The children came in the front door, chattering cheerfully, and went upstairs. A moment later, Catherine
stepped into the parlor, the maid following her with a
tea tray. Emma put the tray on the table in front of the
couch, and Alexandra gave her the letters to employees,
asking her to summon a jackaroo to distribute them. As
the maid left, Alexandra saw down on the couch with
Catherine, handing her the letter from Eureka.

Catherine read the letter, smiling as she scanned the
lines. "At last!" she exclaimed. "This was definitely Jeremy, Mistress Kerrick."

"Yes, there's no question about that," Alexandra
agreed, pouring the tea. "At least we now know that he
was well and safe at the time he was in Eureka, and we
know that he's with a reliable adult. Judging from what
that letter has to say about him, Jeremy was fortunate
to have met up with this Jarboe Charlie."

Catherine pursed her lips and studied the letter again,
having some reservations. "Well, Mistress Harrison
made a point of stating that both Jeremy and the man
were orderly in conduct and hard workers. However, the
man is harboring a runaway boy, which doesn't speak
well for him."

"We don't know what Jeremy told the man about himself," Alexandra pointed out, then laughed. "Children can be inventive, and as a girl, Deirdre could be absolutely convincing while spinning the most outrageous tales. You'll recall that on one occasion, she was Lady Deirdre Augusta Juliana Hanover, granddaughter of King George III. And she had been exiled to Australia to prevent her from challenging Queen Victoria for the throne."

Catherine laughed, handing the letter back and taking her cup of tea. "Indeed, I shall never forget that, Mistress Kerrick. It won't be long until Jonathan takes Justine to Sydenham Academy, and he could go to Eureka to see if he can find out more. If Jeremy and that man are traveling about the gold towns, Jonathan may be able to locate them."

Alexandra nodded happily, taking a drink of her tea. Now that she'd had news of Jeremy, she was optimistic about finding him. An inner voice still warned her against expecting too much, but it was difficult for her to keep her hopes from soaring.

Chapter Seven

When a rider came into view down the track, Jeremy had few misgivings about meeting the man. During the past weeks, he and Jarboe had run short of supplies and had gone to the home paddocks of stations for rations. Each time, no one had been curious about them, which largely relieved the boy of his burden of worry and made the journey more enjoyable for him.

As the rider drew closer, Jeremy saw that his appearance was unusual. He wore a suit and greatcoat, with a sporty but highly impractical bowler hat. Judging by his hunched posture on his saddle, his greatcoat was inadequate protection from the icy wind sweeping the track, but Jeremy was very comfortable in his thick sheepskin coat that hung to his ankles.

The man reined up and spoke in greeting, then made a wry comment about the weather. "G'day to you," Jarboe said. "Aye, the wind is brisk, but at least it's not raining. Do you have far to go?"

"Indeed I do," the man replied. "I'm an engineer at

Broken Hill, and I'm en route to Sydney to talk with the company manager. The riverboats stopped running because the river is flooded, and my business can't wait. How is the track east of here?"

"The track itself is good enough," Jarboe told him. "There are a few creeks in level land that have spread out. But most of your trouble will come at the Lachlan River, unless it's subsided considerably. It gave me and the lad here quite a time."

The man nodded, glancing at Jeremy, then pursed his lips reflectively as he looked more closely. "Who is the boy?" he asked.

"The son of a friend of mine," Jarboe replied. "He's been attending a boarding school, and when I had to make a trip to the east, his pa asked me to bring him home to the station. Why do you ask?"

"He fits the description of a runaway boy," the man mused, studying Jeremy. "A boy named Jeremy Kerrick. His father is Sir Morton Kerrick, and the family owns Tibooburra Station. There was a notice in the newspapers about him, offering a reward of five hundred guineas."

"Well, this lad's name is Jones," Jarboe answered smoothly, laughing. "And his pa's station might be the size of the home paddock at Tibooburra Station. Many boys of his age resemble each other."

"Not many have eyes like his, though," the man observed. "In fact, the only other time I've seen such eyes is when I happened to meet Sir Morton Kerrick while I was in Sydney on business."

Jarboe shrugged dismissively and commented that others in the Jones family had similar eyes. Jeremy struggled to appear unconcerned while quailing inwardly as the engineer continued studying him. Then the man nodded and spoke a word of farewell, turning away. Jarboe replied, then he and Jeremy walked on down the track, the wind tugging at their sheepskin coats.

There was a tense silence between himself and Jarboe. Jeremy knew that the man was indifferent about the reward, but not about other things. He would do what he considered right, and the boy was uncertain of what that would be. The silence made him intensely uncomfortable, but he was afraid to speak.

Finally, the man sighed heavily and spoke, his voice barely audible over the wind: "A peer's son," he muttered. "I've been harboring a runaway boy who is a gent's son. A peer's son with bunyip eyes."

"Yes, but as I told you, I'm a bastard," Jeremy said quickly. "My father doesn't like me and wants nothing to do with me."

Jarboe sighed again, shrugging. "It's as common as flies in December for lords and gentlemen to have children on the wrong side of the blanket. As for liking you, that's neither here nor there. If your family didn't want you, they wouldn't be offering a reward, would they?"

"My grandparents knew my mother was leaving without me. They planned it with her, and they didn't tell me. Also, while I was with them, I was always afraid of tipping things over or breaking something."

"You'd need a wrecking bar to break anything they couldn't replace with their pin money," Jarboe commented dryly. "And people often do as they see fit without explaining it to children, Jeremy. I'm not saying that's the best way of doing things, but it's often the case."

"Do you fear getting into trouble over me, then?" Jeremy asked.

Jarboe snorted scornfully. "I can deal with trouble," he replied firmly. "In any event, the chances of it are small. Of all the people we've met, only that engineer fellow suspected who you are. Many can't read, and many who can don't remember what they've read in newspapers." He shook his head somberly. "No, there's a right and wrong to sort out here. And mayhap what I'd like to do and what I should do are on different tracks."

Jeremy desperately tried to think of something that would sway Jarboe in his decision, but nothing occurred to him. Silence fell between them again, the bleak, wintry day matching Jeremy's mood. The gray brush and trees

tossed in the gusty wind that scudded thick, dark clouds
across the sky. Kookaburras in brush near the track flew
away as they passed, the characteristic cries of the birds
that always sounded like shrill, insane laughter seemed
to the boy to be mocking him.

The silence continued, even though they spoke to each
other. When they camped near dusk, they exchanged necessary comments about the tasks to be done. Those terse
remarks emphasized the absence of their usual lively
conversation, making the suspense of waiting for the fateful decision even more racking for Jeremy. He had
learned that appeals unsupported by reasons were
wasted on Jarboe, and he said nothing on the subject,
even though the silence continued through the following
day, making it long and tormenting.

The next day, they had been tramping down the track
for several hours when Jarboe brought the matter up
himself. "My problem in making up my mind is that I
want so much to keep you with me," he admitted. "Yet,
I feel that you rightfully belong with your family...."
His voice faded, then he began again, "No, it's because
you're not an ordinary boy. You'll do important things
in life, and that would come about best with your family's
help."

"But I want to do things on my own, not with them!"
Jeremy exclaimed. "I want to go on my own walkabout
and find the place where I belong. I want to seek my own
heritage, just like you're doing!"

The outburst came without forethought, which made
it a protest against being sent back to his family rather
than a reply. However, it also reflected his deepest feelings, and it appeared to be meaningful to Jarboe. The
man suddenly stopped on the track, studying Jeremy for
a moment and weighing what he had said. Then they
continued walking down the track.

The silence and onerous suspense in Jeremy's mind
resumed, lasting through the rest of the day. Then, after
they camped that evening, Jarboe brought up the subject
once again. A note of finality in his voice revealed that

he had made a decision, but he approached it in a round-about way. He talked about Jeremy's need for education and its role in what he would do in life.

"I can already read, write, and do sums," Jeremy told him quickly.

"So can I," Jarboe replied, stirring the pans on the fire. "I taught myself to do a bit of each. You need to know more, though."

"I don't understand why."

"You will within time. There must be a school in Menindee where we can get you a share of books. You can already read, so you should be able to learn whatever is in them. That way, you can continue with your learning and stay with me. I've known several fellows who had as much learning as any professor, and they had gleaned it themselves from reading."

Jeremy exclaimed in delight and eagerly agreed, the uncertainty ending in the outcome for which he had anxiously hoped. As they continued discussing it, the boy realized that the solution Jarboe had found was in fact more an excuse so they could stay together. The man had sought and found a means whereby he could convince himself that he was fulfilling a responsibility that would have been accomplished by the Kerrick family.

One side issue of the subject remained undiscussed until the following day, and Jarboe mentioned it as they were walking down the track. He acknowledged that he had failed to ask Jeremy about his family name, but pointed out that the boy should have told him. "You knew it was something that I had a right to know," Jarboe added. "Mates always tell each other things that are important, so don't do that again."

"No, I won't, Jarboe. I should have told you, and I'm sorry that I didn't. There's something you haven't told me, though. For some reason, you always look people over, and you like to stay away from those who might be emancipists. Is the reason for that something I should know?"

Jarboe frowned soberly, making no reply for a long

moment, then he spoke reluctantly: "Aye, it is," he said. "I used to be a tracker. When a convict escaped, I was one of those who found him and brought him back. I wouldn't want to meet up with one of those I brought back."

Jeremy was astonished, even though he had been sure that some unusual circumstances had to be involved in the man's behavior. He knew that Jarboe's last comment was an understatement, because any emancipist who recognized the man would have help from all sides. The convict system itself was widely hated, even though the transportation of convicts to Australia had long since largely ended, and many who had never been convicts would avidly join an attack upon someone who had been a tracker. "No, you certainly wouldn't," the boy agreed emphatically. "Why did you become a tracker?"

Jarboe thought about the question, then smiled wryly. "Not because I liked what often went on in the prison compounds," he said, "because I certainly didn't. Many convicts were the most vile sort one could find, but not all by any means. They were sometimes ill-treated, because some guards and compound commanders were cruel men. But when the worst sort of convicts escaped, they became bushrangers, preying on innocent people. I stopped many of them, and I believe I can be proud of that."

"Yes, you can. Why did you decide to give up being a tracker? Was it just because you wanted to go on your walkabout?"

"Aye, more or less," Jarboe replied tersely.

Jeremy realized that the answer was an evasion, but the man's tone of voice discouraged further questions on that specific issue. However, what he had said about himself explained other facts in addition to his caution about meeting people. Knowing that the man had pursued and arrested escaped convicts, Jeremy understood the reason for his aggressive self-confidence and mannerisms similar to those of a constable.

The revelation about Jarboe also opened up a new,

broad subject of conversation, that of his experiences as a tracker. Among the other things that he and Jeremy discussed during the following days, the man explained how he had gone about finding convicts and told Jeremy what had happened during particularly noteworthy searches. What he related occasionally touched upon the time when he had given up being a tracker and left Van Diemen's Land. At times he seemed to be on the verge of talking about it, then he changed his mind and went on to something different.

Several days after they had first discussed the subject, Jarboe finally revealed why he had stopped working for the authorities. He and Jeremy had finished eating their evening meal beside their campfire, and he fell silent as he puffed on his pipe. Then he abruptly spoke again. "I gave up being a tracker because of a man I killed," he said quietly.

Jeremy was taken aback, as the remark was only indirectly related to what they had discussed before. "One you tracked down?" he asked.

"Aye, one I tracked down," Jarboe replied gravely. "He was more a boy than a man, but he was as mean as two death adders lashed together. He came at me, and I had to kill him to stop him." He shook his head as he continued, his voice barely above a whisper, "But when he was lying there dead, he didn't look mean. He looked like a boy, a dead boy."

The man's dark eyes shone with tears in the firelight, making Jeremy feel a compelling need to defend him and what he had done. "That man wouldn't have regretted killing you, Jarboe," the boy said emphatically. "There was no way for you to avoid doing what you did."

Jarboe puffed on his pipe, staring into the fire, and slowly nodded. "There was one way, mate. I could have avoided it by not being a tracker, so I packed it in. I haven't touched a firearm since then, and I won't ever again. And that made me decide it was time to go on my walkabout."

The boy tried to think of something further to say that

would vindicate Jarboe, but it was unnecessary. The man immediately shrugged off his despondent mood and began talking about their journey. They had covered most of the distance to Menindee, but they were starting to run short on supplies again. Jeremy lay down in his blanket, then fell asleep while they were talking about stopping at another station within the next week or two.

When he thought about it later, Jeremy was certain that Jarboe had never revealed his feelings about killing the man to anyone else. Jarboe had never had another friendship as close as theirs, and the circumstances had been special. Sharing a campfire with a friend in the vast, dark cavern of the Australian night stripped away the restraints of other times and places. It unshackled private feelings, confessions, and moments of shame.

Several nights after that, Jarboe mentioned the books they had to get at Menindee, and he again talked about the need for Jeremy to have more than a basic education. The boy agreed, even though he failed to share Jarboe's sense of importance on the issue. Then he told the man about the various subjects that he had studied at the school in Sydney.

The conversation led to a more general discussion of Jeremy's life in Sydney, the boy relating what he had done from day to day. Then, suddenly, he was sobbing bitterly and trying to express his feelings of confusion and despair when his mother had left. Jarboe put an arm around him and held him, saying nothing, but it was unnecessary for the man to say anything. He listened in sympathy, which was all that Jeremy needed from him.

The moment worked a subtle change in their relationship, adding a new, close bond. One practical result of the change was that Jeremy became more concerned about the man. When they turned in at a track leading to a home paddock to ask for supplies, the boy was less worried over being identified himself than he was about Jarboe's being recognized by some emancipist.

Neither happened, however. The sign beside the track

identified the place as Forbes Station, and their reception was much like that at stations where they had stopped before. The home paddock was similar to the others they had seen, the track ending at a large opening in the surrounding miles of brush and forest. A house flanked by wooden water tanks and cottages was set back across a wide yard from the shearing shed, barracks, and other buildings. The cold gusts of wind stirred up dust in the yard, where the head stockman was giving work orders to other men.

The head stockman had the character of the home paddock, an orderly, functional place that was austere and bare with its absence of foliage and its stark, unpainted wooden buildings. His gaunt, leathery face reflected resignation as he listened to Jarboe, and then complied with the traditional code of generosity to those traveling the tracks in the outback.

Cupping his hands around his mouth, the man shouted at the storeroom, and the storekeeper opened the door and peered out. "Give them enough rations to reach Menindee," the head stockman called, pointing to Jarboe and Jeremy. "And bear in mind that it's not far from here."

Jarboe thanked the head stockman, then he and Jeremy crossed the yard to the storeroom. It was a large building, with blended odors of foodstuffs, leather, and rope wafting from its narrow aisles between barrels and crates. Jarboe and Jeremy opened their dilly bags and took out the cloth bags in which they kept their flour, salt, rice, and other things.

The storekeeper, an old, impish-looking man with a pink face and bald head, was less concerned than the head stockman about the station owner's expenses. With a broad wink at Jeremy, he filled the bags completely and cut a generous square of salt pork. He also gave them a wedge of cheese, a rare treat among rations handed out by a station. Jeremy and Jarboe thanked him, then the boy strained to carry his dilly bag as though it was light while they crossed the yard past the head stockman and went back toward the track.

* * *

Their dilly bags were still heavy with rations several days later when Jeremy and Jarboe began passing farms on both sides of the track. Late in the following day, on a bleak, bitterly cold July afternoon, they reached the crest of a hill and saw Menindee ahead.

In the near distance, the entire landscape was split by the broad, roiling surface of the Darling River. Its flooded condition had evidently subsided, because smoke rose from a riverboat that was fighting the current and edging toward the town. Other riverboats were docked at the waterfront, where there was a clutter of warehouses and other structures. The center of the town was more tidy, the streets lined with large buildings. On the outskirts, a network of roads wound past scattered houses and small farms.

A short distance off to one side of the track, Jeremy and Jarboe found a sheltered place below the crest of the hill to camp. Jarboe's first thought was to obtain school books for Jeremy to study, and he took his crowbar with him as they returned to the track. He stacked stones at the edge of it to mark the location of their camp for when they returned after dark, then they went on down the track toward Menindee.

As they entered the town, Jarboe guided on a church spire that rose above the roofs and trees. With dusk settling under the thick overcast, they went through quiet residential streets lined with large houses. Then they turned in at an alley, one side of it flanked by a tall stone fence at the rear of the spacious grounds around the church and its associated buildings.

A gate in the wall opened onto the rear of the cemetery. As it closed behind him with a squeak of rusty hinges, Jeremy peered around uneasily in the twilight at the crypts and headstones. He and Jarboe walked down a path through the cemetery toward the buildings. Windows in some of them glowed with light, and the sound of vespers came from the towering church.

"Are you sure this isn't stealing, Jarboe?" the boy asked

quietly. "How can we give a fair return for a share of books?"

"It's already been done for you," the man replied. "I daresay many of the people in New South Wales would be more than happy if they could earn as much as the Kerrick family gives to the church in tithes. Which one of these buildings do you think is the school?"

Jeremy pointed out one with dark windows near the vicarage, speculating that it was the school. He and Jarboe crossed the lawns, staying in the shadows and making their way to the rear of the building. Jarboe lifted him up to a window, and the boy saw desks inside. Then the man used his crowbar to open the window as Jeremy shed his bundlesome sheepskin coat.

Jarboe lifted Jeremy again, and the boy climbed in the window. Breathing the familiar smells of a classroom, he crossed it to the shelves of texts and peered closely at them in the dim light coming through the windows from the vicarage. He moved along the shelves, taking down tomes on history, geography, and mathematics. Then he returned to the window. Jarboe reached up to take the books, and Jeremy jumped down to the ground.

As they left the church grounds, Jarboe was pleased that they had the books, and he commented in satisfaction on how easy it had been to obtain them. Jeremy made a noncommittal reply, never having been enthusiastic about the books, and now he regretted having them. Being in the classroom had brought back his memories of tedious, boring schoolwork, which would intrude upon his freedom to study the far more interesting things on the tracks.

When they reached the track, the darkness was so thick that Jeremy could hardly see his hand in front of him. Walking beside the sound of Jarboe's footsteps, the boy asked the man how he would find the stones that marked the location of their camp. "It's hard to explain," Jarboe replied, searching for words. "In the far outback, there are many areas without landmarks. When you travel there, you become accustomed to knowing how far and in what direction you've gone without having to think about it."

Knowing something without thinking about it seemed a contradiction in terms to Jeremy, but it became evident that Jarboe could indeed return to a given spot in the darkness. An hour later, he searched about at the edge of the track for a moment and found the stones, then led the way through the brush and trees to the campsite. While kindling a fire and putting on food to cook, they discussed stopping in Menindee for a few days. Jarboe wanted to earn enough money to buy a large supply of tobacco, as well as a knife, flint and steel, and other necessities for Jeremy.

"Those are things we can't get on the tracks," he added, "and this will be our last chance to buy them."

Jeremy shook his head worriedly. "Many more people will see us than on the tracks. I only hope that none recognizes either of us."

"No one recognized us in Eureka," Jarboe pointed out. "In any event, I've given it considerable thought, and I don't see that we have any choice. We have to stop here if we're going to buy those things, mate."

Jeremy agreed, wanting his own knife and other equipment. After they ate, Jarboe suggested that the boy study his texts. Jeremy reluctantly reached for them, foreseeing many tiresome hours in the future, but he was pleasantly surprised. When he began reading aloud from the geography book, Jarboe was fascinated by the descriptions of other places. Instead of toil, reading became a keen pleasure for Jeremy. Occasionally stumbling over words, he continued reading by the firelight until well past the time when he was usually asleep, as Jarboe puffed on his pipe and listened.

At the first gray light of the raw, cold dawn the next morning, they went back down the track to the town. When they reached it, Jeremy's fears about their being recognized faded to a degree, because the townspeople looked neither right nor left as they hurried along the streets in the blasts of icy wind. He and Jarboe passed

the residential area where the church was located and
went through the center of the town toward the waterfront.

Situated hundreds of miles from any other community,
Menindee had the atmosphere of an outpost of civilization. The residential and business districts were similar
to those of Bathurst and other towns in agricultural and
grazing regions, and the waterfront had something of the
Sydney dockside about it. Back from the warehouses, a
narrow, grimy side street was lined with cheap, shabby
hostels and small taverns, and several dozen men were
going from one to the other in a clamor of loud voices
and laughter.

Jarboe eyed the men, tugging his hat lower. "Many of
that lot look like old lags," he remarked quietly. "Let's
not loiter here."

Jeremy nodded, glancing warily at the men and hurrying on down the street with Jarboe. It led into the
frontage street between a line of large warehouses facing
the river and the wharves, where three riverboats were
docked and their cargo was being unloaded. Gangplanks
were in place at each end of the large vessels, and men
were carrying crates and rolling barrels down to the
piers, then along them and across the street into warehouses.

The riverboat that had arrived the previous evening
was just starting to be unloaded, its deck cargo still
aboard. Eight men were moving between the deck and
a warehouse, a man in a captain's coat and cap super-
vising them and lending a hand with heavier crates. Jarboe studied the men, as he and Jeremy went down the
frontage street toward the vessel. Satisfied with what he
saw, Jarboe led the way down the pier to the captain.

The beefy, ruddy man nodded in satisfaction and
brushed aside Jarboe's explanation of why he and Jeremy
were together. "I'm Captain Kinney," he introduced himself, "and if you want work, I've aplenty of it. With only
my crew unloading cargo, I'll be here much longer than

I like, and it's impossible to hire extra workers in this town."

"I saw a number of men about the hostels and taverns down the street," Jarboe told him. "They all seemed to be at loose ends."

"They're pick-and-shovel men awaiting transportation to Broken Hill," the captain said in disgust, "and they won't turn their hand at anything else except to swill rum and tucker. The pay's eight shillings a day, with tucker and a warm place to sog. My cook and stoker are unloading cargo for extra pay, so I need someone to look after the fires in the engine room and galley. I'll pay the boy a shilling a day for that, if he'll do it right."

"He'll do it right," Jarboe assured the man. "This lad can be trusted with any sort of task. Where do we put our swag?"

"In the engine room, where you'll sog with the crew," Captain Kinney replied. "Come on, and I'll get you and the boy settled in."

Jeremy followed the two men up a gangplank, edging past others rolling casks down it. The captain led the way through a hatch into the engine room, a cavernous space filled with a maze of pipes and machinery. Dimly lighted by portholes, it was warm from the heat radiated by the massive, gurgling boiler and its firebox. The crewmen's belongings were tucked here and there, and the captain pointed out an empty corner for Jarboe and Jeremy.

Jarboe left to join the crew, and the captain showed Jeremy the cords of wood and how to use a long steel rake to keep a smoldering fire spread evenly in the firebox. The boy then followed the captain back up through the hatch and into a small, cramped galley in the after section of the deckhouse. A large kettle of stew simmered on the stove, with a wood bin at one side that was kept filled with smaller billets from the engine room.

When the captain left, Jeremy set to work, keenly aware of his responsibility for the fires and determined to prove Jarboe's expression of confidence in him. As he

moved between the engine room and the galley, he was
struck by the fact that the choice of a place to work had
been an excellent one for him and Jarboe to avoid being
recognized. They were largely isolated from others in the
town, with only the riverboat crew around them.

Their safety from being recognized was further borne
out at midday, when the crew gathered for the noon meal
of stew, ship's biscuit, and tea. Three crewmen were
white, and the others were Lascars and half-Aborigine.
All were taciturn men, evidently having reasons to say
little concerning themselves, and they showed no curiosity about Jarboe and Jeremy.

The stew was a mixture of rice, peas, and dried beef,
and when the meal was finished, Jeremy asked the cook
to show him how to refill the kettle for the evening meal.
The afternoon passed swiftly, the boy stirring the kettle
occasionally as he went back and forth from the engine
room to the galley. After the evening meal, he washed
out the kettle so it would be ready to make porridge the
next morning, and the stoker showed him how to bank
the fires with ashes so the coals would stay hot through
the night.

The following morning, Jeremy was up before everyone
else, stoking the fires and then putting on a kettle of
porridge. By the time the crew came to the galley, the
porridge and tea were ready, and Captain Kinney announced that he would start paying Jeremy two shillings
and sixpence each day. The boy was pleased about the
money, but that was far overshadowed by his satisfaction
from Jarboe's smile and nod of approval.

While he was moving about the refilling of the kettle
after the midday meal, Jeremy noticed wagons drawing
up to the ferry landing at the cluster of houses and small
farms on the other side of the river. A short time later,
the ferry crossed the river with the men going to Broken
Hill. That evening, when Jeremy and Jarboe went to a
store in the center of town, the side street where the
hostels and taverns were located was much quieter.

The first things that Jarboe bought were a knife and a

flint and steel for Jeremy. The next time they went to the store, the man bought each of them a hatchet, then spent the rest of the money he had on tobacco. After that, Jarboe bought mostly figs of tobacco, filling cloth bags with dozens of them and storing the bags in his dilly bag.

The days passed in a busy routine for Jeremy, and during meals and other relaxed moments, Captain Kinney talked with the crew about his plans. He had cargo aboard for Wilcannia, some one hundred miles upstream. After delivering it, he planned to continue on up to the head of navigation at Bourke, an additional two hundred miles up the river. The town was the market center for cattle stations on the Darling Downs, the region whose streams were the headwaters for the river, and he intended to load cattle to take back down the river to the stockyards at Adelaide.

His plans were contingent upon the river not becoming too flooded again for riverboats to travel, but it remained at the same level while the days passed and the cargo disappeared into the warehouse. At the end of the eighth day, when the last of the cargo for Menindee had been unloaded, the captain was in a jolly mood as he talked about leaving for Wilcannia the next day.

Jeremy was in equally high spirits that evening. The riverboat had become a home of sorts to him, as well as the scene of interesting insights on the operation of the vessel, but he was more than ready to continue on to the west with Jarboe. They went to a store in the town, where Jarboe put aside money for his and the boy's ferry fee, then spent the rest of their wages on tobacco for himself and sweets for Jeremy.

The following morning, they made their farewells with the captain and crew, then went up the frontage street to the ferry slip. Several people were waiting there, bundled in thick coats and shivering in the icy wind off the broad river, and the ferry was returning from the other side with four wagons and a dozen men aboard. One man among the people who were waiting remarked to another that those on the ferry had come from Broken Hill to pick up supplies from the warehouses and take them back to the mining site.

When the ferry was halfway across the river, Jarboe broke off talking with Jeremy and peered closely at the men on the low, rectangular vessel. "I know two of those men," he said quietly. "I remember them well."

"Are they ones you tracked down?" Jeremy asked anxiously.

The man nodded grimly as he and Jeremy gathered up their swag and went on up the frontage street, Jeremy peering apprehensively at the men on the ferry. A moment later, he saw which ones were the two emancipists whom Jarboe had noticed. One man nudged another, pointing toward Jarboe, then they both studied him closely. They recognized him, discussing him angrily, and the rest of the men gathered around them to listen.

Farther up the street from the ferry slip, a number of small boats were tied up at the piers and nosed up onto the river bank. At one on the edge of the bank, a man in farmer's garb and an apprentice from a store in the town were loading tools and other things from a merchant's cart into the boat. The farmer was a chubby man with a round, good-natured face, and he talked affably with the apprentice as they moved back and forth.

"If you're going to the other side," Jarboe said to the man, "I'll row the boat in exchange for a ride for myself and the lad here."

"Done, or my name's not John Biggs!" the farmer replied cheerily. "I brought my boat because I begrudged the florin that the ferryman would charge, and I've been thinking that I made a poor bargain with myself. But you've more muscles by far than I, so come right ahead, my friend."

Jeremy and Jarboe put their swag into the boat, then began helping John and the apprentice. While carrying boxes of nails and other things, Jeremy watched the men on the ferry as it drew closer to the slip down the street. As the boy had anticipated, the two emancipists among them had the full, enthusiastic support of their ten com-

panions. All of the men had gathered at the near side of
the craft, and they were talking among themselves and
glaring furiously at Jarboe in readiness to rush at him.

The last few things were put into the boat just as the
ferry docked in its slip. The men on it abandoned their
wagons, bursting through those who were waiting, and
the people raised a storm of protest as they were knocked
aside. Jeremy and John stepped into the stern of the boat,
Jarboe putting his wide shoulder to the bow and shoving
it into the water.

As the boat glided away from the bank, Jarboe leaped
into the center of it and gathered up the oars. The men
from the ferry raced up the street, shaking their fists and
roaring in rage. "Damn your eyes, Jarboe Charlie!" one
voice rang out over the others. "Now I'll get even with
you."

Jarboe spun the boat in the water and turned it toward
the other side of the river with one powerful tug on an
oar, then he began rowing. The boat skimmed across the
water as he heaved his weight against the oars, plying
them rapidly. John Biggs glanced all around in perplexity at the commotion, and Jeremy looked back at the
men, watching them apprehensively.

They stopped, bellowing curses in frustration, then one
pointed to a boat tied up at a pier. As they raced down
the pier and began untying it, two men who evidently
owned the boat ran out of a warehouse and followed them
down the pier, shouting angrily. The encounter turned
into a scuffle, fists flying and some of the men from the ferry
jumping down into the boat.

In their haste and fury, they overloaded the boat. Eight
of them were in it as it swung away from the pier, leaving
bare inches of freeboard. At the last moment, one man
apparently realized the danger and tried to jump back
to the pier. As he put his weight on the gunwale, it dipped
under the water. All of the men began scrambling about
in alarm when the boat shipped water, and it overturned,
dumping them into the river.

His fear changing to relief and amusement, Jeremy

laughed heartily at the men flailing and splashing about in the water. Their companion had watched the goings-on in amazement, and he turned to Jarboe. "What in the name of Saint Geoffrey was that all about?" he asked.

"I've had trouble with some of those fellows," Jarboe replied, pulling the oars in a steady rhythm. "They wanted to even the score."

"Well, that's no good, is it?" John remarked cheerfully. "People should let bygones be bygones and dwell on the pleasant things in life. Speaking of which, the sun has at long last come out, hasn't it?"

Jeremy looked up at the opening in the clouds, the first one in several weeks of solid overcast. With the sun beaming through, the day had suddenly become brighter, as though in acknowledgment of their narrow escape from the emancipists and their rowdy companions. Then he looked at the river bank ahead, happily reflecting that the danger that he or Jarboe would be recognized would be much less in the sparsely populated region to the west.

When the boat was pulled up onto the bank below John's small farm, he invited Jarboe and Jeremy to his house. They declined, making their farewells with the man, and went down the path to the ferry landing and the houses clustered around it. On the other side of the tiny community, a wide, well-traveled track stretched northwest toward Broken Hill. A narrow track led straight to the west, and they set out down it.

Within less than an hour, all signs of the river and those who lived beside it were left behind. The only indication of human activity was the thin ribbon of the track, reaching ahead through a wilderness. The terrain was more rugged than east of the river, unfit for farming and less suitable for grazing. It was a more austere land, with gnarled trees clinging to hills whose flanks and jagged crests were outcroppings of black rock.

The scene looked pleasant enough to Jeremy, with the sky continuing to clear and weak winter sunshine bathing the landscape. He and Jarboe talked and laughed about the men from Broken Hill, and the men's antics when they had fallen into the river. The boy expressed satisfaction that the greatest danger of their being recognized was now past, and Jarboe agreed with him, but added that they still had to be watchful.

During late afternoon, they climbed a hill that was higher than others. From its crest, the landscape opened out all around in enormous dimensions, a seemingly endless expanse of hills and valleys. Jeremy knew that when they reached the farthest point he could see, the land would still stretch on and on ahead of them. He was suddenly struck by a sense of being surrounded by distances so vast they staggered the imagination, of spaces on a scale that reduced human beings to insignificant motes.

The boy realized that the feeling had lurked in the back of his mind for months, awaiting some culminating moment to reveal itself. Awareness of it brought another, still more intense reaction. Even with a companion, he had a sensation of being at a far remove from other people. More than mere loneliness, it was a sense of isolation that could chill the soul. He was untroubled by it, but he understood why others found the outback unbearable.

He now saw the land in a subtly different way. Just as though a hazy film from his life in Sydney was gone from his eyes, he had a new, more revealing perspective. The land lacked the sentience of a living creature, yet it was something more than inert. It had moods and rhythms. While it was uninviting, it fell short of being hostile, because it was indifferent. More than old, it felt inconceivably ancient, as well as weary and wise. The spiny stone crests and flanks of the hills were like the very bones of the earth, where the soil flesh had wasted away over countless millennia.

Jeremy also knew that it was his land. In time he would go on his own walkabout, and somewhere in this vast expanse, he was certain that he would find his heritage, the place where he belonged. "We're certainly in the outback now, Jarboe," he said quietly as they walked on down the track. "Now we're in the far outback."

"Aye, indeed we are, mate," the man agreed. "We're well and truly deep into the outback now."

Chapter Eight

The wild boar appeared without warning, bursting out of the brush a few yards from Jarboe and charging toward him. He was at the edge of the billabong where he and Jeremy had stopped to camp, some fifty feet from the nearest tree large enough to hold his weight. But as he raced toward the tree with the boar gaining on him rapidly, his first thought was of Jeremy. "Get into a tree, Jeremy!" he shouted. "Climb into a tree!"

Jeremy was standing among the trees where he had been gathering firewood, paralyzed by shock and fear. The boar was an ugly, terrifying creature, looking almost entirely unlike its fat, lazy domestic counterpart. A large, powerful beast, it was also very fast and agile, and long, deadly tusks jutted up from its hairy snout.

Then the boy was galvanized into movement as he realized that Jarboe had no chance of escaping the boar. He dropped the wood and snatched out his sling, looking for stones. Sliding his forefinger into the loops at the end of the rawhide thongs, he grabbed up two stones, one the size of a grape and the other larger than an egg. He placed the small stone on the leather and began swinging the sling around at arm's length.

The boar was right behind Jarboe, slashing its long, gleaming tusks at the man's legs. They were over sixty feet away, and Jeremy knew that the sling had to be spinning smoothly for an accurate cast at that distance. With a wrenching, sick feeling in the pit of his stomach, the boy saw the boar gouge a tusk deep into Jarboe's leg, and the man fell.

The sling was finally spinning in a smooth rhythm, Jeremy moving only his wrist and forearm as it spun in a blur and made a droning noise. Jarboe scrambled about on the ground in a frantic attempt to get away from the boar as it snorted in savage triumph and gored his legs. Jeremy carefully judged the rhythm of the spin, then let a thong slip off his finger.

The stone shot through the air and struck the boar's flank with a loud crack. The animal squealed in pain and rage as it wheeled around, blood from Jarboe's legs dripping from its tusks and snout. Then it charged at Jeremy, grunting and snorting ferociously. The boy slipped the loop back onto his finger and started to place the larger stone on the leather. The stone slipped from his fingers, and he snatched it up again.

"Get into a tree, Jeremy!" Jarboe screamed hoarsely. "I can see to myself! Do as I say, Jeremy! Now climb into a tree!"

Jeremy ignored the man's shouts, placing the stone on the leather. It was heavy, and he recalled other times when he had broken a sling while attempting to cast relatively large stones. For an instant, he was torn with indecision, wondering if he should find a smaller stone. Then he realized that he might not have time to cast the one he had, with the boar racing toward him. He began swinging the sling at arm's length.

Jarboe stormed frantically at Jeremy to climb into a tree, his voice almost drowned by the enraged snorting of the boar pounding toward the boy. The lean, muscular beast's tiny eyes gleamed with mindless, brutal savagery as it swung its head from side to side, ready to slash and rip with its tusks. Jeremy began spinning the sling rapidly. It turned into a blur and hummed softly as he spun it with his wrist and forearm, judging the rhythm. Then he let a thong slip off his finger.

The boar was bare yards away and lowering its head to attack when the stone struck it between the eyes with the sound of an ax slamming into a tree. The skin between its eyes burst open and blood exploded from the animal's nose as the impact stopped it in mid-stride and knocked it to the ground. Its mouth opened wide in a shrill, deafening squeal of pain and fury, and it floundered blindly about, trying to get back to its feet.

Jeremy hoisted a large, heavy stone and ran forward, heaving it at the boar's head. The stone thudded on its head and bounced off in a spatter of blood as the animal's squeals became louder. Jarboe hobbled toward the boar, dragging one leg and carrying a larger stone. He lifted it high and slammed it down on the animal's head. Blood gushed and bones cracked, and the squealing was choked off. The animal's limbs twitched, then it was still.

Jeremy ran to Jarboe as the man collapsed, his trouser legs bloody and torn. The man propped himself up to a sitting position, tugging at his trousers. Jeremy helped him pull them up, and the boy cringed inwardly as he saw the wounds. Blood oozed from several gouges in the man's muscular legs, but the worst one was on the calf of his right leg. It was a deep wound over four inches long, with blood flowing from it.

"That's where he got me the first time," Jarboe said, his voice hoarse with pain as he clamped a hand over the wound to control the bleeding. He glanced around, then nodded toward a thornbush. "Fetch a handful of thorns from that bush, Jeremy. Get them from the top of it, because those near the bottom will be dried out and will break, and get long ones."

The boy ran to the bush and plucked several of the long, sharp thorns from its wiry limbs, scratching his hands on them in his haste. He returned and showed them to the man, who nodded in satisfaction. "**Right,** now sew up that cut with them, Jeremy."

"I can't do that, Jarboe!" the boy protested. "It'll hurt you!"

"It'll hurt me worse if you don't, mate, and I can't reach it myself."

Jeremy hesitated, then drew in a deep breath and steeled himself as he nodded. "Very well, Jarboe. What do I do?"

"Push each one through one edge of the cut, then turn it and push it through from the other side. It'll be easy, Jeremy."

The boy found it anything but easy, probing gingerly with a sharp thorn and shrinking from driving it into the man's skin. Then, the knowledge that he was causing even more pain made him summon his determination. With measured force, he pierced the torn skin on one side of the wound, then the other. Jarboe nodded in encouragement, holding the edges of the wound closed with his thumb and forefinger. Jeremy turned the long, supple thorn and pushed it through from the other side.

After the first one, it was somewhat easier. Blood smeared the boy's hands as he worked his way up the wound, closing it with the thorns. When the last one was in place, Jarboe nodded in satisfaction. "You did a good job, Jeremy," he said, "and you got it sewed up before it could swell very much. Now go wash your hands and fetch some cobwebs, but don't wad them up. Keep them open as much as you can."

The boy ran to the billabong and rinsed his hands, then began looking for cobwebs. Dusk was settling, and he peered closely in clumps of brush, finding a large cobweb. He lifted it out and carefully carried it to Jarboe, who pointed to the wound on his calf. The boy laid the cobweb over the wound, and the blood immediately began clotting.

The wound stopped bleeding after Jeremy placed another cobweb on it, then he brought others to put on the

smaller wounds. It was almost dark when he finished
and helped Jarboe slide to where they had put their swag.
The man propped himself up against a tree, and Jeremy
moved about, kindling a fire, bringing water from the
billabong, and putting on food to cook.

Where the dead boar lay several yards away, there
were furtive sounds and movements in the darkness. "It
didn't take the dingoes long to find him," Jarboe remarked. "If it hadn't been for you, they would be eating
me now instead of the boar. You saved my life, Jeremy."

"You were doing the same thing for me," Jeremy
pointed out, stirring the pans. "You were more worried
about me than yourself."

"Aye, we're mates, aren't we?" Jarboe replied, smiling.

Jeremy smiled and nodded in agreement. He made tea
and filled their plates, then handed Jarboe's to him. The
man was in intense pain and forced himself to eat, sighing in relief when he finished. Unrolling his blanket, he
tucked it around himself and then filled his pipe. He lit
it and puffed on it as Jeremy took out his textbooks.

The man was always interested in readings from the
history text, but most of all he enjoyed the geography
book. He took pleasure in hearing the descriptions of
other places over and over, and Jeremy had read some
of them aloud several times. He opened the book to where
he had left off the last time and began reading.

When he finished smoking his pipe, the man interrupted Jeremy. "That's enough for tonight," he said.
"You'd better get some sleep now."

"You can't sleep, Jarboe, and I don't mind reading
some more."

"No, I'll sleep fine just like this, mate. You go ahead
and sog."

Jeremy hesitated, sure that Jarboe was in too much
pain to sleep, then he did what the man had said. After
putting away his books, he unrolled his blanket and lay
down in it beside the fire. He was wakeful for a time,
images of the boar attacking Jarboe flowing through his

mind as he listened to the dingoes feeding on the animal, then he fell asleep.

The man moved and made an involuntary sound of pain at dawn, waking Jeremy. The boy sat up, shivering in the early morning chill, and stirred the ashes of the fire. "How does your leg feel?" he asked.

"I know it's there," Jarboe replied dryly.

The boy smiled, putting wood on the hot embers. Then he gathered up the billys and took them to the billabong. The boar was hardly recognizable, its carcass chewed and entrails scattered about. Kites and other birds swarmed over it in the early light, taking their turn at feeding.

After the breakfast of tea and leftovers, Jeremy took the dishes to the billabong and washed them. When he returned to the fire, Jarboe had dragged himself to his feet and was leaning against the tree where he had sat. The man pointed to a sapling that forked some five feet from the ground, asking Jeremy to cut it down and make a crutch.

"But you can't travel, Jarboe," the boy protested.

"Aye, I must," the man replied grimly. "Anyone who lies about when injured takes twice as long to heal. Make the crutch for me, mate."

Jeremy reluctantly took his hatchet from his dilly bag, then stepped to the sapling and cut it down. After chopping off the branches, he trimmed the bottom of it to a length that was comfortable for Jarboe. Gathering up their swag, Jeremy started to carry Jarboe's, but the man insisted on carrying it. Then they moved toward the track, Jarboe leaning on the crutch.

Their pace was so slow that after an hour, Jeremy could look back and see where they had camped. Jarboe's face had a grayish tinge and was lined with pain as he moved his right leg stiffly, each shuffling, labored step covering only a few inches. When the spring day in September became too warm for their sheepskin coats, they stopped to roll the coats and sling them on their backs with rope, then continued on down the track.

In addition to their slow pace, the day was different because they were silent, a marked change from their usual lively conversation. At midday, when they stopped for Jarboe to rest, he pulled up his trouser legs and examined the wounds. None was bleeding, and the calf of his right leg was massively swollen, but the thorns were still firmly in place. After the man had rested for a time, they set out down the track again.

At the end of the day, when they stopped at a marshy spring beside the track and camped, they had covered no more than six miles. Jarboe was weaker and in even greater pain the next morning, barely able to drag himself to his feet. The man grimly endured the suffering and struggled to the track on his crutch, then slowly shuffled on down it.

On the third day, the pain was more manageable for Jarboe. His main concern became the possibility of festering infection, which could be more dangerous than the wounds themselves. However, the swelling in the calf of his leg began subsiding during the following days, with no sign of infection. The thorns dried out, and Jarboe said they would eventually break apart and fall away from the wound while it was healing back together.

The pace of travel increased, Jarboe resting more of his weight on his leg and relying less on the crutch. He and Jeremy covered more distance each day, conversing once more as they went down the track. While they were talking one day, the discussion turned to Jarboe's destination in his walkabout. Jeremy had always assumed that it consisted of an entire region far to the west, but he learned that it was a very small area.

"You can stand on it," the man told him. "It's no bigger than that."

"What makes that one small place so special to you?" Jeremy asked.

"It's the place on a Songtrail where I came alive," Jarboe explained. "The first time I moved in my mother's stomach, she was passing that spot. As I told you, the elders know the Songtrails by heart, and one of them looked at the place and told her that it was there that a creator sang the red goshawk into being during the Dreamtime. So it was the red goshawk spirit that made me come alive, and I can't ever kill one of them."

"Does it bother you when someone else kills one of them?"

"No. Some people are brought alive by spirits of edible animals. They can't eat that particular animal, but they don't care when others do.'"

"And the elders can tell what spirit brings each person alive? They certainly know many things, don't they?"

Jarboe agreed emphatically, and the conversation moved on to other subjects. Jeremy avoided mentioning one topic, even though it was of much concern to him, because he had found that it was a sensitive one for Jarboe. The boy worried about meeting up with another wild boar, but on the single occasion when he had discussed it with Jarboe, he had learned that the man was disgusted with himself over the attack. He believed he should have detected the boar before it had a chance to attack him.

His attitude toward the incident was the same as his frustration when he had been unable to make a firestick, and similar failures when he had tried to demonstrate skills that he had lost over the years. One such skill that would have been very useful if they happened upon another boar was how to make Aborigine weapons. A few weeks before, when he had found pieces of flint, he had tried and failed to fashion one of them into a point for a spear.

However, during the single conversation with Jarboe about wild boars, Jeremy had learned that not all of them would attack. Just as often, they would move away unless they were molested. In addition, as well as being careful to avoid poisonous snakes and spiders, Jeremy had become more watchful for boars, and he saw that Jarboe had done the same.

The man's leg continued healing, and he began walking part of the time without using his crutch. A line of ten

large drays passed them one day, the teamsters waving
and calling out greetings. They were making the rounds
of stations in the region, collecting the wool clips and
delivering supplies. With their own supplies diminishing, Jeremy and Jarboe talked about stopping at a station
within a few days to ask for rations.

On the day that they used up the last of their tea at
breakfast, they came to a track leading to a home paddock, the sign beside it identifying it as Burrangong Station. The sign was almost illegible, and the post that had
supported it had rotted out of the ground and had been
carelessly propped up against a tree. The first impression
of the station was unfavorable, but it would probably be
several days before they reached the next one, so Jeremy
and Jarboe walked up the track.

When the home paddock came into view, it matched
the first impression of the station. The buildings were
ramshackle, pens were in disrepair, and the horses in a
pen looked half-starved. The reason for the condition of
the station was evident. There was none of the purposeful
bustle at other stations, and most of the stockmen in view
were lazily idling about.

Three men sitting beside a pen pointed out a man at
the shearing shed when Jarboe asked for the head stockman. "That's Wilbur Lukin, the manager," one of the
men said. "The owners live in Melbourne, and a hired
manager runs this place. Lukin does more walking than
running, though."

The three men laughed at the sarcastic remark as Jeremy and Jarboe stepped toward the shearing shed. Lukin
was a burly man in his forties with a bulging stomach
and features that reflected an ill-tempered disposition. His
appearance was as slipshod as that of the station, his
clothes grimy and a ragged growth of stubble on his face.

At first Jeremy thought the man was going to refuse
when Jarboe asked if there were rations to spare, the
phrase always used by swagmen. Scowling irately, Lukin
started to shake his head as he glared at Jeremy and

Jarboe. Then he paused, studying them more closely, and nodded. "Go over to the storeroom," he said, pointing to a building. "I'll find the storekeeper and send him over to measure you out some rations."

As he finished speaking, the man turned and walked toward the dilapidated house without acknowledging Jarboe's thanks. Jeremy stepped toward the storeroom with Jarboe, puzzling over Lukin's attitude and behavior. "I thought for a moment that he was going to send us on our way," the boy said. "But stations always give out rations to people on the tracks, don't they?"

"The odd few might be willing to be known as misers for the pence they'd save," Jarboe replied absently, pondering and glancing around.

They reached the storeroom, and Jarboe took another look around before he followed Jeremy inside. It was cluttered with supplies that had been recently delivered by the drays but not yet sorted out and stored. Barrels of flour, casks of dried peas and rice, flitches of salt pork, and other provisions were piled about at random. Jeremy gazed at the plentitude of rations as he and Jarboe put down their swag and waited for the storekeeper.

A minute passed, then another. Jarboe frowned thoughtfully as he stepped to the window, Jeremy following him. It had shutters instead of a pane, and Jarboe unlatched and opened them. The window faced the pens where the three men had been sitting, but now they were gone.

Jarboe closed and latched the shutters, then returned to their swag. "I don't like the feel of this place, Jeremy," he said, gathering up his things. "Ever since we talked with Lukin, I've felt uneasy. It might be wise for us to get back to the track without delay."

"Do you think someone here recognized one of us?" Jeremy asked, looking at all the rations regretfully. "We're out of tea and almost out of other things, and the next station will be several days down the track."

"Aye, I know, and I'm not sure what I think," Jarboe

replied. "But we can eat bush tucker. That might be our best course ..."

His voice faded as scurrying footsteps outside rushed toward the door, then it burst open. Lukin dashed in, some eight or ten men crowding in behind him. "Grab them!" he shouted gleefully. "That boy is worth five hundred guineas to us! Don't let him get away!"

Jarboe reacted with blinding speed, flipping a flour barrel onto its side and rolling it into the men. Then the storeroom was a scene of confusion as some men scrambled to avoid the barrel and it knocked others into a tumble of flailing limbs. Jarboe had his swag, and Jeremy's first impulse was to get his own—his knife, water bottle, and other things precious to him. He started toward it, then sprang back as men reached for him.

The boy turned to join Jarboe, who was backing toward the window, but men were in his path. They were grappling with Jarboe and reeling away one by one as his heavy fists struck them. Jeremy felt someone behind him grab the collar of his canvas coat, and he tried to wriggle away. Jarboe shoved aside the last man trying to seize him, then turned to the window.

Instead of pausing to open the shutters, Jarboe went through them. His wide shoulder crashed into them, breaking them into splintered boards flying in all directions. Then he vaulted through the window and was gone. A couple of the men he had knocked down clambered to their feet and ran to the window, starting to climb out and chase after him.

"Let him go!" Lukin shouted as he took a fresh grip on Jeremy's coat. "I've got the one who'll fetch the money!" He spun Jeremy around and scowled, studying the boy. "Is your name Jeremy Kerrick?" he demanded.

Seething with resentment, Jeremy silently glared at the man. Lukin's stubbled face flushed with anger, and he grabbed the boy's shoulders and shook him viciously. "Tell me your name, or I'll beat it out of you!" he bellowed.

"Leave off, Lukin," a man objected. "That boy might

well be who you say he is, and if he is, he's going to be
treated right. If there's anything we don't need, it's trouble with the Kerricks."

Other men spoke up in a chorus of agreement, and
Lukin nodded as he took a ragged, folded newspaper from
his coat pocket. "Aye, it's money we want, not trouble
with anyone," he said, opening the newspaper. He read
the reward notice on the front page, glancing at Jeremy,
then he handed the newspaper to another man. "I remembered reading that as soon as I saw him, and it's
him right enough. There can't be many boys about with
those snake eyes, and the rest of the description fits like
scales on a fish."

The other men studied the reward notice, one of them
reading it aloud for the benefit of those who were illit-
erate. They agreed that Jeremy was the boy referred to
in the notice, then talked with Lukin about how to proceed about collecting the reward. A man mentioned the
long distance that some of them would have to travel to
contact the Kerrick family, since Wayamba was the next
station to the north, then Tibooburra Station was north
of it.

"That much money is more than worth a long ride,
though," the man added. "Do you want some of us to
saddle up and start out now, Lukin?"

"No, it's too late in the day to get far before nightfall,"
the burly station manager replied. "It'll take several days
to get there, and a few hours won't make much difference.
Two of you can set out early tomorrow morning, with a
pack horse to carry supplies. While we're waiting for
them to come after the boy, we'll keep him in the tool
shed. That's the strongest building here, and with his
hands tied, he won't get out of it."

"What if that Aborigine comes back for the boy?" a
man asked. "And why was this boy traveling with him?"

Silence fell as all of the men looked at Jeremy, who
said nothing. Then one of them suggested that Jarboe
had been intending to collect the reward. "Aye, that must
have been it," Lukin agreed, and the other men nodded.

"He found the boy, and he was probably heading straight north. Well, in event he comes back, you can take turns standing guard at the shed."

"Not by ourselves," a man put in quickly, others emphatically agreeing with him. "I'm not going to try to fight that man by myself."

"He can't fight bullets," Lukin said, grinning maliciously. "I have a pistol, one of the best made, and I'll fetch it out." He pointed to Jeremy's swag on the floor. "Two of you come with me and bring that sheepskin coat for him to use in the shed. Leave the bag and the rest of it, because there'll be things among it that he could use to get loose. You other men tidy up in here and get some shutters made to cover that window."

The men began moving about and restacking the casks and barrels that had been overturned during the melee. Lukin grabbed Jeremy's collar again and led the boy outside, two men following and one of them carrying the sheepskin coat. They went toward a small building near the shearing shed, and as he looked at it, Jeremy gave up all hopes of escaping by himself. It was weathered but still very strong, constructed of thick, heavy timbers.

Lukin kept a tight grip on Jeremy's collar as one of the other men went for a rawhide thong to tie the boy's hands. The second man opened the tool shed and carried out sheep shears, axes, and other tools that Jeremy might have used to free his hands. When they were all stacked beside the shed, Lukin shoved the boy inside and tossed the coat in, then the man closed the door and fastened the latch on the outside.

Prowling about in the shed, Jeremy found only wool rakes and other tools that were useless for cutting the rawhide on his wrists. He sat down, feeling very forlorn and racked with worry about Jarboe. The boy knew with absolute certainty that Jarboe would return for him, and he earnestly hoped that it occurred to the man that the guard at the shed might be armed.

The light coming through cracks in the shed was that of sunset when the door opened. A man stepped in with a plate of food, while another man stood in the doorway to keep Jeremy from darting out. As the first man started to untie Jeremy's hands so he could eat, the boy refused the food. "You won't get any more tucker until tomorrow morning," the man warned.

"I said that I don't want it!" the boy barked, glaring angrily.

The man shrugged, turning back to the door with the plate. "He's enough of a brumby to be a Kerrick," he remarked to the other man. "And the looks from those snake eyes of his would set wood on fire."

The two men laughed, closing and latching the door. The temperature dropped after sunset, and Jeremy fumbled with his sheepskin coat, finally managing to get it unrolled and pulled around his shoulders. When dusk fell, Jeremy saw the gleam of a lantern in front of the shed and heard Lukin's voice. The boy stepped to the door and peered through a crack.

The man was giving instructions to the first guard of the evening. As he looked at the guard, Jeremy remembered what Lukin had said about his pistol. It was in a holster on a belt around the guard's waist, and in the light of the lantern, the boy saw that it was the most modern and lethal type available. Instead of a common cap-and-ball pistol, it was a revolver that would fire five times before it needed to be reloaded. Gripped by anguished fear for Jarboe, the boy sat down again.

After the home paddock had settled for the night and the other men were in bed, Jeremy hoped the guard would fall asleep, but he remained alert. From time to time he circled the shed with the lantern, its light shining through the cracks as he stepped around the building. Jeremy had no thought of sleep, and his harrowing worry over Jarboe was keeping him awake in any case.

The hours wore on, and during the middle of the night, the guard changed. The second guard also circled the shed at intervals as Jeremy listened to his footsteps and to the sounds of the night outside. The hauntingly dismal wailing of dingoes in the distance made the sheep dogs at the house restless, and they barked occasionally. Then Jeremy heard another noise.

A board at the rear of the shed squeaked very faintly, the nails gradually pulling out of the wood. The boy crept to the back of the building. Moonlight filtered through the cracks, and Jeremy saw a wide board moving slightly as Jarboe slowly worked it loose with his crowbar.

Panic gripped the boy as the lantern moved, and the guard walked around the shed once more. When the glow of the lantern reached the side of the building, Jeremy was just on the point of calling out in warning when the board stopped squeaking. The guard stepped on around the building, evidently seeing nothing suspicious. A moment later, the board began moving again.

The minutes seemed very long to Jeremy until Jarboe finally lifted the board aside. Jeremy squeezed through the hole, and while Jarboe was untying the rawhide around his wrists, he whispered a warning about the pistol that the guard had. Jarboe nodded, softly replying that he had seen it.

They moved quietly around the shed, Jeremy following Jarboe. At the front corner, Jarboe's knife gleamed in the moonlight as he took it out, then stepped to the guard with long, quick strides. The guard was just starting to turn when Jarboe seized him, his knife at the man's throat.

Pulling the guard back to the shed, Jarboe unbuckled the belt around the man's waist, and it felt to the ground with the holstered pistol at the corner of the shed. "What's your name?" Jarboe asked softly.

"Tom Edwards," the guard whispered, his voice quaking with fear.

"Very well, now listen to me, Tom," Jarboe said quietly. "I don't like to harm anyone in any way, but if you try to raise an alarm, it'll be the last thing you'll ever do." He turned to Jeremy. "Fetch my swag, mate. I left it over there at the near side of the shearing shed."

The boy hurried across the yard between the buildings and peered closely in the deep shadows beside the shearing shed. Finding the swag, he gathered it up and returned to Jarboe. "Just put the rest of it down," the man said, taking his dilly bag and slinging it over his shoulder. "While I'm at the storeroom, carry the lantern around the shed. That way, if any of the others happen to stir and look out a window, they'll be less likely to think that anything is amiss. I'll be back in a few minutes."

Jarboe limped on his injured leg as he stepped toward the storeroom, pushing Tom ahead of him and keeping his knife at the man's throat. Jeremy went back into the shed for his sheepskin coat, then he picked up the lantern and began walking slowly around the shed. Peering at the dark house and barracks, he was less than confident that anyone who looked out would be deceived upon seeing the lantern moving around the shed.

At the corner of the shed, he almost stumbled over the belt and pistol, and he realized that it would be protection against anyone who came out of the house or barracks. It also occurred to him that the weapon would serve the same purpose against wild boars. He picked up the belt and the long, heavy pistol in the attached holster, and walked on around the shed.

He knew that Jarboe disliked firearms, but the man had shown in numerous ways that he expected Jeremy to form his own opinions. Opening a leather pouch opposite the holster on the belt, the boy saw that it contained extra bullets. He closed the pouch, then fastened the buckle and slung the belt over his shoulder, feeling much less vulnerable.

The two men returned from the storeroom, Tom carrying Jeremy's swag. The dilly bag bulged with rations, and the dilly bag hanging from Jarboe's shoulder was also full. He asked what Jeremy was doing with the pistol, and when the boy explained, Jarboe dismissed the subject with a nod as he gathered up the rest of his swag. Jeremy took his from Tom, then they crossed the yard toward the track, Tom again walking in front of Jarboe's knife.

As they went down the track in the moonlight, Tom

overcame his fear for his life. Instead, he worried aloud about Lukin's reaction over losing both his valuable pistol and the reward for Jeremy. "Tell him that the fault was his own," Jarboe suggested. "Placing a guard with a lantern in front of that shed was foolish. A guard should be in the dark, and what he's guarding should be lighted. A child could have done what I did."

Showing no inclination to point out Lukin's mistakes to him, Tom fell silent as they walked on down the track. When they were near the main track, Jarboe stopped and told Tom to take off his boots. "That's to slow you down in getting back to the home paddock," he explained. "If Lukin decides to lead a chase after us, I'd like to have a head start. I'll leave your boots where you can find them easily on the main track."

Tom removed his boots and went back toward the home paddock, stepping slowly and gingerly in stocking feet. Jarboe carried the boots as he and Jeremy went on to the main track. In order to mislead Lukin if the man did indeed decide to pursue them, Jarboe led the way to the east for a short distance. He hung the boots in a tree, then he and Jeremy turned and hurried down the track to the west.

When the moon set and the night grew dark, Jarboe's injured leg had become very painful and he was limping heavily. He and Jeremy climbed a slope overlooking the track and lay down in their blankets among thick brush. At daybreak, Jeremy was ravenously hungry, but a fire would reveal their location from miles around. He and Jarboe ate handfuls of dried peas as they went on down the track, watching behind for riders.

The day passed with no sign of pursuit. By late afternoon, it had become evident that either Lukin had been misled by the boots and was searching eastward, or he had decided against following them. Jeremy and Jarboe camped beside a billabong and cooked a large meal of salt pork, rice, and peas, with damper and tea. After they finished eating, Jarboe filled his pipe and lit it, and Jeremy took the pistol out of the holster to examine it.

Although he wanted nothing to do with the pistol himself, Jarboe was thoroughly familiar with firearms and perfectly willing to teach Jeremy all about the weapon. The man explained how the mechanism worked, how to aim and fire the pistol, and how to keep it and the bullets free of corrosion. After they had discussed it at length, Jeremy wrapped the belt around the holstered pistol and put it in his dilly bag. The boy then took out his books and read aloud from the history text until it was time to go to sleep.

The next day, the pistol and all of the rations made Jeremy's dilly bag very heavy, but the boy hardly noticed the additional weight. His muscles had hardened during the past months, and it had become easy for him to carry a heavy burden and keep up with Jarboe, even before the boar had injured the man. In addition, Jeremy was growing rapidly, his boots now fitting him comfortably with only one pair of stockings.

After they passed a home paddock track two days later, the main track narrowed. It still had deep ruts from the drays that transported supplies and wool, but the following day, there was another indication that the region was becoming more remote. Jeremy glimpsed a cluster of sheep at a distance from the track that had long, thick wool from being unshorn. He had seen a few other woolies—sheep that had strayed from flocks—and their feral offspring, but never so many at one time.

"There must be twenty or more," Jeremy remarked, pointing them out. "They're carrying so much wool that it would be more than worthwhile for one of the station owners hereabouts to collect them."

"Aye, if the station owner or his stockmen could find them," Jarboe replied. "Not everyone has your sharp eyes. More than that, you've learned to look where animals are inclined to go. Many graziers spend a lifetime working with animals and don't learn to do that."

"Station owners might also consider it a waste of time to search for woolies," Jeremy suggested. "Dingoes must kill most of them."

Jarboe agreed, adding that only a ram or a large ewe could fight a dingo, which prevented woolies from multiplying rapidly. The conversation continued, he and Jeremy discussing other domestic animals that escaped from stations and became feral. Jarboe commented that brumbies and dunnocks—wild horses and cattle—were particularly well suited to surviving in the wilderness. They could readily defend their young from dingoes, and they thrived in areas that were too arid for graziers to establish stations.

When they camped at a billabong that evening, Jeremy found what appeared to be the hoofprints of dunnocks in the mud at the edge of the water. He was unsure about them, because they were mixed among the tracks of the oxen that had drawn the drays down the track and back. However, shortly after he and Jarboe set out the next morning, the boy saw a half dozen wild cattle grazing in deep spinifex in a valley a mile from the track.

He and Jarboe glimpsed other feral offspring of domestic animals during the following days, and native animals became more plentiful. Scarcely an hour passed without a kangaroo bounding through the brush or an emu scurrying away as they approached. The terrain opened out, the hills falling behind, and it became more arid as spring began changing into summer. With the water holes farther apart, the foliage around them teemed with small animals and with birds that gathered to drink and roost at sunset.

On an early summer day, Jeremy and Jarboe came to the end of the track. A brushy meadow lay to the west of it. "Well, now we're off into the never-never, mate," Jarboe said. "There'll be no more stations to stop at for rations, so we'll have to get used to bush tucker."

"Yes, but not for another week or two," Jeremy pointed out, laughing. "Thanks to Wilbur Lukin, we still have a goodly supply of rations, but I'm sure that he wishes we would choke on them."

Jarboe laughed and agreed as they left the track behind and started across the meadow. When they stepped off into the unmarked wilderness, the boy was conscious of passing a milestone beyond which few had ventured. Others followed beaten tracks of both a literal and symbolic nature, and in both senses he was setting out into the unknown.

Jeremy accepted that fact with anticipation for what lay ahead. He loved the outback, and when he went on his own walkabout, he was certain that he would eventually find the one place where he belonged somewhere in its vast spaces.

The manager of Burrangong Station was still angry when Alexandra Kerrick talked with him. He allowed his anger to overcome his better judgment to the extent of making a reply that bordered on sarcasm to one of her questions, which brought a quick, stern retort from her son: "You keep a civil tongue in your head, Lukin!" Jonathan snapped. "If you speak one more word in that tone, I'll step down from this horse and close your mouth with my fist!"

The color drained from Lukin's sullen face, a pallor of fear replacing his angry flush as he realized his mistake. At just over six feet and two hundred pounds, Jonathan had his father's muscular frame and bold, handsome features. He also had the same commanding presence about him that gave his disapproval the impact of a physical force.

Elizabeth and Sheila Garrity, sitting on their horses beside Alexandra, were equally intimidating. They wore stockman's clothes and wide hats, and their coiled stock whips almost seemed a part of their right hands. Elizabeth ruled Wayamba Station with iron control and had a steely, compelling presence of her own. She was slender and tall, but small compared to Sheila, who was six feet. Sheila had inherited her height and Anglo-Saxon features from her father, Patrick Garrity, while her black hair and eyes and her smooth, ebony skin were from her Aborigine mother. Her and Elizabeth's eyes were fixed on Lukin in silent, glowering menace.

As the owners of Wayamba and Tibooburra stations, there was also an aura of authority and respect associated with the Kerrick and Garrity names, which Lukin had transgressed. The stockmen who had gathered behind him snickered at his chagrin, bringing a frown back to his face. He glared over his shoulder, silencing them, then turned back. "I meant no offense, mo'm," he assured Alexandra. "That pistol was one of the best made, a revolver. It cost me over eighty guineas, and the boy took it with him."

"Yes, so you've said several times now," Alexandra replied. "If you had sent word of this to Tibooburra Station in a timely fashion, I would have assumed responsibility for your loss. But I had to hear about it in due course from a swagman who had heard of it from others on the tracks, so your loss has nothing to do with me. What sort of man was with the boy whom you believed to be my grandson?"

Lukin looked away, muscles working in his jaws as he controlled his anger and voice. "The man was an Aborigine," he grumbled. "A big man, sixty-odd years old, but he could move about lively enough. He called himself Charlie Jarvis, or something of the sort."

"Jarboe Charlie?"

"Aye, that was it," Lukin replied, the stockmen behind him nodding.

Alexandra exchanged a glance with Jonathan. The fact that the boy had been Jeremy was now established with certainty. She turned back to Lukin: "Was there any indication of where they went from here?"

Lukin nodded morosely. "Aye, they went toward Menindee. Tom Edwards was guarding the boy, and the Aborigine took him down to the main track with them. He made Edwards take off his boots so he would be longer in getting back here, and we found the boots down the track to the east."

"I'd like to speak with this Tom Edwards."

"He's not here, because I got shot of him. After what

he let happen, I told him to roll his swag and bluie off this station.''

Alexandra continued questioning the man and listening to his surly replies, concealing her heartbroken disappointment. Logic had warned her that the possible sighting of Jeremy at Burrangong Station held little promise, but that had failed to restrain her soaring hopes.

Now those hopes were crushed. Too much time had passed, and the evidence indicated that Jeremy was farther from her reach than ever before. Lukin had been deceived by a simple ploy into thinking that Jeremy and Jarboe Charlie had gone to the east, but she was sure they had gone westward.

Deciding there was nothing more to be learned from Lukin, Alexandra ended the conversation. "As I said," she told him, "if you'd informed me of this, I would have assumed the responsibility of reimbursing you for the loss of your pistol. But you didn't, so I'll simply thank you for the information—if not your attitude—and bid you a good day.''

The man scowled and started to turn away when Elizabeth spoke, stopping him. "There is one other thing," she said. "Whilst riding into this shambles of a station, we passed a flock that looks as though it has scab amongst it. You get on a horse and go look into that. If scab spreads to the flocks in my southern paddocks, I'll torch this station and turn it into one great, smoking cinder. Do you understand me?''

Lukin turned crimson with rage, glaring at her, but there was also a gleam of fear in his eyes. The stockmen behind him, no longer amused, gazed at Elizabeth and Sheila apprehensively. "Aye, I'll go see to it," Lukin choked, his voice trembling with fury.

Elizabeth and Sheila wheeled their horses around. Alexandra and her son followed them, Jonathan leading two pack horses. Along with her disappointment, the decrepit state of the home paddock depressed Alexandra. It was more or less what she had expected, because stations always deteriorated when a hired manager rather than an owner was in charge. But it violated her sense of order and respect for any sheep station, and the surroundings had made her frustration and sorrow over Jeremy even more tormenting.

When the home paddock fell behind, a dim track led northward through rugged hills baking in the intense, scorching heat of the summer sunshine. The horses maintained a fast canter, pounding around the curves and over the broken stretches in the track. Alexandra had been a skilled rider since her childhood, but she had to concentrate to keep up with Elizabeth and Sheila. The two women rode as though they were a part of their horses, and at a hard, driving pace that was a reflection of their personalities.

She was more than friends with the women, their relationship one of sisterly love. That bond with Sheila reached across the years, from when the tall woman had been a girl. With Elizabeth it was more recent, dating from when she had married Sheila's brother, Colin. The fact that she was well-educated and a minister's daughter was reflected in her diction and manners, but not in her disposition. Her warning to Lukin about torching Burrangong Station had been a statement of intention, not a threat.

As the hours passed, the hills became less bleak and rocky. When the track ended, Elizabeth and Sheila led the way on northward through the hills to the southern border of Wayamba Station. There the landscape opened out into rolling terrain blanketed by thick grass and brush that was excellent sheep graze, with scattered stands of eucalypts and other trees.

On the horizon to the east was a line of hills at the southern border of the station that was a landmark, rising well above its surroundings. At the center of the hills, Alexandra saw a haze of smoke from cooking fires rising above a deep notch between two of them. It was Broken Hill, the mining site where Elizabeth had sent stockmen to construct a long, tall wooden fence and wall off the mining operation from the station.

Late afternoon came as they rode northward into Way-amba Station, its expanse measured in square miles rather than acres. From the crest of a rise, Alexandra saw a billabong in a large, open stand of trees ahead glinting in the sunset. A few minutes later, when they rode in among the trees, the moist shade was refreshingly cool, and peppermint barks among the eucalypts made the air fragrant with their spicy scent.

Alexandra and the other two women kindled a fire and began preparing dinner while Jonathan hobbled the horses and released them to graze. When darkness fell, he joined the women at the fire as they cooked and discussed Jeremy and Jarboe Charlie. Alexandra explained her certainty that where the stockman's boots had been placed on the track had been a ruse.

"From letters we've received," she said, "Jeremy and the man have been heading steadily westward. An engineer named John Hastings met them on the track west of the Lachlan River. A Sarah Biggs in Menindee wrote and said that they crossed the Darling River in her husband's boat. I'm sure they've gone on to the west from Burrangong Station, perhaps to cross the wilderness to Port Augusta or some other town on the southern coast."

Sheila shook her head doubtfully, stirring the simmering stew of dried beef and vegetables. "I think they've gone westward, but not to the coast. From all I've heard of him, this Jarboe Charlie is an old man who's spent most of his life among white fellows. Aborigines in that situation will often decide it's time for a walkabout. If that's the case, they've gone off into the never-never, not to the towns on the coast."

The woman's voice was sympathetic, but that did little to ease Alexandra's remorse. She had contemplated flooding the towns on the coast with reward notices, and now she dismissed that idea. "What is a walkabout, Sheila?" she asked. "I've heard the term mentioned for years, but I've never been sure of what it means."

"I'm not certain myself," the tall woman replied. "My ma used to talk about such things, but they had naught to do with sheep or graze, so I paid little attention. It has to do with someone finding where they belong. More than that, it has to do with finding themselves. In any event, if this Jarboe Charlie is with his tribe, he'll stay there. I could take a dozen stockmen and some Aborigines for trackers, but the chances of finding them are practically nonexistent. The fact is, Alexandra, I think you're faced with coming to terms with something you can do naught to change."

Alexandra nodded, dismissing the subject. Jonathan and Elizabeth joined in the conversation around the fire as it turned to the likelihood of severe grass fires, the condition of the graze, and other topics of constant interest at sheep stations. Talking with Elizabeth and Sheila was always a keen pleasure for Alexandra, and eating dinner beside a campfire brought back fond memories of her first months with David. But this time her enjoyment was smothered with sorrow, and she forced herself to eat, because traveling with the Garrity women demanded a maximum of energy.

When she lay down beside the fire in her blanket, a troubling thought kept Alexandra awake for hours. More than a boyish impulse, what Jeremy had done amounted to a determined, concentrated effort to avoid being reunited with the family. That suggested animosity toward her and the rest of the family, which hurt her worse than not having him with her.

They were up before dawn the next morning, Jonathan attending to the horses while Alexandra and the other two women made tea and heated the leftovers from dinner. They set out just as the sun was rising, and the day was the kind that reminded Alexandra that she was no longer a young woman.

The Garrity women were not inconsiderate, but they shared something of the harsh, remote quality of the outback. It failed to occur to them that others might lack their driving impatience with delays or the endurance of their slender, wiry bodies. The horses pounded northward through the long, sultry hours of the day, and Alexandra's legs ached from clinging to her sidesaddle. She knew the women would apologize and gladly slow down, but pride kept her from asking, and she felt immensely relieved when the home paddock of Wayamba station finally came into view at sunset.

The home paddock was entirely functional, as well as meticulously neat. The station house in the deep shade of towering trees that lined a creek was different only in size from the adjacent cottages for married stockmen. Farther down the creek were vegetable gardens and an Aborigine village.

The acres of pens, shearing shed, and other station buildings were set out from the house into a huge, bare yard. The head stockman and two other men came to the horse pen as Alexandra and the others dismounted. The two men began unsaddling the horses, and the head stockman told Elizabeth that her husband had taken their three sons out into the paddocks.

"There was a small fire in Windorah Paddock," the head stockman explained. "No sheep were killed and little damage was done, and Mr. Garrity thought it would be good for the boys to help clean it up."

"I agree with him entirely," Elizabeth said wryly. "Perhaps they'll learn something more useful than how to create mischief. Come, Alexandra, and we'll get you settled in your usual room. Jonathan, you'll join us at the house for dinner, won't you?"

He nodded and replied that he would, taking his blanket from behind his saddle. At Wayamba Station, women and children stayed at the house, while men went to the barracks. It was a custom of years before at sheep stations, and Elizabeth adhered closely to traditions. Alexandra and the other two women collected up their things and went toward the house as Jonathan crossed the yard to the barracks to find himself a bunk.

The house was as spartan and functional as the home paddock, with heavy, homemade furniture and no curtains, rugs, or other frills. However, it had a warm, comforting atmosphere of hospitality that made it more pleasant than many lavishly decorated, luxurious houses that Alexandra had visited. She put her things in her room and freshened up in the bathhouse behind the house, then joined the Garrity women and Jonathan in the dining room,

The cook was a married stockman's wife, and the roast pork with vegetables and plum duff for dessert was the same food that the stockmen had at the cookhouse. The tableware was also the same, consisting of tin plates and pannikins, with old-fashioned two-tine forks. During the conversation, Elizabeth made a remark that seemed very curious to Alexandra. For several years, supplies had been delivered and the wool clips taken away by steamboats that docked at Wilcannia. Elizabeth commented wistfully that she would like to return to the old method of using drays.

"What would be the point?" Alexandra asked. "The drays would come to Wilcannia, as before, and take weeks longer than riverboats."

"No, I'd have a track made south of the one to Wilcannia and north of the track to Menindee," Elizabeth replied. "It would be a matter of simply joining up the tracks between the stations in that region. I don't like that intrusion at Broken Hill—riverboats, and other things that are happening. I feel that I'll wake one morning and find a railroad in my home paddock."

"Come now, Elizabeth," Alexandra said. "I agree and sympathize with you about Broken Hill, but the other things are simply progress."

"Yes, they are," Elizabeth said. "But those who are caught up in progress lose control of their circumstances. That won't happen here. I didn't take charge of this station just to rule over the passing of a way of life."

Alexandra nodded and dropped the subject, reflecting that it was another example of Elizabeth's attachment to tradition. Presently, when the meal was finished, they went out the front door to the verandah. Jonathan returned to the barracks to join the men gathered in front of it, and Alexandra sat on the verandah bench with Elizabeth and Sheila.

A cool breeze stirred the trees around the house, and moths fluttered about the lantern hanging on the verandah as Alexandra talked with the two women. It was a pleasant moment for her, marred only by the sorrow over Jeremy that hovered at the back of her thoughts. After a few minutes, the mournful groaning of didgeridoos came from the Aborigine village down the creek. The sonorous rising and falling notes were joined by the clatter of rhythm sticks, then by voices harmonizing in a chant.

"What is the corroboree about, Sheila?" Alexandra asked.

The tall, dark woman turned, listening to the chant for a moment, then laughed. "Great lots of naught," she replied. "All they're doing is going on about the games they have at times."

"Games?" Alexandra asked, puzzled.

"Aye, when they get together to see who can fling a spear or a waddy and such the farthest," Sheila explained. "In the chant, they're saying that the farther a boomerang flies, the more certain it is to return. A boomerang must return in order to count as a score in their games."

Alexandra thought about the explanation, wondering if the chant had a deeper meaning than Sheila's literal interpretation. There had been instances when it had seemed to her that Aborigines had mysterious ways of knowing about things. They often appeared to be aware of events removed from them in space or time, with no logical way of having learned about those events.

She wondered if the chant was a message for her. And if it was, she wondered how long she would have to wait for her beloved grandson to return.

Chapter Nine

Sweat streamed down Jeremy's face as he sat on a stone in the blistering sunshine and watched Jarboe trying to converse with an older man among several Aborigines. Jarboe was using a combination of words and gestures, as he had with other Aborigines whom he and Jeremy had met along the way, and he and the older man appeared to be communicating to an extent.

Some twenty other Aborigines were standing about, ranging in age from older men and women to small children whose blond hair contrasted sharply with their dark skin. At first there had been only four, a couple with their children. Then the others had evidently perceived in some fashion that something unusual had happened, and had gathered.

They had appeared almost like magic on the vast, stone-strewn plain that was cut by gullies and virtually devoid of vegetation. Heads and then people had popped up here and there, then they had collected around, wearing scanty loincloths and carrying weapons, grass dilly bags, and other paraphernalia. Their attention was divided between Jeremy and Jarboe's attempts to converse with the older man, but mostly they stared at Jeremy's eyes.

None sat, and they had a curious way of standing. The men leaned on spears and the others on long digging sticks, and they stood on one foot, with the other tucked behind the knee of the leg on which they were standing. The boy also observed that they seemed untroubled by the withering heat. As for himself, he felt as though he were in an oven, with the rocky soil reflecting the glaring, torrid sunshine at him from all directions.

Jarboe finished conveying what he wished to say, then gathered up his swag to leave as the man spoke to the other people. Jeremy stood, picking up his swag. As he and Jarboe walked away toward the west, they exchanged waves with the people who were scattering over the plain again. Jarboe had made himself a spear from a grasstree shaft, the tip sharpened and hardened over a fire, and he used it as a walking staff as he and the boy picked a path between the deeper gullies in the arid, parched soil.

"I told him where we're going, and so forth," Jarboe explained. "We're crossing their territory, so that's the polite thing to do."

"Their territory is certainly hot just now," Jeremy remarked wryly.

"It feels hotter to you because you were sitting down," Jarboe told him. "If you'd lain down, you'd have been hotter still. When the ground and rocks are hot, you shouldn't touch them any more than you must, mate."

Jeremy pondered for a moment, then nodded. "So that's why those people were standing on one foot. I've learned something."

"Aye, you have," Jarboe agreed, laughing. "But trying to stand on one foot in boots would be more of a problem than they have barefoot. We'd better start looking for some tucker and firewood."

Jeremy took out his sling and veered to the left, Jarboe

angling away to the right. When they were some two
hundred yards apart, they continued wandering westward while searching in gullies and around stones. From
the very beginning of their journey, they had traveled at
a leisurely pace, their destination so distant that haste
had been pointless. During recent weeks, they had slowed
even more, hunting food along the way.

The gullies had been gouged by runoff from rains that
swept up from the coast to the south at intervals of years.
Among the rocks in the gullies, Jeremy found bits of driftwood, desiccated sticks bleached white by the sun and
as light as cork. The boy gathered the wood as he climbed
through the gullies, watching on every side for the movement of an animal.

After an hour, he had seen nothing. The sun-baked
plain was almost totally lifeless, and not a single bird
flew across the sky. It was also absolutely silent, with an
eerie, gripping stillness that felt as though it had been
undisturbed for centuries. In that oppressive quiet, the
boy's breathing and footsteps sounded jarringly loud to
him.

The plain tilted slightly, sloping westward at an angle
of a few inches over a span of miles. It was sufficient to
incline the gullies to the west, and they gradually became
more shallow and wider as the hours passed. During mid-
afternoon, Jarboe shouted and held up a two-foot goanna
lizard that he had speared. It was sufficient for the day,
and killing another animal would be taking too much
from the land. Jeremy put his sling away and continued
collecting bits of wood from the gullies.

When late afternoon came, the boy rejoined Jarboe.
The gullies disappeared, opening out into an ancient
lakebed. It was an enormous, perfectly flat expanse of sediment that had washed out of vast miles of gullies over
a span of eons. The sprigs of wiry foliage that dotted it
were brown and dry, waiting through the years for another rain that would make them explode into a frenzy
of producing seeds. Jeremy and Jarboe walked out onto

the lakebed, their footprints and wind ripples the only marks on it.

Far out into the flatland, they stopped just before sunset to camp for the night. Jarboe had also collected a bundle of wood, and Jeremy kindled a fire with his flint and steel while the man cleaned and skinned the goanna. They talked about the Aborigines they had met that day, and Jarboe expressed his opinion that the people were the only ones in the desert region.

"This land can't support very many," he explained. "People have only as many children as the land will feed, and that's few here."

"From what you've said, the Aranda territory is much better."

"Aye, much better indeed," Jarboe replied, placing the goanna over the fire. "There are good and bad years, depending on how much rain falls, but it's always much better than this. In my portion of the tribe, there are about a hundred people—or there were when I left."

The man continued talking about his tribe, Jeremy listening with keen interest. The topic had become one of more frequent conversation during their past weeks of progress toward Aranda territory, and Jeremy looked forward to reaching it. Ever since leaving civilization behind, each day of the journey had been more enjoyable for him.

Foraging off the land had given him a deeply satisfying sense of being self-sufficent, and a feeling of interaction with the outback. The sights and sounds had taken on a new richness and depth of meaning for him, making him more acutely aware of his surroundings. He felt a part of the land, blending with the range of plant and animal life instead of simply being there.

Jarboe turned the goanna to roast the other side, then cut off portions for himself and Jeremy. Weeks before, in an area where the vegetation and animal life had been plentiful, they had gathered a large supply of quandongs. They took out handfuls of the small, red fruit and then ate. Jeremy had long since overcome any qualms about the nature of the food, and he ate with a hearty appetite, the goanna tasting delicious to him.

The last glow of sunset faded into darkness while they were eating. Even before the light faded, the level horizon on each side seemed a vast distance away to Jeremy. After nightfall, with the flat expanse of sediment reaching off into the darkness from the pool of light around the fire, the boy had a sense of being surrounded by spaces on an unimaginable scale. The feeling was heightened by the vast sweep of the sky, where millions of stars twinkled with dazzling brilliance in the clear desert air.

After eating, Jeremy took a measured drink from his water bottle, Jarboe drinking from his flask. They pulled their blankets around their shoulders and stoked the fire, for the temperature plummeted rapidly after nightfall in the desert. Then Jarboe filled and lit his pipe as the boy took out his books. Jeremy selected the man's favorite, the geography text, and read aloud from it until time to go to sleep.

Dawn came swiftly the next morning, a characteristic of the flat terrain. At one moment it was still dark, then daylight spread abruptly across the landscape and the sun lifted above the horizon. Jeremy and Jarboe ate the remainder of the goanna and a handful of quandongs, taking drinks of water, then gathered up their swag and set out again.

In the seeming illimitable vastness around them, they trudged toward a steadily receding horizon. On the other side of the expanse of sediment were more gullies, then a dry river bed that channeled the runoff from another stretch of gullies. Nothing moved on the landscape except shimmering waves of heat as the sun rose higher and the temperature soared.

During the intense heat of the day and after their meal that evening, Jeremy and Jarboe drank most of their remaining water. The following day, they spent the morning digging a soak. At one side of a dry river bed, where the floodwaters had exposed an edge of layered volcanic stone, they began digging. When the hole was five feet deep, Jeremy climbed down into it and continued digging, passing the sandy dirt up to Jarboe.

The soil was damp at a depth of six feet, and wet at seven. A few inches deeper, the boy struck the granite bedrock that the volcanic stone had indicated would lie underground. It was impermeable to water, holding moisture from floodwaters of past years in the soil. The water collected at the bottom of the hole from the surrounding soil, and Jeremy dipped it up with a billy. When his bottle and Jarboe's flask were full, they drank all they could, then they filled in the hole and continued on their way.

The following day, the stark monotony of the landscape ended when sloping domes of red sandstone rose on the western horizon through the heat waves. They were more distinct the next day, backed by dark, stony mountains, and the vegetation became more plentiful in the desert. The next time Jeremy and Jarboe needed water, they dug at the edge of a stand of desert oaks whose deep roots reached down to wet soil that yielded a pool of water.

When they reached the mountains, they found an Eden compared to the desert. The deep gorges and canyons below the barren stone ridges were thickly forested with pines and eucalypts, and teemed with animals. Water was plentiful from the springs and billabongs scattered through the valleys. Jarboe speared a fat possum one day while they were passing through the mountains, and Jeremy brought down an emu with his sling the next day.

They saw numerous goannas, but Jarboe told Jeremy that it was forbidden to kill any kind of reptile in the mountains. He explained that according to an Aborigine tradition, the mountain range was formed by a giant serpent called Arkaroola, whose spirit remained and guarded all reptiles.

"This isn't the territory of your tribe," Jeremy pointed out. "How do you know about the traditions here?"

· "Some are known far and wide," Jarboe explained. "Like the fact that these mountains are here is known far and wide. This is the Flinders Range, and Port Augusta and Port Pirie aren't all that far from here. Also, my tribal territory isn't too far away now."

"What would happen if we killed a goanna?" Jeremy asked.

"I don't know," Jarboe replied, then laughed. "Or I should say that I don't know what Arkaroola might do. But Aborigines who saw us with one would crack our heads open, and plenty of them will be about here."

The point was illustrated later that day, when they met up with a group of Aborigines. The encounter was the same as others, an initial half dozen people being joined by some twenty more. Jarboe spent a few minutes with an older man, explaining that he and Jeremy were passing through the mountains, and the other people stared curiously at the boy's eyes. Then Jarboe and Jeremy moved on, exchanging waves with the Aborigines.

The following day, they came to a clearing with a circle of mounded earth and stones in the center of it and a path leading from the circle into the thick foliage at one side. Jarboe immediately turned back, and as they made a wide detour around the area, he told Jeremy that the clearing was where the local tribe assembled. Called a bora grounds, it consisted of the circle they had seen, and a smaller, secluded one.

"The circle you saw is where the tribe gathers," he explained. "The path from it leads to the little one. That's where the elders meet."

"Do the other people ever go to the small one?" Jeremy asked.

"Only when the elders summon them," Jarboe replied. "The people at large aren't even supposed to see the little circle, and those who aren't of that tribe shouldn't loiter around any of it. It's like a combination of a church and a Government House for them."

Jarboe continued, explaining other things about the bora grounds. Somewhere near the small circle was where the elders of each tribe kept the tribal tjuringa safely hidden away. Extremely sacred objects, tjuringas were made of carved wood and passed down through generations of elders. They represented the heart and soul of the tribe, and for one of them to even be seen by anyone except the elders was extremely rare.

The man also commented that the size of the bora grounds they had seen indicated that the tribe was fairly large, which was borne out during the following days. While going on through the mountains, Jeremy and Jarboe met up with two more groups of Aborigines and saw signs of others, for the lush valleys supported a substantial population.

When they left the mountains, they entered a more austere and forbidding region, where rainfall was sparse. Stretching toward the center of the continent, it was an unchanging landscape of low, rocky hills and arid plateaus covered with scattered brush, scrub forest, and the omnipresent eucalypts. Creeks and most billabongs were surfaces of dried, cracked mud at the end of summer, the foliage wilting in the torrid heat.

A few billabongs surrounded by river gums retained an inch or two of water, however, and there were bottle trees that could be tapped for the cysts of water they contained. Wildlife was plentiful, with rock wallabies in the hills, euros and red kangaroos roaming the brushy lowlands, and a wide range of small animals. There was also a large variety of edible plants, and in the stands of mulga, Jeremy found honey ants in their tunnels under the brush. The ants had sacs on their backs as large as small grapes that were filled with deliciously sweet liquid made from mulga sap.

The region was sparsely populated, and long intervals passed between the times when Jeremy and Jarboe saw Aborigines. The reach of civilization extended deep into the wilderness, because the people had steel tips on their weapons and other items obtained through trade with coastal towns to the south. In one respect, the contact with the towns was more tenuous than Jarboe would have wished. His supply of tobacco was diminishing, and he carefully rationed the amount he put into his pipe each night.

The weather turned cooler, February passing and summer changing into autumn. The early mornings and evenings became chilly, with a haze in the sky that was a harbinger of precious rain. Jarboe believed they were very close to Aranda territory, and he was annoyed with himself because he was unsure of precisely where it began. The man's uncertainty seemed understandable to Jeremy, however, as all the landscape looked much the same to him from one day to the next as they traveled to the northwest.

The end of the long journey came one afternoon, surprising Jeremy. At first it seemed to him much like any other encounter with Aborigines, Jarboe seeing a half dozen in the brush at one side and turning toward them. Others stepped through the brush and gathered around, then Jeremy noticed that Jarboe was talking fluently with an older man among them.

Jarboe broke off, turning to Jeremy with the good news: "These are my people, mate!" he said happily. "They're Arandas!"

Jeremy exclaimed in delight, sharing the man's pleasure at being rejoined with his tribe. Then, as Jarboe continued talking with the leader of the group, the boy observed that the reaction of the twenty or so people who had collected was much the same as that of others whom he and Jarboe had met along the way. They were mostly curious about Jeremy's eyes, commenting quietly among themselves, and there was little or no evidence of satisfaction over the return of a tribesman after a long absence.

The leader, a lean, wiry man about Jarboe's age, had a similar attitude. After talking with Jarboe for a few minutes, he beckoned two men. He spoke to them briefly, then they hurried away, one going north and the other in the opposite direction. The remainder of the group moved toward the west, Jarboe and the leader still talking, and Jeremy followed them. The boy saw that he was the topic of conversation at least part of the time, because the leader occasionally glanced back at him with an in-scrutable expression.

An hour later, they came to a village of bark wurlies beside a billabong with a shallow puddle of water remaining in it. The people had goannas and other small game, along with edible plants they had gathered during the day. The women rekindled fires in front of the bark huts to prepare the food, and Jarboe continued talking with the leader. Jeremy sat down with his swag at one side, not quite knowing what to do with himself.

Presently, when Jarboe stepped over and joined Jeremy, the man seemed disappointed over his reception, but he said nothing about it. "His name's Juburli," Jarboe said, referring to the leader. "Those two men who left are messengers, and the tribe will gather at the bora grounds. Juburli is one of the elders, and he wants the other elders to know about us. We'll set out for the bora grounds tomorrow and reach it the next day."

"Very well, Jarboe. The people aren't very excited over the fact that you've returned, are they?"

Jarboe gazed at the people moodily and shook his head. "It's not like I expected it would be, but I probably expected too much. I must have known Juburli before I left here, because we're of a like age, but I don't remember him. Nor does he remember me, as far as that goes."

"This may be the wrong tribe," Jeremy suggested, recalling that Jarboe had said there were several Aranda tribes. "Perhaps that's why you don't remember each other."

Jarboe shook his head morosely. "No, it's the right tribe. I mentioned the names of those who were the elders when I left, and Juburli remembers them, as I do. We just don't remember each other."

"Well, it's been many years, hasn't it?" Jeremy pointed out, trying to make Jarboe feel better. "Much has happened since then."

"Aye, I suppose so," Jarboe replied, sighing despondently. "In any event, Juburli seems agreeable enough. He told me that he's willing to let you stay with the tribe.

The other elders have a say in it as well, but he told me that he'll ask them to permit it."

"Let me stay?" Jeremy exclaimed, surprised. "I didn't think there would be any question about my staying."

Jarboe sighed again, shrugging. "I didn't either, Jeremy, but this hasn't turned out like I expected." He forced a smile, patting the boy's shoulder. "But it'll be all right, mate. When we get to the bora grounds, I'll probably know the other elders, and they'll be glad to see me. I daresay we'll have a corroboree and spend a few days there, and I'll get to know everyone again. There's naught to worry about."

Jeremy nodded and said no more about it, but he was worried because Jarboe seemed uncertain himself. The man talked about the tribe, saying that it still consisted of five groups of about the same size, as it had years before. He went on to other things that he and Juburli had discussed, and Jeremy listened absently as he anxiously wondered what he would do if the tribal elders decided against his staying with the tribe.

When the food was cooked, a woman brought pieces of roasted goanna and bandicoot to Jarboe and the boy, along with a handful of tiny, nutty-tasting burrawong seeds. As they ate, Jarboe continued talking about his discussion with Juburli. The leader had mentioned that a trading party had set out toward the towns to the south a few days before. Jarboe ruefully commented that if he and Jeremy had arrived sooner, he could have asked those in the trading party to bring him a few figs of tobacco.

The others gathered in a quiet murmur of laughter and conversation over their meal, while Jarboe and Jeremy sat at one side and ate. That isolation continued when the group set out for the bora grounds the next day, with the man and boy remaining more or less apart from the others. The people were friendly, more than willing to provide food and to be helpful in any way that they could. However, their attitude made it clear that they regarded both Jarboe and Jeremy as different from themselves.

The people wore kangaroo and possum skin robes on the brisk autumn day, and the women carried water in wooden bowls called coolamons. Two had firesticks, which Jarboe had been unable to make months before. The firesticks were stems of combungi, a type of bulrush, and wisps of smoke rose from embers smoldering in the pith. The group spread out, gathering food as they moved toward the bora grounds. Jarboe and Jeremy were left by themselves during the day, and at the camp that night, they sat apart from the others.

The situation increased Jeremy's worries about what he would do if the elders decided against his remaining with the tribe. He was sure that Jarboe would never abandon him in the wilderness, but the last thing the boy wanted was to further alienate Jarboe from his tribe. The man was already deeply troubled by their attitude, which made Jeremy equally unhappy.

The following morning, the group remained together and proceeded at a fast, steady pace toward two hills that were a landmark, set close together and rising higher than the surrounding hills. A few hours later, they filed out of the brush into a wide clearing at the foot of the hills. In the center of the clearing was a circle of mounded earth and stones, with scores of people milling about it. A stone-lined path led from the circle into the tangle of brush and trees in the narrow cleft between the hills.

Amid the hubbub of greetings, Jeremy saw that Juburli's group must have been the last one to arrive, because at least eighty people were already at the clearing. That was confirmed a moment later, when the confusion began settling and most of the people sat down at the circle. Juburli spoke to Jarboe, who led Jeremy to one side of the clearing.

The man put down his swag at the edge of the brush and pointed for Jeremy to sit down. "You're to wait here while we get this straightened out," he said. "But there's naught to worry about, mate. We'll have it cleared up presently, then everything will be all right."

Jarboe's attitude lacked the conviction expressed by

his words, betraying some uncertainty about the outcome. The boy nodded worriedly and then sat down with
his swag as Jarboe went back across the clearing. He
joined those at the circle, who collected around him and
began talking with him. Juburli and four other older men
stood at one side, talking quietly and peering at Jeremy.
Then they went down the stone-lined path and disappeared into the thick foliage in the ravine between the
hills.

A few minutes later, Juburli stepped back into view
and beckoned Jarboe. After the man went down the path
with the elder, the attention of the people in the circle
became focused on Jeremy. They gazed at him and commented among themselves while the boy waited anxiously. He noticed rhythm sticks and the long, dark tubes
of didgeridoos in the crowd. The people were prepared
to have a corroboree, as Jarboe had said they might.

However, there was no corroboree, and the tribal gathering ended abruptly. The elders returned and spoke to
the people, Jarboe following them. A murmur of disappointment passed through the crowd, and they began
collecting up their paraphernalia to leave as Jarboe
crossed the clearing, his face like a thundercloud. The
man irately grabbed up his swag without saying a word,
then turned to follow Juburli's group away from the bora
grounds. Jeremy hastily gathered up his things and hurried after Jarboe.

When they were a hundred yards from the clearing,
Jeremy could wait no longer, and he asked if the elders
had agreed that he could stay. "Aye, and they said that
I could as well," Jarboe growled bitterly.

"You?" Jeremy exclaimed without thinking. "But
you're a member of the tribe, and there shouldn't be any
question about it."

Jarboe made no reply, and Jeremy immediately regretted having spoken. The boy saw that it was the reason
that Jarboe was both deeply hurt and resentful. They
trudged on in silence, following the people. Presently, the
group spread apart and began moving more slowly, hunt-

ing and gathering food. Jeremy took out his sling and began looking for small animals, he and Jarboe left by themselves again.

The day became dark and cloudy as the hours passed, matching Jeremy's mood. Jarboe spoke only once during the afternoon, and then he sounded as though he was talking to himself. "I've forgotten the words for many things," he mused sadly, "and how to do many everyday tasks. I always meant to come back, but I suppose I waited too long and forgot too much."

Jeremy was unable to think of any suitable response, and Jarboe said nothing more. During late afternoon, light rain began falling. When the group reassembled to camp for the night, the people were jubilant over the precious moisture. However, it merely seemed miserably cold and damp to Jeremy as he and Jarboe sat in silence at one side of the group. In contrast to the pleasure and excitement that each day of the journey had provided, its end was a crushing disappointment.

Chapter Ten

At the village the next day, Jeremy and Jarboe built a bark wurlie for themselves, then settled into the daily routine of the group. Each morning, at least some of the people set out to hunt for animals and to collect edible plants. When a kangaroo or a substantial number of small animals had been brought in during the previous day or two, people remained at the wurlies to work on weapons, garments, and other tasks. Jeremy and Jarboe hunted each day, always bringing back at least their share.

Although he was unable to understand the language, Jeremy quickly began learning facts about the group from observing their actions. There was a distinct ladder of status within the group, the older and more experienced hunters ranking next to Juburli. In that respect, the leader and the others regarded Jarboe in much the same way that they did the youths, because he had to have help in making a spear and in doing other things.

It galled Jarboe, making him silent and morose. However, as he had indicated in his remarks on the day they had returned from the bora grounds, he regarded it as his own fault. While he was bitter, he had no animosity toward any of the people, particularly Juburli. He had only the utmost respect for the leader, and even veneration toward some of the elders. But when they sat beside their fire at night, Jeremy read his books silently now, because Jarboe was too engrossed in his remorse to be interested.

The man had little interest in anything else and remained desperately unhappy as the days passed. While he and Jeremy were hunting one day, Jarboe stopped at a level spot on the side of a hill, staring at the ground. After a moment, he pointed to it. "That's it there," he said quietly.

Jeremy looked at the ground, seeing nothing but stones and straggling weeds. "That's what, Jarboe?" he asked.

"The place where I came alive," the man replied listlessly. "It's one thing I can remember, because my mother often brought me here when I was a lad. A Songtrail comes down the hill there, and here is where one of the creators sung the red goshawk into being during the Dreamtime."

The boy looked again, seeing nothing about the place that would set it apart from anywhere else, and Jarboe also seemed indifferent. He was as moody as before, and if the end of his long walkabout brought him any satisfaction, his attitude failed to reveal it. He walked on past the level spot, Jeremy following him, and they resumed hunting.

Jarboe showed more emotional reaction that evening, when he was unable to indulge in a habit he had acquired from the British. He rummaged through empty bags that had once contained tobacco, looking for shreds to put in his pipe. Finding none, he angrily hurled the pipe into the darkness, then he pulled his blanket around himself and lay down to sleep.

At dawn the next morning, Jeremy searched for the pipe and finally found it. It had struck a stone, shattering the clay bowl. While they were hunting that day, Jeremy mentioned a solution to the situation. He told Jarboe that they could leave and travel back to the east.

"I don't know what to do," Jarboe replied. "I don't want to spend my last years there, because I'm not a white fellow. But my people don't seem to think that I'm an Aborigine any more. I don't know what to do."

"We were much happier when we were traveling," Jeremy pointed out. "We could be swagmen and live on the tracks."

Jarboe made no reply, remaining silent for a time. Then, later in the day, he commented that many places they had crossed during their journey would now be flooded, making travel difficult and dangerous. That suggested he might consider leaving during the spring, when the weather improved. However, Jeremy knew that Jarboe could go anywhere at any time he wished. As he had said, the man was unable to decide.

A few days later, while they were hunting, they heard others shouting for everyone to collect together. The entire group was searching for food that day, and as they were spread out over a mile or more, it took several minutes for everyone to assemble where Juburli was waiting. When they did, the leader led the way toward the village at a rapid pace.

It was still early afternoon on the cold, windy day, hours before they usually returned to the village, but Jarboe shook his head in perplexity when Jeremy asked him what had happened. Presently, when the billabong came into view, the boy saw a man from another group at the wurlies. The man was evidently a messenger, so tired that he was lying down.

After the man climbed to his feet and spoke with Juburli, things began happening so quickly that Jeremy was still left in the dark for a time. As the leader snapped orders and people scrambled about and collected up belongings, Jeremy followed Jarboe into their wurlie. They gathered their swag and joined the others, and Juburli led the group toward the bora grounds at a fast pace. Then Jarboe told Jeremy what the messenger had said.

The man had reported that the trading party that left before Jeremy and Jarboe arrived had returned much earlier than expected, and only part of the men had made it back. From what they had said, they had met three white men coming north. Those men, carrying knives, hatchets, and other trade goods, had been ill. The trading party had turned back, bringing the white men with them.

"But the white fellows died," Jarboe went on, "and then those in the trading party began getting sick. Out of the ten men in the trading party, only four got back, and they're very sick."

"The white men may have had some bad rations," Jeremy speculated, "and those in the trading party may have eaten some of them."

"That's possible," Jarboe agreed. "The messenger doesn't know what's wrong with them, but many people have died from eating rancey meat. Those in the trading party said that one of the white fellows was wearing big bracelets. That sounds to me like manacles with the chains broken off."

"A convict ship enroute to Perth could have put in at a port to the south for some reason," Jeremy suggested, "and a few convicts could have escaped."

"And broke into a store to get rations and trade goods," Jarboe added. "Aye, it could have happened that way, and the rations they got were bad. We'll soon find out more when we get to the bora grounds."

Jeremy nodded in agreement, still wondering about one point. There was no logical way that Juburli could have found out that a messenger was waiting at the village, yet somehow he had known. But when the boy asked about it, Jarboe shrugged and replied that elders had inexplicable ways of knowing things, particularly important facts.

The group moved rapidly through the brush and trees until dark, then camped. Little food had been gathered during the day, and Jeremy's share was part of an ooboon lizard and several baked towacks—small, potato-like vegetables. Nothing was left for breakfast at daybreak the next morning, when the group resumed its fast pace toward the bora grounds.

They arrived at mid-morning, filing into the clearing. The rest of the tribe was there, gathered around a large wurlie that had been built at one side of the clearing, and the greetings between the people were muted by concern and perplexity. Juburli joined the other elders near the wurlie, and Jeremy followed Jarboe through the people to peer into it.

Then dread gripped the boy. At a glance, he knew that the four men on pallets in the wurlie had a far more deadly disease than food poisoning. Along with their crusted, infected eyes and racking coughs from pneumonia, the eruptions on their skin revealed that they were in the final stages of smallpox. It was the most virulent and highly infectious of all diseases, and the entire tribe had been exposed to it.

Jarboe also recognized the disease and shouted in warning. The crowd was motionless for an instant as he spoke rapidly, then it exploded into motion, the people fleeing across the clearing in panic. Only the elders remained, their stern, aged faces impassive. They began questioning Jarboe, and he pointed to the men and the scars on his face as he explained.

One of the elders pointed toward Jeremy, asking a question, and Jarboe turned to the boy. "They want do know why you're not afraid of catching it," he said. "You've been vaccinated with cowpox, haven't you?"

"Yes," Jeremy replied, pushing up his sleeve to the scar on his forearm. "A doctor vaccinated me when I was very small."

Jarboe turned back to the elders, talking with them again, then he spoke to Jeremy once more. "They want to know if there's any way other than vaccination to prevent smallpox. I've never heard of any, have you?"

Jeremy started to shake his head, then hesitated. "Well,

no, I know of no other way to actually prevent it. But in school, I read that before vaccination with cowpox was discovered, doctors sometimes inoculated people with smallpox. They took fluid from a blister on someone who had smallpox, and put the fluid in a scratch on people's arms."

"But all that did was give them smallpox."

"Yes, but within a few days instead of the usual two weeks or so after being near someone with it. That meant they were stronger when they became sick, and they became well again much more quickly. It killed some, but far fewer than if the people had caught smallpox in the usual way."

Jarboe translated what Jeremy had said, and when the man finished, the elders were silent and motionless for a moment. Then, moving as one, they stepped toward the path that led to the small circle hidden in the ravine. Juburli beckoned Jarboe to go with them, and as he followed the elders away, he told Jeremy to wait at the large circle in the clearing.

The rest of the tribe had gathered at the circle in an atmosphere of apprehension. As he joined them, Jeremy cringed inwardly with horror over what the disease would do to the tribe, because very few would have a natural immunity. Typically, less than half would survive, and he earnestly hoped the elders would inoculate the people.

An hour passed, the people muttering uneasily among themselves. Juburli came back up the path, wearing only a loincloth; stripes of white clay on his limbs, chest, and face that made him look strikingly different. The effect was dramatic, giving him a fierce, formidable aspect. Then the boy glanced twice at the heavyset man with the leader before recognizing Jarboe, also in a loincloth and with white stripes on his body.

The leader began giving the people orders. Jeremy gathered up his swag to help with whatever was to be done, but Jarboe told him to wait there. The boy sat back down, reflecting that he was evidently wanted at hand in the event the elders had more questions about inoculation. The people left the clearing, and Jarboe went back down the path with the leader.

Part of the tribe had been assigned to gather firewood, and they brought load after load to the clearing as the dark, cold afternoon passed. During late afternoon, the remainder of the people returned from hunting and gathering plants. When the women began cooking, Jeremy's hunger pangs reminded him that he had eaten nothing since the previous evening.

One of the women carried food part of the way down the path, calling out, and Jarboe stepped up the path to take it. A woman brought Jeremy a juicy chunk of roasted wallaby and several small, onion-like nyiri bulbs, and the boy ate hungrily. As dusk fell, the clearing was dimly illuminated by fires around the circle, where all the people had gathered to eat.

After the meal, Jarboe and Juburli came up the path to the circle. Jarboe began talking to the people, and he was interrupted by an outburst of dismay. Both he and Juburli shouted sternly, quieting the uproar, then Jarboe continued talking. Jeremy was relieved. The reaction indicated that the elders had decided to inoculate everyone in the tribe.

The people were disciplined, voicing their objections only once and then accepting the decision. Jarboe and Juburli went back down the path, and the people took out didgeridoos and rhythm sticks from among the things they had brought from their villages. Six men sat down with the didgeridoos, facing a dozen women with the rhythm sticks.

One after another, the didgeridoos began sounding their deep rising and falling notes. The rhythm sticks started tapping in cadence with them. After a moment, a man in the crowd began chanting. Then the other people joined in, the men's and women's voices harmonizing.

The volume of noise was deafening, but it had a velvet quality that kept it from being uncomfortable for Jeremy. The blend of sounds was pleasant, and the throbbing beat touched a responsive chord at a deep emotional level within him. The boy listened in fascination, gazing around at the dark people swaying in the flickering firelight as they chanted.

Jarboe stepped up the path, beckoning Jeremy. The boy stepped toward him, thinking that the elders were ready to talk further about inoculation. But when he reached the man, Jeremy learned that he was mistaken. Jarboe bent down to him, speaking over the sound of the corroboree, and told Jeremy that the elders wanted him to inoculate the people.

"Me?" Jeremy exclaimed in dismay. "No, it'll make some of the people die, and I don't want to be the one who kills them. That's the responsibility of the elders. I'm only a boy, and not even an Aborigine."

"You're the one who knows about it, though," Jarboe replied. "To the elders, that makes it your magic. They'll give you power to help you keep people from dying, and few if any will do so."

Jarboe looked different in a loincloth and with white stripes on his body, but he was still much the same, with his warm, affectionate manner. Jeremy had no faith at all in any supposed power from the elders, but he was unable to refuse what Jarboe wanted him to do. The boy reluctantly nodded, then went down the path with Jarboe. It led back through the dense foliage that choked the narrow ravine, with the steep, rocky flanks of the hills closing in on both sides.

The foliage muted the sound of the corroboree, reducing it to a loud background of noise echoing through the ravine. The path opened out into a clearing around a small circle of mounded earth and stones, a fire burning in the center of it. Four of the elders sat on the far side of the circle, and Jarboe seated Jeremy on the near side.

The elders were motionless and silent, the firelight making dark shadows in the hollows of their wrinkled, bearded faces as they gazed fixedly at Jeremy. In that setting, it was harder for the boy to reject the idea that the aged, wise men might possess ancient secret ways of bridging the void into the supernatural and drawing forth mysterious, awesome powers.

Jarboe handed the boy a small wooden bowl with a few ounces of liquid in it. "That's a kind of rum made from the sap of bottle trees," he said. "It's used only for ceremonies. Drink all of it."

Jeremy almost choked as he began drinking the bitter liquor, its powerful, alcoholic sting making him gag. He forced himself to swallow it, and the liquor burned its way down to his stomach as he handed the bowl back to Jarboe. Then a tingling warmth spread through the boy's limbs, seeming to permeate every fiber of his body.

Juburli stepped out of the shadows at the rear of the ravine. He carried a square object the size of a large book, with skins wrapped around it. The leader removed the skins as he stepped around the fire toward Jeremy, and Jarboe spoke softly: "That's the tribal tjuringa," he said reverently. "Be careful with it, and don't let it touch the ground, Jeremy."

The boy nodded, remembering that Jarboe had said that a tjuringa was extremely sacred, representing the very heart and soul of a tribe. It was a thick board, black with age and every inch of it covered with intricate carving. Juburli took Jeremy's hands and placed them on each side of the tjuringa so that the boy was holding it out in front of himself. One of the other elders picked up a grass dilly bag and stepped around the fire. He knelt in front of Jeremy, took a carved, polished bone the size of a finger from his dilly bag, then pointed it at the boy.

A whisper of sound came from the elder's aged, wrinkled lips. It grew louder, becoming a rhythmic, wordless singing that blended with the corroboree. The effects of the liquor continued coursing through the boy's veins and made him feel lightheaded. The scene took on an unreal, dreamlike character for him as he gripped the tjuringa, the elder's singing and the corroboree seeming to combine into a pulsing force within him.

Something of that feeling remained with Jeremy when the elder finished and put the bone back into his dilly bag. He returned to his place beside the other three, Juburli taking the tjuringa from Jeremy. The leader replaced the skins around the carved board and stepped back into the shadows at the rear of the ravine. Jarboe disappeared up the path.

A moment later, the corroboree ended, and Juburli emerged from the shadows again. The other four elders stood up and filed toward the path with Juburli, who beckoned Jeremy to follow. A bustle of activity had replaced the corroboree, and when Jeremy reached the end of the path with the elders, he saw that the people were kindling a fire in front of the wurlie where the four ill men lay. He followed the elders toward it.

At the wurlie, Jarboe handed Jeremy a tuft of possum fur and a stick that had been sharpened to a keen point, then began forming the people into a line. Kneeling beside one of the ill men, Jeremy opened a blister with the tip of the stick and pressed the fur against it, sponging up the fluid. Then he stepped to the line of people, the elders at the front.

The boy scraped tentatively at the first elder's arm with the stick, hesitant to inflict pain. The old man's dark, penetrating eyes suddenly reflected friendly amusement. Jeremy pressed harder on the stick, making a scratch with beads of blood oozing from it. The old man nodded in approval, and the boy swabbed the fur across the scratch.

After the first few, it became a mechanical routine for Jeremy. The line inched forward, the people indifferent to pain but some eyeing the fur with shrinking apprehension. Some hesitated fearfully, and Jarboe spoke to them impatiently, motioning them forward. There were muscular arms and slender, feminine ones, as well as squirming babies with blond hair and oldsters who stood in stoic indifference as they held out a bony arm.

The line gradually grew shorter, those who moved away returning to the circle and settling down for the night around the fires. By the time Jeremy finished with the last one, the effects of the liquor had turned into a strange, overpowering fatigue. He tossed the fur and stick into the fire in front of the wurlie, then wearily crossed the clearing to the circle. Pulling his blanket around himself, he lay down beside a fire.

The boy had never felt as drained of energy in his life, but for a time, a consuming worry overcame his exhaustion and kept him awake. He lay and wondered how many he had consigned to a lingering, painful death from the ravages of the disease before he finally fell asleep.

On the same day that the initial signs of illness appeared among the people, two of the men from the trading party died. That seemed a bad omen to Jeremy, a harbinger of massive mortality to come. The sickness began with the very young and very old, then it spread like a grass fire driven by torrid summer winds. The people had built wurlies in preparation, and over a period of hours, they were filled with those who had become weak and feverish.

Several became only slightly ill, while four women and two men were among the fortunate few with natural immunity to smallpox, and they escaped the disease entirely. Those, together with Jarboe and Jeremy, had the task of bringing in food, keeping fires burning, and attending to almost a hundred people in the wurlies at all hours of the day and night.

Jarboe wore his stockman's clothes again, leading the men out to hunt every day. Little food was brought back even on the best days, because human activity at the clearing had driven most animals from the vicinity. Jeremy occasionally glimpsed red kangaroos at a distance, but they were large, swift creatures, extremely difficult for the most experienced hunters to spear, and his sling was useless against them. Rain fell intermittently, providing ample water, but food became more and more scarce.

After the first few days, Jeremy was constantly numb with fatigue from hunting during the day and spending much of each night with the ill people. He drew energy from his tormenting anxiety over how many would die, feeling a compelling need to do everything he could to help. He continued seeing red kangaroos from time to time, and he began taking his pistol when he went hunting, hoping he would get close enough to shoot one.

His opportunity came on a rainy afternoon, when he was going around a hill and glimpsed a red kangaroo little more than a hundred yards away. It was at a time of dire need, with virtually no food at the bora grounds, and he and the others had hunted since dawn without success. The boy took out his pistol and crept through the brush toward the kangaroo.

The animal was exceptionally large, one that would end the food shortage for at least several days. When he was a hundred feet from the kangaroo and could see the outline of its head and neck through the thinner tops of the brush, he eased the hammer back on the pistol and cocked it. Then, doing as Jarboe had shown him, he looked down the barrel and placed the sight on the animal's head. Then he slowly squeezed the trigger back.

The pistol roared and bucked in his hand, belching a cloud of smoke. The animal dropped to the ground, killed instantly. As the boy stepped forward, Jarboe came running over the hill to find out why Jeremy had fired his pistol. When he saw the large kangaroo, he whooped in delight and hurried down the hill, one of the other men following him.

"Good on you, mate!" he exclaimed joyfully. "This will end the empty stomachs among the people for a good while to come."

"Yes, it will," Jeremy agreed happily. "I was very lucky to happen upon this kangaroo." He thought about the people, his satisfaction fading. "But some of the people are so weak that they can hardly eat. It seems certain that several of them will die."

Jarboe smiled patiently, shaking his head. "As I've told you, you shouldn't worry about that, Jeremy. Many would have died if you hadn't inoculated them, and I still believe that few if any will die." He pointed to the kangaroo. "As you said, you were lucky to find this 'roo.

That's probably a sign that we're going to have good luck all around now."

Jeremy forced a smile and nodded, feeling doubtful but hoping that Jarboe was right. The other man plucked stems of tough grass and tied the kangaroo's feet together as Jarboe took out his hatchet and chopped down a sapling to use as a pole. Then, with the heavy kangaroo making the pole sag, the two men carried it toward the bora grounds, Jeremy following them.

At the clearing, the kangaroo brought cries of joy from the four women who had been unaffected by the disease, and the few others who were moving about. They had been joined by two men who had been less ill than most, and were now able to take feeble steps. Jeremy was encouraged by that, but only to a degree, because scores of people remained very ill.

The next day, it appeared that Jarboe's prediction of good fortune might have been correct. Jeremy hit a rock wallaby with a stone from his sling, stunning it long enough for Jarboe to get to it with his spear, which further eased the food shortage. When they returned to the clearing, a woman who had been bedridden had left her wurlie and was moving about.

During the following days, those who were very ill began improving. The first ones were the elders, who seemed to regain their strength through force of will. The same appeared true for women with small children, their determination to look after their young ones giving them energy. Then others began tottering weakly about, and even the two surviving members of the trading party began recovering.

At last it became clear to Jeremy that the tribe had experienced exceptional good fortune. It would take months for some of the people to fully regain their strength and health, and the evidence of the disease would remain for many decades in the telltale scars that it was leaving on many. However, all of the people were recovering, and none would die.

The scarcity of animals and edible plants in the vicinity

of the bora grounds became an increasingly severe problem, with only small portions to go around at each meal. On the day that the last few people were able to leave their wurlies, the elders ordered everyone to make preparations to return to their villages. At dawn the following morning, the people assembled with their belongings at the circle in the clearing.

The people held their robes close as they shivered in the cold gusts of wind that were scudding low, dark clouds across the sky. Jeremy and Jarboe were warm in their sheepskin coats, waiting with the others for the elders to lead the groups away from the bora grounds. The five men were standing and talking in front of the circle, and Juburli summoned Jarboe. He joined the elders and spoke with them, then beckoned Jeremy out of the crowd.

The boy stepped to the men, and the murmur of conversation among the people faded as one of the elders began speaking to the crowd, Jarboe translating for Jeremy. "He's telling the people that from now on, your name in the tribe will be Jinturpi," Jarboe said happily. "It's a short form of a sentence that means someone who saved the tribe."

A loud roar of agreement rose from the people as the elder spoke, and the five stern, aged men gazed at Jeremy in warm approval. Then the elders stepped toward the crowd and it began breaking up, the people sorting themselves into the five groups. Amid a bedlam of farewells, the groups moved out of the clearing in different directions.

After the bora grounds were left behind, Juburli's group spread out over a mile or more as usual, hunting and gathering plants. However, there was a difference that Jeremy noted with great satisfaction. During the crisis, Jarboe had been placed in a position of authority within the tribe, which had changed the way in which he was regarded by the group. Juburli kept Jarboe near him, and Jeremy hunted within earshot of the two men. The people were still weak and moved slowly, but an-

imals and plants were much more plentiful at a distance
from the bora grounds. The women found a patch of
murnongs, a parsnip-like yam, and the men speared a
wallaby. The meal that evening was a bountiful feast
compared to those of the past weeks, and Jeremy sat with
Jarboe among the others beside the fire.

The following day, the group settled back into the village. When the routine of daily activities resumed, Jarboe's intense dissatisfaction of before was gone. His
acceptance among his people on terms appropriate to his
age made him perfectly content, and Jeremy was bliss-
fully happy over the change in the man's state of mind.

During the evenings, Jarboe again enjoyed listening to
Jeremy reading aloud from his textbooks, but he was
different in other respects. He never mentioned tobacco,
evidently no longer wanting it, and he conformed more
closely to the ways of his ancestors. His water flask, billy,
and tin plate were coveted by the others, and he traded
them for spears, a possum skin cloak, and other traditional belongings of his people.

The final and most fundamental change came one
morning, when Jeremy woke to find that Jarboe and all
of his swag were gone. The boy dressed, then put on his
hat and sheepskin coat as he went outside. The people
were huddled around the fire in the grey dawn light as
the women stoked it and heated food, but Jarboe was not
among them. Juburli and another man moved to make
room for Jeremy beside the fire, and he shook his head.

"Jiburdarli?" the boy asked, speaking Jarboe's Aborigine name and then shrugging to indicate perplexity.

"Nymbunja," Juburli replied, he and other men pointing northward.

The word was the Aborigine term for a red goshawk,
and Jeremy thought about it for a moment, then realized
what the men had meant. He started to turn away, and
one of the women called him back and handed him a
piece of possum from the food that was heating. Jeremy
nodded in thanks, then munched the meat as he walked
away from the village toward the north.

At midmorning, Jeremy reached the hill where Jarboe had said that the red goshawk had been sung into being during the Dreamtime. However, instead of finding Jarboe at the level place he had pointed out, the man was at a sheer stone face higher on the hill. Wearing his possum skin robe, he was folding up his stockman's clothes and putting them into a niche in the stone with his swag. Jeremy climbed up the hill toward the man.

Jarboe smiled in greeting, putting his boots and stockman's hat into the niche. "I won't use these any longer," he said, "but it's no good to let them go to waste, is it? In the event they're ever needed again, this will be the best storage place that one could find. With the climate we have here, nothing will rot as long as it's protected a bit."

"That's true," Jeremy agreed. "Would you like for me to help you?"

"No, I'd rather do it myself, mate," Jarboe replied. "I'm grateful for the offer, but this is something I want to do alone."

Jeremy nodded in understanding and stepped on around the hill to a tree. He settled himself comfortably under it, pulling his thick coat closer against the cold wind stirring the foliage on the hill, and watched Jarboe. After he finished putting his things into the niche, Jarboe went down to the foot of the hill, where the soil was still wet from rains during the past few days. He piled mud on a slab of bark and carried it up the hill.

Jarboe found rocks that would fit together across the front of the niche and cemented them in place with the mud. After that, he plastered a thick layer of mud over the rocks, sealing the opening completely. When he finished and the mud began drying, it took a close look to find the niche, since the soil was almost the same color as the stone around it. The man then picked up his spear and went down the hill to the level spot.

He sat beside it, tucking his robe around himself, then gazed at it. A movement up the hill from the man caught Jeremy's eye. It was a red goshawk that had alighted in a tree. The boy studied it, reflecting that the bird had probably chosen that vantage point to watch for prey, but it took very little stretch of the imagination to believe that it was looking at Jarboe.

Jeremy sat and waited, leaving Jarboe undisturbed. The boy knew that while Jarboe had finished his walkabout weeks before in a physical sense, it had only just ended in the man's heart and mind. That morning, he had truly concluded his walkabout and returned to his heritage.

The boy looked out over the wilderness and thought about his own heritage, a place where he would know within his heart that he belonged. While he knew it would be in the outback, the vast land that he loved, that was all he knew. In time, he would go on his own walkabout to find it, but his adulthood was still years away. For now, he was in the outback and with his friend, and he was content to wait.

PART II

Chapter Eleven

"It's been eleven years since we last had any word of Jeremy," Alexandra Kerrick mused, looking down at the baby on her lap. "But I still think of him frequently and wonder what happened to him."

"So do I, Mother," Morton replied despondently. "One of the things I reproach myself about most is how brutally cruel I was to that boy."

Alexandra shook her head, regretting that she had spoken her thoughts aloud. Years before, Morton would have shrugged off the remarks, but now he was a far more thoughtful man. "Brutally cruel?" she echoed. "No, that's being too harsh on yourself, Morton. Indeed, you could have been more affectionate toward the boy, but I would go no further than that."

"Well, I would, and I do," Morton said emphatically. "He's my son, and I didn't even acknowledge him. That's a dastardly way to act to a child."

"It's also flotsam in your wake, and you shouldn't torment yourself with things in your past," Alexandra told him. "Life is too precious to waste a single moment of it in needless misery." She smiled, changing the subject. "Here it is time for me to leave, and we've barely discussed your business affairs while I've been here, Morton. Has the loss of the income from your gold mine caused you any difficulty?"

"No," he replied. "I knew the vein of ore would end eventually, and I was prepared for it." He laughed, shrugging. "What gave me a drubbing was the American Civil War. I was very heavily invested in cotton mills in, England, then the war came along and cut off the supply of cotton. I only managed to recover sixpence on the guinea, and I was fortunate to do that."

Alexandra smiled in response to his jocular manner, even though she sympathized with her son over the immense loss. She knew that the financial setback was directly related to the change in his personality, because years before, the onset of the war would never have caught him by surprise. But he now had a wife whom he loved deeply, and he had become a family man. In doing so, he was much less of a shrewd, driven businessman.

He was still wealthy, however, and Alexandra listened as he continued talking about his business activities. He had offered to make a loan to the station to cover the purchase of ten thousand thoroughbred Merino sheep that had been bought to improve the bloodline of the flocks, and he mentioned it once more. As before, Alexandra declined with thanks.

"That's kind of you, Morton, but we don't need it," she told him. "We'll be without a cash reserve for a year or two, but we can manage. For most sheep stations, that is a normal state of affairs."

He nodded, dropping the subject again. Hearing a bustle in the entry, Alexandra knew her baggage was being taken outside to the carriage. Along with the stir of footsteps, she heard Morton's wife talking to the servants as they carried out the luggage. Characteristically, Julia had quietly and efficiently organized every detail of having the bags packed and taken to the carriage. More than a gracious hostess, Julia was one of the most thoughtful and caring human beings whom Alexandra had ever met.

A moment later, Julia came into the parlor. In her mid-thirties, she was an attractive, slender woman whose beauty was enhanced by the radiant good nature her well-formed features reflected. She was the principal reason for the change in Morton's personality, because his adoring love for her had transformed him. For that alone, Alexandra would have been deeply fond of Julia, but the woman's endearing personality made her very easy to love. Moreover, with a practical, judicious side to her nature, Julia was also Morton's best friend and advisor, a perfect companion in life.

Her blue eyes sparkling in a warm smile, Julia stepped toward Alexandra. "Shall we let the nurse take your grandson now, Mistress Kerrick?" she asked.

"I'd love to hold him forever." Alexandra replied, lifting the baby and kissing its cheek. "But it's almost time for me to leave, so I suppose that I must give him up for now."

"There's no cause for hurry," Julia said, taking the baby and handing it to the nurse, who had followed her into the room. As the nurse left with the baby, Julia sat on the couch beside Morton. "I wanted to claim a bit more of your time and enjoy your company myself. We have so precious little time together, and your visit has seemed very short."

Alexandra agreed emphatically, saddened by the rapidly approaching end of her visit with her loved ones. The previous day, she had attended the baby's christening, and she again thanked Julia and Morton for their choice of names for the child. "It was so thoughtful of you to name him David Alexander," she said. "It's such an honor, and I'm ever so pleased."

"It is he who is honored," Julia assured her. "Matching the example set by those who had the names before him will be a worthy goal in life. We're so happy that you were able to attend the christening."

"No happier than I was to attend, and it was the main reason that determined the timing of my visit to Sydney," Alexandra replied. "I enjoyed it entirely as much as I knew that I would."

The discussion moved on to other things, and Alexandra asked about a man who had been briefly mentioned in conversation a few times. It had been in disparaging terms each time, making her curious about him, and Morton shook his head scornfully as he replied: "Aldous Creevey is a businessman who recently arrived in Sydney," he told her. "It didn't take him long to make himself known to everyone as a perfect monster."

"Indeed it didn't," Julia agreed. "He's revolting, both in character and appearance. His wife, Beverly, is a pretty, personable young woman, and he keeps her as a virtual prisoner in his house. He must have forced her to marry him through some foul scheme."

"And one that involved money," Morton added. "He's been in business in England, Canada, and elsewhere, and he's as rich as Croesus. Though it's no wonder he's rich, because he'll engage in anything. While in Canada, he had agents prowling the Civil War battlefields in America and pulling out the teeth of the dead with pliers. He boasts that he got barrels of them."

"Good Lord!" Alexandra exclaimed in horror. "Whatever for?"

"To sell to manufacturers of false teeth. I understand it's very lucrative for anyone willing to be involved in it. Creevey's goal must be to have more wealth than anyone else, by whatever means."

Julia shook her head, disagreeing. "No, it isn't that, Morton. His great desire is for power, such as he wields over his poor wife."

"Well, whatever his goal," Alexandra put in, "it's clear that he's a man to avoid. I trust that you aren't involved with him in any way, Morton."

"No, certainly not, Mother," he replied. "If I can possibly prevent it, I never will be, because I want nothing to do with his sort." He took out his watch and glanced at it, sighing ruefully. "As much as I regret it, it's time for us to leave. Deirdre will meet us at the train station, and she said she would bring Eudora from Sydenham Academy."

Alexandra nodded. She and the others stood, and they went out into the entry. As they put on their coats, hats, and gloves from the closet, Alexandra mentioned her daughter's photographic studio: "Deirdre has always told me that it provides a good profit," she said. "However, I've wondered if that hasn't been dissimulation to prevent my worrying about her."

Morton laughed heartily, shaking his head. "Her studio is profitable, but she spends the profits as quickly as she gets them. Whenever she reads about a new lens or some other contraption, she sends for it. She loves her work, perhaps too much to pursue it as a business."

"She doesn't want for anything, though," Julia added. "We visit often, and I know her circumstances to be comfortable enough. In addition, she is happy in what she is doing, which is more than many can say."

Alexandra agreed, satisfied on the point concerning Deirdre. As they went outside, the April wind had the biting chill of a cloudy autumn day, and she pulled her coat closer. The carriage was waiting, her baggage stacked and tied down on top of it. She and the others stepped into the carriage and continued talking as it moved away from the house.

"How is Father's health?" Morton asked. "In his letters, he insists that he's hale and hearty, but I know that he's had chest pains at times."

"Your father is almost seventy years old," Alexandra pointed out. "For a man of his age, his health is remarkably good. Concerning his chest pains, he saw a doctor in Wilcannia and got some medicine."

Morton nodded, and the conversation moved on to the others at Tibooburra Station, but David's chest pains worried Alexandra more than she had revealed. The medicine he had obtained from the doctor was laudanum, which merely dulled the pains. She tried to dismiss the nagging worry, glancing out the window as she talked with Morton and Julia. During the past forty years, she had seen Sydney grow from little more than an outpost for convicts into a thriving, cosmopolitan city. She greatly preferred the outback, but she was fond of the city, with its shady residential streets and beautiful parks.

As the carriage made its way through the center of the city, Alexandra saw Benjamin Tavish on the street. He waved vigorously, a grin wreathing his handsome features, and Alexandra smiled and waved. His sisters had married successful prospectors and left Australia with their husbands, but at thirty years of age, Benjamin remained unmarried.

"It's not for want of women who set their cap for him," Morton said when Alexandra mentioned it. "He's sensible, and he's waiting until he has the means to provide a family with comfortable circumstances. That shouldn't be long now, because he's one of my senior clerks."

Morton continued talking about Benjamin, and Alexandra noted with satisfaction that her son's voice and manner revealed fondness for the man. He had a special interest in Benjamin, evidently regarding him more or less as a younger brother, which pleased Alexandra intensely.

A short time later, where George Street became Parramatta Road at the old brickyards, the carriage turned off the street into the wide plaza fronting on the train station. It was a large, imposing stone structure, with a neo-Gothic facade and clock tower. As the carriage drew up at the entrance, Alexandra saw Deirdre and Eudora waiting in front of it.

At thirty-five, Deirdre was a radiantly beautiful, aggressively independent woman. She had never shown serious interest in any man, even though many men had, and still did, in her. Alexandra would have preferred her daughter to have a loving companion in life, but it was a subject she had never broached with Deirdre, leaving the issue entirely to her.

Alexandra exchanged a hug and kiss with her daughter, then with her granddaughter. Eudora—Jonathan and Catherine's youngest daughter—was seventeen. Along with a facial resemblance to her father, she had her mother's raven hair and striking green eyes. While carefully avoiding any show of favoritism, Alexandra had always been especially fond of Eudora, because she was the most vivacious and spirited of the three sisters.

The coachman and porters carried the baggage into the train station, and Alexandra and the others followed them inside. In the large, vaulted waiting room, Morton went to attend to the baggage and ticket, while Alexandra talked with the women. A week before, Eudora had received a letter from her sister, Justine, who had married an army officer two years before and gone with him to Singapore. In the letter, Justine had stated that she was pregnant, which was a topic of excited conversation between Alexandra and the others.

"I shall look forward to being a great-grandmother," Alexandra said. "And I hope I'll be able to see Justine's child at some time or other."

"Yes, as we all do," Deidre replied. "Julia and I will be grandaunts, and we're certainly looking forward to that."

Alexandra nodded, thrilled over the coming new generation in her family, even though the child would be many miles away. As she and the women continued talking, the conversation turned to the possibility of further additions to the family, although far away. Anastasia, the third sister, was also married to an army officer and had gone with him to England.

Morton returned with the receipt for Alexandra's baggage and her ticket, and she put the receipt away as she and the others filed out onto the platform, where baggage was being loaded into a freight coach and people bustled about as steam hissed softly from the engine. Alexandra's ticket was for the first-class coach, which was divided into compartments, and she protested about the extra expense.

"It amounted to very little," Morton replied, shrugging it off. "You'll have privacy, which will be worth many times the expense, Mother."

An awkward silence fell, no one finding anything to say during the last moments before leavetaking, then Eudora suddenly burst into tears. Deirdre put an arm around her and smiled in a silent comment on the girl's weeping, but she also blinked tears out of her own blue eyes. Alexandra was dismally sad, recalling past times when she had blithely departed from loved ones, certain of seeing them again in due time. At sixty-three years of age, however, there was no such certainty.

Mercifully, the engine whistle hooted and the conductor called out, ending the tortured moment. Alexandra exchanged hugs and kisses with her family. No one had dry eyes, and she barely kept herself from weeping as Morton helped her into the compartment and closed the door. She waved through the window as the engine snorted and the train jerked into motion. Then it moved away from the platform, and she wept.

After a few minutes, Alexandra dried her eyes and, searching for cheerful things to concentrate upon, thought about the child that Justine would have. But in her depression, the dark side of the situation occurred to Alexandra. Jonathan and Catherine would be grandparents, but they had yet to produce an heir to assume the stewardship of Tibooburra Station after they were gone. Unless they did, what she and David had spent their lives building might eventually fall into ruin under a hired manager.

Alexandra sighed in impatience with herself and shrugged off her melancholy. She looked out the window, but the view did little to improve her mood. The raw earth of cut banks alternated with overgown wasteland and glimpses of ramshackle houses. The railroad led to Parramatta, but the view was depressing compared to the enjoyable drive of years before.

Parramatta was a pleasant, attractive town, and a personal association made it even more appealing to Alexandra. Almost forty-five years before, when she had been nineteen, it was there that she had met David for the first time. But she was unable to see Parramatta from the train, because the tiny station was beside stockyards on the outskirts of the town.

The view finally became enjoyable after the train left Parramatta, with the landscape opening out into the valley of the Nepean River when the train chuffed across Prospect Hill. It was entirely different from the first time Alexandra had seen it. The open forest and sheep paddocks of those years had been replaced by farms and pastures. Penrith had sprung up as a village, then grown into a town. Through all the years, however, one place was unchanged. South of the Bathurst Road, a dense forest beside the river was just as it had been on a fateful day in her life decades before.

The engine whistle shrieked and the bell clanged as the train entered Penrith, isolated houses and then streets passing the window. Then the brakes squealed and the train slowed, approaching the station. A journey that had once taken a day or more with wagons had been accomplished in less than two hours. Alexandra acknowledged that it was convenient, but all in all, she preferred a slower, more enjoyable pace in life.

As she stepped off the train, she saw Ruel Blake and Eulie Bodenham among the other people. Both men were in their fifties, old friends as well as employees. Jackaroos followed them toward Alexandra, all of them lifting their hats, and she greeted them as she took out the receipt for her baggage.

"The landlord at the Nepean Inn has a room for you, mo'm," Ruel said, taking the receipt. "We'll bring your baggage over there. The horses and the wagons are all ready to leave for the station."

"Very well, we'll leave tomorrow morning," Alexandra told him. "I want to walk around for a bit, so I'll meet you at the inn presently."

Ruel nodded, he and the others lifting their hats as Alexandra crossed the platform to the door. She went through the station and out onto the main street of the town, and as she walked down it, it turned into a road beside the river that led to the Bathurst Road.

In addition to being a commercial center for the area, Penrith had a thriving timber industry, and Alexandra saw spots where trees had been felled on both sides of the river. South of the Bathurst Road, trees had been cut on the west side of the river, but that large, thick forest on the east bank that had been the scene of pivotal events in her life was untouched.

People had ended work for the day and were coming up the road toward Penrith. One of them, a man in his late fifties, carried a broadaxe and was evidently a woodcutter. Alexandra stopped him and asked why no trees had been cut in the woods on the other side of Bathurst Road.

"No one wants to get into trouble," the man said, laughing, then explained further, "Years ago, a man named Wilkinson owned a great stretch of land south of the road. When he died, his heirs sold it to the Mac-Arthurs, but the deed was flawed. It covered that patch of forest, but the government is supposed to have an easement on both banks of the river. All that happened well before your time, of course."

Alexandra let the last remark pass without comment, even though it was the second error in what the man had said. Despite her white hair, people always judged her to be much younger than she was. "So that parcel of land is in litigation, then?" she summed up.

"Do you mean that lawyers are haggling over it?" the man replied with a laugh. "Aye, they were at it when I first started cutting wood here, and I daresay it won't be settled when my grandchildren are my age."

Alexandra thanked the man for the information, then walked on down the road. The first error in what he had said had been the name of the original landowner, which had been Williamson, not Wilkinson. The remainder agreed with what she knew, because decades before, she had heard that John Macarthur had bought the land from Frank Williamson's heirs.

She crossed Bathurst Road, pulling her coat closer against the cold breeze. Then she looked at the forest. When he had been a convict, David had spent his Sundays there, planning to go to the outback and establish a sheep station. Jonathan and Catherine had gone there with a lunch and a bottle of wine, and it was there that Catherine had agreed to marry him.

It was also there that Alexandra had been left tied for a time, just after she had been kidnapped by bushrangers. During recent years, however, she had come to terms with that incident. It had been an ordeal, but it had set the circumstances leading to her now richly enjoyable, fulfilling life. As she looked at the forest, the breeze rustling the thick foliage, she hoped that no ax ever touched a single one of the trees.

Thousands of miles to the west, Jeremy Kerrick mentioned the same forest as he talked with Jarboe Charlie about when they had first met. "I was going through the trees toward the river," Jeremy said, "and I didn't know anyone was about. Then I suddenly came upon you, and you frightened me."

"You scared me too," Jarboe replied, struggling to laugh. "Seeing those bunyip eyes for the first time would scare anybody."

The man's voice was weak and his words were slurred, barely understandable. During the afternoon, he had suffered a seizure more severe than the one of three days before, leaving him almost completely paralyzed. At his request, he had been carried to where the red goshawk had been sung into being, wanting his life to depart at the same place it had entered him. Then the others had returned to the village, leaving Jeremy with him.

The strain of talking exhausted Jarboe, and he fell silent, breathing shallowly. As the glow of sunset began fading, the gusty wind stirring the brush on the hill was colder. Jeremy pulled his kangaroo skin cloak around himself, wearing only it, a loincloth, and kangaroo-skin moccasins. Then he leaned close to listen as Jarboe muttered something.

The man's condition appeared to be worsening rapidly, because his breathing was labored and his slurred voice was barely a whisper. After he repeated himself several times, Jeremy finally understood that he wanted a fire to ward off the gathering darkness. Jeremy stood up, gathering his cloak around himself, and went down the hill to collect firewood.

While he was there, two boys from the village came through the brush, carrying food and a firestick. They offered him the food, and he shook his head. "You eat it, because I want nothing," he told them.

"Juburli said we are to stay with you, Jinturpi," one of them said.

"Then build a fire and stay here in the valley, where it is warmer."

The boys began gathering up sticks as Jeremy carried his firewood back up the hill to the level spot. He kindled a fire and watched its pool of yellow, flickering light spread out into the thickening darkness. Jarboe appeared to be either sleeping or unconscious, because his eyes were closed. Jeremy sat down beside the fire and waited.

The hours passed, and sorrow tormented Jeremy as he stared into the fire and thought about his years with Jarboe. For more than a year, he had remained with the Arandas only because of Jarboe. At nineteen, he was six feet and two inches, and one hundred and ninety pounds of bone and sinewy muscles hardened by the daily struggle for survival in the arid wilderness. Along with adult stature, he had a compelling urge to go on his own walkabout and find his place in life.

Jarboe had encouraged him to go, but as he gazed at the flames and pondered, Jeremy was thankful that he had remained. If he had left, he knew he would have always wondered about the man who had been such a powerful influence upon him. Having remained, he could try to comfort Jarboe in his last hours. In another way, however,

Jeremy wished he had gone so he could have avoided the wrenching anguish of seeing Jarboe die.

Late in the night, Jarboe stirred, trying to talk again. Jeremy leaned over him, listening to the faint, distorted whisper and at last understood what the man was trying to say. Jarboe was telling him to leave and go in search of his heritage, the place where he belonged. "I waited too long to go on my walkabout," the man muttered. "You mustn't do the same...."

"No, I won't, Jarboe," Jeremy replied. "I'll go very soon."

The man continued, making slurred sounds and haltingly forming words. "Take the swag and clothes I left up on the hill," he told Jeremy. "The reason I left them there was so you would have them...."

"Yes, I know. I'll take them, Jarboe."

The effort of talking had drained Jarboe's last strength, and his breathing became rapid and labored. After a moment, it stopped. Moreover, Jeremy felt a subtle change in the atmosphere of the night. Before, he had been with his companion of many years, and now he was alone. Jeremy went down the hill toward the glow of the boys' fire in the thick darkness.

The boys were asleep beside the fire, and Jeremy awakened them. "Go and tell Juburli that Jiburdarli is gone," he said.

The boys raced away into the night, and Jeremy went back up the hill to his fire. The Aborigines believed that upon death, the life force returned to its origin, to the spirit that had instilled it into an unborn child in its mother's womb. Jeremy knew only that the man who had meant so much to him was gone. Tears of grief spilled from his eyes as he stared into the fire.

Dawn was dull and grey, thick clouds covering the sky. A short time later, the people arrived, Juburli leading them through the foliage toward the hill. The leader had become more emaciated with age, but he still had wiry strength and his step was light. He stopped in the valley below the hill, pointing and giving orders. The people had brought didgeridoos and rhythm sticks, and they gathered firewood.

After kindling a fire, they put green mulga brush on it. As the thick smoke billowed up, the didgeridoos began their mournful dirge, the rhythm sticks tapping. The people chanted as Juburli led them up the hill. It was a single sentence repeated over and over, imploring the spirit of the red goshawk to take back the life force it had given Juburdarli.

The internment took only a few minutes. Jarboe's forehead, hands, and feet were coated with red ocher, then he was placed in the earth that had nourished him. When it was finished, the corroboree ended. Juburli evidently realized what Jeremy intended to do, because the old man told the people to go while he remained behind to talk with Jeremy.

As the people filed down the hill and toward the village, Juburli agreed when Jeremy said he must leave. "The other elders and I would like for you to stay," he continued, "but it is better that you go. Juburdarli remained too long among those who were not his kind and became unlike his kind. You should not do the same. Where will you go and what will you do?"

"Somewhere to the east, and I will work so I will have the necessities of life. At the same time, I will go on a walkabout and search for the place of my spirit where I will be content."

"You will find it," Juburli stated positively. "You will search for a time, but it awaits you even now." He rummaged in his dilly bag and took out an intricately carved piece of bone an inch wide and some four inches long. A hole had been bored in one end, and it hung on a thong made of tough animal tendon. "The other elders and I have known that you would leave. The last time we were together at the bora grounds, we made this for you."

"What is its purpose, Juburli?"

"To protect you," the old man replied, standing on tiptoe to put the thong over Jeremy's head. "If you have an enemy whom you must destroy, point it at him and then destroy the amulet. Then he will be destroyed also."

Looking at the amulet, Jeremy was more than doubtful that it would do what Juburli had said. Over the years, he had seen instances when the elders apparently knew of events at a distance, with no logical way of having learned of them. There had also been times when situations had taken surprising turns, but precisely as the elders had wished. He still remained skeptical about supernatural powers, however, preferring to believe that circumstances of which he had been unaware had been involved.

At the same time, he was grateful for the old man's concern for him. "It was very kind of you and the other elders to make this for me," he said, touching the amulet. "Until I have an enemy whom I must destroy, I will keep it to remind me of the people who allowed me to share their land."

The old man placed a hand on Jeremy's shoulder, silently smiling in farewell, then he turned and went down the hill. Jeremy climbed up it to the vertical face of rock where Jarboe had stored the clothes and swag so many years before. The niche was still sealed as solidly as on the day that Jarboe had covered it with stones and mud. Jeremy picked up a stone and broke it open.

The clothes were loose on him, but the hat fit. After years of wearing moccasins, the boots felt cumbersome. Jeremy put his pistol, knife, and other things into the canvas dilly bag. He slung it over his shoulder, along with the rolled blanket and the water bottle that Jarboe had covered with leather years before, then went back down the hill.

When he was at the foot of the hill, a movement in the sky caught his eye. He looked up, seeing a red goshawk circling overhead. As he watched it, the thought that the goshawk might be something more than a bird seemed fanciful to him. Even so, he took off his hat and waved it.

The goshawk began climbing into the cloudy sky. It

spiraled higher and higher until it was only a speck against the clouds. Then it disappeared. Jeremy put his hat back on and set out toward the southeast, taking long, quick strides. His walkabout had begun.

Chapter Twelve

Morton Kerrick was flustered when he arrived at the Bank of Securities and Trust for a directors' meeting. He had always prided himself on punctuality, but he was late for the meeting. More important, he was distracted because his son was ill, which was the reason for his tardiness.

A clerk in the drafty hall outside the conference room took Morton's hat, cane, and greatcoat. Then, when Morton opened the door and stepped into the conference room with an apology on his lips, he was struck speechless with surprise. Along with the other directors and Henry Newcomb, the bank manager, Aldous Creevey was seated at the long table.

"Ah, there you are, Sir Morton," Henry called cheerily. "We've waited for a few minutes, because I was sure you would be along presently."

"I'm very sorry for the inconvenience," Morton apologized, closing the door and stepping to the table. "I was detained at home for a time this morning, because David Alexander, my son, is ill."

"Indeed?" Henry said, concerned. "Nothing serious, I trust."

"My wife doesn't think so," Morton replied, exchanging nods with others around the table as he sat down. "But then, she isn't a physician."

"Well, the weather we're having gives rise to complaints, doesn't it?" Henry commented. "You've observed, of course, that we have a new director. Mr. Creevey purchased shares in the bank that were held by smaller stockholders. The total is ten percentum of the shares, so under the provisions of the bank charter, he automatically becomes a director."

The explanation amounted to an introduction, but Creevey made no response to Morton's cool nod. The man was enormous, not tall but a breadth more appropriate to a massive hog rolling in fat. A half dozen chins buried his collar, and his eyes were almost hidden behind his heavy eyelids and fat brows. His banana-like fingers were laced together, his hands folded and resting on his bulging stomach.

The man's bulk overflowed his chair, and something about him seemed odiously different to Morton than simply a large quantity of human flesh. Morton was reminded of an incident of years before, when he had been at the docks at the time that a body was fished out of the water. It had been obscenely swollen by putrifaction, and Creevey's girth also seemed to come from something other than an overabundance of food.

Henry Newcomb shuffled through his papers and began going down the items on the agenda. It was a routine meeting, as most were, but they were still time-consuming. With the exception of Morton and one other director—and now Creevey as well—the directors were elected to their positions at meetings of small stockholders. As men of relatively modest means who were involved in the management of a large, highly profitable financial institution, they were inclined to be voluble at the meetings.

However, Henry kept the meeting moving on down the agenda by looking at his watch frequently when one of the elected directors propounded too long on some point. Morton said little and accepted Henry's recommendations on each item. They were good friends, and years before, Morton had been friends with Henry's father, Giles Newcomb, who had also been a bank manager.

The meeting became other than routine when they reached the last item, concerning eight mortgages in arrears. Henry recommended that they be extended, because the mortgagors had been customers of the bank for years and were in temporary financial difficulties. "No, they should all be foreclosed," Creevey said, his voice bizarrely high and thin for his huge bulk.

Discussion began on the point, which astonished Morton, because it was so contrary to good business sense. Then he saw that Creevey had intimidated the elected directors, which was easy enough to do; all of them were awed by wealth. However, as he watched and listened, Morton saw that something else was involved.

Most people had limits on what they would do to others. Even the most depraved usually had some spark of humanity that set boundaries to their iniquity. Creevey's attitude and his eyes suggested that he had none. His eyes had opened wider, and they were totally remorseless, reflecting savage, inhuman evil. More than intimidated, the elected directors were frightened of what the huge, ugly man might do to them.

It stirred Morton's temper, and he saw that Henry was losing control of the meeting. "This is absurd!" Morton snapped. "Why are we discussing whether or not to cut off our noses to spite our faces?"

Henry looked relieved, turning to him. "Would you like to explain your position on the issue, Sir Morton?" he asked.

"No, I'd like an immediate vote on it, Mr. Newcomb,"

Morton replied formally. "I vote shares amounting to twenty-six percentum of the stock in favor of accepting your recommendation on these mortgages."

Henry glanced around the table, and the other director who was a principal shareholder silently nodded. Then two elected directors hesitantly joined in, taking it over fifty percent and closing the vote.

It also ended the meeting, and the others began leaving the table and filing out of the room. Creevey stared at Morton just long enough for it to be either a challenge or a warning, his eyes now like two discs of dark glass. Morton stared back, knowing that his pale blue eyes were more effective than most in a contest of wills. The huge man then heaved himself up from his chair and ponderously waddled out.

After most meetings, Morton chatted with Henry for a time, but he was anxious to check on his son. "I quite understand," Henry said when Morton explained, "but I'd like to delay you for just a moment, if I may, Sir Morton. John Whitney told me that he'll be unable to make the mortgage payments on his property on Grace Street. I'm sure he would like to sell it so he could recover some of his investment."

"Grace Street?" Morton mused. "That's in the older section of Wooloo, where some very valuable properties are located."

"Yes, this house is fairly old, and it's been unoccupied for years. It's adjacent to Mr. Creevey's home. After seeing his manner in the meeting today, I believe if the property is openly advertised for sale, he might browbeat John Whitney into selling it for a pittance."

"He very well might," Morton agreed. "John Whitney is a good man, but he's a bit timid. I'll have Benjamin Tavish take a look at it to examine its condition, and I'll see what kind of offer I can make."

"Any reasonable offer will buy it," Henry said. "Naturally, I'd like to keep my involvement in this private. I wouldn't want it known that I had provided profitable information to only one bank director."

"Yes, of course. Let me have the keys, and I'll deal directly with the owner. Moreover, he won't know how I knew to ask for the keys. I could have very well learned about the situation from Benjamin, because he keeps a close eye on all of the real estate in the city."

Henry nodded in satisfaction, gathering up his papers. As they went out into the hall, Morton collected his hat, coat, and cane. He followed Henry downstairs to his office, where the man gave Morton a key ring and then looked up the amount of the mortgage in the bank records.

Morton held his hat on in the gusty, bitterly cold wind as he left the bank and ducked into his carriage at the curb. While it moved through the streets toward his office building at Kings Cross, he mused anxiously about his son, as well as another matter. That morning, Julia had urged him to go to work instead of waiting at the house for the doctor. He had become almost sharp with her before leaving, which he deeply regretted.

When the carriage drew up at Kings Cross, Morton hurried into the large, central office on the ground floor to see if there was word from his wife about their son. Albert Loman, the tall, austere head clerk, stood up from his desk and handed Morton a folded paper. "Lady Julia sent this note by a maid, Sir Morton," he said. "It arrived a short time ago."

Morton hastily unfolded the note and read it, then stiffened in anger. "A mild fever and no reason to worry?" he exclaimed. "That doctor should be attending swine and goats, not human beings." He sighed, shoving the note into his coat pocket. "I'd better go and check on David Alexander, and perhaps call another doctor. Is there anything important at hand?"

"Well . . . yes, there are some matters that require your attention, Sir Morton," Albert replied hesitantly. "Some are quite important."

"I'll return as quickly as possible, then," Morton said, and turned to Benjamin Tavish across the room at his desk. "Come with me, Benjamin."

Benjamin took his hat and coat off the rack, and put them on as he followed Morton outside. Morton told the coachman to take him home by way of Grace Street, then he and Benjamin stepped into the carriage. As it moved through the streets toward the Wooloo district, Morton gave Benjamin the key ring and related the substance of his conversation with Henry.

"The house may be in poor condition," Morton continued. "It'll probably take you a few days to search for structural defects and compute repair costs. We'll need an accurate figure so we'll know how much to offer."

Benjamin nodded, replying that he would make a careful analysis. A few minutes later, the carriage stopped at the end of Grace Street, and Benjamin stepped out. Then the carriage moved on through the residential district toward Morton's house as he thought about his son and how to phrase his apology to Julia for his impatience that morning.

The lock on the foot gate in the stone wall fronting on the property was caked with rust, as was the gate itself. Benjamin shivered in the wind as he patiently worked with the key, finally getting the lock open. The hinges on the gate protested shrilly as he stepped inside.

The front garden was a wasteland of weeds and overgrown shrubbery, but Benjamin disregarded it as a minor point, studying the house. Three stories tall, it was an old mansion in classic, formal Georgian style, the single block design without wings. True to form, it was absolutely symmetrical, built of brick with courses and cornices of white local granite.

Making his way around one side of the house, Benjamin looked it over. When he reached the rear corner, he saw that the rear garden was a wilderness. Trees and shrubbery were overgrown, arbors were sagging under the weight of roses gone to vine, and flower beds were patches of rank weeds. Here and there, pieces of statuary jutted up among the mass of foliage, and the weathered roof of a summerhouse was visible in back of the garden.

Benjamin pushed past shrubbery overhanging the path and went down it to look back at the roof at the rear of the house. Halfway down the path, an opening through the foliage gave him a clear view of the summerhouse. He froze, transfixed by what he saw. The lattice on the near side of the summerhouse had fallen down, and a young woman was sitting inside it.

Bundled in a heavy winter coat, she had a book opened on her lap. Instead of reading, however, she was gazing away, her profile to Benjamin. She was ravishing, the most rapturously beautiful creature he had ever seen, with finely etched, classically beautiful features. In the setting of the overgrown garden, she almost seemed unworldly, like an exquisitely charming fairy in her secret, isolated hideaway. Her expression was pensive, making her appear vulnerable and even more appealing.

In her reverie and with the wind in the foliage masking his footsteps, she failed to notice him until he reached the summerhouse. Then she sprang to her feet in surprise and fright, her book tumbling to the floor. "Please do forgive me," he apologized contritely, stepping into the summerhouse and picking up her book. "I most sincerely regret that I startled you."

"No, the fault is mine," she said breathlessly, taking her book at arm's length. "I will leave."

Her blue eyes were wide and her cheeks pale, and she seemed like a delicate, graceful doe trembling in terror of a brutal hunter's gun. Benjamin was stricken with remorse. "No, no, please don't," he begged her, moving away. "I'm truly sorry I disturbed you. If I'd had any idea that I'd drive you away, I wouldn't have come down the path this far."

"No, I shouldn't be here," she replied softly, edging toward the front of the summerhouse. "I shall go now."

"Please don't," he pleaded, backing out of the small structure. "I'll go away and not disturb you further. If I'd known—" He broke off as his foot slipped off the threshold, and he staggered backward out of the summerhouse, windmilling his arms to keep from falling.

A lively, girlish sense of humor suddenly revealed itself in her, her shy expression disappearing into a radiant smile of amusement and her large blue eyes sparkling. Then she shook her head apologetically as he recovered his balance. "I didn't mean to make sport of you," she said.

Benjamin laughed and shrugged, willing to do anything to bring that smile to her lovely face again. "You didn't, because at times I fall over my own big feet." He took off his hat. "Please allow me to introduce myself. My name is Tavish. Benjamin Tavish."

"Mine is Beverly," she replied, "and I must go now. It's kind of you to tell me to stay, but I'm trespassing here."

"It is inconceivable that you could trespass anywhere, Beverly," he assured her firmly. "Anyone who would try to deny you the right to go wherever you wish should be hanged, drawn, and ..." His voice fading, he considered the expression too gory to use in her presence and belatedly amended it. "They should be punished severely."

"Well, hardly," she commented, disagreeing with his extravagant statement but pleased by it. She glanced around. "I've been coming here for several months, ever since I found this place. This disorder is somehow quite appealing to me, and it's very pleasant to sit here."

Benjamin studied her well-educated English accent and mannerisms, speculating that she might be a hired companion for some rich old shrew in one of the nearby mansions. "And it provides private, restful moments away from your mistress?" he ventured, searching for more information about her.

She hesitated, pursing her lips, then replied, "I neglected to tell you my full name, didn't I? It is Beverly Creevey."

Benjamin was struck speechless. He had heard that Creevey had a young, attractive wife, but it seemed a terrible wrong for this adorable woman to be married to the man. Noting his reaction, she became sadly resigned, and he struggled to overcome his bewilderment. "Yes,

I've heard that you and your husband have a home nearby, Mistress Creevey," he said.

"Beverly will do quite well, Benjamin," she told him, dismissing the subject of her husband. "Is this house yours, then?"

"No, no," he replied, laughing. "I'll own properties like this one day, but for now I manage real estate for my employer. He's interested in this property, and I came here to look it over."

"Who is your employer?" Beverly asked, sitting back down on the bench that ran around the inside of the summerhouse.

Benjamin told her as he stepped inside the small building and sat on the bench. He explained what he did for Morton, then he began talking about his plans to eventually become an investor himself. It occurred to him that he might be boring her, even though she seemed attentive enough. "This is probably of little interest to you, though," he suggested.

"On the contrary, it's quite interesting," she said. "What sort of real estate will you buy at first?"

"Commercial properties," he replied. "The profits are less, but more readily forthcoming. That will allow me to build up the capital to expand into residential real estate, and eventually into land."

Beverly nodded, and Benjamin continued explaining what he planned to do. Her occasional questions revealed a good grasp of what he was saying, indicating at least some interest in the subject. More than that, however, Benjamin suspected that she was desperately lonely, yearning for companionship and conversation about anything at all.

She was a shy and even a timid woman, but he sensed that she had an inner strength that would do credit to the most brawny, brawling porter at the docks. The discussion moved on to other things, Benjamin telling her about himself and his family. Beverly talked about her family in England, but said little about her life in Sydney. From the few things that she did say about her life in the Victorian mansion next door, it was a strange, solitary existence. Her husband prohibited her from making friends or visiting others, even though he took her to church and at times to the theater to display his beautiful wife. The rest of her time—virtually all of it—was spent in crushing loneliness.

Why she had married Creevey was a bewildering enigma to Benjamin, as well as a topic he avoided. There were many other things to discuss, and their lively conversation never lagged as the hours passed. He hardly felt the cold, and she also appeared perfectly comfortable. Talking with her was like an ecstatic dream from which he never wanted to awaken as he studied her lovely face and listened to her sweet, melodious voice.

Beverly was warm and responsive to him, and from time to time while they talked, a charming flush rose to her cheeks and she looked away. After hours had fled by and she had to leave, he asked her to meet him there the next day. "I shouldn't," she said softly, blushing.

"Please do, Beverly," he begged her. "I'll be here at the same time tomorrow. Please meet me here so we can talk again."

"I'll think about it," she replied, moving away. "Goodbye, Benjamin."

He spoke in farewell, wishing it was a word he had never needed to say to her. She disappeared into the dense foliage as she hurried down the path toward the wall at the rear of the garden. Benjamin went back toward the house, fervently hoping she would meet him the next day.

Thinking of practical matters, he looked at his watch and saw that inspecting the house would have to wait. He had other things that had to be done, and he liked to visit the Merchants Exchange each day. It was a club of sorts for businessmen, where current data on insurance rates, ship arrivals and departures, and other information was kept posted on boards. He put his watch away and went around the house toward the street.

He had always thought that love for a woman would

develop over a period of time. Instead, it had exploded to full, rich life within him during that moment when he had first seen her through the foliage. Now it seemed to him that the world had changed, and everything was subtly different from what it had been before that moment. Colors appeared brighter, people were friendlier, and even the raw, dark winter day was more pleasant.

At the Merchants Exchange, however, Benjamin was sharply reminded of another side to the joy that had entered his life. He overheard two men discussing someone who had sold a small amount of stock in the Bank of Securities and Trust to Creevey. At first the man had declined to sell it, then Creevey had found some way to utterly crush the man's will, forcing him to sell the stock at a much lower price than the first offer.

That night, Benjamin was sleepless for hours as he lay in bed at his lodgings and relived his moments with Beverly. Then, during the early hours of the morning, he was awakened by a storm that had swept down on the city. At daybreak, he worriedly looked out the window at the gusts of wind driving sheets of rain down the street and wondered if the combination of the weather and her misgivings would make Beverly decide to stay at home.

Wearing his best suit, and with oilskins over his greatcoat, he made his way down the rain-drenched streets to Kings Cross. After attending to essential work at the office, he went back out into the pelting rain and across the city to Grace Street. He arrived early and waited in the summerhouse, the roof leaking rivulets as he checked his watch every few minutes.

At the precise moment that he had arrived at the summerhouse the day before, Benjamin glimpsed the bright yellow of oilskins through the foliage. Beverly hurried on down the path from the back wall of the garden, pushing through overhanging growth. With an excited smile wreathing her lovely features, she looked angelic. As she stepped into the summerhouse, Benjamin took her hands in his, silently gazing down at her in delight.

Beverly smiled up at him, then looked away as a bright

flush began spreading over her face. "The weather is so dreadful that I wondered if you would be here, Benjamin," she said.

"Nothing on earth could have kept me away," he assured her. "Would you like to go into the house? There's very little difference between being in this summerhouse and being outside in the rain."

Beverly laughed and nodded, and they went down the path to the rear door of the house. Benjamin found the right key on the ring and opened the door, its hinges squeaking noisily. Inside was the central hallway, with a laundry room on one side and a large, old-fashioned kitchen on the other. Benjamin and Beverly left their oilskins hanging in the laundry room and went down the hall toward the front of the house.

It was frigidly cold and had the quiet of unoccupied houses, the wind outside emphasizing its stillness. Their footsteps and voices echoed through the hall as they peered into the rooms, in some of which were pieces of furniture under dust covers. After looking through the rooms on the first floor, they went up the wide staircase.

As they stepped into a room just off the landing, Beverly exclaimed in pleasure. It was a cozy, elegant sitting room, a private nook for reading or quiet contemplation. A marble fireplace was at one end of it, and two large windows looked out onto the back garden. Most of the furniture was still there, with a daybed against one wall, a couch near the fireplace, and chairs scattered about. Benjamin left Beverly taking the dust covers off the furniture and went back downstairs to look for firewood.

The large wood box in the laundry room was full of old, seasoned logs from years before. Benjamin carried an armful up to the sitting room and kindled a fire. The room quickly became comfortably warm, and he and Beverly put their coats aside. They sat on the couch near the fireplace and watched the rain stream down the windows as they talked.

Beverly told him about her family in England, who

had once owned a small factory where vellum and other high quality paper had been produced. She had worked in it herself, and she explained how the paper was made. Her voice became sad as she said that her brother had sold the factory when her father died. Then she shrugged off her mood, and they talked about other things, Benjamin glowing with happiness over being near her.

It had seemed to him that nothing could have improved upon the day before, but the sitting room had brought them closer physically as well as in their feelings. Benjamin was uncertain of what form their relationship would take, but there seemed to be little hope that it would develop as he wished. He had finally met his love in life, but she was already married.

Their mutural attraction was an overtone in the atmosphere between them that was as tangible as the wind outside, but their conversation remained that of friends. Benjamin's love for her was the most compelling force he had ever experienced, and she was bewitchingly beautiful. While he yearned to take her in his arms and make love to her, keeping her trust, regard, and companionship was far more important to him.

When it was time to leave and they went back downstairs, Benjamin told her that he would bring a bottle of wine the next day. "I would bring one," she said, "but the housekeeper has the keys to the cellar. And by my husband's orders, she takes her instructions only from him, never me." Her tone and attitude became bitter over being treated like a prisoner in her own home, but then she shrugged it off and changed the subject. "Surely your employer will begin wondering why you are gone so much."

"No, in seeing to matters concerning properties, I'm often out of the office. There is a certain amount of work I must do there, but what I can't get done during the morning, I can always attend to by working late during the evenings. So I'll be here every day if you will."

Her warm smile was her reply, and it made her so beautiful that his love was a poignant ache within him.

They stepped into the laundry room and put on their oilskins, then went outside and down the path together. They exchanged a word of farewell at the gate in the wall at the rear of the garden, and Benjamin walked back up the path to the house.

Before he left, he spent an hour looking through the house and examining it as he pondered a forthcoming problem. He could delay the resale for a time if Morton bought the house, but eventually he and Beverly would lose their rendezvous place. If someone else bought it, the same thing would happen immediately. A way of postponing the problem for several months occurred to him, but he disliked it, because it involved deceiving Morton.

The next day, Benjamin explained it to Beverly while they were sitting in front of the fireplace in the small, upstairs room. Although she was acutely distressed over the possibility of their losing their meeting place, she readily understood why misleading Morton would make Benjamin's conscience trouble him. They discussed the situation and tried to think of alternative places where they could meet, but there was none.

Then, when they were preparing to leave, Benjamin helped Beverly with her coat. As he breathed the alluring scent of her perfume, he was unable to resist kissing a wisp of hair that had slipped loose from the gleaming brown tresses pinned up on her head. She turned, lifting her lips to his. They tasted of the wine he had brought, but were sweeter than the most costly vintage and more intoxicating that the most powerful rum.

Beverly ended the embrace, touching his face with the tips of her fingers and then moving away. As they went downstairs, Benjamin decided what he had to do. While he disliked deceiving Morton, it was infinitely more acceptable than ending the rapturous joy that had entered his life.

The following morning, he went upstairs to Morton's office and talked with him about the house, explaining that some repairs would be needed. "That will include replacing some of the slate on the roof," he continued, "and other things that can't be done until the weather improves. It would be an excellent investment, but for leasing rather than for resale."

"Why only for leasing?" Morton asked.

"As I mentioned, it's an old Georgian, and the nearby houses are all Victorians. People with funds to buy a house in that price range want a modern, fashionable house. Those who lease are less particular."

"That's true," Morton agreed. "What about cost and profits?"

"I believe twelve hundred would be a fair offer. Two hundred should see to the repairs, particularly if some are put off until spring, when they'll be cheaper and easier to do. It should lease for about three hundred per annum, so it would pay out the investment fairly quickly."

Morton made notes on a piece of paper, giving no hint of how he felt about buying the house, then the discussion turned to other properties. When he left the office, Benjamin had no idea if Morton would make an offer on the house. During previous years, when funds had been flowing in from the gold mine on the Murray River, decisions on such matters had usually been made instantly. Now they were studied carefully.

Benjamin told Beverly about the conversation that afternoon, explaining that the issue was unresolved. She was just as anxious as he, and even less patient. When nothing had changed by the next day, she suggested that Benjamin ask Morton about it. However, Benjamin knew that would be a serious mistake, because the keen mind behind Morton's pale blue eyes would immediately suspect that something else was involved.

The following day, the matter was resolved in a way that again reflected Morton's more limited financial resources. Instead of buying the house outright, as he would have done in the past, Morton took over the mortgage and paid the owner the balance. But the financial arrangements were irrelevant to Benjamin, and to Beverly. When he told her about it that afternoon, she threw herself into his arms in her ecstatic happiness.

With the problem resolved for the present, Benjamin settled into a daily routine of attending to his work before and after meeting Beverly. They became closer and more affectionate, always greeting each other and parting with kisses. During their conversations, however, one subject remained closed: Beverly avoided any mention of why she had married Creevey.

On the day she finally talked about it, Benjamin knew that something was wrong as soon as he saw her. He was waiting for her in the summerhouse, and when she came down the path, she had been crying. As he rushed to her, she ran on down the path and threw herself into his arms.

Almost bursting into tears again, she told Benjamin that her husband had burned a letter from her brother before she had read it. "I learned that he'd kept it three days after reading it," she went on. "When I asked him to give me my letters more promptly, he threw it into the fire."

"After reading it?" Benjamin echoed angrily. "Why should he read your letters at all? And why would he even want to?"

"To prove that he can," she replied. "That's the way he is, Benjamin. His great joy in life is to dominate people. His great hunger is for power over people. I look forward so much to letters from my brother, and it'll probably be months before another arrives."

Benjamin ground his teeth in rage, so furiously angry that he could have gleefully killed Creevey. Then he kissed Beverly and turned toward the house with her. "Come, let's get in out of the rain and have a glass of wine."

They went on down the path and into the house, leaving their oilskins in the laundry room, then climbing the stairs to the sitting room. Benjamin had already kindled a fire, and he poured glasses of wine after they had put their coats aside. With the rain pattering against the window, Beverly sipped her wine as she explained how she had come to be married to Creevey.

The first time she had seen him had been at an industrial exhibit, where her family had put samples of their paper products on display. After staring at her fixedly for a time, he had approached her and told her that she would marry him. Then he had threatened to immediately destroy her family and their business if she told anyone what he had said, and to do the same thing over a longer period of time if she refused to marry him.

The incident had been so extraordinary that she had wanted to dismiss Creevey as an eccentric. But he had been too menacing for that, and she had heard talk at the exhibit about him, people saying that it was unwise to make an enemy of him. During the succeeding days, it had been on the tip of her tongue several times to tell her father or mother, then later she had been thankful that she had kept silent about it.

Mysterious fires and accidents had occurred at the paper factory. Profits had plummeted when customers had received shipments of paper ruined by water and other means. The factory employees had been persecuted by unknown vandals, rocks hurled through their windows in the night and their children threatened by scruffy, evil-looking strangers.

Then, when her engagement had been announced, her family had strongly disapproved of Creevey, but the trouble had stopped. "Worst, of all," she continued, "my father died not long after the wedding. I was grief-stricken, because I loved him with all my heart. But in addition, what he and my mother had spent their lives building was lost when my brother sold the factory. I can't fault my brother, because his interest was never in the factory. But my father trained me in every aspect of the trade, and if I had been there, we could have kept the factory."

"I'm amazed at what you endured all by yourself," Benjamin said in wonder. "Keeping silent and submitting to that man's demand to marry him was an ordeal that few could endure. You have immense strength of character."

"No, I was sustained by my great love for my family and the need to protect them," she replied. "And there was no option, because my husband is very cunning. He uses hirelings with whom he has no direct contact to work his evil, and he can't be brought to justice for his crimes."

"He may come athwart the Kerricks here," Benjamin remarked. "If he does, he'll get his just deserts sooner or later, because that family always sees that right wins out. That aside, your ordeal continues, doesn't it? And now those remaining of your family are far away."

Her pensive mood faded, a radiant smile wreathing her features. "But now I have you to sustain me, Benjamin," she said softly.

He smiled, taking her into his arms as she moved closer on the couch. Her large blue eyes had an intensity in them that he had never seen before as she gazed into his eyes and lifted her lips. The kiss and embrace were also different. Her mouth opened under his, her lips and tongue caressing his as she pressed herself against him in closer contact.

His desire swelling, Benjamin clasped her to him and kissed her passionately. As their kisses and embrace became more ardent, he fumbled for the buttons on her bodice. Her hand guided his, unfastening her clothes. He caressed the silky, yielding warmth of her breasts, then lifted her in his arms and carried her to the daybed at the side of the room.

A moment later, their clothes were scattered on the floor, and Beverly's thick, fragrant hair pillowed their heads on the daybed. In the soft light through the rain-streaked windows, she was a vision of beauty, her nipples and the shadow of darkness at her thighs contrasting with the milky sheen of her slender body. Lifting himself over her, he controlled his raging desire so as to be gentle. She clasped his face between her hands and gazed into his eyes as she opened her thighs and poised herself to meet him.

As they joined, he met with a close resistance. Beverly tensed, her smooth legs over his, and took him with a supple movement as her lips parted in a sigh. Then she smiled at the surprise in his eyes. "My husband's lusts are of an entirely different nature," she whispered in explanation. "He is content to dominate me and own me for display. My joy knows no bounds that you are the first, because you are my first love."

Somehow the moment also took on a more special significance for Benjamin, even though it was already the most vivid instant of his life. As he moved and she arched up to meet him, gazing into his eyes, it was more than lovemaking. Passion fueled by pure, adoring love brought them ecstasy that created a world of their own, and the rest of creation was left at a far remove.

In their private universe of rapture, the union between them took on a life of its own, his faster rhythm answered by the swifter pivoting rise of her hips. Ascending plateaus passed in surges of bliss, and they grasped for a final peak. Then they reached it and passed over it in a gushing tide of ecstasy, her cry of pleasure smothered against his lips.

When the surrounding world returned to Benjamin, the only sounds in the room were the patter of rain against the window, the crackling of wood in the fireplace, and the soft breathing of his love as she slept in his arms. The cold, harsh reality of their circumstances was brought back to Benjamin as he thought about what could happen if her husband found out.

Benjamin knew he had stolen the choicest jewel among Creevey's possessions, an ultimate cause of wrath from a man who was immensely powerful and utterly without remorse. Fearing only for his loved one, he resolved to be very cautious. He hoped that would be enough.

Chapter Thirteen

One of the woolies was a large ram that kept charging at the dogs, and Jeremy turned his horse toward it. He uncoiled his stock whip in a back stroke and snapped it forward, cracking it over the ram's head. The ram bleated in fright and ran back to the other sheep, a dog nipping its heels in revenge for having had to dodge its heavy horns.

Only sixty odd sheep were in the flock, but the dogs had to work hard because the terrain was difficult to drive sheep across. It was the rugged, austere landscape west of the Darling River and far south of Broken Hill that he remembered from years before. However, several years of low rainfall had made it even more arid since then. Winter rains had been falling during the past months, but the foliage was still sparse.

The drought was the reason that the work Jeremy had found was temporary, because the owner was abandoning the station. He intended to sell his flocks in Menindee, then join his brother on a cattle station in Queensland, a new state that had been formed a few years before from the northern reaches of New South Wales. The owner was giving up in disgust, but Jeremy had seen that what had happened was the man's own fault. Instead of conforming to the land, he had tried to bend it to his will, and it had defeated him.

The sheep ambled between two jagged, rocky hills, going up a ravine that opened out into a wide valley. At its center was a grove of river gums around one of the few remaining billabongs on the station after the years of drought. Some two thousand sheep grazed at the far end of the valley, dogs scattered around them, and a stockman sat on his horse near the flock.

The stockman turned his horse and rode up the valley to meet Jeremy. A short, portly man in his sixties, he had a grey beard and mustache and a red, bulbous nose. His exceptionally large, protruding eyes had given him the only first name by which he had ever been known.

Buggie Dobkin whooped in delight as he reined up, casting a glance over the sheep in swift, expert appraisal. "Sixty-two more!" he crowed. "Jeremy, you can find woolies under rocks and hanging in trees!"

"These are the last ones that I'll find in this paddock," Jeremy said, laughing. "I've searched everywhere sheep might be."

"You've searched where no one else thought to look," Buggie replied. "I've heard that there were a few woolies scattered about in this paddock, but you've found scores of them."

The stockman continued talking with Jeremy as they followed the sheep. During the two weeks they had worked together, he had shown Jeremy how to control the dogs and a flock. Despite their differences in age and experience, however, Jeremy was the natural leader between them. From the beginning, the older man had looked to him for every decision.

"It would be nigh onto sunset if it wasn't so cloudy," Buggie commented. "Do you want me to go build up the fire and start some tucker cooking?"

"Yes, if you wish. I'll bring the flock to the fold."

Buggie turned away, riding toward their camp near the billabong, and Jeremy drove the sheep on down the valley. A few brief instructions from the stockman had been sufficient for Jeremy to learn how to herd sheep, and he had needed no advice at all about riding and controlling a horse. After his years of being at one with the land in the far outback, he had an affinity with animals, and he keenly enjoyed working with them. Wherever his walkabout ended, he had decided that he would have his own station there.

The woolies reached the flock and blended into it. Jeremy rode around the flock, whistling to his dogs and those that Buggie had left posted to watch over the sheep. He motioned the dogs into position at the sides of the flock, then cracked his stock whip. The sheep began moving toward the billabong, the dogs trotting at the flanks of the flock.

After the sheep drank, Jeremy drove them into the fold made of rope and poles. By the time he finished hobbling his horse and released it with Buggie's and the spare horses to graze, cold winter twilight was falling. He carried his saddle toward the fire, its glow bright and inviting in the gloom. The dogs had gathered around it in anticipation of their meal, part of the mutton roasting over the fire.

Buggie was stirring pans of rice and peas, a pan of damper was browning, and the billys boiled on the hot coals. "I put the rest of the mutton from that carcass on the spit," he said. "There's no reason to save any, because you said we're leaving for the home paddock tomorrow, didn't you?"

"Yes, that's what we agreed on," Jeremy replied, sitting down. "We have them all mobbed together now, so there's no point in delaying."

Buggie nodded and continued talking in his usual jolly, voluble way, his large eyes shining in the firelight. Jeremy liked the old man because he had a disarming warmth and candor. He was always cheerful, in contrast to other stockmen on the station. Knowing they would shortly lose their jobs, some had become surly. The one who had been attending the flock that was in the fold had simply deserted the sheep and left, and Jeremy and Buggie had been sent to gather the sheep and bring them to the home paddock.

"Frank Biven will be over the moon when he sees all those woolies," Buggie remarked happily, referring to the station owner. "You know, he'll need some help getting his wagons and horses to Queensland. As good as you've done here, he might want to keep you hired to go there with him. I certainly wouldn't mind going there with him."

"You could always go there by yourself," Jeremy pointed out.

Buggie shook his head; he was reluctant to strike out on his own. Then he had another thought and looked at Jeremy hopefully. "I'd be glad to go with you, Jeremy. Are you thinking about going to Queensland?"

"I've given it some thought. You say you've been there?"

Buggie nodded, cutting up part of the mutton and feeding the dogs as he talked about a sheep station where he had worked years before. It had been in the Darling Downs, the vast, fertile region watered by the streams that formed the headwaters of the Darling River. "When steamboats began coming up the river to Bourke," he continued, "that changed everything. Most of the stations began raising cattle to drive to the market in Bourke."

"That's a long distance to drive cattle, isn't it?"

"Aye, it is. Brisbane is much closer, of course, but it's on the other side of the Great Divide. There's not even a footpath across there, much less a track where cattle could be driven."

"Are cattle stations still being established there?"

Buggie shook his head, taking the pans off the hot coals. "No, all of the good land has been taken up," he replied, filling their plates. "The Darling Downs is big, but there's only so much of it, and people have been settling there for many years. The land west of it is even worse than here, too dry to be useful to anything except 'roos and dingoes."

Jeremy nodded and, taking his plate, he began eating hungrily. During his journey through the Flinders Range and on to the east, he had traveled at a rapid pace from before dawn until after dark each day. He had hunted and gathered only enough food to maintain his energy, and he was still regaining a few pounds he had lost during the long, hard trek.

As he and Buggie ate, they continued talking about the Darling Downs. Jeremy was interested in it, wondering if it was there that he would find a place where he would have a sense of belonging. In addition, a remark that Buggie made remained at the forefront of Jeremy's thoughts when they lay down in their blankets. The man had said that some cattle strayed while being driven to Bourke, and Jeremy knew they must have since multiplied, producing dunnocks that would now be running wild in the arid land west of the Darling Downs.

At dawn the next morning, Jeremy and Buggie breakfasted on leftovers, then took down the fold. After loading the rope from it and their other equipment on the spare horses, they began driving the sheep toward the home paddock to the south. Buggie was unsure of the precise location of the single billabong on the way to the home paddock, and he offered to ride ahead and find it, but Jeremy had seen it once and knew where it was. In the far outback, he had acquired an accurate sense of distance and direction, and he could unerringly find his way back to any place where he had been.

Near midday, the sheep flowed across a saddle between two hills, and the billabong was straight ahead. Buggie laughed and shook his head in wonder. "You're like a homing pigeon, Jeremy!" he exclaimed. "People who've worked on this station for years can't find their way about on it like you can. You know, it's easy to see why Frank Biven is pulling up stakes. Even though it's been raining, there's still very little water here."

Jeremy nodded to acknowledge the remarks, but he had seen that there was enough water about for anyone who knew how to find it. Some of the hills that flanked dry watercourses had outcroppings of igneous rock. That was a sign of granite bedrock and subterranean soaks in the watercourses.

After the sheep drank and grazed for a time, Jeremy and Buggie resumed driving the flock through the hills. They turned southeast, toward the track that led from the home paddock to the main track to the Darling River and Menindee. By mid-afternoon, they had turned onto the track, the long column of sheep streaming out down it.

A few hours later, the buildings and pens of the home paddock came into view ahead. Other sheep that had been brought in from the paddocks were grazing in a large, grassy mustering yard set back from the shearing shed and pens, and Buggie rode ahead to open the gate.

Frank Biven rode out from the buildings to watch as the flock entered the mustering yard. A lanky, bearded man, he had a reserved, hard-bitten manner from his years of struggling against the invincible outback. After closing the gate behind the flock, Buggie happily pointed out the number of woolies to Frank and boasted about how Jeremy had found them.

Not given to compliments, Frank merely grunted in reply, but he was impressed. Some two weeks before, he had been offhand during the brief conversation when he had hired Jeremy, but now he was more interested. "Are you any kin to the Kerricks who own Tibooburra Station?" he asked.

"Not any that I claim," Jeremy replied.

Frank waited for further comment, then dropped the subject when Jeremy said nothing more. "Well," he mused, "you seem to be a good man to have about. I'll keep you on wages to help get my wagons and horses to my brother's station, if you want to go. If I can't give you a job when we get there, I'll give you two good horses and a month's rations instead."

"I'll agree, if the same offer goes for my mate here," Jeremy told the man, turning a thumb toward Buggie. "And when we get there, we'll just take the horses and the rations. We won't need a job."

Frank stroked his beard and thought about it. Buggie glowed with delight and waiting anxiously for a reply. Then the station owner nodded. "It's a bargain," he said. "We'll start sorting out things to load into the wagons tomorrow, because I want to be gone from here within the week."

As Frank turned his horse and rode away, Buggie was overjoyed. His bulging eyes glowing with happiness, he stammered his heartfelt gratitude. Then, when he and Jaremy rode toward the horse pen to unsaddle their mounts, Buggie had another thought. "There might be trouble with some of the other stockmen," he remarked worriedly. "Some of them might get their wind up when they find out that we're keeping our jobs for now."

Jeremy shrugged indifferently. He regretted that a couple of the stockmen would be out of work, but as for the rest of them, he had been disgusted by their surly, pettish attitudes. As far as the possibility of trouble with them was concerned, he was also indifferent.

After unsaddling their horses, Jeremy and Buggie carried their swag to the barracks and went to the bathhouse to clean up. That was a perfunctory matter for Buggie, but Jeremy was meticulous about cleanliness. He disliked a beard, and had sharpened a knife to a keen edge to use as a razor. It was late afternoon by the time he finished cleaning up and shaving, and he and Buggie went to the cookhouse for dinner.

The other five stockmen were seated at the long table in the cookhouse, and the aged former stockman who was the cook worked over his pots and pains at the fireplace. The one who had complained most about losing his job was a brawny, slovenly man in his forties named Otis Cullen. Word had already spread about Jeremy's agreement with the station owner, and Cullen was grumbling loudly about it. His two mates beside him on the

NAME:_____

ADDRESS:_____

_____

_____

TELEPHONE:_____

E-MAIL:_____

_____ I want to pay by credit card.

__ Visa   __ MasterCard   __ Discover

Account Number:_____

Expiration date:_____

SIGNATURE:_____

Send this form, along with $2.00 shipping and handling for your FREE books, to:

Historical Romance Book Club
20 Academy Street
Norwalk, CT 06850-4032

Or fax (must include credit card information!) to: **610.995.9274.**
You can also sign up on the Web at www.dorchesterpub.com.

Offer open to residents of the U.S. and Canada only. Canadian residents, please call 1.800.481.9191 for pricing information.

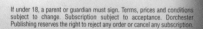

bench were emphatically agreeing with him, while the other two stockmen sat quietly on the opposite side of the table and waited for their meal.

Cullen's thick, coarse features were scarred and his nose misshapen from brawls. He scowled and looked straight at Jeremy as he continued, "It ain't bloody right. Somebody who showed up here a fortnight ago keeps his job, and some of us won't even get to stay long enough to load the wagons. There ain't nothing bloody right about that."

"Perhaps Frank is tired of listening to your grizzling, Cullen," Jeremy suggested. "After a time, hearing a grown man sniveling like a mewling boy will raise anyone's gorge."

The blunt retort dismayed Buggie, whose protruding eyes looked as though they were about to pop from his head as he turned to Jeremy in alarm. Cullen leaped up from the table, his battered face flushed with rage, and his two mates followed him as he stamped toward Jeremy. "By God, I'll teach you that nobody talks to me like that!" he bellowed furiously.

Jeremy waited until the man was halfway across the cookhouse, then moved with the sudden, swift determination that had at times provided the margin between survival and death in the far outback. His full strength was behind the fist that slammed into Cullen's paunch, doubling the man over. Cullen reeled back across the table and benches, and they toppled with a crash that shook the building as the other two stockmen scrambled out of the way.

Buggie gamely charged in to help with Cullen's mates, but was quickly knocked aside in the melee of flying fists. Jeremy dodged and parried blows, looking for openings. Finding them, he punched one man in the stomach and then the other in the face. Both men stopped flailing their fists, one bending over and the other wobbling on his feet.

Jeremy followed up the job to the man's face with a hard blow from his right fist that had his weight behind it. Blood exploding from his mouth and nose, the man staggered back and fell. Jeremy gripped the other man's hair, driving his knee into the man's face. The impact of the blow jerked the man's hair out of Jeremy's hands, and the man collapsed.

Cullen was untangling himself from a bench and starting to climb to his feet. Jeremy knocked him down again, then bent over and gripped the man's head, thumping it firmly against the floor. When the man's eyes became dazed, Jeremy hauled him up from the floor and heaved him toward the other two. Cullen spun across the cookhouse, his knees sagging under him, and sprawled across his two mates on the floor.

Bare seconds had passed since the fight began, and Buggie, the cook, and the other two stockmen gazed in astonishment at Jeremy and the three men on the floor. Jeremy lifted the table to its legs and was putting the benches back into place when Frank Biven charged into the cookhouse. "What's all the ruction in here about?" he demanded.

"What ruction?" Jeremy replied, sitting down on a bench.

As the cook, Buggie, and the other stockmen started to explain in a babble of voices, Frank motioned them into silence. He studied Jeremy musingly, then shrugged in sardonic amusement. "Well, Cullen never did have enough brains to know the difference between an ordinary horse and a brumby," he commented. He bent over the three men, beckoning the stockmen. "Give me a hand getting them to the barracks."

As the station owner and the stockmen dragged the three men out, the cook turned to Jeremy. "You say you're not kin to the Kerricks who own Tibooburra Station?" he asked, laughing. "You deal with trouble like they do."

"I'm not related to them in any way that makes a difference to me," Jeremy told him. "Don't let the tucker burn on the fire."

The cook turned back to the fireplace, he and Buggie

talking about the fight. Jeremy pondered the continuing questions concerning his kinship with the Kerrick family, which had come from Buggie as well as others during the past two weeks. His denial of close relationship with the family had been only to avoid any special notice or consideration from others, because whatever ill feelings he had ever harbored toward them had faded.

More important, he had consciously put his past behind and was looking forward to finding the place where he would have a sense of belonging. However, he occasionally thought of the Kerricks. His memories of his father were disagreeable, but those of Deirdre were pleasant. He thought of his grandmother most often, remembering her as a beautiful woman with a compelling personality who had always been very affectionate toward him.

Alexandra Kerrick writhed inwardly with crushing grief as she stood in the cemetery at Wayamba Station. Soft, cold rain pattered on her oilskins as darkness fell, and the somber twilight was even more dismal against the background of the corroboree that had drummed incessantly in the Aborigine village for the past three days and nights. The mournful dirge of the didgeridoos, the rhythm sticks tapping in cadence, and the chanting voices combined to sound like the wailing of lost souls.

Elizabeth Garrity was only an arm's length away, but in a sense, Alexandra was a vast distance away and all alone in her sorrow as she faced three fresh graves. A jackaroo was buried in one, and a stockman in another. The third was where Sheila Garrity had been buried an hour before. They had been encircled by the flames while trying to rescue sheep from a freak winter grass fire started by sparks from the stack of a riverboat on the Darling River. It had happened during one of the rare, isolated instances when Sheila and Elizabeth had been separated from each other.

Over the sound of the corroboree and the rain, a murmur of women's and children's voices came from the

house, and conversation among dozens of men carried
from the barracks and the shearing shed. People had traveled from other stations and from Menindee and Wilcannia to pay their respects to a deceased member of the
legendary Garrity family, the pioneers of the region. Little more than an hour before, the cemetery had been
crowded with people while the minister read the burial
service. Then they had abruptly left.

With the service over, there had been no reason to stay.
In addition, standing in the rain with night coming on
had been uncomfortable. Most of all, however, they had
left because of Elizabeth, and they had departed in an
atmosphere of keen embarrassment. All during the wake
and even while the minister had been reading the burial
service, Elizabeth had spoken aloud to Sheila as though
she were still alive, cursing her furiously for allowing
herself to be caught in a grass fire.

"You stupid bloody cow," Elizabeth snarled causti-
cally, speaking again after several minutes' silence.
"How many grass fires have you fought in your life, you
daft slut? And then you were that much of a pewling
ninny to let one encircle you. Were you such a bloody
lame get of a sick goat that you had to have me at your
bloody side every flaming minute?"

As the bitter tirade continued, Alexandra turned her
face up to the dark sky and let the rain mingle with her
tears. The people from other stations and the towns had
come prepared to help soothe heartbreak over the death
of a loved one. But they had been unprepared for this
raging grief of such savage intensity that it brought forth
strange behavior. The best they had been able to do when
the outbursts occurred during the wake and burial had
been to act as though they were hearing nothing.

Elizabeth's husband, Colin, had also left the cemetery,
taking their three sons. Like the other people, he had
never comprehended the complex nature of the attachment between his wife and his sister. However, Alexandra had long understood that they had been one, the two
of them a single entity as different and bizarre as other

creatures of the outback. They had been like Siamese twins with shared organs, each sustained by and nourishing the other. Now, although her eyes were dry, Elizabeth was suffering just as though her vitals had been ripped from her body.

After nightfall, Elizabeth was a disembodied voice in the thick darkness and rain, Alexandra remained, even though she was unsure if Elizabeth even knew she was there. Light shone through the gloom from the windows in the house and other buildings. A lantern moved toward the cemetery, and as it drew closer, Alexandra saw that Jonathan was bringing it to her.

Her son silently handed Alexandra the lantern, then went back into the night. As she continued waiting with Elizabeth, Alexandra wished that David had been able to come to Wayamba Station with her. He had wanted to, because he had known Sheila from when she was a girl, her hair still streaked with blond like that of a pure Aborigine child. During the past few weeks, however, he had been going through one of the increasingly frequent periods when any exertion gave him severe chest pains.

In her agony of sorrow, Alexandra lost track of the time. Her grief over the death of a beloved friend was multiplied by knowing that another friend just as dear was enduring sheer torture. Then, suddenly, Elizabeth turned to leave. Alexandra lifted the lantern to light the way. Elizabeth gave no indication of noticing Alexandra as they went toward the house.

It was congested with women and children, the parlor carpeted with sleeping pallets. The children and some women were asleep on them, and other women were talking quietly near the fireplace. Silence fell as the women gazed at Elizabeth, but she went through the parlor and down the hall toward her room. The women then looked to Alexandra as an alternate hostess, because Wayamba and Tibooburra Stations were closely related in everyone's mind. Alexandra stepped to the fireplace and sat on the wide hearth among the women.

The conversation dwelt on funerals, all the women reminiscing about and extolling the virtues of the deceased, yet it was less sincere than usual. None of the women had really known Sheila, who had been intensely close to very few and a total stranger to everyone else. Alexandra sensed that while the people had been disturbed by Elizabeth's behavior, they had far from regretted it. In years to come, during discussions around fireplaces and over campfires in lonely paddocks, their story of when they had attended Sheila Garrity's funeral would be more dramatic through descriptions of Elizabeth's profane, one-sided conversations with the burned body in the coffin.

With the corroboree continuing as a pulsating background of sound, Alexandra talked with the women for a time, then went to the bedroom she always used at the house. It was also full of pallets, and Alexandra lay on hers at one side of the room. She expected to merely rest and remain awake, but somehow she slept. An hour before dawn, she was awakened when the corroboree finally stopped. The others were starting to stir, and Alexandra went back outside into the rainy, early morning darkness.

A temporary cooking shed to feed the crowd was set up in the wide, bare expanse out in front of the house. Fires roared beside it, where the station cook was heating up the remainder of the whole beef and the pigs that had been roasted, along with large pans of beans, peas, and rice. The cook had also made a kettle of porridge for those who wanted it and gallons of tea.

Alexandra drank a pannikin of tea as the milling crowd talked sleepily and ate their breakfast. When the wet, dreary dawn came and the people began saddling horses and hitching teams to wagons, Elizabeth was still in the house. Alexandra took Jonathan and joined Colin to thank the visitors for coming to the funeral and to wish them farewell.

The vehicles and horses moved away on the tracks radiating out from the home paddock, hoofs and wheels splashing through the mud. When the last of them were gone, the grief-stricken Colin thanked Alexandra and Jon-

athan for their help, then went into the house to sit with
his sons. Jonathan left to saddle his and Alexandra's
horse, and she started toward the house to spend a few
minutes with Elizabeth before leaving.

Then she stopped as Elizabeth came out of the house,
wearing her stockman's clothes and hat and carrying her
stock whip and rifle. She stepped briskly across the verandah and paused on the steps, shouting to the head
stockman at the shearing shed: "Ross! Assemble five
stockmen and ten jackaroos! Have them saddle horses
and draw two weeks' rations from the storeroom, and
pass out rifles and ammunition to the stockmen!"

The head stockman touched his hat and hurried away
to do what she had said. Her boots splashing through
puddles, Elizabeth came across the yard toward Alexandra. The woman appeared normal except that her face
was deathly white under her tan, and her eyes revealed
excruciating pain. She also looked incomplete without
Sheila at her side.

"Alexandra, tell David that I hope he soon improves,"
Elizabeth said in a normal, conversational tone. "And
tell him to look after himself."

"Yes, I will."

Elizabeth nodded as she continued talking in the same
tone, which under the circumstances, seemed more jarring to Alexandra than anguished screams. "I certainly
don't wish to make problems for David as the magistrate,
but I must do something about those riverboats and the
danger of grass fires they pose. They've placed stacks of
wood for their boilers on this side of the river to pick up
whenever they need it. I'm going to throw all of it into
the river. Also, I intend to post stockmen along the river
to put rifle bullets through their stacks until they stay well
out into the river."

"You must do what you must do, Elizabeth."

"That's the way I perceive it. Also, I intend to open up
that track to the east for drays to bring our supplies and
haul the clip away. I should have done that years ago,
but at least I can do it now."

"You can't turn back the calendar, Elizabeth."

"No, but I can protect this station from the slime and muck that leaks into it from the outside," Elizabeth replied. "What has happened may be progress, but it's also the death knell for a way of life that is more than worth preserving. And from now on, progress stops at the boundaries of Wayamba Station." She started to leave, then turned back. "In time, I'll again be able to kiss you and tell you that I love you. Because I do love you with all my heart. But at the present, Alexandra, my heart is gone."

"I understand, Elizabeth. Truly, I understand."

Elizabeth walked away, her strides brisk and determined. Jonathan led the saddled horses across the yard to Alexandra. He helped her mount and stepped into his saddle, then they rode away from the home paddock.

As the horses moved up the track at a slow canter, Alexandra thought about Elizabeth's frame of mind. When word had first arrived at Tibooburra Station about Sheila's death, Alexandra had considered the possibility that the tragedy might crush Elizabeth's spirit, plunging her into such despair that she would lose interest in the station. Elizabeth's inner strengths had met that challenge, however, and the heritage that Patrick Garrity had established for succeeding generations would be preserved.

Alexandra wondered if as much could be said about the heritage that she and her husband had established. She spoke, broaching a subject that she had never before mentioned to her son. "Jonathan, do you think that you and Catherine will have more children?"

"No, she hasn't wanted to ever since she lost that baby years ago," he replied. "Nor have I wanted her to. Why do you ask, Mother?"

"I wonder who will take over the station after you."

"I haven't taken it over myself yet," he pointed out, shrugging dismissively. "That's many years away, Mother."

Alexandra hoped that his lack of concern was justified,

but the funeral had made her keenly aware of the uncertainties of life. The future stewardship of the station worried her, and in the back of her mind, a warning voice told her that her fears were well-founded.

Chapter Fourteen

"Before the meeting adjourns," Aldous Creevey said in his strangely thin voice, "there is another matter I'd like the directors to consider."

The man's puffy face revealed nothing, but Morton was immediately suspicious, expecting nothing favorable. Henry Newcomb nodded, politely attentive. "Yes, of course," he said. "What is it, Mr. Creevey?"

The man's huge body remained immobile, only his beady eyes moving in the folds of flesh around them as he addressed the directors as a whole. "I would like to recommend that the employment of the present manager of the bank be terminated." he said. "Further, I would like to recommend the hiring of a well-qualified individual of my acquaintance as manager."

Just as Morton started to angrily demand an explanation, one of the elected directors quickly spoke up. "This is very unusual, Mr. Creevey," Lester Utley said unctuously. "On what basis do you recommend terminating the employment of Mr. Newcomb as the bank manager?"

"For unethical conduct," Creevey replied, pointing a sausage-like finger at Morton. "He told one director about a house that was available for purchase from a bank customer who was in financial difficulties. No other director knew of it, and the way the situation was dealt with didn't serve the best interests of the customer. The man might have received more for his house if others had known about the situation."

Utley frowned somberly, turning to Henry. "This is a very serious charge, Mr. Newcomb," he said. "Would you like to say something in rebuttal or explanation before the matter is put to a vote?"

Years of experience in concealing his reactions during business discussions enabled Morton to mask his feelings, but he was totally bewildered. Henry Newcomb's response, however, was more than evident; his face paled and his hands trembled in distress as he gathered his papers and stood up from the table. "A vote won't be necessary," he said quietly. "I'll resign immediately as manager of the bank. Good day, gentlemen."

Even though events had moved rapidly, catching Morton off guard, he automatically assessed the situation. Utley had conspired with Creevey, as had as at least four other directors, because their gaze shifted away from Morton's as he glanced around the table. Creevey's beady eyes gleamed with gleeful triumph at the result of his carefully plotting to implement Henry's removal as bank manager. Morton burned with remorse, because he felt responsible for what had happened, but he had been powerless to protect Henry.

It was the first defeat that Morton had suffered for many years. Worse still, he had no idea of how it had been done, because he was at a complete loss to understand how Creevey had found out the details concerning the house. It had also been a costly defeat, for Morton knew that he had lost all of his influence over the decisions taken by the directors. Creevey had collaborators among them and would control the meetings in the future.

That was illustrated immediately after Henry left. Utley stepped out into the hall and brought in a man who had been waiting there, further evidence of how carefully Creevey had planned his moves. The man, named Nevin Moule, had eyes that were set close together, giving him a sly appearance. After only a few moments of discussion, a vote was taken on making Moule the manager. It went over fifty percent of the shares before it reached Morton, no one wanting to challenge Creevey, then the meeting ended.

Morton went downstairs to the manager's office, where Henry was cleaning out the desk to leave. The man was so distraught that he was almost in tears. "I can't tell you how sorry I am that this happened, Henry," Morton said despondently. "There's no way to undo it now, of course, but there are other possibilities for you. Come and see me tomorrow."

A proud man, Henry shook his head. "No, it isn't necessary for you to find me a job in your firm, Sir Morton. I'll find something."

"No, I wasn't referring to hiring you myself Henry, because I know you wouldn't accept that. I have contacts here and there, and perhaps I can help you find another position in banking. I'd at least like to try, so please do come and see me tomorrow."

Henry nodded and replied that he would, and Morton left. As he returned to his offices, Morton seethed with anger, as much at himself as at Creevey. Even though how Creevey had found out the details about the house was a disturbing puzzle, he knew that being caught off guard had been his own fault. If he had made it a point to see the other directors every few days, as he should have, he would have detected that something was wrong.

Although he made a concentrated effort to keep business problems from interfering with his unfailingly pleasant evenings at home, in this instance Morton was unsuccessful. When he went home, he kept thinking about what had happened, which made him absent-minded during conversation with Julia over dinner. Later, while they were sitting in the parlor and Morton was holding the baby on his lap, she asked what was troubling him.

After he explained, Julia loyally insisted that it had not been his fault. "How could you know what people are whispering about behind closed doors?" she pointed out. "I'm very sorry to hear about it, though. It's a dreadful situation for Henry and Amelia Newcomb."

"Indeed it is," Morton agreed, sighing remorsefully. "But I should have at least had forewarning, my dear. Plots almost create an odor that one can detect when talking to people. I shouldn't have been taken by such surprise in the meeting. As you may imagine, I felt like a helpless fool."

"Yes, I'm sure you did, dear Morton," Julia said sympathetically. "Well, what do you intend to do now?"

"First I must try to help Henry find another position," he mused, looking down at the baby on his lap. "Then I'll divest myself of shares in that bank. I'm a director at the Bank of Commerce, so I'll concentrate my financial interests there." He smiled at the baby, stroking its face gently with the tip of a finger, then shrugged. "And I'll start keeping a closer eye on all of my business affairs. In doing so, perhaps I'll even find a way to dispose of some of that New Zealand flax rope that I'm still accumulating."

"Are seamen still reluctant to buy that rope, then?" Julia asked.

"They absolutely refuse to buy it," Morton replied. "I have great quantities of the stuff that no one will buy."

"Well, a possibility occurred to me," Julia said. "Flax can be dyed, you know. Spring isn't too long away, and those who own yachts will soon be putting them in order for summer. They might like pretty red, blue, or green rope for their yachts. Also, when I visited Eudora at Sydenham Academy a few days ago, she mentioned that some of the girls there own sailing boats. They might like yellow or pink rope for their boats, mightn't they?"

Morton was at first astonished at the idea of brightly colored nautical rope, then he exploded into such hearty gales of laughter that the baby began crying. Julia stepped to the door and summoned the nurse, who came and took the baby out. Still amused, Morton sat on the couch with his beautiful, beloved wife, and as they began talking about other things, the problems with his business affairs seemed much more remote to him.

They returned in full force the next morning, when Morton went to his offices. He pondered what to do for Henry, but the only possibility that came to mind seemed a very paltry position compared to the one the man had lost. Henry arrived at mid-morning, deeply depressed and his eyes red from a sleepless night, and Morton hesitantly described the one potential opening for employment that had occurred to him.

Henry was enthusiastic about it, his mood quickly improving. "In Auckland?" he said. "That sounds very interesting, Sir Morton. My wife's family lives there, and she often comments about how much she misses them."

"She does?" Morton replied, pleased by the man's reaction. "Well, I can certainly understand how that would make it more attractive for you. But it's a small bank, and the remuneration would be less than you received before."

Henry smiled, shrugging. "As long as it's a reasonable amount, it would suffice. Living expenses are much less in Auckland than here. But how do you know that the position is open, Sir Morton?"

"About two months ago, I received a letter from Charles Vail, who was in business here for years. He and several others had chartered the bank and were searching for a capable manager. The interim manager was a retired banker who was attending to it as a favor for Charles."

"That sounds very promising, doesn't it?" Henry remarked cheerfully. "Shall I write to Mr. Vail and inquire about the position?"

"No, let me contact him. I can be more free with complimentary remarks about you, and I've known Charles for years. I'll write the letter immediately, and we should hear from him very soon."

Henry thanked Morton effusively and then left, eager to tell his wife about the possibility of moving to Auckland. Morton wrote the letter to Charles Vail, giving Henry a glowing recommendation, and took it downstairs to the main office. He gave the letter to the head clerk to post, then put on his coat and hat as he left to attend a meeting at the Sydney Maritime Assurance Company, in which he was a principal partner.

The meeting was routine, consisting of a review of transactions since the last time the partners had met. The company manager issued insurance policies on outbound ships, charging premiums that were based on the seaworthiness of the vessel and the insurance rates posted at the Merchants Exchange. Even though the weather had been severe, the company had experienced no losses, promising a substantial profit for the month.

After the meeting, Morton went to look in on other business ventures, but not the ropewalk he'd discussed with Julia. A year before, an acquaintance in Wellington had sent him a length of rope made from New Zealand flax, which was far stronger than the common hemp rope. Anticipating a ready market, he had ordered a large supply of raw flax from New Zealand and had bought a ropewalk that had been verging on bankruptcy.

However, he devoted less time and energy to business affairs than he had years before, and he had failed to fully investigate the market. Seamen were rigidly conservative about the stores they bought for their ships, and they insisted on having the hemp rope that had been used for centuries. The ropewalk employed nine men, all with families, and Morton had been reluctant to spend more and convert it back to hemp. He had kept it operating, even though the workers turned out the unsaleable rope at such a maddenly furious pace that it had been necessary to rent a warehouse to store the rope.

What he had thought would be an outlet for the rope had turned out to be barely less than a financial disaster. He had bought a dry dock and offered shipowners a lower cost for reconditioning ships if they would accept flax rope for the rigging. All had chosen the higher cost and hemp rope. The dock was in poor repair and only marginally profitable, but Morton had also kept it operating because it employed several men with families.

The monthly financial loss was manageable, but the series of miscalculations he had made was a constant irritant to Morton. Weeks had passed since he had last visited the ropewalk, because going there was only an occasion for self-reproach, and now he avoided it once again and went to his dry dock at the waterfront. When his carriage turned down the street leading to the waterfront at Walsh Bay, Morton saw that a barque was in the dock, even though it was to have been finished and refloated the previous week.

The dock foreman, a master shipwright named Virgil Handley, was constantly apprehensive that Morton would close the dock. As the carriage drew up under the long spars of the barque overhanging the side of the dock, Virgil ran to open the door. He grinned anxiously and spoke in greeting as Morton stepped out, holding his hat on in the gusts of icy wind off the bay.

"The dock flooded during a high tide last week," he told Morton, explaining the delay in finishing the barque. "We had to patch the leak and pump out the dock again. We'll finish this one in three days now."

Morton nodded wearily. Leaks in the eroded walls of the dock were a common cause for delays. "Why don't you take some vessels larger than this barque? There are full-rigged ships waiting at docks smaller than this one. Refitting them would bring in more revenue than small vessels, and we might even be able to get some of them to take flax rope."

Virgil hesitated, then reluctantly pointed down into

the dock. "It's those stocks, Sir Morton," he said apologetically. "They're a bit old and rickety, and I wouldn't want to put too much weight on them."

Morton peered down into the dock at the massive timbers that supported the hull of the vessel. "How much would it cost to replace them?"

"Less than a hundred guineas," Virgil replied eagerly, delighted that Morton had broached the subject. "If we could replace those stocks, we would be in excellent shape, ready to take any ship afloat."

Morton sincerely doubted that, and he knew that Virgil had deliberately underestimated the cost. Turning back to the carriage, he thought about his shares in the Bank of Securities and Trust, which should bring several hundred guineas. "I'll see if I can find the money," he said. "In the meantime, do try to get some of the shipowners to take flax rope."

Virgil nodded happily and replied that he would do his best. Morton also doubted that, because he strongly suspected that the foreman disliked the flax rope just as much as any seaman. He stepped into the carriage, telling the driver to take him to the Merchants Exchange.

The carriage moved through the streets, returning to the central business district. As it went down Bent Street, the Royal Botanic Gardens were at one side, with Farm Cove coming into view through openings between the trees. Several yacht clubs were located in the cove, and Morton glanced idly at the rafts of small vessels beside floating docks.

Morton looked more closely at the yachts, thinking about what Julia had said. It still seemed more amusing than practical, but he was approaching a point where he would try almost anything to dispose of the rope. Thumping on the floor of the carriage with his cane, he shouted for the driver to take him to the cove. The carriage turned onto Mrs. Macquaries Road, which led down the narrow point of land on the east side of the cove.

The carriage drew up at the fleet steps, and Morton studied the yachts at the docks. With slender, graceful lines,

they were decorated with extra brass fittings, and the
designs of the portholes and other features on many were
unusual. Morton thumped his cane on the floor of the carriage, shouting for the driver to take him to the ropewalk.

It was a long, narrow building on a street of ship chandlers and shipping offices near Circular Quay, the main
freight and passenger docks for the city. Short lengths of
cordage were attached to the sign over the door, dis-
playing the various diameters available for sale. They
were the pale grey of New Zealand flax, a sharp contrast
to the dark brown of hemp.

His visits were very rare, so work stopped as Morton
entered the tunnel-like building with its enormously long
work benches. The foreman was a grizzled, rawboned
man in his fifties named Isaac Tulk. As he stepped toward
Morton, touching a knobby hand to his forehead, the
other eight men followed him. "We're still selling some
hanks of grocer's twine now and again, Sir Morton,"
Isaac said cheerfully. "I take the money to the bank and
send a paper to Mr. Loman at your offices, just like he
said to do."

Morton nodded, knowing all about the sales, which
amounted to almost a guinea on a good month. He leaned
on his cane, searching for words. While he had been looking at the yachts, dyeing the rope had seemed almost
sensible. Now, with the nine men in wrinkled work
clothes staring at him and waiting for him to say something, it seemed utterly absurd. He plunged in. "You
know of the Beasley Dye Works on Hickson Road, don't
you?"

Isaac blinked, then slowly nodded. "Aye, I do, Sir Morton. I ought to, because it's been there since I was a boy."

"Very good. Go there and talk to the foreman, and find
out what sort of supplies and procedures they use. When
you've found out what you need to dye this rope, take a
list to Mr. Loman, and he'll authorize the expenditure.
If you have any trouble in finding out what you need to
know from the foreman, let me know and I'll speak to
the owner."

Nine pairs of eyes gazed suspiciously at Morton, the men automatically wary of any departure from the traditional practices of their craft. Then the foreman suddenly chuckled. "To dye this rope brown like hemp," he summed up, shaking his head. "It won't fool nobody, Sir Morton. Hemp has a strong, hearty feel, and this rope feels more like a lady's unmentionables, if you don't mind me saying so." All the men laughed, Isaac shaking his head again. "Dyeing this rope brown won't fool nobody into thinking it's hemp."

"No, not brown," Morton said.

The laughter choked off, the dark frowns returning as silence fell. "What color did you have in mind, then?" Isaac muttered warily.

Morton adjusted his hat and moved his cane on the floor, feeling ridiculous. "Well, red," he suggested uneasily. "Some blue as well. Green, and perhaps a bit of yellow." He cleared his throat uncomfortably and tugged at his collar with a finger. "And pink," he added weakly.

The frowns turned into glares of outrage, and the foreman trembled in a fury of indignation. "Pink?" he gasped in disbelief. "You want us to make pink cordage? *Pink*?"

His temper flaring, Morton drew himself up to his full height. "I want you to dye rigging cordage in the colors I have stated," he said crisply. "Further, I want a length of each color to be displayed on the sign outside. Now have I made it sufficiently clear as to what I want?"

"Aye, you have," Isaac growled, his rugged features like stone as he lifted a bony hand to his forehead. "You want us to dye rigging cordage in daft colors and hang some of it outside the factory where we earn bread for our families by the sweat of our brow. And even though it makes us the fools of the town, you're our employer and we'll do what you want."

Morton turned on his heel and stamped out, slamming the door behind him. As he stepped into the carriage, he told the driver to take him to the Merchants Exchange. Then he threw himself down on the seat in the carriage, fuming with anger over the flax rope. It had become the bane of his life, and he earnestly wished he had never heard of it.

His visit to the Merchants Exchange did nothing to improve his mood. He had anticipated that word of the developments of the day before at the bank would spread, and it had. A few with whom he had clashed over the years could barely conceal their glee, while others shared Morton's misgivings about Creevey's influence upon the business climate in the city.

In addition, his tentative inquiries about selling his shares in the bank failed to draw even a lukewarm response. He had expected little enthusiasm, as well as offers well below the nominal value of the shares, because any upheaval in the management of a bank made its shares unattractive. However, some businessmen evidently wanted no involvement with Creevey, and others seemed to fear that buying the shares from Morton might be interpreted by Creevey as their having aligned themselves against him.

Morton was unable to shake off his discontented mood until that evening, when he was sitting in the parlor with Julia and holding the baby on his lap. As he stroked its smooth face with the tip of a finger, the baby opened its mouth and bit his finger, and a sharp pain stabbed through it. "A tooth!" he cried exultantly. "David Alexander has a tooth!"

Julia smiled, telling Morton that the tooth had appeared two days before, and she had decided to let him discover it for himself. Morton gingerly lifted the baby's lip and admired the tiny bump on its gum, his aggravations of the day completely gone. His worries about Creevey and other problems were completely lost in his wonder over the fact that his son had a tooth.

Morton's problems diminished the next day, when his business affairs improved. While at the Merchants Exchange, he sold his shares in the Bank of Securities and Trust for only slightly under par. The buyer was a recent arrival in the city whom Morton barely knew, and he managed to disregard his suspicions that the man might be acting as Creevey's agent. Among the other transactions of the day, the head clerk authorized the purchase of dyes, chemicals, and large wooden casks for the ropewalk.

The weather also improved, a warm breeze from the north replacing the cold offshore wind. It continued into the following and subsequent days, bringing spring to Sydney. By week's end, parks in the city were turning into riots of color. Boronias and mallee banksias were starting to blossom in their range of bright colors, the tiny yellow flowers of geebung appeared, and the large, magnificent scarlet warathas were opening.

On the day he received a letter from Charles Vail in Auckland, Morton hastily opened and scanned it, then heaved a sigh of relief. He sent an apprentice for Henry, and the man arrived breathlessly a short time later. Henry was tearful with joy as he read the letter and thanked Morton effusively, then he left the tell his wife and begin preparations for his family's move to Auckland.

Work began on replacing the stocks in the dry dock, and other affairs followed a seasonal routine. Spring brought a surge in the number of people arriving at and departing from Sydney, with a consequent rise in real estate activity. It occurred to Morton that work on the house on Grace Street was taking a long time. However, the house had such unpleasant associations for him that he disliked even thinking about it, and he made no mention of it on the occasions when he talked with Benjamin Tavish.

Morton tried to concentrate more closely on his business affairs, but he found it very difficult. Spring was his favorite time of year, the days sunny but still pleasantly cool for him to take Julia on drives down the scenic coast road. This year was even more enjoyable, because they had their son to take with them, and Morton left work for a few hours on three or four days of each week to take Julia and the baby on a drive.

When Henry and his family left for New Zealand, Morton and Julia went to Circular Quay to see them off. After the ship moved out of the bay, Morton took Julia home and then went to his offices. As he entered the building and started to go upstairs, the head clerk told him that Isaac Tulk had asked to have an apprentice clerk assigned to the ropewalk.

"To take care of cash receipts and back orders," Albert Loman explained. "They've become quite complicated. I put a note on your desk yesterday afternoon about the increase in sales at the ropewalk."

"I haven't had time to go through everything on my desk," Morton said absently, weighing what the head clerk had told him, then: "Back orders?" he exclaimed in astonishment. "There are back orders for flax rope?"

"In some colors, yes," Albert replied happily. "The cash sales began about a fortnight ago, and they've grown to four guineas a day or more. That's certainly good news, isn't it, Sir Morton?"

"Indeed it is," Morton agreed emphatically, turning back to the door. "Let's have an apprentice there by tomorrow at the latest."

Albert nodded, replying that he would see to it. Morton rushed back out to his carriage and told the driver to take him to the ropewalk. Then he stepped into the carriage and sat down with a sigh of satisfaction, feeling as though a great burden had been lifted from him.

The most common vehicles on the street of ship chandlers and shipping offices were delivery carts and wagons, but five carriages were parked at the ropewalk when Morton arrived. Inside, he found a beehive of activity. At the far end of the building, the workmen were dyeing lengths of rope in casks and hanging them on racks to dry. Customers were looking at coils of brightly colored rope stacked at one side, while Isaac sorted through a pile of receipts and other papers on one of the tables. Morton was acquainted with all of the customers and exchanged greetings with them.

"Excellent idea, Sir Morton!" one of the men called

cheerily, the others nodding emphatically in agreement. "The best idea anyone has had for ages, in fact. This cordage is absolutely perfect for yacht rigging."

"I'm pleased that you like it," Morton told him, "but my wife is due credit for the idea. It was entirely hers."

"Then I'll certainly express my appreciation to Lady Julia," the man said. "I'll send around a bottle of wine with a note of thanks."

"Allow me to suggest a good Camden Park Chardonnay," Morton replied, slapping his stomach as though in anticipation. "She would enjoy a glass of that, and I'll be glad to dispose of the rest of it for her."

The men laughed, Morton laughing with them as he stepped toward Isaac. The foreman was frustrated over working at an unfamiliar task as he sorted through the papers with his large, bony hands. "An apprentice will be here tomorrow to attend to that for you, Isaac," Morton said.

The foreman smiled wryly and nodded. "I'll be grateful for that, sir Morton. You know, now that me and the men have got into this dyeing of cordage, it's not half bad. And speaking of being grateful, that's how we all feel for you keeping us hired when this place was only a drain on your funds. There's not another employer in the city who would do that."

"Well, that's ended now, hasn't it?" Morton observed. "And when we're fully organized on this, I'll see about raising the wages here."

"That's very good of you, considering this place was only an expense on you for so long. But we'll be glad of it, and we'll earn it."

Some of the customers had made their choices from the stacked coils of rope, and as the foreman stepped toward them, Morton exchanged a word of farewell with them and left. On his way back to Kings Cross, he thumped his cane on the floor of the carriage for it to stop at a goldsmith's shop. When he went in and the merchant put out a selection of wares, a brooch set with diamonds immediately caught Morton's eye. It cost over forty guineas, more than he could afford for a present, but he bought it.

That evening, Julia was delighted with the brooch. However, as Morton had known she would be, she was even more pleased that her idea had turned the ropewalk into the source of a monthly profit. She was also just as happy as Morton that Henry and his family were en route to a new home and a new beginning, and all of Morton's other problems seemed very distant.

He was strongly reminded of them, however, while he was at the Merchants Exchange the next day. As he studied the board on which revised insurance rates had just been posted, he heard a thick floorboard creak behind him, then Creevey's soft, falsetto voice. "We could cooperate, you know," the man said, speaking quietly to prevent others from hearing. "Perhaps I misjudged you, In any event, we're now at odds with each other, but we needn't be. There is ample here in Sydney for both of us, and together we could have all of it."

Morton glanced over his shoulder, then turned. The man looked like a wall of clothed flesh, his beady eyes peering out from folds of fat. "Indeed you have misjudged me," Morton told him. "You and I cannot cooperate on anything. I have principles that I follow, and you apparently have none."

The man's large, puffy face remained immobile, but his eyes glinted with anger over the rebuff. "Principles?" he sneered. "That's pretty speech to come from the son of an old lag."

"Yes, my father is an emancipist," Morton acknowledged. "He is also a man with very high principles. I love my father, and I also respect and admire him. Are you able to say as much about yours? And will your children be able to say the same about you?"

Creevey's piggish eyes revealed nothing but rage, and Morton realized that the terms he had used had been merely empty words to the man. The concepts had no meaning to Creevey. The huge, bloated man turned and lumbered ponderously away, leaving the Exchange.

Silence had fallen in the large room, and conversation began again as Morton turned back to the insurance rate board. It was a buzz of speculation, because no one had heard the conversation. Morton knew why the bloated man had kept his voice low, avoiding a public confrontation: Creevey preferred stealth, a knife in the back rather than open conflict.

Morton also knew that Creevey would create more trouble, and only its nature remained to be determined. That revelation came two days later, when he was summoned to a hastily convened meeting at the Bank of Commerce, where he was a principal shareholder and a director. The bank maintained depository accounts and provided other financial services, but its main activity was in business loans. That morning, the Bank of Securities and Trust had lowered its interest rates for those, as well as for all other types of loans.

The other directors wanted to do the same, but Morton was adamantly against it. He explained that if they did, it would take very few defaulted loans to put the bank below a margin of profit. Creevey had begun operating his bank at a loss, but it would be senseless for them to do the same. Some of the directors wanted to lower the rates temporarily, but Morton rejected that, telling them how it would be far more harmful than beneficial.

All during the conversation, no mention was made of why the other bank had lowered its rates, because everyone knew: Creevey had begun an attempt to control banking in Sydney, and he was willing to lose large amounts of money to achieve that end. If he could drive marginal banks into insolvency and weaken others so they would follow his lead, he would dominate the situation. Banking was the keystone in commercial activity, and through it, he could largely control the business community in Sydney.

When the meeting ended, Morton had convinced the others to do nothing at present, but he knew he had more persuading to do. A number of banks had been chartered since the gold rush began, many of them small ones whose directors lacked extensive experience. If they lowered their rates, that would exert even more pressure on other banks to do the same. After the meeting, Morton went to the Merchants Exchange and saw several men there who were directors at banks. He talked to them, recommending against lowering interest rates, then began calling on others at their businesses.

It took a few hours of each day over the next several days, in between other work and the time that Morton spent with his family. Through talking with the directors of virtually every bank in the city, he successfully formed a united opposition that would make it more difficult and expensive for Creevey to continue what he was attempting to do. However, all of the directors preferred to remain in the background, none wishing to join Morton and incur Creevey's wrath by openly drumming up support against him.

During the conversations, Morton learned that Creevey had also begun buying up mortgages from other banks, another tactic to gain control. It was another costly one, because Creevey was having to pay the premiums that banks charged when selling their mortgages. Morton still had a mortgage on the house on Grace Street, which was held by the Bank of Commerce. He paid it off to prevent Creevey from buying it, even though that took all of the remainder of the money he had received from selling his shares in the bank that Creevey had taken over, together with other funds.

In addition to making a deep inroad into his cash reserves, paying off the mortgage reminded Morton that for some reason, the house on Grace Street was still not ready to lease. He returned to Kings Cross, intending to immediately talk with Benjamin about it. However, as soon as Morton went through the entrance of his office building, Benjamin crossed the main office and asked if they could speak privately.

Benjamin was obviously very troubled, wanting advice. Morton took the man up to his office and seated him in the chair beside the desk, asking what was wrong.

"I've been seeing a lady," Benjamin muttered sadly. "I love her with all my heart, but she's married. And now she's with my child."

Morton sighed and shook his head, both sorrowful and angry at Benjamin. "Why couldn't you have learned from my mistakes?" he demanded. "Somewhere I may have a son who's now a man, but I don't even know if he's alive. Now you've fathered a child that you'll never be able to claim as your own." He sighed and shook his head again. "Well, who is she?"

"Mistress Beverly Creevey," Benjamin mumbled despondently.

Morton sat bolt upright, gaping in dismay. "Beverly Creevey?" he exclaimed. "Have you taken total leave of your senses? Of all the women in Sydney, you pick the only one who—" Morton broke off, getting up from his desk and stepping to the door. He closed it, then returned to the desk and leaned over Benjamin, glaring at him angrily. "As you well know, I'm hard put to scotch that man's conniving business schemes. How did you expect me to protect you from his revenge for trifling with his wife?"

"Protect me?" Benjamin stammered blankly.

"Of course, protect you!" Morton retorted, throwing himself down in his chair. "Did you think I'd let you face him alone? He'd swat you like a fly." Morton rubbed his temples with the tips of his fingers, controlling his temper. "How long has this been going on, Benjamin?"

"Several months, since last winter."

Morton frowned thoughtfully, surprised by the length of time. "Well, you've been sly about it," he mused. "If he hasn't twigged by now, he probably won't as long as you're careful. Mark my word, a time will come when you'll be tormented with remorse over not being able to claim—" He broke off as Benjamin shook his head. "What is it?"

Benjamin squirmed uncomfortably in his chair, searching for words. "Creevey never does..." He hesitated, then began again: "Creevey isn't and never has been a proper husband, if you take my meaning, Sir Morton."

"Yes, I do," Morton replied grimly. "And it puts us in a pretty pickle, doesn't it? Well, we'll have to think of some remedy...."

His voice faded as the only possible solution came immediately to mind. Then, in order to conceal the tears that suddenly filled his eyes, Morton stood up and stepped to the window, as though looking out and thinking. He had failed to realize just how very fond he had become of Benjamin, and he intensely regretted what he had to do.

Morton blinked away the tears, then stepped back to his desk and sat down. "I'll have to send you away, Benjamin," he said. "I certainly don't want to, but there's simply no alternative."

"I can't leave without Beverly, Sir Morton," Benjamin replied quickly. "She means more than life to me, and I can't—"

"Of course not," Morton interrupted briskly. "She'll go with you, but this must be done in such a way that Creevey will never find out what happened to her. Now, do you know anyone in Auckland?"

"Only Mr. Newcomb, Sir Morton. No one else."

"Good, then that's where you'll go. Certainly no one there will know her, because very few here know her. You'll go there as a married couple, under assumed names. John and Mary Hawthorne will suffice for names. I'll write to Henry Newcomb and ask him to help you get settled and find work. Has anyone in the office remarked on how downcast you've been?"

His mood the opposite of before, Benjamin smiled and nodded. "Mr. Loman and several others have asked me what was wrong. I told them that I was a bit unwell, but they seemed doubtful that was the reason."

"Excellent. When you go back downstairs, tell them that you received a letter from Roger Haynes in Bombay. When he was here, he often remarked to me what a promising young man you were. You're to say that Roger has offered you a partnership, but you were distraught because you were reluctant to leave here. Now that you've discussed it with me, it's all sorted out in your mind, and you're going to Bombay."

"That's wonderful, Sir Morton!" Benjamin exclaimed happily. "When I leave, everyone will think I've gone there. Beverly will simply disappear, which will have no connection with my departure, as far as anyone will know. But how can we leave together without being seen?"

"I noticed old Captain Jude Barnes on the street yesterday," Morton mused, "and he constantly sails between here and New Zealand. I'd trust him with my life, because he's absolutely discreet, and he was sailing the waters in this region before I was born. When you've related your story to everyone downstairs, go to the seamen's hostel and see if you can find him. Make arrangements for me to meet him in some quiet place tomorrow."

Benjamin nodded happily, his face flushed with joy and gratitude as he and Morton stood up. Both of them were at a loss for words to express their feelings, and they spontaneously hugged each other affectionately. Then Benjamin left and Morton sat back down at his desk, reaching for pen and paper to write the letter to Henry Newcomb.

Morton dipped the pen into the inkwell, sorrowful over having to send Benjamin away, perhaps to never see him again. However, the question that he had intended to discuss with Benjamin was fully answered, because it was now obvious why the house on Grace Street was still not ready to lease. Smiling in amusement over that, Morton began writing the letter.

Choosing words carefully, he described "John Hawthorne" in such a way that Henry would know it was Benjamin, and his identity had to be kept secret. When the letter was finished and Morton took it downstairs to have it posted, the main office was abuzz with talk of Benjamin's good fortune at being offered a partnership in Bombay. Benjamin was gone, and when he returned later in the day, he came up to Morton's office. Benjamin had found and talked with Captain Barnes, and Morton's meeting with the seaman was set for the next day in a small tavern near the seamen's hostel.

The following day, Morton went to the tavern. At the early hour, it was deserted except for the aged seaman at a corner table. In his seventies, Captain Jude Barnes was a large man with a flowing white beard and features that were textured like aged leather. The man reminded Morton of his father in being a powerful, authoritative figure despite his advanced age.

Morton paid for two brandies at the bar and carried them to the table, and his business with the captain was finished before the drinks. Captain Jude's ship was loading cargo, which would take three more days, and he intended to leave for New Zealand on the early tide the following day. Discreet to a fault, he had no curiosity about the two passengers or the unusual request on how to take them aboard. Morton paid the cabin fee, shook hands with the captain, then left.

On his way back to Kings Cross, Morton stopped at the Merchants Exchange. News about Benjamin's supposed partnership had spread, and several men commented to Morton about it. Looking at the board that listed ship departures, he saw that on the morning that Captain Jude was leaving, a ship was setting sail for Trincomalee, in Ceylon. When he returned to his offices, Morton told Benjamin to tell everyone that he was going on that ship, intending to take passage onward to Bombay from Trincomalee.

Other arrangements proceeded just as smoothly as those with Captain Jude. Benjamin closed out his bank account and gave notice at his lodgings, and packed his belongings. He made plans with Beverly, and told Morton that her only problem would be in concealing her exultant joy until it was time to leave. On the last afternoon, Morton sent out for wine so the staff could drink toasts and wish Benjamin good fortune in his new life.

The next morning, Morton rose hours before dawn, moving about quietly to avoid waking Julia. After shaving and dressing, he went to the stables and harnessed a horse to a buggy. Thick fog blanketed the city, combining with the darkness to make the coach lamps virtually useless. Morton almost became lost several times as he drove slowly through the streets, but he finally found his way to the house on Grace street.

As he reined up at the carriage gate, Benjamin and Beverly emerged from the foggy darkness. Benjamin stacked their baggage behind the seat as Beverly thanked Morton so effusively in a joyful whisper that he was embarrassed. Then, with the three of them crowded onto the seat, Morton drove the buggy toward the Royal Botanic Gardens. When he turned onto Mrs. Macquaries Road, the fog was so thick that Benjamin had to get out and lead the horse. Presently, a gleam of light came into view and gradually brightened into a lantern that a sailor was holding at the top of the fleet steps.

When the buggy drew up at the steps, a second sailor joined the first to help him carry the baggage down to the boat. Morton made his farewells with Benjamin, the two of them hugging, and then he turned to Beverly. She threw her arms around him and kissed him. "Benjamin and I will never be able to repay your great kindness, Sir Morton," she said. "But you will always be in our hearts, our thoughts, and our prayers."

Morton kissed her, then Benjamin took her arm as a sailor returned with the lantern to guide them down the steps. They and the light disappeared into the murky darkness. A moment later, oars splashed and squeaked faintly in their locks. When the sound faded under the swishing of waves against the jetty, Morton stepped into the buggy and drove away.

Dawn came with a breeze that scattered the fog as Morton returned home. When he reached his house, he found that his efforts to avoid waking Julia had been futile. She was up and about, and had woken the cook early. Over a hearty breakfast of eggs, gammon, and toasted rounds of bread, they discussed what Morton had done that morning.

Morton had told Julia about the situation on the same day that he had first learned about it himself. She had been intensely happy that Beverly was escaping the bondage of her marriage, but Julia had advised Morton to be cautious. Morton was certain he had done that, arranging matters in such a way that Creevey could never find out what had happened. "Everything worked out just as I planned," Morton said in said in satisfaction. "I'm sure that Creevey will never know what happened to his wife."

"No, you can't be sure, dear Morton," Julia told him. "Until you find out how he learned the details concerning the house on Grace Street, you can't be absolutely sure of keeping anything secret from him."

"But in this instance, the only ones who know what happened are Benjamin, Beverly, and myself. And you, of course. Everyone else believes that Benjamin left for Bombay. To anyone aside from we four, Beverly has simply disappeared, with no connection to Benjamin's departure."

"We are the only ones who know *everything* about what happened," Julia corrected him. "Isolated facts are scattered among others. For example, the sailors on Captain Jude's ship are aware that a man and woman boarded this morning in a most unusual fashion. But it's certainly true that far less is known at large about this than was the case with the house." She smiled and shrugged, dismissing the point. "Benjamin and Beverly should be very happy in New Zealand. I've heard that it's a very pleasant place."

Morton agreed and began talking with Julia about New Zealand. At the back of his thoughts, he felt slightly uneasy and wished that she were more positive about Creevey's never finding out what had happened. In numerous instances, Morton had found that Julia's keen mind intuitively identified possibilities in situations that he overlooked himself.

Chapter Fifteen

"You were right, Jeremy!" Buggie called happily from the bottom of the hole under the stone ledge. "There's water down here!"

Jeremy dropped his makeshift sledgehammer and stepped over to the hole at the side of a dry watercourse and under a ledge of igneous rock that had revealed the presence of granite bedrock several feet under the earth. The hole was over six feet deep, and water was puddling in the wet, sandy soil around Buggies boots. "You should hit bedrock within another foot or so," Jeremy told him. "Then we'll have a good soak there."

Buggie nodded and continued working, loosening the dirt with a sharp stick and piling it on a slab of bark to heave it out of the hole. Jeremy returned to the large, flat rock where he had been working and picked up his hammer, which was a large chunk of igneous rock tied in the split end of a thick stick. The flat rock was softer conglomerate stone, and Jeremy resumed slamming the hammer down on it, chipping away pieces in the center and making a large depression to hold water.

The warm, late spring sunshine of November beamed down on the wide channel cut by floodwaters as Jeremy pounded the rock with his hammer. Two saddle horses and two pack horses were tethered on the other side of the watercourse to graze on mallee that had sprouted there since the last heavy rain. But the horses only nibbled at the foliage, because they were very thirsty, having had no water since the previous day.

A short time later, Buggie shouted again, calling out that he had struck bedrock. Jeremy surveyed the depression in the stone, satisfied with it, and tossed his hammer aside as he stepped to the hole again. It was some seven feet deep, and Buggie was standing in several inches of water. Jeremy leaned down into the hole, grasping the man's hand, and pulled him out.

Buggie brushed dirt from his long hair and beard as he walked over to the flat rock. "Aye, now this will make a very good water trough for animals," he remarked. "But how will we get the water into it?"

"Fetch the extra canvas and rope, and I'll show you," Jeremy replied.

Buggie went toward the horses, and Jeremy picked up his hatchet and stepped to the cluster of saplings where he had cut down one to make a handle for his hammer. He chopped down two short, slender trees and trimmed them, then bent each into a circle and tied the ends with branches he had trimmed off. When Buggie brought the canvas and rope, Jeremy cut pieces of canvas and pushed them down into the hoops, then punched holes around the edges with his knife to lace the canvas to the wooden rings with rope.

With a rope tied to the wooden rim to lower the rings into the hole, and a rock in the bottom of the canvas to make it sink into the water, they were serviceable, makeshift buckets. Buggie smiled in wonder as he watched. "You certainly learned a lot amongst the Aborigines, Jeremy," he said. "You find water where there isn't any, and you can make all manner of things."

"Well, Aborigines don't have canvas," Jeremy replied, laughing. "But I learned to make do with what I have at hand, which eliminates the need for tons of equipment. The horses will break loose as soon as they smell the water, so bring them over and I'll start dipping up some."

Buggie stepped toward the horses again, and Jeremy took the buckets to the hole and tossed them into it. After they sank, he hauled them out on the ropes and carried them toward the flat rock, water dripping from them. Buggie was leading the horses across the watercourse, and the animals charged frantically toward the water, dragging the short, portly man.

Jeremy poured the water into the depression, and the horses jostled each other as they crowded around the small puddle to drink. Buggie took one of the buckets, and he and Jeremy carried more water to the horses. After they had made several trips back and forth, Buggie asked if the water from the hole could ever be exhausted.

"Not as far as I know," Jeremy told him. "But Aborigines always put the dirt back into the holes or covered the soaks to keep the water from evaporating. We'll cover it with brush and bark."

After the horses drank their fill, Buggie led them back to the mallee, which they grazed more eagerly than before. Jeremy climbed out of the watercourse to the mallee and mulga that grew beside it, and began chopping brush and tossing it down the steep bank. Buggie climbed up the bank and went to the scattered eucalypts, gathering slabs of bark they had shed.

By the time they finished collecting brush and bark, the dirt had settled in the water at the bottom of the hole. Jeremy dipped up a bucketful, and after he and Buggie quenched their thirst, he filled his leather-covered bottle and Buggie's metal water flask. The bottle was an old-fashioned container for water, and Buggie often commented about it.

"I used one of those years ago," the man remarked.

"You say that fellow Jarboe Charlie covered it with leather for you?"

"Yes, that's right. According to Aborigine beliefs, it may contain something of the spirit of the first one who owned it."

"Do you believe that too?"

Jeremy laughed and shook his head in reply as he and Buggie placed brush over the hole under the ledge. They covered the hole and mounded the bark on top of the brush, then went to the horses. Leading the pack horses, they rode up the steep bank and away from the watercourse.

The remote outback of Queensland stretched to the horizon in all directions, untouched by the least sign of civilization. The thick brush that blanketed the hills and valleys was broken by occasional patches of savannah, where open forest grew among tall, lush spinifex. The wildlife was unaccustomed to humans, and red kangaroos, blue racers, and emus paused to peer curiously before scurrying through the growth ahead of the horses. The sky teemed with lyrebirds, currawongs, mopokes, honey eaters, and large flocks of noisy, colorful parrots in a wide range of species.

The landscape was similar to the outback of New South Wales, and Jeremy loved it just as much. It was his natural environment, where he felt a part of his surroundings. However, he sensed no more personal affinity toward it than toward any other part of the outback. When he had first seen it, he had known that his heritage, the place where he belonged, lay elsewhere. He had decided to remain for a time, then continue his walkabout.

He reined up on the crest of a hill and scanned the terrain. A few miles to the north was a stand of river gums, indicating the possibility of water. He and Buggie rode down the hill, turning toward the trees. A mile from the hill, a dunnock ran out of dense brush ahead of them. Thin and fast compared to domestic cattle, it was a young, solitary bull that had been driven away from a small herd by another, dominant bull.

During the past few days, Jeremy and Buggie had seen several woolies and brumbies, along with scattered dunnocks. More important, they had seen tracks at waterholes that indicated fairly large numbers of the animals about. When another young bull that had been chased from a herd ran through the brush in front of them, Buggie smiled and nodded in satisfaction. "We're seeing more and more dunnocks, Jeremy," he remarked.

"Yes, and we haven't been actually looking for them. When we do, we should be able to find all we want."

"I know you'll be able to find them," Buggie said, laughing. "I've seen you find woolies. How many do you want to herd together?"

"About a hundred, with their calves. From what the men at Biven Station said, cattle bring ten or twelve shillings each in Bourke. Fifty or sixty guineas will be good pay for a few weeks' work."

Buggie agreed emphatically, smiling happily. A short time later, as they approached the river gums, the setting sun gleamed on a billabong in the trees. Jeremy saw that it was a small, shallow pond that would dry up during warmer weather, like almost all of the billabongs they had seen.

He and Buggie unsaddled and hobbled the horses to graze in the deep grass among the trees, then kindled a fire. Buggie began preparing dinner, and Jeremy walked around the billabong and studied the tracks in the damp soil, finding some made by dunnocks. At dusk, he returned to the fire, where Buggie was taking the pans off the hot coals and filling their plates.

As they began eating, Buggie commented about how fertile and well-watered the land was in the Darling Downs region. Jeremy shrugged; other things were far more important to him. "I've hardly ever seen more crowded land, except around cities," Jeremy said. "Some prefer that, but I want fewer people and more land about me, like we have here."

"Aye, you're a man of the outback, no doubt about that," Buggie remarked. "Well, those at Biven Station didn't have anything good to say about coming out here in the drylands to find dunnocks, did they?"

Jeremy laughed, nodding in agreement. All of the men, including the station owner, had considered it totally impractical. They had believed that the dunnocks would die of thirst before they could be herded out to the Downs. Moreover, the men had regarded the venture as perilous. They had viewed the remote outback as a strange, hazardous place, where it was very easy to become lost and die of thirst and starvation. They had also considered dunnock bulls to be just as dangerous as wild boars.

That last point troubled Buggie. "We haven't seen any bulls with herds," he said apprehensively, his bulging eyes shining in the firelight. "Those are the ones that will put us at risk."

"Then I'll shoot them if we can't deal with them in any other way," Jeremy told him. "I'm not worried about anything those men said, because they were too wrong about too many things."

"Well, they're not outback men like us, are they? And especially not like you. We won't have to worry about water, will we?"

"No, we can water dunnocks at the soak we dug today, and that will last them until we reach that big billabong south of here. From there, we can drive them to that small creek we found, then we'll be in the Darling Downs. Moving on to the north and west of here, we'll either find water or dig a soak everywhere we'll be stopping overnight with dunnocks."

"What'll we do for a holding pen to keep those we've found while we're searching for others? It'll take us weeks to build a big pen."

"When we need a pen, we'll devise something."

Buggie nodded, content to leave it at that, and the conversation moved on to other things. One statement that Jeremy had heard at Biven Station had intrigued him, and he continued to think about it. The station owner had said that cattle sold for thirty shillings or more in Brisbane, where except for a few raised locally, they had to be brought in by ship. A rugged stretch of the Great Divide lay between the Darling Downs and Brisbane, and everyone considered it impassible even on foot. However, Jeremy knew there had to be Aborigine trading trails through the mountains, some of which might be adequate for a small herd of cattle.

When the meal was finished, Jeremy and Buggie lay down beside the fire in their blankets. They were up again before dawn the next morning, making tea and heating leftovers for breakfast. At sunrise they saddled their horses and rode to the northwest, searching for another source of water.

After several hours, they found a billabong that would retain water through the summer. The next day, the search continued into late afternoon, and Jeremy began thinking about digging a soak Then, noticing animal trails that converged on a rocky hillside, he followed and found what he was looking for. At the foot of the hill was a spring, the rocky ground around it bare of foliage that would reveal the presence of water from a distance.

The following day, they had to dig a soak, then another on the day after that. As they continued riding northwest, the terrain became more arid and the billabongs even more infrequent. The dunnocks were more numerous, and Jeremy glimpsed small herds occasionally. He began looking for a way to eliminate the necessity of building a holding pen.

He discovered it early one afternoon, and found a billabong at the same time. After riding about since sunrise, he and Buggie had reached a narrow valley between two hills. At one side of the valley were trees and lush foliage that indicated water, and as they rode toward the hills, Jeremy noticed that the sides flanking the valley were too steep for dunnocks to climb.

Other features that made it perfect for his purposes became evident to Jeremy as he and Buggie drew closer and then rode into the valley. It was no more than two hundred feet wide at the near end, then it opened out into about twenty acres of tall spinifex and trees. At the far end, it was barely wide enough for the stream that flowed during rains and left the billabong filled when the surrounding valley became a dry creek bed.

The billabong was a large, deep one that would retain water during the summer, and across the valley from it was a stand of boxwoods, a good type of tree for making rail fences. After setting up camp beside the billabong, Jeremy and Buggie took out their hatchets, crossed the valley to the thicket, and began cutting down trees. During late afternoon, Jeremy saw a small herd of dunnocks coming toward the billabong, then the animals turned away, frightened by the chopping noises.

When sunset came, Jeremy and Buggie had felled and trimmed a score of the tall, slender trees. The next morning, Buggie continued chopping down the trees and cutting off the branches as Jeremy dragged them to the wider end of the valley to enclose it. While stacking the ends of the poles in a zigzag pattern, he recalled the night years before when Jarboe Charlie had shown him the best way of constructing a rail fence.

By sunset on the third day, both ends of the valley were enclosed by rail fences, with a makeshift gate in the shorter fence. The following morning, Jeremy and Buggie rode out of the valley at dawn. Jeremy knew that dunnocks began grazing early in the day and preferred spinifex over other foliage, From the crest of a hill, he saw a large expanse of savannah several miles away, and he and Buggie rode toward it.

A small herd grazing in the tall grass included ten cows, four stirks, and a half dozen calves. There was also a large, aggressive bull with wide, keen horns. It pawed the ground and bellowed threateningly as Jeremy and Buggie circled around the dunnocks and then rode slowly toward them, snapping their stock whips to drive the animals toward the valley.

"You'd best go ahead and shoot it, Jeremy," Buggie suggested nervously, his bulging eyes wide with apprehension.

"No, first I'll try to drive it away," Jeremy replied,

reluctant to kill any animal except out of necessity. "Perhaps it'll run off if I sting it with my whip. Move back so it won't charge at you."

More than eager to comply, Buggie reined his horse around and put fifty yards between himself and the bull, then watched anxiously. The rest of the herd raced away into the brush as the bull roared, shaking its long horns and ripping up clods as it pawed the earth with its powerful forelegs. Jeremy's horse was frightened, and he held the reins tight and nudged its sides with his heels as he moved toward the bull, snapping his whip.

The bull lowered its head and charged, and Jeremy's horse tried to bolt. He pulled hard on a rein to turn the horse in a circle, looking back and snapping his whip. The bull was too large and muscular to be as nimble as the horse. It skidded to a stop and charged again as Jeremy veered from side to side. He slashed the tip of the whip across the animal's shoulders, but it merely roared in rage and redoubled its efforts to catch the horse.

The horse became more difficult to control in its fright, its eyes glaring in terror as it fought the reins. Jeremy finally gave up, dropping his whip and pulling out his pistol. He cocked it and took quick aim, then squeezed the trigger. At the sharp report of the pistol, the bull's legs folded and it rolled on the ground, shot through the head.

"That was a rare sight to watch!" Buggie exclaimed as he rode over to the bull. "And you're very good with that pistol."

"An expert taught me how to shoot it," Jeremy replied, dismounting and picking up his stock whip. He coiled it and climbed back into his saddle. "Now that I had to kill that bull, we can't let all of it go to waste. If you'll skin it and cut off part of the meat, I'll find the herd."

Buggie nodded as he dismounted and tethered his horse, and Jeremy rode in the direction in which the dunnocks had fled. At first they had scattered, leaving a fan of trails through the brush. Within a few hundred yards, they had stopped running and their herding in-

stinct had drawn them back together. Jeremy followed
the trail and found them where they had stopped two
miles away in a grassy clearing, peacefully grazing again.

By the time Jeremy returned to Buggie, the man had
skinned the bull and wrapped the tenderloins and other
choice cuts in the skin. He tied it behind his saddle, then
he and Jeremy rode to the dunnocks. They were much
more difficult than sheep to drive, but manageable. Some
kept trying to turn aside as the rest of the herd moved
toward the valley, but they rejoined the others when Jeremy or Buggie rode around to the flank.

When the herd was a mile from the valley, Buggie rode
ahead to open the gate. The dunnocks hesitated at the
fence, then crowded through the gate as Jeremy cracked
his whip behind them. After closing the gate, the two
men rode down the valley to their camp. They stretched
out the skin to dry and hung the beef in a tree under
canvas to protect it from flies, then they mounted their
horses and rode out of the valley again.

It was midday, a time when Jeremy knew that most
dunnocks would be lying in a quiet place and chewing
their cud. He and Buggie searched in thickets, finding
another herd during midafternoon. The bull was less aggressive than the first one, racing away when Jeremy
stung it with his whip. Then he and Buggie drove the
rest of the herd toward the valley.

The following day, Jeremy and Buggie found only one
small herd, but they drove two herds to the valley on the
following day. During the succeeding days, the number
of dunnocks grazing in the valley steadily increased. At
first the animals remained as far as possible from the
camp beside the billabong, then they gradually became
less frightened of Jeremy and Buggie. The dunnocks were
also thin and bony from ranging far over the terrain in
search of forage and water, but they began gaining
weight from grazing the lush grass and resting in the
confines of the valley.

When there were a hundred odd cows and stirks, along
with half that number of calves, Jeremy decided that was

all he and Buggie could manage. For two days, he waited for the last arrivals to become less apprehensive of people, and he and Buggie occasionally rode their horses around the dunnocks as they grazed. At the end of the two days, the animals had stopped bolting away from the horses. That night, Jeremy and Buggy had only a few hours of sleep, because they were up hours before dawn to dismantle sections of the fence so animals could get into the valley freely and drink at the billabong. When dawn came, the two men herded the dunnocks out of the valley.

That was the first of many nights of little sleep for Jeremy and Buggie as they drove the herd down the winding route between the waterholes. Dunnocks had a much weaker herding instinct than sheep, making them more inclined to wander off by themselves when the herd was bedded down at night. Dingoes trailed the herd, causing further trouble. Though they were unable to fight a fully grown dunnock, they preyed upon the old, sick, and young ones. Their howling could be heard from all sides each night, which made the cows with calves restless.

It was easy for the dingoes to keep up with the herd, because Jeremy set a slow pace so the dunnocks could graze and continue gaining weight along the way. The animals began resembling domestic cattle in appearance and behavior, becoming fatter and more tame. They also grew completely accustomed to having Jeremy and Buggie near them, and on nights when the herd stopped at a soak, the two men were almost trampled as they hurriedly dipped up water for the thirsty dunnocks crowding around on all sides.

After the first nights of virtually no sleep, Jeremy tried to divide the nights with Buggie, but he found it was impossible. During his years with Jarboe Charlie, he had acquired the man's characteristic of devoting his full energy to everything he did. At any unusual stir among the dunnocks at night, he was awake and on his feet before he realized what he was doing. Buggie always strived to do more than his share, and each time Jeremy went to check on the herd, the bearded, portly man was at his side.

Jeremy bore his fatigue stoically, as he had other hardships in the past, and there were factors that fueled his reserves of energy. He knew that Buggie was suffering even more, being older and not as strong. The man sagged wearily and his bulging eyes were tinged with red, but he plodded on about his tasks with grim determination. Jeremy did as much and more, feeling compelled to make the journey as easy as possible for the old man.

An important milestone in the journey was passed at the first soak they had dug. After that, the terrain rapidly became less arid. The next evening, they stopped at a large billabong surrounded by lush, green grass for the dunnocks to graze before they bedded down for the night. The following day, they reached a creek, the first flowing water they had seen for weeks.

Two days later, they reached the first track they had seen for weeks, and it led down into the alluvial plains in the southwest of the Darling Downs. In its luxuriant foliage, the area reminded Jeremy of the Nepean River valley, but there was no comparison in size. The region cut by streams that formed the headwaters of the Darling River was vast, comprising tens of thousands of square miles. Villages were scattered here and there, and the cattle and sheep stations alternated with large farms planted in wheat and other grains. In the settled region, the dingoes shadowing the herd fell behind. The cows with calves were no longer restless at night, and Jeremy and Buggie were able to sleep for four or five hours on most nights.

Near the town of Dargawarra, the track led into the broad track used by drovers to take herds to Bourke. The cattle track was flanked by wide, grassy verges that provided graze for livestock, and the drovers had established good campsites at intervals. There was also an abundance of water in the many creeks and small rivers that

the track crossed as Jeremy and Buggie drove the herd
down it during the balmy early summer weather. Most
cattle were taken from the stations to Bourke much later
in the year, and the only other traffic on the track consisted of swagmen and travelers.

It was still too congested for Jeremy, and the area was
too settled. Most stations were hardly larger than the
farms, and they passed several set back from the track
in the course of a day. He readily acknowledged that it
was a fertile, bountiful region, but he greatly preferred
the austere, sparsely settled vastness of the remote outback.

At a ford in the Barwon River beside the town of Mun-
gindi, the track crossed over into New South Wales. It
gradually curved to the west, and after a few days, the
Darling River was a short distance to the north, still
collecting water from tributaries for its long journey to
the sea. Their supplies began running short, and Jeremy
traded a stirk to a farmer for bags of early vegetables, a
bag of freshly milled flour, and a flitch of bacon.

The end of the journey came into view one afternoon,
when they caught sight of Bourke lying a few miles
ahead. The town was the head of navigation on the river,
and three riverboats were at the docks. Bourke was large,
spreading back from its waterfront in a maze of tree-
lined streets, with church spires and taller buildings jutting above the foliage. South of the town was an open,
grassy expanse of several acres, the mustering grounds
for the herds.

The sun was setting as Jeremy and Buggie drove the
herd onto the mustering grounds and camped beside it.
The next morning, three buyers from stockyards in the
town came to view the herd. They appeared bemused as
they crossed the mustering grounds, gazing at the animals, and Jeremy knew why. Herds from the stations
always consisted of mature cows and bullocks, while his
ranged from calves through stirks to cows. In addition,
the dunnocks now looked more or less like domestic cat-

tle of mixed breeds, but they had no brands or ear-notches to identify ownership.

Immediately after the introductions were exchanged, Jeremy replied to the familiar question about his relationship to the Kerricks of Tibooburra Station, and explained the origin of the herd. "It's the same name," he said, "but no more than that to me. These are dunnocks. We gathered them in the outback to the northwest of the Darling Downs."

"Indeed they are dunnocks!" one of the men exclaimed. "Now that you've said that, I can see that they're a bit shaggy and wild-looking. But they're fat and in excellent condition. How did you get them out of the outback? The waterholes there are days or weeks apart, aren't they?"

"For the most part, we dug for water," Jeremy explained.

The men laughed, taking the reply as an evasive answer. "So you dug wells in the outback?" one of them remarked jocularly. "No one can fault you for keeping your methods to yourself, because it was undoubtedly a hard task to get them out of the outback even with sufficient water. I greatly admire you, and I daresay few could have done it. Unfortunately, though, my employer wants only mature stock, and he won't buy calves."

"Mine will," another man put in. "He'll buy any sort of stock if the price is right." The man glanced over the herd again with an expert eye as he continued, "I can offer ten bob for the cows, eight for the stirks, and five for the calves. Call it sixty-five guineas for the lot."

"I'll pay seventy for the lot," the third buyer said.

The one who had made the first offer took another look at the herd, pursing his lips as he pondered, then shook his head and declined to raise the bid. Jeremy turned to the man who had made the higher offer. "Done," he said. "Where is your stockyard located?"

"It's near the docks," the man replied. "I'll send out two men who work in the pens to show you the way and to help you with the herd. Your money will be waiting at the office when you get there."

The three buyers left, and Buggie commented gleefully on the amount of money they had been offered for the herd as he and Jeremy began gathering up their cooking utensils and other things where they had camped. Jeremy was also more than satisfied with the amount, and he discussed plans with Buggie. Neither of them wanted to remain at the town any longer than they had to, so they agreed to buy supplies and other necessities, then set out back up the track.

By the time the horses were saddled, the two workers from the stockyard had arrived. The workers took the flanks of the herd, forming it into a wide column and guiding it toward a road leading from the edge of the mustering grounds into the town. After a hundred yards, the houses at intervals on each side closed together, and the road turned into a wide street that led around the north side of the town. When a stockyard beside the river came into view, one of the workers rode ahead to open the gate in a pen.

In the office at one side of the stockyard, the owner counted out seventy guineas in gold from a strongbox. As he and Buggie left the office, Jeremy started to hand over half of the money, but Buggie declined to take it, preferring for Jeremy to keep it and pay for everything. On the way to the stockyard, they had passed a smithy, and they rode back up the wide street toward it to get their horses' worn shoes replaced.

While the blacksmith was shoeing the horses, Jeremy made extra sets to take along in the event the horses cast shoes in the outback. The burly smith nodded in approval, noting the expert way that Jeremy formed the shoes on the anvil. "You could do your own smithing if you had a mind to," he told Jeremy. "Have you worked as a blacksmith?"

"No, I had a mate years ago who showed me how to shoe horses," Jeremy replied. "But if I did my own smithing, I'd need an extra pack horse for my anvil, then another for my forge, tools, and iron, wouldn't I?"

The blacksmith laughed heartily, agreeing. When the

horses were shod, Jeremy paid for the work and the iron for the extra shoes, then he and Buggie rode into the center of the town. The pace of activity on the noisy, congested streets appeared frantic to Jeremy.

There was also a lack of the respect and courtesy toward others that was the rule on stations and in the outback, and the men seemed timid to him. In the dry goods shop where he and Buggie went to buy new clothes, two large, muscular roustabouts from a riverboat were using foul language as they laughed and talked loudly. Several men were present among the women in the shop, but they merely frowned and made no move to come to the assistance of the shopkeeper, who was trying in vain to quiet the roustabouts.

Jeremy turned on the two men, furiously angry. "Either have done with that scavvy, or get yourselves out of here!" he barked.

Silence fell in the shop as Jeremy glared at the two men. For a moment, one appeared to consider making a retort, his lips twisting in a sneer, then he changed his mind and they left the shop. But the situation soon became embarrassing for Jeremy, because the shopkeeper and customers gazed at him in admiration as they thanked him effusively. He hurriedly paid for his and Buggie's new dungaree shirts and trousers, and they left.

Stopping in other shops, they bought new hats and boots. In a hardware, they picked out an ax and other tools, a new water flask for Buggie, and cooking utensils to replace those that had become too battered. Jeremy chose a razor from a display, then laughed and shook his head when the shopkeeper took out a tray of watches to show him. "No, that's the last thing I'd ever need," he said. "I can see for myself when the sun rises and sets, and those are the only times that I need to know."

The man laughed, putting the tray away again. He added up the prices of the items on the counter, and Jeremy paid him. Jeremy and Buggie carried their purchases out and went on down the street to a general store to buy bags of peas, rice, tea, and other foodstuffs.

With their pack horses carrying heavy, bulging loads, they rode out of Bourke. Shortly after midday, they reached a grove of trees beside a brook that crossed the track. It was a quiet place, well away from the congestion and confusion of the town, and they stopped to sort out their purchases and camp until the next morning. After their supplies and equipment were organized into neat loads for the pack horses, they kindled a fire.

Jeremy sat beside the fire and counted the remaining money as Buggie filled the billys at the brook and placed them in the hot coals. Nodding in satisfaction, Jeremy put his purse back into his pocket. "We still have more than half the money left," he said, "and we have everything we need to bring in another herd of dunnocks. That's a good profit, but I believe we could make a much better one with the next herd."

"How?" Buggie asked, keenly interested.

"By taking it to Brisbane," Jeremy replied. "Frank Biven's brother said that cattle sell for upwards of thirty shillings there."

Buggie's protruding eyes grew still wider in astonishment. "But Brisbane is on the other side of the Great Divide, Jeremy!" he exclaimed. "There isn't even a footpath across it within hundreds of miles of Brisbane."

"I know where Brisbane is," Jeremy told him, laughing. "And I know that people say there's no way of getting across that part of the Great Divide. But Aborigine trading parties have been crossing just about every part of it for donkey's years. There must be a trail there that we could use."

The billys began boiling, and Buggie set them off the fire and sprinkled tea into them as the conversation continued. Jeremy had a private reason for wanting to go to the coastal plain, one that was far more important to him than additional profits for dunnocks. He wanted to find out if it would have the special appeal for which he was searching, a quality of affinity for him that would make it the place where his walkabout would end.

The conversation turned out as usual, with Buggie

agreeing to whatever Jeremy wanted to do. "How will you find a trail?" Buggie asked. "Will you ask some of the Aborigines who live up in the mountains about it?"

"No, I speak only Aranda, and those in that area will have a different language," Jeremy replied. "And those who live near villages and speak English probably wouldn't know anything about the trails. We'll take the track to Toowoomba, which is well up into the mountains and due west of Brisbane. From there I'll look for a trail we can use."

"Well, if anyone can find one, you will," Buggie observed confidently. "If we can make enough money, do you think you might buy or start a station somewhere? I'm not getting any younger, and I'd like to think that the time will come when I'll have somewhere to rest my bones."

"Yes, I'll have a station sooner or later. When I do, you'll always have a place with me, and you can do whatever you wish there."

Buggie glowed with satisfaction as he began drinking his tea. Jeremy took a drink of his and set the billy back down. When he did, his elbow passed over his water bottle, which was beside him with his blanket and other swag. Even though he felt no contact between his arm and the bottle, it toppled over with a clatter of glass shattering, and water gushed out of the broken neck of the bottle and the leather cover.

Jeremy looked at it in disbelief, then in consternation. "Damn!" he exclaimed. "How in all that's holy did that happen? I've dropped that bottle off a horse onto rocks, and it didn't even chip or crack. But I didn't touch it, and it simply fell over and broke."

"It could be that your sleeve brushed it and knocked it over," Buggie suggested sympathetically. "Perhaps it was already cracked, and you didn't notice it. That happened to a water bottle I had years ago."

The explanation seemed inadequate to Jeremy, but he was unable to think of any other as he looked at the broken bottle remorsefully. "Yes, I suppose that could be why it broke," he replied doubtfully, gathering up the pieces of the broken neck of the bottle and putting them into the leather cover with the rest of the shattered glass.

After he had collected all of the bits of glass and put them into the leather cover, Jeremy was uncertain about what to do with it. It was absolutely useless, but the thought of simply discarding it was intolerable to him. Buggie evidently understood how Jeremy felt, because he untied their new shovel from one of the pack horse loads and stepped to a tree a few yards from the fire. He dug a shallow hole under the tree, then turned expectantly to Jeremy.

In a way, burying the leather cover and broken glass seemed absurd to Jeremy. But in another way, it was very appropriate, the only suitable means to dispose of something with so many vital associations for him. He stepped to the hole and placed the leather cover in it, then Buggie shoveled the dirt back into the hole and smoothed it over with the back of the shovel.

They returned to the fire, and as Buggie replaced the shovel on the pack horse load, he mentioned what Jeremy had once said about Aborigine beliefs concerning the water bottle. "According to them, it might have some of the spirit about it of the one who first had it, didn't you say?" he asked. "If that was true, what would it mean when the bottle broke?"

Jeremy sat down beside the fire, starting to say that he had no idea what it would mean, then he thought again. He recalled that Jarboe had told him about a carved stone that one tribal elder had given another, and when it had broken, the one who had possessed it first had died. Then he shrugged off the thought. "Superstitions don't mean anything, Buggie," he said.

"Aye, that's true," Buggie replied, sitting on the other side of the fire. "You can have my new water flask. That won't replace your bottle, because I know how much you liked it, but it'll provide water. My old one will suffice me for a while longer."

Jeremy shook his head. "No, I'm grateful, but I'll use

your old one for now. I can get another one in Too-woomba."

Rummaging in his swag, Buggie took out the flask and passed it across the fire. Jeremy nodded in thanks and set it aside, wanting to talk about other things. "We should be able to gather a herd much faster this next time, Buggie," he said. "Now we have waterholes ready and waiting, and the best holding pen that anyone could ever want."

Buggie smiled happily and agreed, and as they began discussing plans for collecting another herd of dunnocks, Jeremy tried to dismiss thoughts of the water bottle. But the link with his boyhood and with Jarboe had been too precious for him to forget so quickly and easily. The thoughts lingered in the back of his mind, creating a feeling of sorrow.

Alexandra Kerrick sat at her desk in the parlor and tried to work on the station accounts. She struggled to concentrate on the fact that the spring wool clip was en route to London, and on hopes that the market would be strong. It was impossible, however, because a corroboree had begun in the Aborigine village earlier in the afternoon.

The throbbing didgeridoos, rattling rhythm sticks, and chanting voices had never sounded more ominous and mournful, but nothing had happened at the village to justify a corroboree. The Aborigines evidently believed that something of vital significance had occurred else-where, and Alexandra had an oppressive sense of fore-boding. For the past few days, David had felt well, with no chest pains at all. That morning, he had gone with Jonathan and several other men to move the flocks about in Pingara Paddock, the one immediately to the north-west of the home paddock.

As the knocker on the front door thumped, her hand holding the pen jerked, and a blotch of ink fell onto the page in the ledger. Controlling her urge to throw down the pen and race to the door, Alexandra carefully blotted the smear of ink and replaced the pen in its holder. Then she left the desk and crossed the parlor toward the front door.

Emma Bodenham was coming down the hall from the rear of the house toward the door, but when the maid saw Alexandra step out of the parlor, she turned slowly back down the hall. The corroboree had infused the household with tense apprehension, and Emma waited to see who was at the door. Alexandra steeled herself, opening the door. Ruel Blake and Silas Doak, the head stockman, were on the porch. At the steps behind them, their horses were sweaty and panting from a long, fast run.

It was the first time that Alexandra had seen either of the two bearded, middle-aged men with tears in their eyes, but they were both crying openly and unashamedly. The two men stared at her and wept, at a loss as to how to begin what they had come to say. Alexandra gripped the edge of the door for support. "Which one?" she asked. "David or Jonathan?"

"Both of them, Mistress Kerrick," Silas replied tearfully. "Mr. Jonathan was afoot, looking at some sheep, and a wild boar ran out of the brush and attacked him. The closest one to him was Mr. Kerrick. He killed the boar, but he had a fatal heart seizure. The boar had already injured Mr. Jonathan terribly bad, and we—well, we couldn't do anything for him."

Instead of beginning an adjustment that would span days or weeks, Alexandra accepted the loss and its full implications within an instant. But that instant seemed infinitely long. The events of her many years with David and their struggle to establish Tibooburra Station in the wilderness flowed through her mind. The final event of that day had turned the results of those decades into ashes that would scatter at the first wind of ill fortune. There was no one to assume the mantle of authority and responsibility, no Kerrick heir to sit at the head of the table.

Her grief over the loss of her loved ones was crushing,

and it was compounded by the fact that what she had achieved in life would now wither away. The generations of her offspring would continue, but all she could leave to them would be a headstone with her name on it. The shock was too much, and she felt out of contact with her surroundings, an empty shell drained of emotion.

She could only respond to her knowledge of what had to be done. As though from a long distance away, she heard herself speaking to the head stockman. "Riders must be sent to nearby stations and to Wilcannia," she told Silas. "The minister from Wilcannia must be brought here."

"Aye, I'll see to that, Mistress Kerrick," Silas replied. "The riders will leave within the hour on the fastest horses in the pen."

"Arrangements must be made to feed and house the guests who will come to the funeral. There will be scores of them."

"Aye, me and Ruel will see to everything," Silas assured her. "And we'll see to it proper and all, Mistress Kerrick. It'll be done so that it'll be a credit to the memory of Mr. Kerrick and Mr. Jonathan. Don't you worry, because me and Ruel will take care of everything."

Alexandra thanked him and closed the door. She went down the hall past Emma, who was leaning against the wall and sobbing brokenly. The maid had told the rest of the staff, and Alexandra heard sounds of grief from the kitchen and scullery. Her eyes dry and her face set in rigid lines, she continued with what had to be done. She went out the door to the garden at the side of the house to tell her daughter-in-law what had happened.

Catherine was in the station cemetery at the far side of the garden, once again cleaning off the grave of her son who had been still-born years before. The corroboree echoed through the gardens, and Catherine knew that some dreadful tragedy had occurred, though she fought against hearing about it. Her attempt at a smile a grotesque grimace, she interrupted as Alexandra started to speak: "I intend to plant flowers here, Mistress Kerrick," she said quickly. "I've often thought of that, and I'm going to do it. Pretty flowers would choke out these terrible weeds."

"Catherine, I must tell you that—"

"I hate these terrible weeds," Catherine interrupted again, plucking furiously at the thin shoots on the grave. "Why should my poor mite's body nourish these ugly weeds? Yes, I intend to plant pretty flowers on his little grave to choke out these weeds that keep growing on it."

"Catherine, listen to me. I must tell you that—"

"No, I don't have time to listen now, Mistress Kerrick," Catherine continued in a strained, quavering voice as she clawed at the surface of the grave with her fingernails. "See, I'm preparing to plant pretty flowers. Every time I look at my poor baby's grave, it's covered with these terrible weeds. I intend to plant flowers that will choke them out."

Alexandra gripped the woman's shoulders and lifted her. "Catherine, Jonathan was killed by a wild boar," she said. "David had a heart seizure. David and Jonathan are dead, Catherine."

"If my baby's body must nourish anything, it will be flowers," Catherine babbled, turning her face away. "All I ever see on his grave are weeds, weeds, weeds!"

"Catherine, David and Jonathan are dead!"

The woman's incoherent words faded to a whisper, then into silence. Her knees sagged, her eyes rolled back, and a blank expression came over her face. Alexandra caught her, keeping her from falling. Her arms around the woman, Alexandra began pulling her down the path toward the house.

When they were halfway down the path, Catherine suddenly exploded into a frenzy. She began trying to pull away, screaming at the top of her voice. With the woman's shrill, deafening screams battering her ears, Alexandra gripped her tightly and tried to drag her toward the house.

The side door of the house flew open and Emma Bodenham ran out, followed by the other maids, the cook, and the kitchen helpers, all of them still sobbing and tears streaming from their eyes. They charged down the path, then gathered around, taking Catherine from Alexandra.

In her violent delirium of grief, Catherine was almost too much for the nine strong women. She fought them, her screams ringing out as she kicked and flailed her arms. They finally lifted her, staggering from side to side with her struggles, and carried her toward the house.

They took her inside and toward her room, her screams resounding through the house. Alexandra stood on the path, the sound of the corroboree and the shrieks of despair from the house blending and swelling to a plaintive, drumming thunder in her ears. Even then, Alexandra was still unable to weep. She could only lift her fists to the heavens in a silent, bitter protest.

Chapter Sixteen

"I can certainly understand your situation, Alexandra,"
Elizabeth Garrity told her. "I don't have enough hours
in the day, and Tibooburra is just as large as Wayamba.
What do you intend to do?"

"Simply see how things go for a time," Alexandra replied. "That's the only way to find out what sort of problems will come up."

"Yes, it is," Elizabeth agreed. "You have an ample
number of loyal, experienced stockmen, which will be a
help."

Alexandra nodded, but she silently doubted that their
help would be sufficient. She was talking with Elizabeth
at the foot of the hill below the house during the last
minutes before the woman left. The other guests at the
funeral had left the previous day, and stockmen were
dismantling the shed that had been used as a cookhouse.
At one side of it, Colin Garrity was talking with Ruel and
Silas as he waited for Elizabeth to finish her conversation

with Alexandra, and the three Garrity sons were with him.

Elizabeth had changed into her stockman's clothes to leave, and she idly tapped her stock whip against her thigh as she spoke. "But whoever makes the decisions must be out in the paddocks, Alexandra, and there's no way around that. At very best, you can keep things in hand only temporarily. Perhaps Deirdre or Eudora will marry a good man."

Alexandra sighed and shook her head doubtfully. "Deirdre appears to have every intention of remaining unmarried, and that's her choice to make. It's unlikely that Eudora will find a man in Sydney who could take charge of this station, and she has no desire whatsoever to live in the outback. It appears that a hired manager will eventually be in charge here."

"I hope it doesn't come to that," Elizabeth said. "Each time I've seen a manager in charge of a station, I've seen a station going to rack and ruin, and I'm sure your experience has been the same." She shook her head regretfully, then changed the subject. "Well, I must be on my way, Alexandra. It's time to start watching for grass fires again."

"Very well, Elizabeth. Thank you for your love and support when I needed it most. Go with God, and I hope to see you again soon."

Elizabeth replied as they hugged and kissed in farewell, Alexandra feeling a warm rush of affection for the woman. Alexandra's tears had finally come during the funeral, and Elizabeth had remained at her side through that night and the following day. Although many things awaited her at Wayamba Station, Elizabeth had remained for as long as she had been needed.

After a final kiss, Elizabeth turned to her horse. Characteristically, she simply stepped into the saddle and rode up the track at a fast canter by herself. When her husband noticed that she was riding away, he and their sons hastily mounted up and rode after her, waving to Alexandra. She waved, then watched Elizabeth. The woman still seemed incomplete without Sheila at her side. Elizabeth disappeared over the hill at the south side of the home paddock, Colin and the boys trying to catch up with her, and Alexandra went up the hill to the house.

From the porch, Alexandra saw that Catherine was in the cemetery. She was planting flowers on the tiny grave, as well as the larger, fresh one beside it. The violent outburst had passed, with no indication that it would be repeated. Over the years, however, a morbid, excessive trait had revealed itself in Catherine, and it had become more pronounced under the stress of grief. Alexandra sighed worriedly and went into the house.

Catherine came in from the cemetery and went upstairs to her room, then remained there. Alexandra ate alone at the long table in the large dining room, forcing herself to consume the food brought by a grieving maid. After dinner, she tried to read for a time, then went upstairs to her room. The bed still had David's poignantly familiar fresh, masculine scent about it. She woke several times during the night, reaching out to him.

The next morning, when Silas Doak came to the house to discuss the station work schedule with Alexandra, it was very frustrating for her. The head stockman was searching for the orders he had previously received from either David or Jonathan, but Alexandra lacked the wealth of detailed knowledge that her husband and son had acquired daily while going about their activities. At the same time, Silas was unwilling to make decisions except on the most routine matters.

One of the topics they discussed was where grass fires were most likely to happen, with a view toward watching those places closely. Identifying the most vulnerable areas required a thorough knowledge of the present condition of the foliage all over the station, but years had passed since Alexandra had been in some paddocks. She tried to talk Silas into choosing the areas himself, but he was unwilling to do more than discuss the issue.

In the end, Alexandra told him to watch those areas where fires had occured during previous years. She knew it varied from year to year, but Silas was satisfied. The next morning, the subject of moving some of the flocks came up. Again Silas avoided making a decision, but readily accepted hers though it was based on inadequate information. It was the same during the following days, the head stockman depending upon Alexandra for decisions and coming to the house every morning, except when he had to go out into the paddocks for a day or two.

Catherine's mental and emotional state was an even more troubling problem for Alexandra. The woman spent her days in the cemetery and her evenings in her room, taking her meals there. She became careless about her appearance, and often went about in an untidy dress and with her hair uncombed. That pointed up how much older Catherine suddenly appeared, her face lined and gaunt, and the streaks of grey in her hair turning into broad bands.

Intensely worried about her, Alexandra tried to talk with Catherine and break her pattern of behavior. It was futile, Catherine nodding in agreement with everything, then continuing as before. On one occasion, she said that she wanted to move to Sydney, which took Alexandra aback.

"But this is where you and I belong, Catherine," Alexandra told her. "Tibooburra Station is our home."

"Eudora is in Sydney," Catherine said dully. "All of my family has either died or moved away, but Eudora is there."

"Well, perhaps we can visit Sydney before too long, and you can see Eudora. But our home is here at Tibooburra Station."

"It isn't the same here as before. At times, everything seems to be waiting for something. It grows very quiet, even the birds falling silent and the breeze dying away. Everything waits for something to happen, and everything seems to be watching me."

Alexandra told her to ignore it, which left Catherine dissatisfied, and the conversation ended inconclusively.

It also deeply disturbed Alexandra, because the sensations that Catherine had described were those experienced by many who were unable to live in the outback. Some stockmen who were hired had to leave, often talking about the silence, the watching, and the waiting of the outback for something to happen.

Love and a family were a bulwark for some. In addition, keeping busy helped, and Alexandra suspected that both of those had been of assistance to Catherine in the past. But now Jonathan was gone, and Catherine had nothing to do except to grieve.

For years, she had been in charge of the station school, where married stockmen's children and those from the Aborigine village attended classes. One of the numerous Bodenham children, Amelia, had since taken it over, and Catherine had helped her from time to time. When she talked with her daughter-in-law again, Alexandra encouraged her to resume helping Amelia, but Catherine had no interest in the school.

Some adjusted to the outback through force of will, and Alexandra hoped that Catherine would do the same once she overcame her grief. Then, as she went to her room one night, Alexandra heard a loud voice in Catherine's room, and she stepped down the hall. Catherine was addressing Jonathan, bitterly criticizing him for leaving her all alone in the outback.

It was entirely different from when Elizabeth had spoken aloud to the coffin at Sheila's funeral, because Catherine's voice had a shrill edge of emotional instability. Deciding to take a firmer hand with her, Alexandra knocked on the door and then opened it. Catherine was sitting on the bed in her nightclothes, and she broke off in mid-sentence.

"Catherine, I'd like you to resume coming to the dining room for dinner," Alexandra told her. "Please be there tomorrow evening."

"No, I'd rather have dinner here," Catherine replied. "When I'm here in my room, everything isn't watching me, and I don't—"

"Come to the dining room for dinner tomorrow evening," Alexandra interrupted curtly. "I'll expect to see you there."

The woman hesitated, then sullenly nodded. Alexandra stepped back and closed the door, then went down the hall toward her room. Behind her, Catherine began talking loudly again. Alexandra went to bed and lay awake for hours, worrying about her daughter-in-law.

The following day, Catherine was in the cemetery until late afternoon, then she came to the dining room for dinner. She was haggard and unkempt, and her behavior had changed abruptly. During the previous days, she had been morose and silent, but now she was excessively cheerful.

"There was a white cockatoo on my window sill this morning," she announced gleefully, a bright, irrational sparkle in her eyes. "A white cockatoo! Isn't that remarkable?"

"Well, curious, perhaps," Alexandra replied uneasily, studying the woman closely. "There are innumerable cockatoos about."

"Not white ones!" Catherine shouted across the table in abrupt rage. "How many times have you had a white cockatoo on your window sill? Never, I'll warrant! You're only jealous because I had one on my window sill. It isn't merely curious, it's remarkable! Truly remarkable!"

Alexandra turned and said to the maid, who was gaping at Catherine in astonished fear, "Leave the room." As the maid scurried out, Alexandra pointed a finger at Catherine. "Either you take control of yourself and stop this foolish behavior," she said in a soft, cold voice, "or I'll thrash you until you do. Do you understand me?"

Catherine slumped in her chair, burying her face in her hands and bursting into tears. "Please don't be angry with me, Mistress Kerrick," she wailed. "Sometimes I feel as though I'm at a great distance from myself, only watching what I do. Please don't hate me."

Alexandra stepped around the table and sat on the chair beside Catherine. "I could never hate you, my dear," she said soothingly, putting her arms around the woman. "I love you, and I always shall. But you must try to control what you say and do. Will you do that for me?"

Catherine nodded, leaning against Alexandra and sobbing. "Yes, I'll try," she replied tearfully. "I'll do my best, Mistress Kerrick."

Alexandra continued holding the woman, talking to her. Catherine stopped crying and became calm, and Alexandra called the maid back in as she returned to her place at the table. Catherine neither did nor said anything out of the ordinary during the remainder of the meal, but she was subdued once again. She sat in silence, eating very little of her food.

As she pondered two facts, Alexandra was just as quiet, and also ate very little. The first was the memory of two new stockmen who should have left the outback, but had remained for too long. David had brought them in from the paddocks and sent them back to the east, escorted by other stockmen. One had been unable to talk, and the other had been violent.

The other fact was her inescapable responsibility for Catherine. In addition to her love for the woman, which created an obligation, Jonathan would have begged her with his dying breath to safeguard Catherine's welfare. Alexandra also knew that it would be wrong to send an emotionally unstable woman to Morton and Julia.

Lying in bed that night, Alexandra pondered a further fact that she had tried to ignore for days, for she had not wanted to leave the station. If he had no member of the family to consult for decisions, Silas Doak would have to make them himself. Some might not be the best decisions, but he was an intelligent, experienced head stockman, and Alexandra knew that she could never find anyone who would be more capable as a station manager.

After a sleepless night, Alexandra waited for him in the parlor. When she talked with him, he was unenthusiastic, but even more reluctant to refuse what she asked.

"Well, I'll take charge as manager if that's what you want, Mistress Kerrick," he said. "And I'll do my best."

"That's all I ask, and no one else could do as well as your best, Silas," Alexandra assured him. "I intend to visit Elizabeth Garrity before I leave, and Catherine and I will take the household staff with us. The house will be closed, with the furniture stored under dust covers."

Silas nodded, asking about arrangements for the journey to Sydney. They discussed the number of wagons that would be needed, and the number of drivers and other employees. When the details were settled, Silas left and Alexandra stepped to her desk to write a letter to Morton. If possible, she wanted to live in the house that her father had once owned.

As she began writing the letter, tears filled her eyes. She glanced around the room, anguished over having to leave her home in the outback. Then she brushed her tears away and continued writing the letter.

When he received the letter, Morton was at first hesitant about reading it. The last one he had received from his mother—and had opened in eager anticipation of news about his family—had informed him that his father and brother were dead. He was still coming to terms with the tragedy, intensely sorrowful each time they came to mind during quiet moments.

Morton opened and began reading the letter, his misgivings fading. He knew his mother would have greatly preferred to remain at the station, but he was certain that he and Julia could make her content in Sydney. Then, reaching a sentence that expressed her preference about a house, he dropped the letter and rushed downstairs to the main office.

The clerk now responsible for real estate was an employee of many years named Harold Fraley, a thin, angular man with a sober demeanor. Morton hurried across the office to Harold's desk. "Is the house in Wentworth Street in the Whitlam district still vacant?" he asked.

"Yes, it is, Sir Morton," Harold replied. "The gentleman who looked at it is undecided between it and a house on—"

"I'm making the decision for him," Morton interrupted. "Under no circumstances is that house to be leased. My mother is moving to Sydney and wants to live there, and that house is to be kept vacant for her."

Harold dipped a pen in his inkwell and made a note on a piece of paper. "Very well, Sir Morton. The house will be kept vacant."

Morton went back toward his office, trying to disregard the vague dissatisfaction that he always felt about Harold in his present position. While he knew it was unfair, Morton was unable to keep himself from comparing how Harold did the work with how Benjamin Tavish had done it.

In this instance, however, Morton acknowledged it was better that Harold had been managing the real estate, because Benjamin would have probably had the house in Whitlam leased out. There was also a more general reason for satisfaction in the present situation: Benjamin was perfectly safe and evidently very happy. A letter from Henry Newcomb that had arrived weeks before had stated that "Mr. and Mrs. Hawthorne" had been comfortably settled in a small, neat cottage on the outskirts of Auckland.

The letter had also stated that it had been unnecessary to assist Benjamin in finding employment. The couple was using one room of their house to manufacture a fine linen paper that had found a ready market among those who wanted high quality stationery. In the meantime, Morton had heard no rumors about the disappearance of Creevey's wife. Beverly had been seen by others only rarely, and her absence had created no curiosity. Creevey apparently remained completely in the dark as to what had happened to her.

Morton finished reading the letter from his mother, then put it in his coat pocket to take home to Julia. He turned to the papers on his desk, which reflected a gradual change in his business affairs. He had advertised the dyed flax rope in newspapers in Melbourne, another location of numerous yacht clubs. Inquiries had been followed by a flood of orders, while the sales in Sydney had remained brisk, and the ropewalk was now producing a substantial income. The other part of what had once been a fiasco, the dry dock, had begun producing a modest profit.

However, the income from his other investments had declined because of a financial slump and widespread unemployment in Great Britain. Overall commercial activity in Sydney had been affected, depressing real estate and other markets, and some had been reduced severely. Exports of commodities to British ports had fallen sharply, and the policies issued by the marine insurance company in which Morton was a partner were at a very low level.

While others retrenched, the business climate was one in which Creevey was thriving. His financial resources were enormous, and his bank was still absorbing losses in a continuing effort to control banking in the city. He had been buying into firms that had been weakened by the downturn, usually as a silent partner. When he had bought the *Chronicle*, a newspaper that had been established during the early years of the colony, the purchase had become public knowledge because the employees had found out and many had resigned.

At the end of the day, Morton had found more reasons for caution than satisfaction in his business affairs, but the situation was the opposite when he went home. His family had never looked more captivating, Julia sitting on a shady lawn in the back garden with the baby on a blanket beside her and the nurse on a bench nearby. He kissed Julia, then took out the letter and handed it to her as he sat down on the grass.

"It's from Mother," he told her. "However, it contains very favorable tidings this time."

"Thank heavens for that, dear Morton," Julia said, reaching over and clasping his hand affectionately. "The last letter brought more than enough sadness to suffice for a lifetime."

Morton lifted her hand and kissed it, grateful for her constant sympathy and comfort after he had received the other letter. Then he began playing with the baby as Julia read the letter. She exclaimed joyfully, then anxiously asked if the house in the Whitlam district was available. Morton replied that it was, and added that it probably would have been leased out if Benjamin Tavish had still been managing the real estate.

Even that innocuous remark about Benjamin brought a warning frown and slight nod toward the nurse from Julia. They avoided discussing Benjamin when any of the household staff was within earshot to eliminate any possibility of making a revealing comment that could be repeated elsewhere, and Julia was more insistent on the point than Morton. He believed that it was becoming ever less likely that Creevey would find out what had happened to his wife, but Julia considered the danger to be as acute as ever.

When the nurse folded the blanket and took the baby into the house, Morton and Julia went inside. Over dinner and then in the parlor, they discussed preparing the house for his mother. Morton knew that she enjoyed gardening and would prefer attending to the flower beds herself, but other things needed to be done. He and Julia made provisional plans about what to do, agreeing to inspect the house together the next day.

The following morning, Morton went to work and took care of the most urgent matters awaiting his attention, then he went to the house in Whitlam. Julia was there, along with several maids who were busy at work cleaning the house. Morton looked through the rooms with her, helping her prepare a list of new and replacement furnishings that were needed.

A few repairs that could have been overlooked for other occupants were also needed, and when he returned to work, Morton gave Harold Fraley a list of them to pass on to the caretaker. The next day, when the cleaning had been finished, Morton took Julia to shops in the city to select the furnishings. Drapes and some of the furniture had to be made, and were delivered piecemeal during the following days. On the afternoon that the last items were brought and set into place, Morton went through the house again with Julia, and they agreed that his mother would be pleased with it.

Shortly after Morton returned to work to finish up for the day, an apprentice came to the office door and started to announce a visitor. The boy broke off with a startled squeak as a hand gripped his collar from behind and jerked him aside. Aldous Creevey stepped into the doorway, filling it. The thick floorboards creaked under the huge man's weight as he stepped into the office, the apprentice peering apprehensively around the doorjamb at him, and Morton motioned for the boy to leave.

Creevey stepped up in front of the desk, his beady eyes glittering with anger. "Where is Benjamin Tavish?" he demanded in his falsetto voice.

Morton concealed his surprise and alarm over what the question revealed, and he shrugged, sitting back in his chair. "Seeking his fortunes elsewhere," he replied casually. "Why do you ask?"

"He took property of mine when he left here."

"Property?" Morton echoed, puzzled. "What sort of property?"

"Clothing. Specifically, women's clothing. There was a woman in my household who was my wife, and I invested monies in clothing for her. Benjamin Tavish took that clothing with him when he left here."

Morton's anger flared at the man's choice of terms, which implied that Beverly was of so little value as to be not worth mentioning. "I'm at a loss to understand you," he said acidly. "Are you telling me that Benjamin Tavish absconded with your wife, or was it only with her wardrobe? And whichever it was, on what basis do you accuse him?"

"On the basis of inquiries during the past weeks," Creevey replied in his thin voice. "He managed your real estate, which included a house adjacent to mine." The man reached into his coat pocket, then tossed a woman's handkerchief onto the desk with his thick, puffy fingers. "That is more of my property, as is the perfume on it, and it was found in the house beside mine. He left Sydney at the same time that my property disappeared, reportedly en route to Bombay on a vessel outbound to Trincomalee. He was not on the ship's passenger manifest, and he is not in Bombay. Now where is he?"

Morton was dismayed by how much the man knew, but he took comfort in the fact that Creevey's investigation had come to a dead end. "This has nothing to do with me," Morton said coldly. "If you have evidence of a crime, you should take it to the attorney general."

For the first time, Morton saw the man's broad, expressionless mask of a face reveal emotion. It twisted and flushed with rage, and his tiny eyes gleamed. "Do you think I'm such a fool as to make myself a laughing-stock in the town?" he hissed. "You would enjoy that, because it would substantiate the tale you will spread, wouldn't it?"

"I intend to spread no tales," Morton replied brusquely. "I have more to do with my time than to gossip."

Creevey grabbed the handkerchief and shoved it into his coat pocket, then pointed a bloated finger at Morton. "You know where Benjamin Tavish is," he snarled. "I intend to destroy you. In every conceivable way, I intend to ruin you and grind you into dust."

The huge man turned and lumbered ponderously out of the office, the floorboards squeaking beneath him. Morton pondered for a time, weighing the implications of the conversation. Then he dismissed it, deciding to wait until he discussed it with Julia and had the benefit of her insights. He turned to the papers on his desk and finished his work for the day.

When he went home, he waited until he and Julia were alone in the parlor before he told her about the conversation. They discussed what Creevey knew, agreeing that he could have learned it through ordinary means. He could have written to an acquaintance in Bombay to find out if Benjamin was there, and the Admiralty Office kept file copies of passenger manifests of outbound ships.

"And it was common knowledge that Benjamin managed my real estate," Morton added. "However, it involved time and trouble for Creevey to inquire into Benjamin's activities that closely. I can't believe he did that on everyone who left here at about the time Beverly disappeared. For some reason, he was suspicious of Benjamin. That's what I didn't expect, and not expecting it led me to think that he wouldn't find out what happened."

"Yes, what made him suspicious of Benjamin to begin with?" Julia mused. "Morton, that suggests that he is aware of what occurs in your offices. The only conclusion I can draw is that someone in your offices is either given to much loose talk, or is passing on information to him. It's past time for you to take a close look at your employees."

Morton reluctantly agreed, not wanting to believe that he would be betrayed by an employee, but the facts indicated it was likely. The conversation moved on to Creevey's threat, and Morton talked with Julia about what the man might do. The possibilities were endless, because Creevey was without scruples. They concluded that all Morton could do at present was to take reasonable precautions to protect his property, while at the same time being watchful for any indication of a plot devised by Creevey.

Of all his employees, Morton had known his head clerk the longest and was absolutely certain that he could trust the man. When he went to work the next day, Morton called Albert Loman up to his office and closed the door to talk with him privately. Making no mention of Benjamin, Morton said only that he believed Creevey was obtaining information from the offices.

"It could be that someone is talking to the wrong people whilst in his cups," Morton continued, "or it could be worse. I don't want to think that an employee would exchange information for coin, but it's at least possible.

The work here is fairly well separated between the different clerks, so what you should look for is someone who is unduly interested in what others are doing and in their files of correspondence."

"And perhaps look into the employees' activities outside the offices," Albert suggested. "Like you, I don't want to believe that we have a traitor in our midst, Sir Morton. However, I'll certainly investigate all of the possibilities. With your permission, I'll have Harold Fraley help me with this. I've known him since we were boys, and I trust him implicitly. He's very discreet, and two can see more than one who looks twice."

"Very well. Most of all, you must proceed cautiously so you won't alert anyone who may be engaged in wrongdoing. If it takes a month, two months, or six, then so be it. And I pray to God that I am mistaken, and that none of our employees is disloyal."

The head clerk agreed somberly as he left the office. Morton began going through the papers on his desk, thinking about what else to do. The previous evening, he and Julia had discussed the chances of sabotage at the dry dock and ropewalk, concluding that it would be characteristic of Creevey. After looking through the papers on his desk, Morton stepped to the door and called downstairs to have his carriage brought around to the entrance.

While talking with the foreman at the dry dock, Morton merely expressed concern about the danger of vandalism and theft of tools, and Virgil Handley replied that he would immediately set about finding a reliable nightwatchman. The workmen at the ropewalk, a more closely knit group with a more proprietary attitude toward their shop, wanted no outsider prowling about it at night. Isaac Tulk said he would schedule the men for extra shifts at night as guards, and Morton agreed to pay them extra wages.

The income Morton received from leased houses was more than that from the dry dock and ropewalk, and the amount invested in them was much greater. However, they were scattered all over the city, and there was no means of protecting them. Morton grimly accepted that risk and then looked for other ways in which Creevey might retaliate.

The papers passing across Morton's desk and the activities in his offices remained routine, with no indication of anything untoward. Later in the week, he had meetings at the Bank of Commerce and at the Maritime Assurance Company, and he closely examined the reports on the activities of the firms. The profits of both were low, but Morton found no evidence of any sort of underhanded plot against either of the firms.

A week went by without any indication that Creevey was fulfilling his threat, then another week passed quietly. Morton remained alert, knowing that the greatest danger was a false sense of security. In the same methodical, painstaking way that the head clerk did everything, he was proceeding about monitoring the activities of the other employees. He was finding nothing in the least suspicious, and Morton was unsure of whether to be relieved or even more worried about how Creevey was obtaining his information.

On the oppressively hot, humid afternoon in February when Morton's mother arrived, Julia sent the stableboy to inform him. She had also sent word to Deirdre and Eudora, and they reached the house at the same time that he did. It was a scene of pandemonium, with stockmen, jackaroos, and the household staff from Tibooburra Station unloading wagons that filled the carriage drive beside the house and overflowed into Wentworth Street.

The staff from Morton's house was also there, helping out and serving the refreshments that Julia had kept ready for the occasion. A large trestle table beside the house was filled with food and tureens of rum and ginger punch for the employees. For the family, there was a buffet of choice delicacies and bottles of wine on ice in the parlor.

During the joyful reunion, Morton's main concerns were his mother's health after the long journey in the sweltering heat, and how she was bearing up under the emotional strain of her husband's and son's deaths. He saw that with the resilient vitality that was so much a part of her character, she had endured both in a way that few could have equaled. The ordeals had taken a much greater toll on his sister-in-law. Catherine was exuberantly happy that they had arrived, but she looked much older than her years.

For the next two days, Julia spent most of her time at the house to help Alexandra and Catherine get settled in. The household was fully organized by the second day, when the stockmen and jackaroos left with the wagons. On the following day, a Sunday, Morton and Julia hosted a family gathering at their home. An hour after everyone had arrived, Morton left Julia entertaining Deirdre, Eudora, and Catherine, and took his mother outside to show her the gardens and to talk with her.

Over the past three days, Morton had observed that Catherine was inclined to be nervous and emotional, and he had concluded that was one reason his mother had moved to Sydney. He referred to it, then continued, "As you well know, Julia and I are delighted that you're here, but we're also mindful of your wishes. We could have provided a home for Catherine."

"No, at least for the present, she needs to be with someone who knows her well," Alexandra replied. "Now that she's living here in the city, she will probably improve rapidly. In any event, her condition is no reflection on her character, because she has endured much."

"Indeed she has. Mother, I've never known you to complain or even air any problems, but I know you'd rather be at the station. Circumstances have placed you here, though, and I do hope you'll be happy."

"You and my other loved ones are here, so I have that many reasons to be happy," she told him. "Silas Doak will have to see to the affairs of the station now, and he'll do a much better job of it than when he felt obliged to come to me for inadequate instructions." She shrugged, laughing. "And I'll have work to keep me busy. I noticed that the flower beds are in a state that will occupy my time in restoring them."

Morton laughed and nodded, knowing that she was looking forward to the gardening. Alexandra asked how his business affairs were progressing, and he told her about Benjamin, Beverly, and the potential for trouble from Creevey. Then he hastened to ease any worries that she might have about the situation, explaining the measures he had taken to thwart the man.

A few minutes later, they went back into the house and rejoined the others. Morton observed that his mother appeared to be correct in believing that Catherine would overcome her emotional problems. As she talked with her daughter and the other women, his sister-in-law was more cheerful and outgoing than she had been since her arrival in Sydney.

Alexandra gave an impression of being in good spirits, but Morton knew that her feelings were mixed at best. He realized that she was grimly resigned to living in Sydney, as well as worried about the future of the station. When she and the other guests left after dinner, Morton discussed his mother's situation with Julia, and they agreed to do everything they could to help her adjust to her new life and to make her happy.

The following day, Sydney baked in the stifling heat of late summer as another week began. Business activities were at an ebb, because the full effects of economic conditions in Britain were beginning to be felt. The commerce between ports in Australia and those from India to the Sandwich Islands had declined, and most of the vessels entering and leaving the harbor were coastal traders or those sailing no farther than New Zealand.

The heat continued on into the week, with no hint of a sea breeze to cool the torridly hot streets and offices. Work was finished on a ship in Morton's dry dock on Tuesday, and no other vessels were scheduled for refitting. Other dry docks and shipyards in the harbor were idle, and most of their workers had been laid off. While there was no reason to believe that conditions would improve in the near future, Morton kept his employees on wages and had them do what they could to repair the leaky walls of the dock.

On Wednesday afternoon, Morton was sitting in his sweltering office in shirtsleeves and with his necktie loosened when a heavy footstep made him look up from the papers on his desk. Aldous Creevey stood in the doorway, awash in sweat. His broad, puffy face gleamed wetly from the rivulets trickling down it, and his coat was darker in spots where the perspiration from his bloated body had seeped all the way through his clothes. When he stepped into the office, a mustily sour odor wafted ahead of him in the breathlessly hot, still air.

"While at the Merchants Exchange and other places that businessmen frequent," he remarked in his falsetto voice, "I've heard no mention of what we discussed during our last conversation."

"I told you then that I have more to do with my time than to spread gossip," Morton said curtly. "What do you want here?"

"I wish to inform you that I will be equally discreet about your personal affairs," Creevey replied. "You are aware that I bought the *Chronicle*, aren't you? Whilst looking through the back issues, I discovered matters that would embarrass you no end. However, I have kept silent about them, and I intend to continue doing so in the future."

Morton was unable to recall any hint of his relationship with Clara Tavish in the newspapers, but he was sure that was what Creevey had discovered. "I have no desire to make little of a generous impulse on your part," he commented acidly, "as astonishing as it may be. And for reasons that you would never understand, I'm heartily ashamed of my conduct in connection with Clara Tavish. However, the facts were known at large long before you came here, including to my beloved wife, and it's of no—" He broke off as Creevey shook his head. "It isn't that? Well, what is it, then?"

Creevey's beady eyes gleamed with sardonic amuse-

ment as he sat on the chair beside the desk. Along with
an acrid odor of sweat, his huge body exuded moist heat,
and the thick legs of the chair groaned as it disappeared
under him. Taking two old, yellowed newspapers from
his coat pocket, he selected one and unfolded it. He
placed it on the desk and pushed it toward Morton, pointing to a notice in the center of the front page.

The first thing that caught Morton's eye was the ob-
solete typography, with a connective *s* that was similar
to an *f*. Glancing at the top of the page, he saw that the
date was nearly forty-five years before, in September of
1821. He reflected that the newspaper could hardly have
mentioned his relationship with Clara Tavish, because
it had been printed almost a year before he had been
born, in June of 1822. Then he read the notice.

It offered a reward of five hundred sovereigns for information on the whereabouts of Alexandra Hammond.
The description was that of a tall, attractive woman,
nineteen years of age. The notice stated that she had been
seen last at Camden Park and was feared to have been
abducted by bushrangers known to be in the area, who
were Enos Hinton, Daniel Crowley, and Frank Snively.
It ended with a request for persons with any knowledge
of her whereabouts to contact her father, Nevil Hammond, at his law offices in Sydney.

"You've observed the date, of course," Creevey sneered,
oozing vindictive glee along with his sour sweat. "Your
mother was kidnapped by bushrangers not much more
than nine months before you were born."

"What are you suggesting?." Morton demanded hotly,
enraged. "I was unaware of this, but a fool could understand why my mother would be loath to discuss it. But
if it had anything to do with me personally, she would
have long since told me. So I won't listen to insinuations
about—"

Morton broke off, the mocking smirk on Creevey's puffy
face revealing that the first newspaper had been only a
preparation for the second one. Creevey unfolded it to
the back page as he placed it on the desk and pushed it

toward Morton. Feeling numb with a fear totally unlike any he had ever experienced before, Morton looked at the newspaper.

It was dated about a year before the first one, and an article at the bottom of the page concerned two of the bushrangers, Hinton and Crowley. The article stated that they had escaped from the convict compound at Parramatta and were suspected of having stolen two horses and foodstuffs from a nearby settlement. Another sentence warned that aiding them in any way was a criminal offense, and there were descriptions of the men. Creevey reached over, his thick finger pointing to that of Enos Hinton.

The man's height had been the same as Morton's. According to the description, Enos Hinton's most obvious identifying characteristic had been a birthmark on the side of his face, and it had been crimson, like the one on Morton's shoulder. Another readily noticeable feature in the description had been the unusually pale blue color of the man's eyes.

"You were fathered by a blackguard, so it's little wonder that you protect blackguards like Benjamin Tavish," Creevey jeered, heaving himself up from the chair and lumbering toward the door. "As I said, I'll not mention this to anyone. I prefer to work quietly, but this is only the beginnging. I told you that I would destroy you, and I intend to do just that."

In his state of shock, Morton barely heard the words or noticed that the man had left. From his boyhood and all through the years when he had been largely indifferent toward other people, one person had still meant everything to him. The devoted love between himself and his mother had been a stable, dependable anchor in his life during all those years.

He had thought that their mutual love had been solidly based on trust and complete openness with each other, but on her side there had been deceit. What he feared most in life was betrayal. And now it had come from the one he had always trusted most, the one he had always loved.

Numbly, he folded the newspapers and then stepped to the door, calling downstairs for his carriage to be brought around. Then, with the newspapers in his coat pocket, he went downstairs. The head clerk said something that was a meaningless sound to Morton, and he ignored it, going outside to the carriage. On the way to the Whitlam district, the stifling heat brought out beads of sweat on his face that blended with his tears.

When the carriage was halfway up the drive and beside the house, Morton thumped his cane on the floor for it to stop. He stepped out and walked on up the drive to the garden behind the house, knowing his mother would be there. She was kneeling beside a flower bed and digging it up with a trowel.

As she stood up, she saw his face. Her smile of greeting changing to an expression of concern, she started to ask what was wrong. Then the words died on her lips and her face blanched with dismay when he took out the newspapers, showing them to her.

Neither of them spoke for a moment. Alexandra silently gazed at the newspapers in stunned consternation, while Morton was rendered speechless by his seething turmoil of emotions. Then he found his tongue. "Why didn't you tell me about this, Mother?" he demanded hoarsely in distress. "Why did you betray me? How could you have done this to me?"

Alexandra searched for words, then burst into tears. "It happened so very long ago, Morton," she sobbed. "By the time you were old enough to understand, I thought it was completely forgotten. Then I thought it would remain in the past, and I could only do what I thought best."

"That isn't an answer!" he shouted, flinging the newspapers to the ground. "That's utter foolishness! How could you have thought it best to deceive me and keep something like this from me? That's absurd!"

"But I believed that no one would ever know, Morton,"

she protested tearfully. "I'm only one of God's creatures, a mortal human being, and I can't see into the future. I thought it was forgotten, and ..." Her voice fading, she put her hands over her face as she sobbed brokenly. "And I was so ashamed! So terribly, terribly ashamed, Morton. My penalty for a moment of poor judgment has been a lifetime of suffering this shame. I wanted to protect you from any part of what I have endured."

Morton shook his head, groaning in anguish. "Protect me?" he echoed bitterly. "Do you call this protecting me? You couldn't have devised a way to make me more vulnerable. I had to find this out from Creevey. From that swine Creevey! Ever since I was a boy, I've always trusted you, because I thought you and I were so close in our feelings for each other."

"We are, Morton, we are!" she cried. "God is my witness, I've opened my heart to you in my thoughts and feelings, as well as my love. I've never kept anything back from you except this, Morton."

"But this was the most important of all. This was—" His voice broke with a sob, then he drew in a deep breath and continued, "I trusted you implicitly, Mother, but you deceived me."

"I'm sorry, Morton, I'm sorry," she wailed, reaching out to him. "God knows I meant only to protect you, and I beg you to forgive me."

"No!" he replied, tears streaming down his face as he moved back. "You betrayed my trust in you, and I can't forgive that. Mother, I would give years from my life if this had never happened, because I love you with all my heart. But I can never forgive such a ..." His voice faded as he began sobbing wretchedly, and he turned away, going back toward the carriage.

The driver had turned it around, ready to leave. Morton pulled his hat low and ducked his head to keep the driver from seeing his face as he went down the drive and stepped into the carriage. It moved toward the street, and he buried his face in his hands, weeping bitterly.

Almost blinded by tears, Alexandra gathered up the

newspapers. In an instinctive reaction from many years of concealing the shameful secret, she folded and tucked them into her pocket to dispose of later. Then, out of a lifetime habit of filling her hours with productive activity, she knelt beside the flower bed and resumed loosening the soil with the trowel.

Across the vast chasm between the world of the living and that of the dead, a vindictive, baneful laugh seemed to ring in her ears. In the seconds before David shot him dead, Enos Hinton had jeeringly told her that she would never be rid of him. And in a very real way, he had told the truth. His evil, corrupt presence was still entwined with her life and those of her loved ones, no matter how she had strived to purge it. After years of illusory victories, she thought she had finally exorcised Hinton from her life completely.

Now he was back. Decades had passed, and now the vile, depraved ghost of Enos Hinton had returned. At other times, some way of fighting his evil had been at hand. But this onslaught had been more successful, totally crushing her. Enos Hinton had won the final victory, because she knew of nothing she could do. She lacked the means of fighting back, as well as the energy.

In her youth and prime, her battles against the specter of Enos Hinton and other difficulties besetting her had been pursued eagerly, even joyously. During those years, her vigor had been inexhaustible, her strides long and her footsteps firm. But fate had reserved the worst blows for her autumn years, when her strength of body and of spirit had waned.

Her husband and younger son were gone. Her elder son had turned against her. The future of Tibooburra Station, the achievement of her lifetime, was seriously in doubt. As she loosened the soil with the towel, she dampened it with her tears. For the first time in her life, she knew utter despair.

PART III

Chapter Seventeen

"Cease your bloody scavvy!" Seton Donley roared, his fist lashing out viciously. "I'll not listen to such talk from you!"

Fiona Donley flinched nimbly, her father's fist just missing her face as she darted around to the other side of the heavy, homemade kitchen table. She struggled to control her temper, trying to talk reasonably. "But I need a shilling or two for the doctor," she repeated. "Dr. Willis will be here this morning, and Mother is almost out of her medicine. It's been weeks since the doctor has had a ha'penny. What am I to tell him?"

"You bloody tell him to come and talk with me," Donley snarled, tapping his chest with a finger. "If he has any complaints, I'll soon end them."

It was his answer for everything, because most people were frightened of him. A large, muscular man with an aggressive, overbearing personality, he enjoyed trouble and tyrannizing others. That created constant friction between him and Fiona, because he was unable to dominate her.

She was wary of him, but never frightened, and he knew it. At eighteen, she had reached the full flush of womanhood, her tall body slim and hard from grueling labor since childhood. Her luxuriant mass of hair was a fiery, shimmering red, and the fable of the disposition that accompanied red hair was fulfilled in her, her temper and will matching her father's.

"You'll get your just deserts, Seton Donley," she said, glaring her hatred with her large, green eyes. "Sooner or later, you'll be brought to account for how you've dealt with your family."

Her use of his full name—the way she always addressed and referred to him—was at once a denial of relationship, a statement of equality with him, and a calculated insult. He ground his teeth in rage, poised to leap at her, but they both knew he would be unable to catch her. Shrugging in dismissal, he stamped out the back door. Fiona stepped to the door to see if her brother was about, knowing he would be a target for their father's anger. Christopher was evidently hiding in a barn or shed until their father left.

Then she saw that Donley was taking another of the pigs that she had been fattening to provide food for the winter. As he had done before, he intended to sell it at the market and then squander the money on drink. Rage exploded within her, and she gripped the doorjamb to restrain herself from running out and screaming at him to find work instead of selling her pigs.

Donley ignored Fiona standing in the kitchen doorway, guiding the pig with a stick as he herded it across the barnyard and past the house to the road leading into Brisbane. When he was gone, her wrath subsided into constant smoldering resentment toward her father. Setting about her work, Fiona went out to the well for a bucket of water and carried it into her mother's bedroom to attend to her.

For as long as Fiona could remember, Mavis Donley

had looked weary, careworn, and much older than her years. Constant drudgery and her husband's cruelties had broken her spirit, and life had been hard on her in other ways. Four of her eight children had been buried in Brisbane Cemetery from childhood diseases, and her two oldest sons had fled from their father's tyranny as soon as they had reached their mid-teens.

Stricken with cancer, now she was pale and gaunt, having lost weight rapidly during the past few weeks. Her voice was a hoarse, weak whisper as she spoke. "Did he hit you?" she asked.

Fiona laughed and shook her head, hiding her reaction to her mother's appearance with a cheery attitude. "No, don't worry about that, Mother."

"Have you spoken with Christopher about leaving?"

"Yes, I did yesterday, and I will again today," Fiona replied, pointing to the bowl on the table beside the bed. "You hardly touched your porridge."

"It's very tasty, but my appetite is poor, love. Perhaps it'll improve as the day wears on, and I'll have a good tiffin and dinner."

Smiling to conceal her worry, Fiona knew it was unlikely that her mother would eat very much more during the day. She washed her mother and straightened the bedclothes, and when she finished, she took a spoon and the laudanum bottle off a shelf above the bed. Her mother's eyes brightened in anticipation of relief from the pain that racked her body.

Fiona carefully filled the spoon, leaving very little in the bottle, then put it to her mother's lips. Within moments, the powerful tincture of opium had taken effect, and her mother sank into a semiconscious state. Fiona carried the porridge bowl and bucket into the kitchen. She emptied the porridge into the bucket of slops for the pigs, then washed the breakfast dishes and put the kitchen in order. Carrying the slops bucket and a milk bucket, she stepped outside and crossed the barnyard.

Her brother had emerged from hiding and was halfheartedly hoeing down the weeds between the rows

of vegetables in the crop fields set back from the barn
and sheds. A tall, thin youth of fifteen, Christopher had
a heavily freckled face and hair that was a more coppery
color than Fiona's brilliant red tresses. As she poured the
slops into the trough in the pigpen, she shouted and beckoned him.

He came toward her, but with chores that filled every
minute of the day, Fiona had no time to stand and wait
for him. She went into the barn, where she put an armful
of fodder into the feed bin in the cow's stall. As it ate,
she sat on her stool and milked it. A moment later, Christopher came into the barn and sat down at the stall door.
He chewed a stem of hay and averted his face, his eyes
avoiding Fiona's.

"Well?" she prompted him, milking with both hands.

"There's a sloop," he said reluctantly. "It's leaving for
Melbourne tomorrow morning. The master is the owner,
and he said that he'd take me as a deck hand. But I'd
best not leave yet, Fiona."

"Why?"

"You can't manage here by yourself. Mother was able
to help with the planting last spring, and I helped out
between jobs. You can't—"

"Stop seeking excuses!" Fiona interrupted angrily.
"Make up your mind to either go or remain here, but
stop searching for excuses!"

He turned away, and the cow shifted uneasily. In her
anger, Fiona had begun putting too much of the wiry
strength in her long, slender arms and hands into tugging
on the cow's teats. Drawing in a deep breath, she controlled her temper as she continued milking. She burned
with envy over Christopher's freedom of action as a male,
but she also loved him.

"Mother wants you to go, love," she said gently. "And
so do I. I know it's frightening for a lad to leave everything he's known, but Calvin and Julian left when they
were about your age. I'm sure they're very happy now,
and you would be as well. But you must decide for yourself."

"What would you do if you were me?"

"I'd go west and across the Divide, climbing with my fingernails and teeth if need be. Then I'd keep going across the Downs and into the outback. I'd find some way of providing for myself and live there, away from all this misery and trouble. But what I've just said is a foolish answer to a senseless question, because you and I aren't the same."

Christopher fell silent until she finished milking, then he stood up and moved aside as she carried the milk out of the stall. "I'll go on the sloop, then," he muttered. "I'll have to do it so Father won't see me."

"Seton Donley will be swilling in the taverns until tonight. Go tell the captain that you'll come aboard this afternoon. I'll give Mother only a bit of laudanum after tiffin so you'll be able to talk with her and say goodbye, then you can collect your clothes and leave."

Christopher nodded and then suddenly began crying. Fiona put her arms around him and held him for a moment, kissing him. Then the youth left the barn, wiping his eyes with his sleeve, and tears stung in Fiona's eyes. Partly due to sadness that her brother was leaving, they were also tears of frustrated anger because she was unable to leave herself.

For over two years, young men in the town had attempted to call on her, but her father had driven them away. Luckily, she detested idleness and enjoyed hard, productive work, and it usually took her mind off her situation. Another escape was reading, her single pastime.

On occasion, a neighbor finished a book from the rental library in the town before it was due and let her borrow it for the days that remained. Fiona gladly went without sleep to read and return the books on time, and she devoured every word of old newspapers and magazines that neighbors gave her. But reading and work were only temporary, incomplete means of escape, and physically she remained chained to her circumstances.

After putting the cow out to pasture, Fiona took the

milk to the cellar. That from the previous day had finished curdling, and she churned it, then scooped off the butter into wooden molds and took most of the buttermilk to the pigs. While she was feeding the chickens and gathering eggs, she saw the doctor's buggy coming up the road, and she went to the house to meet him.

Dr. Oliver Willis was an amiable, softly-spoken man in his fifties, his face always lined from too little sleep. He went into the bedroom to examine Mavis, and Fiona heated water in the iron kettle on the fireplace hob to make tea. When the doctor came into the kitchen and sat at the table, he was more somber than usual, and Fiona's heart sank.

She poured the tea, asking about her mother, and the doctor replied that very little time remained. "But only a fortnight ago, you said that she had several months left," Fiona protested.

An honest, modest man, the doctor nodded and admitted that he had been wrong. "I was judging by another patient who had the same type of cancer," he continued. "That was years ago, when I had a practice in Sydney, and her name was Mistress Clara Tavish."

"She lived longer? Why?"

"Perhaps because she had a reason to," the doctor replied. He took a drink of tea, then shrugged as he set the pannikin down. "The will to live is much better medicine than that any doctor can provide, Fiona. Mistress Tavish had several children, as I remember, but only one was small. She wanted to make arrangements for the child's care, then she intended to return to Scotland to save her children the grief of seeing her pass away. So while she had a reason to live, her strength remained. It appears that your mother doesn't have that will to live."

"There's God's truth," Fiona remarked bitterly.

The doctor sighed, reaching over and patting her hand. "It's certainly no secret that your father is a cruel man, so I know that your life is far from easy either, my dear. Is there anything I can do to help you?"

"By looking after my mother, you've done what I want

most, Dr. Willis. In any event, there are others with a worse life than mine. I have my work and a bit of reading now and again, both of which I enjoy."

"Most would consider your work here a very hard life indeed," he told her, smiling wryly. "Your father doesn't realize how fortunate he is." The doctor finished his tea, then took a bottle of laudanum out of his black bag as he stood up. "I noticed that you have very little laudanum left."

Fiona took the bottle, embarrassed because she had no money. "I'll try to pay you the next time, Dr. Willis," she said apologetically.

He dismissed it with a smile. "I'll collect an extra florin from the next rich merchant I treat for gout from over-indulgence. Remember that your mother is to have only three spoonfuls a day. More would be dangerous."

Nodding in understanding, Fiona thanked the doctor, then saw him out. It was almost midday, and she began preparing tiffin when she returned to the kitchen. She worked furiously hard to suppress her sorrow over her mother's rapidly worsening condition. In addition, a practical concern that had been distant had now drawn closer. Her mother had inherited the farm, and the terms of the will prevented its sale until after her death.

On many occasions, Fiona had heard Donley curse the farm for being so far from his work as a laborer at the docks. He was presently unemployed, because he was known as a troublemaker, and he had been one of the first to be laid off when fewer vessels had begun arriving at the port. However, after her mother's death, Fiona feared he would sell the farm and rent one of the hovels in the alleys around Petrie Bight, where many dock workers lived.

When she finished preparing tiffin, Fiona took a tray to her mother. Mavis had emerged from the effects of the laudanum, her face drawn with pain, but she smiled as Fiona told her about Christopher's decision. "I'm very pleased," she whispered weakly. "When does he leave?"

"Tomorrow morning, and he'll board the sloop this

afternoon. I'll give you only a small amount of laudanum for now so you can talk with him."

"Very well. I'm so worried about you, Fiona. What will you do?"

"I'll abide, Mother. Don't you worry about me."

Mavis nodded doubtfully, trying to smile. Fiona sat on the edge of the bed and fed her mother. Mavis ate only a small amount, and after half a spoonful of laudanum, she sank into a stupor. Fiona took the tray back to the kitchen and ate quickly, having little appetite herself.

During early afternoon, a grocer's apprentice came with a cart for the eggs and butter. Fiona had no idea of how much the grocer was paying for them, because Donley collected the money. She helped the apprentice carry them to the cart, then went to the crop fields as the boy left.

It was time to select choice vegetables to use for seed the next year, and Fiona marked them with stakes. While examining vegetables and occasionally pushing a stake into the soil beside one plant, she was haunted by a fear that it would be someone else who planted the fields the following spring. Then, seeing Christopher coming up the road, she hurried to the house.

Her passing concern that he might have changed his mind faded when she saw his forlorn expression. She put tiffin on the table for him while their mother recovered more of her awareness, but he wanted nothing to eat. He bundled his belongings in his room, then went to talk with their mother.

When he came out, he was crying brokenly. Fiona also wept as she held and kissed him, and led him to the front door. Standing in the doorway, she watched him trudge down the road. After he was lost from view, she went to her mother's room. With tears streaming from her eyes, Mavis opened her lips eagerly for the other half spoonful of laudanum. Fiona waited until it took effect, then she returned to the crop fields.

At sunset, she milked the cow again and did the other evening chores.

While dinner was cooking, she mended clothes by the fire, then took a tray to her mother. Mavis ate more than usual and talked with Fiona for a few minutes before taking her laudanum, seeming very much at peace in her mind now that Christopher had left. Fiona ate dinner in the kitchen and put a plate of food for her father on the hob before going to bed.

She woke when he came home late in the night, stumbling about drunkenly, then she fell asleep again. At dawn the next morning, Fiona went into the kitchen to start breakfast, and the food was still on the hob. She emptied it into the pail of slops for the pigs, reflecting that it was being put to better use there, and filled the kettle to make porridge.

Donley was up earlier than usual, moving about his room and muttering. Then he stamped into the kitchen, his eyes bloodshot and a strong odor of rum eddying around him. "Where the bloody hell is Christopher?" he demanded. "I met a bricklayer last night whose hod carrier fell and broke an arm. If that whelp will get his arse down there and talk to the bricklayer, he might get the job. Where the bloody hell is he?"

"He's gone," Fiona replied. "He left home."

"Gone?" Donley thundered. "Left home? Just when he might have brought in a fair wage for a change! Where the bloody hell did he go? And why the bloody hell didn't you tell me so I could stop him?"

Fiona resisted suggesting that he work for the bricklayer himself, not wanting her mother disturbed by another loud argument. "He left as a deck hand on a ship," she said. "I learned about it only yesterday, when he left, and I didn't know where you were."

Donley threw himself down on the bench at the table, holding his head in his hands and cursing. Then he sat up and began eating as Fiona put a bowl of porridge and pannikin of tea on the table. She filled another bowl and took it through the house to her mother's room.

In the instant before she entered the room, Fiona knew that no one was there. As she stepped inside, the first thing she noticed was the laudanum bottle on the table beside the bed. During the night, her mother had found the strength to get the bottle off the shelf, and it was half empty. Fiona stepped to the side of the bed and put the bowl on the table.

Her mother's calloused hands were cold as Fiona folded them together on her mother's chest. She closed her mother's eyes and kissed her, then wiped away the tears that had fallen on the gaunt, wrinkled face. Then she picked up the bowl and went back toward the kitchen.

Donley looked up from his breakfast as she put the bowl on the washstand and stood gazing out the window. "What's wrong with you?" he growled.

"Mother has passed away," Fiona said quietly.

He stood up with a grunt of effort and tramped heavily toward the bedroom. Fiona looked out at what had been a very ordinary day only a short time before. Now it was profoundly different from any other day of her life, even the sunshine seeming to have an unusual character. A precious bond that had been a joy in her life from her earliest childhood memories had been broken, and nothing would ever be quite the same again.

Donley returned and sat down, then resumed eating. "I'll go see about an undertaker," he growled. "That'll cost a pretty penny."

Fiona went outside and crossed the barnyard to the tool shed. She took out a hoe and carried it to the crop fields. Then she began chopping down weeds, lifting the hoe high and slamming it into the ground with all of her strength while tears streamed down her face.

The funeral arrangements were frugal, but neighbors prevented it from appearing miserly. Dozens from surrounding small farms and the workers' row houses down the road came to the funeral with flowers to cover the cheap coffin, and a stone mason among them had made a headstone for the grave in the far corner of the cemetery. Fiona understood why none had ever offered her mother help—no one wanting to do anything that might cause trouble with Donley—and she was grateful that they had made the funeral more reverent.

During the days that followed the funeral, Fiona's grief was tempered by the knowledge that her mother was at peace, free of the sheer misery that had been her life. For several days, Fiona saw little of Donley except at breakfast. He had papers with him at times, and she presumed that he was seeing to legal matters and securing the deed to the farm.

Then, while cleaning out the barn one day, she saw him leading the team of horses in from the pasture, and she asked what he was doing. "I'm taking them to the stockyards to sell them," he explained. "I had to go into debt for the funeral, and I have other expenses that must be paid."

"How can I till the fields to plant them next spring without horses?" she asked. "I can't pull a plow and a harrow myself."

"That's next spring, and I need money now," he replied, leading the horses away. "We'll worry about next spring when it gets here."

Fiona then knew that he intended to sell the farm. Even though she had anticipated it, the certainty was a crushing disappointment. She tried to think of somewhere she could go or something she could do to avoid moving to a hovel in Brisbane, but she had no alternatives. Trapped by circumstances, she could only endure what Donley decided to do.

In the meantime, she had her work, and she concentrated her thoughts as well as her energy upon it. Because of that, a few days passed before she analyzed and drew conclusions from what Donley was doing. In a distinct change of behavior, he became concerned about his appearance. He spent part of the money from the horses on clothes, he kept his beard trimmed neatly, and he wanted a shirt ironed from time to time. When she detected a faint scent of perfume about him at breakfast one morning, Fiona considered all the other facts and realized that he was courting some woman.

Her meeting with the woman was brief and conclusive, and it took her by surprise. She returned from feeding the pigs one day, and Donley was sitting at the kitchen table with the woman. He introduced her, his eyes warning Fiona to be friendly. Violet Slattery was a frowsy, bawdy-looking woman in her fifties with a mean, calculating face and gaudy clothes.

"Is that a slops bucket you have there?" she asked, her jovial smile not reaching her narrow eyes. "Does Seton make you attend a piggery?"

"He has no need to make me. It's honest work, which I enjoy."

"You could do much better, deary. With a bit more flesh on your bones, your looks and that hair would draw men like flies to honey. Working in a tavern, you could fill it to overflowing every night."

"I don't consort with riffraff."

The cold, hard expression in the woman's eyes spread over her face, and she silenced Donley with a glare when he started to erupt angrily. Then she turned back to Fiona. "Riffraff?" she barked. "You little vixen, I'll have you know that I own a tavern!"

"Well, it's never too late to mend, as Mr. Reade points out in his book of that title. You could always dispose of it and buy a millinery or some other business of a respectable sort."

"Enough of your bloody scavvy!" Donley roared, leaping up from the table. "By God, I'll still your wagging tongue with my fist!"

Violet grabbed the table and caught herself, almost falling as Donley tipped over the bench under her. Then she turned away, dismissing Fiona with a gesture of disgust. "Leave it, Seton," she said. "Let's go."

"No, by God!" he stored. "This is my house, and I—"

"I said to leave it!" the woman screamed in his face. "In my business, the one lot I have naught to do with is the goodwives of the town, and I know one when I see one. She might be your whelp, but she's a different sort entirely. Now I'm going. If you want to go with me, come on!''

They stamped out, Donley shaking his fist at Fiona in a threat of what he would do later. She set the bench back upright and went on with her work, but she remained alert in the event he returned unexpectedly.

Donley came home at sunset, completely sober for once, and what happened was much less than Fiona had expected. He merely ranted, raved, and threatened, after which the incident with Violet Slattery seemed to be ended. The next morning, he was no more brusque than he usually was when in a bad mood and faced with some problem he was trying to resolve.

Thinking about it later, Fiona realized that a tide had turned in their relationship. All of her life, he had been a burden to her, but now the situation was reversed. Violet Slattery wanted nothing to do with her, and she had become a burden to him in that she was an obstacle to his romance, such as it was.

Nothing happened for a few days, Donley evidently seeking a solution to his problem, but then another change of an entirely different type occurred. When she stepped out of bed one morning, Fiona knew that the first touch of autumn had arrived. Through her close harmony with the cycles of growing things and to the flux of nature, she could feel the difference throughout her body. The foliage looked the same, and the day was just as warm as the one before, but she knew that the season of harvest had begun.

That night, the heavens exploded in a dazzling display of lightning as a thunderstorm swept across the landscape toward the mountains to the west. It was an opportunity for a bath that Fiona enjoyed much more than in water from the well, because rain seemed much more clean and fresh to her. When the first drops struck the roof, she sprang out of bed, grabbed her pot of soap and washcloth, and ran to a large rock beside the barn.

It was a warm, heavy downpour, the kind of rain that infused the seeds in the fertile furrows in the crop fields with burgeoning life during the growing seasons. When she finished bathing, Fiona stood with her feet apart and her arms outspread to the pure, wholesome flow of rain that laved her body. She felt one with the rich, heady forces of nature amid the crackling flashes of lightning and pounding roars of thunder.

Bathing in the rain usually lifted her spirits for several days, but this time, Fiona was confronted by a disagreeable situation two days later. Donley had decided upon a solution to his problem, and Fiona suspected that Violet Slattery had participated heavily in the decision. He had determined that the logical solution was for Fiona to have a husband.

He had brought cronies to the house on occasion, all of them very similar. Coarse, loud men, they had all tried to ape Donley in being as much of a bully and troublemaker as he. And, ever since Fiona had been twelve or thirteen, they had also leered at her. Vernon Slocum was much the same as all the others.

A muscular man in his thirties, he had craggy, ugly features that were scarred from brawls, and his nose had been broken several times. As soon as Fiona saw Slocum, she understood why Donley had brought him. The man had made himself presentable by his standards, wearing a suit in a garish check. In addition, he appeared reluctant to be there and doubtful about what he would find. But as soon as he saw Fiona, he became eager.

He also assumed the patronizing attitude that his kind usually took toward women, as though she were a child, which infuriated Fiona. She greeted him curtly when Donley introduced them, then went to make tea. It was an obligatory courtesy for a visitor, and in this instance she resented it. When the tea was made, she took it to them and then turned to leave.

"Bring a pannikin for yourself and join us," Donley ordered. "I must leave in a few minutes, and Vern would like to talk with you."

"I don't wish to talk with him," Fiona replied, including Slocum in her glance as she turned back. "He's your friend, you talk with him."

Donley's face flushed with anger, which she expected. However, Slocum appeared insulted by her lack of interest, a reaction that wryly amused Fiona as she walked out and went to do the evening chores. When she returned to the house, Slocum had left. Donley was in the parlor, and as she gathered up the pannikins and took them to the kitchen, he followed her.

"I'm not an old man by any means," he grumbled, "and I have many good years ahead of me. But I can do naught until I get shot of you. You're like a bloody millstone about my neck."

Fiona shrugged, putting the pannikins in the basin on the washstand. "That's easily remedied," she told him. "You've no interest in farming or this farm, so sign the deed over to me. I'll never trouble you again, even to the extent of speaking to you if I pass you on the road."

Donley laughed sourly and shook his head. "You'd like that, wouldn't you? No, with a house, barn, and sheds such as these, this farm will bring me a tidy sum. Enough so that I can go into business with Violet. For the past couple of years, Vern has been down in the gold fields, and he managed to put his hands on more than a few quid to lay by. He's a good catch for a woman, and plenty have set their caps for him."

"They're more than welcome to him," Fiona replied.

"Who the bloody hell are you to be so bloody choosy?" Donley bellowed in sudden anger. "You feed stinking pigs and scratch potatoes out of the dirt, and yet you consider yourself so precious that you turn up your nose at the likes of my friends! You want to get your head on straight!"

"Growing food to feed oneself and others is honest, honorable work, Seton Donley!" Fiona shot back. "And far more respectable than skulking in taverns with riffraff! And how did Vernon Slocum get money in the gold fields? By picking pockets rather than by work, no doubt!"

"Aye, you're a mistress high and mighty, aren't you?" Donley snarled sarcastically. "Your mother was the same when I married her, but she soon came to heel." He leaned toward her, raising his voice and stabbing a finger at her for emphasis. "And you will too, by God! The next time I bring Vern here, you'd bloody well better be more sociable! If you defy me on this, I'll give you the fisting of your life! Then I'll make your life so miserable that you'll wish you were dead!"

Shouting his last words over his shoulder, he turned on his heel and stamped out. Fiona stood unmoving beside the washstand, one hand gripping it so tightly that her fingers were white. His reference to her mother had brought back her memories of the times when her mother had silently endured his abuse. Fiery, speechless rage had exploded within her, and at that moment, she could have killed him.

Fiona continued with the rest of her work for the day, then prepared dinner and forced herself to eat. After she went to bed, she lay awake for a time, racked with worry over the situation closing in on her from every side. She had no intention of repeating her mother's mistake and condemning herself to the bondage of a loveless marriage to a brutal, worthless man. However, she knew that Donley would and could do just as he had threatened, making her life so miserable that she would wish she were dead.

Chapter Eighteen

The following day was laundry day, and Fiona went out into the dawn light to fill the big copper kettle behind the house with water and kindle a fire under it. She went back into the kitchen and prepared breakfast, and when Donley came in, she put his on the table. He gulped it down, then got up to leave.

Then he turned back in the doorway, glaring and pointing a finger at Fiona. "You'd best remember what I said last night," he growled. "When I bring Vern here today, you be sociable with him. You'll have either a smile or my fist on that high and mighty face of yours."

He left, and Fiona sat down at the table. On the point of bursting into tears of anguish, she felt completely helpless and all alone in the world. Then she drew in a deep breath and stood up again, disliking idleness even when she was tortured by anxiety. She went through the house and gathered up the bed linens and all of the dirty clothes.

Fiona put the laundry into the copper pot and poured

in soap, then went to do the morning chores. When she returned to the house, she noticed that something out of the ordinary had happened west of the farm. People were hurrying up the road toward the foothills, but she saw no smoke from a house or barn on fire, the usual reason that brought people running.

Going around the house toward the road in front, Fiona saw a man from a neighboring farm coming down the road. His name was Thomas Mansley, and she called to him, asking what had happened. "Two men brought a herd of cattle across the Divide!" he shouted back. "They have the cattle pastured at the Markham place, up the road!"

"Across the Divide?" Fiona echoed in astonishment, walking closer. "They brought a herd across from the Darling Downs?"

"No, much farther than that," Thomas replied. "They brought the cattle all the way from the outback. They're outback men, particularly the young fellow in charge. His name is Jeremy Kerrick, and one can tell from a glance that the outback is his home."

Listening raptly, Fiona was thrilled by the extraordinary event. The opening of a track across the Great Divide was a long-awaited development to everyone in Brisbane. To her, however, the most intriguing fact was that the men and cattle were from the legendary outback. The name that Thomas had mentioned was instantly familiar to her, but it also puzzled her.

"The man is from Tibooburra Station?" she asked. "That's a sheep station, not cattle. And it must be nearly a thousand miles from here."

"No, I understand he doesn't claim kin to that family of Kerricks," Thomas told her. "But he more than lives up to the name." He lifted his cap, walking on down the road. "G'day to you, Mistress Donley."

Fiona thanked him for the information and turned back toward the rear of the house. She yearned to go and see the men and cattle from the outback, for anything associated with that fabled land fascinated her. However, she knew that if Donley returned while she was gone, he would have an excuse to berate her, placing her at a further disadvantage.

The laundry had boiled, and Fiona began lifting it out of the copper wash pot with a long stick and dropping it into a tub of water to rinse it. As she worked, she noticed that the people had satisfied their curiosity about the men and cattle. The road was busy for a time with people coming back down it, then it returned to its normal state of calm broken only by an occasional passer-by.

After rinsing the laundry, she wrung it out and put it into a basket, then carried it to the clothesline at the side of the house. While hanging it on the line, she saw two riders coming down the road. From a distance, she recognized one of them as Matthew Harrison, the owner of a stockyard. The other one was much taller, with wide shoulders. A young man, he wore a stockman's hat and dungaree clothes. Fiona had never seen him before, and she realized that he had to be Jeremy Kerrick.

As he drew closer, she studied him from the corners of her eyes. He was clean-shaven, his strong, handsome features revealing a pleasant disposition. His appearance, posture, the way he rode his horse, and other characteristics bore out what Thomas Edward had said. With an air about him that was evocative of vast, open spaces, he was indeed a man of the outback.

Then she saw that he was staring at her, which made the stockyard owner grin. They reined up on the road beside the fence, Matthew lifting his hat. "G'day," he greeted her. "I believe you're Mistress Donley, aren't you?"

"Yes, I'm Fiona Donley, Mr. Harrison."

"This is Mr. Jeremy Kerrick, Mistress Donley," Matthew said. "He and his mate brought a herd of cattle across the Divide."

As she exchanged greetings with Jeremy, the self-control that Fiona had developed while dealing with her father served her in good stead. His glowing smile was one of open, ardent admiration, and he had the most beautiful eyes she had ever seen. They were the pale blue of the spring sky, the season that made her feel vibrantly alive in her awareness of nature bringing forth fresh new life all about her.

Fiona managed to maintain an outward calm, even though her heart was racing and blood thundered in her ears. "I'm sure you're weary of being asked how arduous your journey was, Mr. Kerrick," she remarked. "But it must have been exceedingly difficult to cross the Divide with cattle."

"It wasn't easy," he acknowledged. "More than difficult, though, it was time-consuming. My mate and I could have driven two or three herds to Bourke in the length of time that it took us to get through the mountains." He pointed to canvas bags behind his saddle. "We ran short on supplies, and I'm just on my way to buy a few things in Brisbane."

"The shops at the market square are the best in the city."

He thanked her for the advice, and the conversation moved on to the size of his herd and other things for a few minutes. Then it ended, the two men lifting their hats and bidding her a good day as they moved away. Fiona replied and turned back to her laundry, her heart pounding in the most confused turmoil of emotions she had ever known.

She felt poised between the threshold of a new life of exuberant joy beyond her wildest dreams, and the depths of crushing despair that had been closing in on her during the past days. Jeremy seemed so perfect in every way that it was almost unbelievable. The admiration in his smile had been perfectly straightforward and undeniable.

However, that was a shaky foundation for blissful expectations. It was anything but unusual for a man to smile admiringly at a pretty woman, and she knew that she was attractive, if somewhat tall and thin. He had as much as said that in the future, he would drive his herds to Bourke. In all likelihood, he would leave in a few days and she would never seen him again.

Her feelings bouncing between buoyant optimism and gloom, Fiona finished hanging up the laundry and went on to other tasks. When the grocer's apprentice came for the eggs and butter during early afternoon, she had given no thought at all to preparing tiffin. After he left, she was hungry, but too agitated to eat anything. The laundry was dry by then, and she took it into the house and put the linens back on the beds.

In the meantime, Fiona tried to stay where she could see or hear the traffic on the road. Each time she glimpsed or heard a rider, she ran to wave if it was Jeremy, but it was always someone else. By mid-afternoon, she was beginning to fear that she had missed him. She was ready to churn the milk from the previous day, and she carried the churn to the side of the house and sat under the clothesline, where she could watch the road.

A short time later, she heard a horse coming up the road on the other side of the house, but the hoofbeats were accompanied by the rumble of buggy wheels. It stopped in front of the house, and her heart sank as she heard Donley and Slocum talking boisterously as they climbed out of the buggy. Their heavy footsteps clumped in the front door and through the house, Donley calling to her, then they went out the back door.

"There you are," Donley said as they stepped around the corner of the house, his voice hearty and his eyes glaring in warning. "I told Vern that you said you're agreeable to seeing him. That's right, isn't it?"

Fiona's temper flared over his putting words into her mouth. "No, it is not, Seton Donley!" she shot back. "You gave me a choice between being sociable with him or being fisted, and I greatly prefer being fisted!"

"Then that's what you'll get!" Donley roared furiously. "By God, I'll kill you if you don't stop defying me!"

"Just a minute, Seton," Slocum put in. "Let me talk some sense into her head." He turned to Fiona with the condescending attitude that enraged her. "Now it's time

for you to bring your foolishness to an end," he said. "I've
hired a buggy to take you for a ride, so you get ready to
go."

Fiona shook her head in disgust. "No, certainly not!"
she retorted.

"And why the bloody hell not?" Slocum growled, becoming angry. "Do you think you're too bloody good for
me? By God, I'll tell you that you're not. You're no better
than a char, working with that churn and such here. Now
I'm a patient man, but I won't have—" He broke off,
glaring past Fiona at the road. "What the bloody hell do
you want?" he snarled.

"I want to know if you'd like to try talking to a man
in that fashion," Jeremy Kerrick replied.

Her joyous relief almost overwhelming, Fiona turned
and saw Jeremy on his horse beside the fence. For an
instant, she felt concerned about what might happen to
him, then her concern faded. He was the same man who
had talked with her before, yet he was different. Now his
eyes were the cold, steely blue of the sky that heralded
the onslaught of a violent, raging storm. Now the inde-
finable quality about him that was suggestive of the outback evoked images of its harsh, forbidding character
and its lethal dangers.

Slocum hesitated, studying Jeremy. His misgivings
were betrayed by a blustering note in his voice as he
replied, "By God, you come across that fence and I'll do
more than talk!" he roared.

Jeremy dismounted and vaulted lightly over the fence.
Slocum rushed past Fiona, his fists knotted as he bellowed threats and oaths. Jeremy silently stepped forward
with his arms at his side and his tanned features set in
grim determination. Then, as they met, Slocum seemed
to run into an invisible wall. Jeremy's right fist lashed
out with blinding speed and crushing force, slamming
solidly into Slocum's face.

Blood exploding from his mouth and nose, Slocum
weaved on his feet as he came to a sudden standstill.
Then he stumbled backward in jerky steps from the im-

pact of Jeremy's fists pounding into his stomach and face. Jeremy followed him, driving him toward the house. Fiona was shoved aside as Donley brushed past her and charged toward Jeremy, whose back was turned as he knocked Slocum to the ground beside the house.

"Behind you, Jeremy!" Fiona shouted. "Watch your back!"

Donley paused to glare over his shoulder at Fiona in apoplectic rage. He turned and rushed forward again, running straight into Jeremy's fist. It thudded into his stomach, doubling him over, then Jeremy hit him in the face. Blood spurted from his nose as he staggered and fell. Slocum was climbing to his feet, and Jeremy turned back to him.

Slocum hunched his shoulders and bent over as he ran at Jeremy, trying to butt with his head. Jeremy stepped lightly to one side, gripped the man's arm, and swung him around in a circle. Slocum yelped in surprise as he ran around the circle, his steps becoming longer and faster until Jeremy hurled him toward the house.

The man tried to stop himself from hitting the house, but his momentum was too great. He crashed headfirst into it with a force that rattled the windows. Then he fell sprawling on the ground. Donley stumbled to his feet, shaking his head to clear it. Jeremy approached him again with both fists swinging. The swift, furious pounding opened cuts on Donley's face; his knees sagged and a final, powerful blow spread-eagled him on the ground.

Jeremy glanced from Donley to Slocum, both of them groaning in semiconsciousness, then turned to Fiona. "Who are these men, Fiona?" he asked.

"That one, I regret to say, is my father," she replied, pointing. "The other one is a friend of his."

"Your father?" Jeremy exclaimed in astonishment.

Fiona shrugged, earnestly wishing her family background had been one that would have made a better impression on Jeremy. "Yes, he's always been a cruel, selfish man." She briefly explained about her mother's death and Donley's plans to sell the farm and remarry.

"So under the circumstances," she continued, "I'm a hindrance to him. He decided to dispose of me by forcing me to marry that one over there."

"Well, I realize it's no comfort to you," Jeremy said, "but I've heard of other parents who were cruel to their children. In fact, I would never treat a child the way my own parents dealt with me."

Once again, his eyes were the color of the spring sky, and he was strikingly handsome as he smiled sympathetically. "I'm most grateful that you came to my assistance," Fiona told him.

"I was pleased to do it," he replied, "and I appreciate your warning me to watch my back." He pointed to the bags behind his saddle, only one of them filled. "I bought some supplies at the shops you recommended, but I didn't get any vegetables. I decided to ask you to sell me some."

"You can have all you want for the asking, because I always have a surplus to feed to my pigs. Bring your horse to the barnyard gate."

His smile as he nodded was radiant, making it seem at least possible to Fiona that his real reason for stopping at the farm had been to see her. Her heart raced as she went around the front of the house to the wide gate on the other side, Jeremy nimbly vaulting back over the fence. He led his horse to the gate and through it, closing it again, and Fiona took a hoe out of the tool shed as they crossed the barnyard to the crop fields.

While they were digging vegetables and talking, Fiona felt certain that his attitude toward her was far more meaningful that mere courtesy and friendliness. However, the most heartfelt longings she had ever experienced in all of her life had been passing whims in comparison to her yearning for him to feel drawn to her in the same way that she was to him. Acknowledging that, she feared that she might be deceiving herself.

In addition, she realized that her judgment was anything but at its best. Being near him kept her in a constant state of keenly pleasant, flushed confusion, particularly when their hands touched while they were gathering up the vegetables. She was also struggling to come to terms with the most profound event of her entire life. Her ardent love for him had come like a bolt of lightning, exploding within her. It was a joyous feeling, but it created an emotional turmoil that muddled her thoughts.

The conviction that he felt the same kept tugging at Fiona because of the nature of the conversation. He guided it, proceeding methodically to their finding out all about each other. An hour passed, and the bag was still not full of vegetables as they talked. Jeremy told her about himself and how he had grown up in the outback, and she was fascinated.

"So you are of the same family that owns Tibooburra station," she said. "Why do you allow people to believe otherwise?"

"It isn't because I have any ill feelings toward them," he replied. "In fact, I admire them for what they've done. I simply don't want others to judge me or draw conclusions about me on the basis of my name."

Fiona suspected there was more, that his feelings about the family were far too complex to be summarized in a brief explanation. He continued, barely mentioning his parents, and when he began talking about the outback and how he searched for feral cattle, his approach to the subject seemed to have a double meaning. He was a modest man, but his emphasis on the hardships of the outback was almost boastful.

In another way, however, his dwelling on the worst aspects of the outback made her heart leap for joy. He seemed to be indirectly telling her that life with him would lack the comforts of a household. Then he began talking about his search for a place in the outback where he felt that he belonged.

"I'll know the place when I find it," he continued, "but I have no idea of when that will be. The only words that I can find in trying to explain it sound senseless even to me, and I've never tried to tell Buggie about it. But I'm fortunate to have a mate like him, because few people would endure wandering about like that, would they?"

His tone was meaningful, asking for more than a conversational opinion. They were stepping from one vegetable patch to another, Jeremy carrying the bag, and Fiona drew in a deep breath to keep her voice from trembling with emotion. "Whenever I've dreamed of escaping from Seton Donley and my life here," she said, "I've always thought of the outback. Others speak of it with dread, but to me it's a grand, great land that offers freedom from all that has ever troubled me. I know I would love it there."

Jeremy dropped the bag and took her hands, turning her to him. "Then will you come with me?" he asked softly, gazing into her eyes. "We've only just met, and I don't want to seem hasty and inconsiderate. However, the situation we're in here is unusual. The first moment I saw you, I fell in love with you. I knew then that I could never be content again unless you were with me. Will you come with me, Fiona?"

Fiona was numb with exuberant joy. His large, warm hands held hers, and the gaze from his pale blue eyes created a far more intense, glowing warmth within her. "Yes, I'll go with you, Jeremy," she whispered.

She was uncertain which of them moved first, but she was suddenly in his arms and they were kissing. The embrace and kiss abruptly triggered an unexpected, unintended reaction. Meant as an acknowledgement of their mutual feelings and the understanding they had reached, it fueled some inner flame that instantly flared into an explosion of passion.

Her lips opened to his as she crushed herself to him, his hands moving over her. Then, at the same moment, they both remembered that they were in the crop fields in broad daylight, where others could see them. They moved apart, Fiona flushed and breathless, and Jeremy's hands trembling as he took out a rawhide thong and tied the top of the vegetable bag. He picked it up and reached for her hand as they walked back toward his horse.

At the gate beside the road, they saw that Donley and Slocum had recovered enough to leave, because the buggy that had been in front of the house was gone. "I can't leave you here by yourself," Jeremy told her. "My dunnocks are pastured at the Markham farm, and they're obliging people. I'm sure they'll be willing for you to stay with them."

"I think not, because people hereabout avoid trouble with Seton Donley," Fiona replied. "But it's irrelevant, because I must attend to my cow, pigs, and chickens. Also, I want to face him alone."

"No, I cannot leave you here by yourself, Fiona," Jeremy insisted. "And it's unwise for you to face him alone. Now that I know what sort of man he is, I don't rule out anything that he might—"

"It isn't your decision to make, Jeremy," Fiona interrupted. "It's my decision, and I intend to face him alone." She smiled to soften her blunt disagreement. "There's no reason for concern, because you'll be there in spirit, and I'm on a different footing with him now."

It was a contest of wills, entirely free of animosity. The persuasive force of Jeremy's strong, compelling personality tugged at Fiona, but she was determined. He relented, kissing her and touching her hair; then he stepped into his saddle. "I'll be back tomorrow morning," he said.

"Bring Buggie with you, and I'll prepare a good breakfast."

Jeremy nodded and smiled, starting to ride away. Then he stopped, his smile fading, and something of his ardent expression after they had kissed returned to his tanned, handsome face. "I love you with all of my heart, Fiona Donley," he said in a soft, fervent tone.

"And I love you with all of my heart, Jeremy Kerrick," she replied.

He waved as he lifted his reins and rode away. Fiona watched him ride up the road, and just before he disappeared around a curve, he waved again. Fiona waved, then turned toward the house.

The entire world seemed to have become brighter and

more cheerful around Fiona, and she felt as though she were walking on air as she rushed about her work. After she finished essential chores, dusk was gathering. Ravenously hungry, she went into the kitchen and began preparing dinner.

Even though she was more uneasy about confronting Donley than she had revealed to Jeremy, it was something she had to do alone. She pondered what might happen, and her gaze moved to the poker, the iron rod used for stirring ashes and turning logs in the fireplace. She took it off its peg and slid the tip of it into the fire, then continued preparing dinner.

When the meal was almost ready, Fiona heard the front door being quietly opened and then closed. A moment later, a floorboard in the parlor creaked, and she moved to the front of the fireplace. Then Donley leaped into the kitchen, getting between her and the doors. He was hardly recognizable, his face swollen and discolored by bruises.

His sneering smile was the same, however, as was the smell of cheap rum. He slowly moved toward her, poised to grab her if she tried to slip around him. "Now we're going to have a reckoning, mistress high and mighty," he snarled. "Now is when you learn the cost of defying me."

When he was almost close enough to seize her, Fiona turned to the fireplace, jerked the poker out of the coals, and whipped it around toward him. He leaped back from the white-hot tip, but Fiona managed to brush his beard with it. Smoke boiled up, along with the stench of burning hair. Donley stumbled back, beating at his beard and cursing in rage. Then he grabbed up a bench at the table and hoisted it to throw at her.

"Think twice, Seton Donley!" she warned him. "You've learned how it feels to be on the other end of a fisting. Your only choice now is between a far better drubbing than the first, or to accept defeat as best you can whilst you stew in your bile."

Donley glared at her, breathing heavily and trembling

with fury as he held the bench ready to throw. Then he hurled it down with a crash and stamped out of the house, slamming the front door behind him. Fiona relaxed and smiled in satisfaction as she replaced the poker on its peg. She set the bench back upright, then finished preparing her meal.

After eating a hearty dinner, Fiona put the kitchen back in order and then went to bed. As she lay and thought about the swift events of the day, her mood of blissful elation made falling asleep impossible. An hour passed, then another as she gazed up into the darkness. Finally, she rose and dressed again, then went through the kitchen and out the back door.

The soft sounds of the night surrounding her, Fiona crossed the barnyard to the pasture fence in the moonlight. As she opened the gate and stepped into the pasture, she heard footsteps behind her and turned. Jeremy came across the barnyard from somewhere near the house.

"I said that I wanted to face him alone," she reminded Jeremy.

"That's what you did, Fiona," he replied, then laughed. "You also did it excellently well. I could smell his beard burning from where I was standing outside the kitchen door."

Fiona laughed, stepping out into the deep, soft grass of the pasture with Jeremy. "He won't offer to cause any more trouble now," she said. "Judging from his past actions, he won't even return until tomorrow. You could have returned to your camp."

"I wouldn't be able to sleep, and I wanted to be near you."

His words echoed her feelings, and the joyous excitement that had kept her awake became an irresistible longing to be closer and to be one with him. They sat down on the grass, Jeremy taking her in his arms. Resting against his chest, she heard the throbbing pulse of his heartbeat as he stroked and kissed her hair, whispering his love. She lifted her lips to his, and they lay back on the bed of soft grass, holding each other and kissing.

Their kisses and caresses became passionate, igniting a demanding need for more intimate contact. Moments later, they were naked in the moonlight, their clothes tossed aside. Fiona pulled at Jeremy, the feel of his hard body beside hers creating a gentle, burning agony of desire within her. He lifted himself over her, and she arched to meet him.

A twinge of pain in overcoming a momentary resistance was followed by a wave of keen, blissful sensation reaching into and awakening every fiber of her body. That passed and became the promise of further pleasure as she responded strongly to his lovemaking. She moved her hands over his smooth, muscular shoulders and back, her lips against his in deep kisses, and she opened herself to an approaching tide of rapture. It engulfed both of them, their bodies surging together in wrenching spasms.

Time seemed to warp, becoming distorted in an eternity of lovemaking. An aftermath of quiescence fled swiftly, kisses and caresses turning it into renewed passion. He lifted himself over her again, and the instants of peaking ecstasy seemed to stretch into hours. Then, when their desire was quenched, the need to remain close remained, and they lay clasped together in each other's arms.

With his strong, warm arms around her, Fiona was beyond joy, suffused by a sense of fulfillment that reached into the very depths of her being. She felt as though the misery and grief during the years of her growth to adulthood had been a cold, harsh early springtime. Now the balmy season of late spring had arrived, and a gloriously beautiful and richly promising summer lay in the future. Having found the love of her life and being loved by him, she was utterly complete and content.

Chapter Nineteen

When he woke in the thinning darkness just before dawn, Jeremy felt as though it was the first day of his life in a new and inexpressibly joyous world. Late in the night, he had persuaded Fiona to come to his camp with him. She was nestled against him in his blanket, her long, thick mass of hair a bright red even in the soft pre-dawn.

His first look at the region east of the mountains had revealed that the place for which he was searching was elsewhere. Instead, he had found joy beyond anything he had ever experienced. Meeting Fiona had created a desperate need within him, a huge abyss in his life that only she could fill. He was still struggling to understand the wondrous event that had changed the world around him, and to accept that she was actually his.

He tried to move away without waking her, but her slow, regular breathing stopped and her eyes opened. Then her white, even teeth gleamed in the dim light in a wide smile. Jeremy kissed her, then stood up and stepped to the fire. Fiona moved off the blanket and rolled it up as he stirred the ashes and put thin sticks and bark on the hot coals. At the sounds of activity, Buggie broke off snoring on the other side of the fire and sat up.

When the portly, bearded man saw Fiona, it appeared that the moment had finally come when his protruding eyes would definitely pop out with astonishment. Jeremy laughed, introducing them. "Fiona is the young lady I told you about yesterday," he added. "We're going to be married."

They exchanged greetings, Buggie clapping his hat on his long, matted hair so he could lift it to her. "Well, this is a fair dinkum turn-up!" he exclaimed happily. "The way you were talking about her, Jeremy, I knew you'd be moping about forever if she wouldn't have you."

"No, I'd court her until she would have me," Jeremy said firmly, smiling at Fiona. Then he turned back to Buggie. "Fiona is agreeable to leaving as soon as possible so we can get back across the mountains before cold weather sets in, and she and I will get married in Toowoomba. Until we leave, she wants us to stay at her farm, which makes good sense. Along with many other advantages, the pasture there is much better than this."

"Let's move your cattle there now, before making breakfast," Fiona suggested. "By the time we get there, I'll need to see to my cow, pigs, and chickens. Breakfast will be late, but it'll be a good one."

Taking out his purse, Jeremy glanced toward the house some two hundred yards away and saw lights in the windows. "Yes, let's do that," he agreed, handing Buggie a florin. "The Markhams appear to be up and about, Buggie. If you'll go pay Mr. Markham for yesterday's pasturage, I'll organize things here and get ready to move the dunnocks."

Buggie set out across the fields toward the house in the early morning twilight as Jeremy started collecting the cooking utensils and other things around the fire. Fiona immediately began bustling about and helping him. The previous day, he had noticed that she was exceptionally industrious. In her stubborn determination to confront

Donley alone, Jeremy had found out that she was strong-willed and independent as well.

Watching her, he reflected that she had to be the most fascinating woman in the world. Her dazzlingly beautiful, flaming red hair had first drawn his gaze from nearly a mile away, and it was a perfect frame from her wide, green eyes and strikingly attractive features. She had an intriguing personality and an earthy quality that seemed to come from working with the plants and animals on her farm. More than anyone he had ever met except Aborigines, she seemed to be at one with the land and the cycles of nature.

When Buggie returned shortly after dawn, Jeremy had just finished tying down the loads on the pack horses. He lifted Fiona up in front of the load on one of them and handed her the halter rope to lead the other one, then stepped into his saddle and rode toward the gate to open it. The dunnocks were docile after the long journey, and as Buggie rode around them and snapped his stock whip, they began moving toward the gate.

The dunnocks flowed out onto the road, Jeremy forming them into a column and heading them down it. Buggie rode out the gate behind the herd, Fiona following him and leaning down from her horse to close the gate. A short time later, Jeremy rode ahead to open the barnyard and pasture gates at Fiona's farm, and to guide the dunnocks through the gates.

When the herd was in the pasture, Fiona tethered the pack horses at the barn and went to the house. Jeremy followed her, wanting to be near if Donley had returned. The man was still gone, and Fiona began carrying his clothes and other belongings to the front door and flinging them out. Jeremy detested Donley more than anyone he had ever met, and he laughed and shook his head in amusement, going back toward the barn.

Jeremy and Buggie stored their supplies and equipment in the barn, then Buggie put the horses in the pasture and went to help Fiona with her chores. Jeremy looked in the harness room and found a sidesaddle for

Fiona that was in good condition, though it was stiff and dry from years of disuse. Taking it to the front of the barn, where he could see the road, he began oiling the saddle with mutton tallow as he watched for Donley.

Shortly after Fiona went to the house to prepare breakfast, Jeremy saw Donley coming up the road. The man stopped, evidently seeing his belongings in front of the house, then he rushed toward it. Jeremy crossed the barnyard to the house. They reached the kitchen at the same time, Donley coming through the house as Jeremy stepped into the back doorway and stopped, folding his arms. Fiona was peeling potatoes at the washstand.

Donley had been very drunk the night before, his clothes disheveled and his eyes bloodshot in his bruised, swollen face. He hesitated warily as he looked at Jeremy, then he turned to Fiona. "Why are my things scattered out in front of the house?" he demanded.

"So they'll be ready at hand for you to gather up and carry away," she told him. "You don't live here now, Seton Donley."

"Don't live here?" he snorted indignantly. "This is my house!"

"No, not for the remaining time that I'll be here. Jeremy and I intend to leave and get married, and until then, I don't want to see your miserable face on the premises. You've no rights here, because you haven't brought a farthing into this house in months. Instead, you've stolen my pigs to sell so you and your riffraff friends would have funds to swill rum."

Donley glared at her in outrage, speechless for a moment. "You can't throw me out of the bloody house that belongs to me!" he spluttered. "I'll fetch the constables here and rectify this, by God!"

"You've spiked your own cannon to that end, Seton Donley," Fiona replied. "Any constable you ask for help will laugh in your face, because they all know you for the vile, slothful wretch that you are. Now begone with you and get back to your own kind. I'm sick of the sight of you."

Donley ground his teeth in fury and turned to leave. Then he wheeled back around, the rage on his face changing to a sneering, triumphant grin. "Whether you bloody like it or not, you're serving my purposes!" he shouted, stabbing a finger at Fiona. "All I want is to be shot of you, and to sell this stinking farm! When you're gone, some dolt who knows naught but digging in dirt and such will pay enough for it so that I can go into business with Violet Slattery! Now what do you say to that, by God?"

Fiona said nothing. Her face and green eyes reflecting disgust, she merely gazed at him. Interpreting her silence as a lack of anything that she could do or say, Donley laughed sarcastically as he turned and stamped out of the house. Jeremy went back toward the barn, suspecting that Fiona had only chosen to remain silent, and Donley had laughed too soon.

When he finished with the saddle, Jeremy found a riding bridle that had hung unused for years in the harness room and oiled it. A short time later, Fiona called him and Buggie to the house. The belated breakfast consisted of thick, succulent rashers of smoked gammon, a platter of fried eggs, and potatoes that had been fried with onions in the drippings from the bacon. There was also a pitcher of zestfully tart buttermilk that was cool from the cellar, along with a pan of light, flavorful barley bread.

As they began eating, Fiona smiled in reply to Jeremy and Buggie's emphatic compliments on the delicious food. "There are hams and flitches of bacon in the smokehouse," she said, "and we may as well eat what we can. I'll give away the rest, because the pack horses will have enough to carry when we set out, and I don't intend to leave it for Seton Donley."

"No, you can take whatever you wish," Jeremy told her. "There are three of us now, so I plan to buy more pack horses. Those vegetables you've grown are the best I've ever seen, and Buggie and I will bag some to take."

"Very well, I'll collect the other foodstuffs together so you can see how many pack horses will be needed. I don't have many clothes, but some of the kitchen utensils have been in my mother's family for generations, and I'd like to take them. When will you sell your cattle?"

"When I get my price," Jeremy replied. "Matthew Harrison has made the best offer so far, but it wasn't enough. I want two hundred guineas, and I believe I'll get if it I act as though I'm in no hurry to leave. I found a sidesaddle and bridle in the harness room for you to use when we leave. The leather was very dry, so I put mutton tallow on them."

"They were my grandmother's," Fiona said, frowning. "My mother's father and mother built up this farm from nothing, and I'm loath to let the fruits of their labor go to riffraff." She shrugged, shaking off her sober mood. "I'll give my pigs, chickens, and cow to neighbors, along with the tools and other things we can't use. Before, the neighbors would have wanted to take them away in the dead of night to avoid any possibility of trouble with Seton Donley, but I expect it'll be different now. Once a bully gets his comeuppance, people are less frightened of him, aren't they?"

Jeremy laughed and agreed, and the discussion moved on to other things they had to do. He was keenly pleased that Fiona and Buggie had liked each other at first sight and were becoming good friends, promising a perfectly harmonious relationship between all three of them. That friendship was furthered when Fiona brought out a plate of apple turnovers she had made to go with tea at the end of the meal, and Buggie smiled happily as he devoured a large share of the deliciously sweet, crisp pastries.

When the meal was finished, Jeremy and Buggie went to the crop fields to dig and bag vegetables to take with them. Buggie marveled over the large vegetables, and Jeremy speculated that their size was due to Fiona's skill and hard work, combined with a favorable climate. Brisbane was in the subtropical zone, and there were mango, pawpaw, and bauple nut trees among the other foliage at the edges of the fields. Somewhere Jeremy had read that an enterprising individual had transplanted bauple trees to Hawaii, where they had thrived and the nuts were called macadamias.

The remainder of the day passed swiftly for Jeremy. After bagging the vegetables, he and Buggie sorted out their equipment, shod horses whose shoes were worn, and worked at other preparations for the journey back to the west. Two more stockyard owners came to look at the dunnocks and to talk with Jeremy, and he and Buggie helped Fiona with her chores. Yet though the minutes flew by, the hours seemed very long until he and Fiona would be alone.

The end of the day came at last, after a delicious, hearty dinner consisting of smoked ham with all the trimmings. Jeremy experienced an additional, piquant sense of intimacy with Fiona from their being in her bedroom, the place where she spent her private, secret moments. She was rapturously beautiful in the moonlight streaming through the window, creating a storm of passion within him that her fiery nature matched.

His passion could be satisfied, but his deep love for her fueled an inexhaustible need to express affection, and he held her close as they talked. She asked about the bone talisman on the thong around his neck, and he explained what it was. "I'll take it off if it bothers you," he offered.

"No, leave it on," she told him. "It doesn't bother me at all. Do you think it has the power that the man Juburli said?"

Jeremy laughed, shrugging. "While I lived amongst the Aborigines, I saw things that would take one aback, but I daresay there was always a logical explanation. I don't believe in magic." He laughed again. "Nor do I believe in leprechauns or pots of gold at the end of rainbows."

"I don't either," Fiona replied, laughing. "But neither do I place total reliance upon logic. Nor do you in your actions, because your search for a place to settle isn't based on logic. From a logical standpoint, many places are much the same and would suffice for you. Your walkabout in search of your heritage is more of the heart and soul than of the mind."

After thinking for a moment about what she had said, Jeremy had to agree. He also noted that it had been a thoughtful observation, which was typical of her. She had mentioned that she enjoyed reading, and it made her entertaining to talk with, for her interests and knowledge reached far beyond her farm. Then the conversation turned to the outback, a topic Fiona never tired of discussing. Jeremy held her close, her head pillowed on his shoulder as they continued talking until they fell asleep.

The next day, Jeremy learned that Fiona was well-liked by the neighbors, whose visits had been limited in the past because of Donley. Word about what had happened between him and Jeremy had spread, along with the news that Fiona was leaving with Jeremy to get married. People came to congratulate them and to wish them well, and Fiona began giving away the animals and farming implements to those who needed them most.

Jeremy saw that Donley's reign as a bully had indeed ended, because the people were unconcerned about what he might think of their coming with wagons to take away crates of chickens, tools, and other things. Fiona sent a boy to tell those in the workers' row houses down the road to come for the remainder of the crops, and a short time later, a swarm of people arrived with bags to dig the vegetables in the fields. Some of the farmers and others brought Fiona a tattered book or a ragged magazine or two as a token gift in exchange, which she accepted with great satisfaction.

Along with the other activity, stockyard owners came to look at the dunnocks and talk with Jeremy. Matthew Harrison arrived and studied the animals once again, then agreed to pay two hundred guineas for the herd. He left to get the money and bring some of his employees to drive the herd to his stockyard, and Jeremy went to the house and talked with Fiona. After discussing the situation, they agreed to leave early in the morning two days later. Fiona began telling the people at the farm, knowing that word of her plans would be talked about in taverns and Donley would hear about it.

When Matthew returned with the money and two employees, Jeremy helped them drive the herd to the stockyard. The road crossed Spring Hill, which gave an overall view of Brisbane. The capital of Queensland, it was some twenty miles from the coast and situated on a deep bend in the Brisbane River. It spread out from its docks at Petrie Point over the alluvial flats and adjacent hills, many so steep that the houses on them were supported by stilts. The road intersected with Boundary Road, which led around the outskirts to Matthew's stockyard at North Quay, on the edge of the city.

Other stockyards, as well as wainwrights, horse copers, and similar businesses were at the quay. When the herd was penned, Jeremy made his farewells with Matthew and went to the horse dealers' yards. At one he bought a young mare for Fiona to ride, and at another he chose three geldings for additional pack horses. Like his other horses, the geldings were tamed brumbies, all three of them large, shaggy animals with bulging, powerful muscles. Jeremy stopped at a saddlery and bought three packsaddles for the geldings, then he rode back toward the farm, leading the horses.

It was late in the day when he reached the farm, and the last of the people had left with the things Fiona had given them. The place looked desolate, the crop fields completely dug up and the doors of the empty barn and sheds hanging open. Fiona had given away the furniture also, and dinner in front of the fireplace was much like that beside a campfire. After the meal, Buggie took his blanket to another room. Jeremy and Fiona spread their blankets in front of the hearth, and the dim, flickering firelight gleamed on her red hair and soft skin as they made love.

The following day was spent in final preparations to leave. While Buggie sorted tools, coils of rope, and other equipment into loads for the pack horses, Fiona changed clothes to go with Jeremy and pick out the additional supplies they needed. She was strikingly beautiful in her best dress and hat, and Jeremy glowed with pride as they rode toward the city, lifting his hat to neighbors as Fiona exchanged waves with them.

When they reached the city, they first went to the cemetery where Fiona's mother was buried so that she could spend a few minutes beside the grave. Fiona's grief was still too fresh for her to talk about her mother, and Jeremy knew very little about the woman except that she had recently died. Presently, Fiona turned away from the grave, wiping her eyes with her handkerchief, and they rode on to the streets of shops at the center of the city.

They went from shop to shop, buying bolts of dungaree cloth, soap, and other necessities. In a general store, the foodstuffs they needed were limited to salt, tea, and a few other items. In addition to the cured pork from the smokehouse and the vegetables, Fiona had put by bags of dried fruit and dried peas and beans for winter, along with wheat, barley, and rye that she milled to make flour. However, she also selected ample amounts of rock sugar, treacle, and honey for making sweets and pastries.

Their last stop was at a bookstore, where Fiona was radiantly happy as she made her selections among the books and magazines. Then her mood became more subdued when they returned to the farm. Jeremy understood that, although she was looking forward with great anticipation to their new life together in the outback, the farm was where she had been born and spent her childhood. It was the scene of many unhappy times for her during those years, but it also had an emotional attachment for her that was painful to break.

Their footsteps echoing through the empty house, Jeremy and Fiona helped Buggie finish sorting out the loads for the pack horses. Fiona grew more and more melancholy as the last day she would spend at the farm passed, and at dusk she prepared dinner while Jeremy and Buggie tied the loads to packsaddles. That night, when they lay in front of the hearth, Jeremy merely held her close and talked about how happy they would be during the coming years.

Before dawn the next morning, Fiona cooked a last

meal in the house while Jeremy and Buggie brought the horses out of the pasture and tethered them behind the house. After breakfast, she washed the dishes and Jeremy put them in a pack, then he and Buggie began loading the pack horses. When they finished with each one, they tied its halter rope to the packsaddle on another one, forming the five horses into a long string.

At the first light of dawn, when they began saddling the riding horses, Jeremy looked around for Fiona. Then he saw her across the barnyard in the dim light, carrying hay from the barn to the sheds. He realized that, as he had suspected, she had merely chosen not to reply when Donley had boasted about having the farm to sell. Instead of leaving the results of her grandparents' labor for Donley to use for his purposes, she intended to leave only the bare ground that they had developed into a farm.

Buggie continued girthing the saddles on the horses as Jeremy went to help her. Destroying what she had also labored to build up was an ordeal for Fiona, and her face was set in grim lines. The house was last, and Buggie had finished saddling the horses when Jeremy and Fiona carried armfuls of hay in the back door and scattered it through the rooms.

They returned to the back door, Fiona almost in tears. "I can't do the rest," she said softly. "Will you do it for me, please?"

"Of course," Jeremy replied, leading her outside. "Come along, love."

He helped her up to her saddle and handed her the reins on his horse. Leading it, she rode around the house toward the gate, and Buggie followed her with the pack horses. Jeremy wrenched a shutter off the kitchen window and pulled a board loose from it. Stepping into the kitchen, he used the board as a shovel to scoop up hot coals from the fireplace.

He began at the barn, spilling hot coals on the straw, then he went to each shed. When he reached the house, dense smoke was boiling from the barn and shed doorways. He dumped the last coals on the hay in the house, and it burst into flames as he went out the front door. Fiona and Buggie were waiting on the road in front of the house. Jeremy vaulted over the fence, and Fiona handed him his reins as he climbed into his saddle.

As the sun rose, flames roared from the windows and doorways of all the buildings, and smoke towered into the sky. Neighbors ran from all directions, some half-dressed and others gulping down bites of breakfast. Fiona shouted at them, telling them to let the buildings burn. They understood her reason and gathered on the road to watch, talking quietly.

Jeremy noticed that Fiona was gazing down the road, and he turned to look. He saw that Donley had indeed heard when they were leaving, and had come to take possession of the farm. Having seen the smoke, he was running up the road toward the farm in rage and shocked dismay. He slowed to a walk as he approached, glaring at Fiona and stepping toward her. Then, glancing at Jeremy, he changed his mind.

Instead of berating her, he vented his fury on the neighbors standing about. He rushed toward a small group of men, swinging his fists. "You scurvy swine!" he snarled. "Do naught but watch while my property burns, will you? By God, I'll teach you to either help or to hide from me!"

Donley expected the men to cower and run in fright, but he was met by a hail of fists thudding solidly into his face and body. He reeled back in astonishment, blood streaming from his nose and mouth. Then he attempted to run himself, and the men caught him, beat him to the ground, and began kicking him. Other men and women joined in until he was buried under a mass of people failing him with sticks, fists, and heavy boots.

When it continued for a moment too long, Jeremy started to intervene, not wanting the people to kill Donley. A tall, heavy-set woman did it instead, pushing into the crowd and calling out, "Why put him out of his misery?" she shouted. "Let him wallow in it!"

The people moved back, and the woman beckoned to

a man and several of the children. "Come on. If we're to have food for the winter, we've work to do." She turned to Fiona: "Go with God, love. And may God grant you a far happier life with your young man than what you had here."

Fiona replied, thanking the woman and wishing her well. The woman and her family left, and others moved away, calling out farewells to Fiona and Jeremy. Presently, the only one remaining was Donley. He lay face down on the road, swearing in frustrated rage and defeat.

The roof and walls of the house collapsed with a crash. A fountain of flames and sparks shot up, then the debris burned hotly. Donley lifted his head and looked, tears making streaks in the blood on his face.

"It's all yours now, Seton Donley," Fiona called. "Some dolt who knows naught but digging in dirt will still buy the land. With good fortune, you may get farthings on the guineas it was once worth. That won't be enough for you to go into business with Violet Slattery, but if worse comes to worst, you can always consider seeking employment to earn money."

Donley looked at her in despair, then buried his face in his folded arms and sobbed brokenly. Fiona lifted her reins, nudging her horse with her heel, and Jeremy turned his horse. They set out up the road toward the mountains to the west, Buggie following them with the pack horses. Smoke from the burning buildings billowed into the sky behind them.

Chapter Twenty

A strong stench of smoke filled the damp, cold air on the rainy day as Morton Kerrick gazed at the ropewalk. Its front wall, as well as part of the sides and roof, were a pile of charred rubble.

The sight had become familiar to him during the past weeks, because eight of his houses let out on lease had been destroyed by fires of mysterious origin. It was different this time in that the destruction had been less than total, and there was no mystery about how the fire had started. One of the hirelings who had set it had been caught and was in jail.

Isaac Tulk and seven of the workmen were standing at one side, watching as Morton viewed the damage. Even before the yachting season had ended, sales from the ropewalk had plummeted because of the severe economic conditions. The men were silent and fearful, worried that Morton would declare it a total loss, and jobs had become very scarce in Sydney.

The foreman stepped toward Morton. "I understand

that there isn't any fire insurance, Sir Morton," he said anxiously.

Morton sighed heavily, nodding. "The parent company in England of the one here that wrote policies on all my properties went into receivership. For all practical purposes, none of my recent losses were covered. Was the employee who was guarding the building last night injured in the fray?"

"No, he was only bruised a bit," Isaac replied. "I told him to go home and get a good rest. He was the one who summoned the fire brigade and the constables to take the man he had caught."

Morton nodded in satisfaction, hoping the man would talk. He was certain that Creevey used intermediaries to keep a distance between himself and those who committed criminal acts, but the situation was far more promising now than after the other fires. If the one who had been arrested could and would identify an intermediary, that man might choose to talk in order to escape punishment, implicating Creevey and bringing him to justice.

"It's good that it was raining," Isaac mused. "That helped the fire brigade put out the fire. It shouldn't be too expensive to make the repairs and put everything back in order, should it, Sir Morton?"

Morton hesitated, pondering. As a businessman he knew he should close the ropewalk, but as a human being he was unable to put the men out of work unless he absolutely had to. "Get an estimate on the cost of repairs," he said. "We'll continue at least until next spring, and with any luck the general economic situation will improve and rope sales will pick up."

Isaac nodded and grinned happily as he touched his cap. Morton stepped into his carriage, telling the driver to take him to the police station. As the carriage moved away, an outburst of joyful exclamations rose from the workmen when Isaac told them the outcome of the conversation. Morton's mood was the opposite of theirs, and had been for months.

His continuing estrangement from his mother tormented him, but he was still unable to understand and forgive what she had done. It was the first subject that he had ever been unable to discuss with his wife, which had created a barrier between them. Julia had stopped asking about it, and they both tried to act as though nothing was wrong. That was impossible, because Julia and his mother visited back and forth often, and he had lost the feeling of precious, total intimacy with Julia.

His business affairs had taken the same path as his personal life, and bankruptcy was no longer something that could happen only to others. With no means of protecting his real estate from arson, he had sold all of it, but the funds had quickly dissipated. In instances when leased houses had burned, he had felt morally obligated to reimburse the people for the unused portions of the leases. Many unanticipated expenses had also arisen, diminishing his cash reserves. The dry dock had begun producing a small profit, but that from the Bank of Commerce remained at an ebb. Revenues from the dry dock and the marine insurance company were barely covering his expenses.

The only favorable development for months had been the arrest of the arsonist at the ropewalk. When his carriage drew up at the police station at George and Argyle Streets, Morton stepped out briskly, but his expectations quickly changed to disappointment. In the booking room, the chief inspector was snarling orders at apprehensive constables who were scampering about. He took Morton to one side to talk with him.

The chief inspector, a large, bluff policeman named Walter Polding, was furiously angry and just as embarrassed. "That prisoner won't be able to tell us anything, Sir Morton," he said grimly. "The man's dead."

"Dead?" Morton exclaimed. "I understood he had only minor injuries."

Walter nodded somberly. "You understood correctly, Sir Morton. However, after he was brought here and put in a cell, he somehow came into possession of a bottle of rum. And it was laced with arsenic." He glared around the room at the constables. "Somehow a bottle of rum laced with arsenic found its way past the guards, the turnkey, and everyone else."

His temper flaring, Morton started to demand an explanation, then he thought again. Walter was already sufficiently angry and chagrined, and Morton knew what had happened—Creevey had found someone who would accept a bribe and had eliminated a potential witness against him.

Morton went back out to his carriage and told the driver to take him to the Merchants Exchange. As the carriage moved down the street, he looked out the window moodily. Even the weather was depressing, because winter seemed to be arriving early, and it promised to be very rainy.

As it had been for months, the Merchants Exchange was quiet, reflecting the continuing slow pace of business in the city. Morton noticed that one of the men present, James Haslett, seemed as downcast as he was himself. A resourceful, hard-working man in his thirties, James was the general manager of Broken Hill Associates, the large mining consortium.

Talking with the man, Morton learned that James was dejected because a large quantity of supplies that he had sent to Adelaide had been lost in a shipwreck in Bass Strait. "I wanted to get the supplies delivered to Broken Hill as soon as possible," he explained. "It appears that this will be a rainy winter all over the continent, and the Darling River may become too flooded for riverboats to get upstream from Adelaide to Menindee."

"Yes, that can happen even during years of average rainfall," Morton observed. "Have you dispatched another shipment yet?"

James smiled wryly, shaking his head. "My staff is working very hard to get that done, but it isn't a small task. The value of the shipment amounted to some two thousand guineas, and it was meant to completely provision well over two hundred men through next spring."

Impressed by the large quantity of supplies, Morton commented that it was a very difficult task indeed. He ended his conversation with James, wishing him well, then talked to a few other men and looked at the boards where the insurance rates and other information was posted. Then he went back out to his carriage, telling the driver to return to Kings Cross.

The atmosphere in his offices was somber, the staff fearful of being unemployed. That feeling had intensified during the past few days, ever since Morton had told the head clerk to make a study of ways to reduce expenses. It was evident to everyone that laying off employees was logical, because the amount of work to be done had diminished sharply.

A tense silence fell when Morton entered the main office and Albert Loman told him that the study was finished. Morton beckoned him, going upstairs to his office, and the head clerk followed him with a sheaf of papers. Morton seated himself at his desk, and Albert sat on the chair beside it as he began going over the various options he had identified.

The first was to combine the work so that two clerks and five apprentices could be laid off. Morton shook his head, determined to retain all of the employees for the present. The head clerk smiled in relief and placed the paper aside. He went on to the next one, which was reducing by ten percent all wages and the amounts paid to pensioners from the firm. "Yes, but not the pensions," Morton told him. "They're little enough as it is. Also lower the amount paid into my personal account by ten percentum."

Albert made a note on the paper, then went on to other options. When he finished, he rapidly totaled up amounts. "That will produce a savings of some thirty guineas per month, Sir Morton," he said. "Incidentally, in regard to private information of the firm getting into the wrong hands, the apprentice Jubal Averly has been acting suspicious."

Morton was surprised, finding it difficult to believe that

the apprentice whom Albert had named could possibly be guilty of anything disloyal. "What has he been doing that seems suspicious?"

"Looking into work that others do, which we agreed was something that would bear careful watching. Moreover, he's been doing it so cautiously that Mr. Fraley and I didn't notice it until very recently."

"But the boy is one of the third-generation employees in the firm. His grandfather is a pensioner who used to work as a clerk for my uncle and me, and his father was a clerk here until he went to his reward."

"Yes, but I'm sure of what I observed, Sir Morton. With your permission, Mr. Fraley and I will watch him in the offices and also in the evenings."

Morton sighed, nodding in agreement, and the head clerk left. Pondering the subject, Morton reflected that it had become more and more evident that Creevey was somehow obtaining information from the offices, because only the sources of income had been struck. The office building, Morton's house, and the one where his mother lived were a drain, a monthly expense for caretaking and maintence, and they remained safe. Sighing again, Morton sat up and began going through the papers on his desk.

Months before, he had acknowledged that at least some of his business difficulties stemmed from insufficient attention on his part. He remained at his desk until late, going home in the rainy, dreary twilight. Being with his family was the joyous pleasure it had always been, but now that feeling was tainted with pain. The rift between him and his mother continued to echo to a slight degree in his relationship with Julia, and the loss of even that small measure of harmony with her made him keenly remorseful.

The strain between them was less evident when they had much to discuss, which they did that evening. Morton told her about the fire at the ropewalk and the murder of the arsonist, discussing all of the ramifications with her. When the discussion moved on to other things, Julia made no direct mention of his mother, but it was evident to him from her conversation that they had visited during the day. Julia talked about Catherine instead, remarking on how much the woman had improved since coming to Sydney.

Morton had noticed the improvement himself, because there were occasions when he saw his mother and Catherine. It was evident that Catherine had recovered her emotional balance and no longer needed his mother's support and companionship. He also knew that his mother would be much happier at Tibooburra Station, yet she remained in Sydney.

Her stated reason was still that the station manager would exercise more initiative in her absence, but Morton wondered if that was partly an excuse. When he had seen his mother, he had observed that she was looking older, and it occurred to him that she may have given up on life. If so, he knew that at least part of the reason was their estrangement. His love for her remained as strong as ever, and the thought that she might have lost interest in life and her will to live kept him awake for hours after he went to bed.

The following morning, the cost estimate for repairs to the ropewalk was on Morton's desk, and he approved it. It was just under a hundred guineas, less than he had feared, but far more than he could afford. That afternoon, when he went to the Merchants Exchange, the clerk was erasing the figures on the board where interest rates were posted in preparation to change them. A moment later, an apprentice from the Bank of Commerce came in, looking for Morton to tell him about an emergency meeting of the directors.

Banks in the city had finally caved in under pressure from Creevey, reducing their interest rates. Some had gone down to eight percent and others to seven, which made the meeting a stormy one. After a lengthy, heated debate, Morton relented and agreed to the lower figure. The next day, however, Creevey's bank reduced its interest rates to six percent.

* * *

A few days later, Morton received a message from the manager of the marine insurance company, informing him that an insured vessel had wrecked on the Great Barrier Reef. Another ship insured by the company had been lost less than three weeks before, which eliminated any possibility of a profit from the company for the next month or two. It was a principal source of income for Morton, and his financial situation was becoming dire. Then, the following week, three more ships were lost in rapid sequence.

During the turbulent meeting of company directors, Morton said nothing. The other directors merely vented their feelings and agonized helplessly, because nothing could be done about the situation, and no worthwhile results came from the meeting. After it ended, Morton went to the admiralty office to research the information that would disprove a suspicion that had occurred to him, but which was unlikely on the face of it.

Instead, he found evidence to support the suspicion. The rash of sinkings had struck only vessels insured by the company, because only one out of the dozens of other ships sailing from Sydney had sunk during that period. In each of the five sinkings, the malfunction of steering or navigational equipment at a crucial moment had caused the shipwreck.

The facts seemed conclusive to him, and when he discussed it with Julia that evening, she agreed. "Scuttling ships seems extreme, but we know that Creevey will do anything to achieve his ends," she said. "Those who did it would be in just as much danger as everyone on the vessel, so it must be expensive to bribe men to scuttle a ship."

"It might not be," Morton replied. "Creevey would need only one hireling aboard a ship to stealthily damage the rudder chains, set the compass awry, or do any of the many other things that will put a ship on the rocks. And when the one who did it returns for his money, he might collect only what the arsonist at the jail did, leaving no witnesses."

Julia acknowledged that strong possibility, and they discussed other aspects of the situation. Morton pointed out that there were three marine insurance companies in Sydney, but only vessels insured by his had been sinking recently. After they talked it over, Julia and Morton reluctantly agreed that he had only one possible course of action open to him.

The following morning, Morton sent an apprentice to the Merchants Exchange to find out the most recent quotes on stock in the insurance company. When he had the information, he sent apprentices to the other directors of the company to summon them to a meeting, and took his stock certificates out of the safe. Then he called for his carriage.

At the meeting, Morton told the other directors what he had found out at the admiralty office the day before. "I have no evidence against Creevey, of course," he continued. "If I did, I'd talk with the attorney general, not with you. However, it's no secret that we're at odds, and his methods are equally well known. So I'm a Jonah in the boat here, and all of you have suffered financially." He took out his stock certificates and tossed them on the table. "To compensate for that, I'll sell my shares to you as a group at seventy-five percentum discount from par. For an investment of five hundred guineas, you should soon recoup your losses, and more."

The other directors listened to Morton in shock and remorse. They were silent for a moment, then with some embarrassment among them, they hastily accepted the offer. Moments later, Morton left with a cheque and took it to the Bank of Commerce to deposit it in his business account.

He went to the ropewalk to look at the repairs in progress, then to the dry dock, his single remaining source of income. A large, three-masted ship that was in the dock would be finished soon, which would cover expenses for a few weeks. While talking with Virgil Handley, the foreman, Morton told him to warn the nightwatchman to stay very alert. Morton then returned to his carriage, telling the driver to take him to the Merchants Exchange.

While he was studying the boards where interest rates and other information was posted, a floorboard behind Morton creaked. Then he heard Creevey's falsetto voice, raised barely above a whisper: "This needn't go on," the man said. "My offer of a partnership still stands. As a token of good faith, tell me where Benjamin Tavish is, then we can be partners. I have an undertaking at hand that will make you a millionaire many times over."

"I'll never sink so low as to be a partner with you, Creevey," Morton replied quietly, not turning.

Creevey laughed scornfully as he walked away. Fuming with anger, Morton finished looking at the information on the boards, then left. Creevey's huge, gaudy carriage was just moving away from the building. Morton stepped into his own carriage, telling the driver to take him to Kings Cross.

Through the rest of the day, Morton tried to devise a strategy to regain his financial stability. Sitting at his desk, he pored over the papers on it and notes from his files, searching for a highly profitable way to use the five hundred guineas. Several ideas occurred to him, but none that had a reasonable chance of success against the formidable combination of Creevey's ruinous plots and the depressed business climate.

As he dismissed each of them and racked his brain for others, Morton was haunted by memories of his uncle, who had suffered defeat and bankruptcy as a middle-aged man. When dusk fell, he lit the lamp on his desk and continued pondering. A short time later, Albert Loman stepped in.

The head clerk began talking about Jubal Averly, saying that the apprentice had been secretly delivering information to someone. Twice each week, he had been going to the public cemetery after dark. The apprentice had been placing notes describing various office activities in an urn beside a crypt, and taking out money that had been left there.

Albert continued, "Mr. Fraley and I lost him numerous times before we learned where he was going. We went there shortly before he did last Thursday and saw that a crown was in the urn, and we left it. Yesterday evening, we waited until he left the cemetery, and saw that he had placed a page of notes on business affairs in the urn, which we also left. I believed that you would prefer dealing with this in private, so I kept him after the rest of the staff went home. He is waiting downstairs to confess his treachery, Sir Morton."

Even though he tried to feel angry, Morton experienced only crushing disappointment and remorse. Being betrayed remained his great fear, and it was a worse blow than the fires, ship sinkings, and other things. Sitting back in his chair, he nodded in grim resignation. The head clerk stepped to the door and sternly called to Jubal Averly. A moment later, Morton heard the apprentice coming slowly up the stairs, weeping.

A husky, bright-faced youth of fifteen, Jubal sobbed brokenly as he came into the office. "I'm dreadfully sorry, Sir Morton," he wailed. "It wasn't for the money. Two men said they would kill my sisters and my mother."

Morton seized on the boy's words, immensely relieved that he had not been betrayed for money: "You were approached by men who threatened your family if you didn't do as they said?" he asked.

"Yes, sir," the boy sobbed. "And if I told anyone about it. At first I didn't believe them, then one morning our dog was dead. Its head was cut off, and its entrails scattered about. My mother and sisters were in a terrible state for days. I didn't know what to do, because my father is dead and my grandfather couldn't help. Then the two men came again, and they said they would do the same to my mother and sisters...."

His voice fading, Jubal wept bitterly, and the head clerk's stony disapproval changed to shocked dismay. Morton stood up and stepped to the window, consumed by the intensity of his burning hatred for Creevey. Folding his hands behind his back, he looked down at the rainy, foggy street in the dim glow of the gaslights without seeing it.

When the apprentice controlled his tears, Morton questioned him. The youth had never seen the two men before or after they had confronted him. He had taken information to the cemetery for a year, and his replies explained many things. That was how Creevey had found out about the house on Grace Street, and was the source of his suspicions toward Benjamin Tavish when Beverly had disappeared. Most recently, it was how he had learned which ships had been insured by the marine insurance company,

"I haven't spent a farthing of the money, Sir Morton," Jubal added. "I'll bring all of it to you tomorrow."

"No, it doesn't make any difference," Morton told him. "You must continue taking notes to the cemetery, or you and your family may be endangered. However, Mr. Loman will tell you what to write."

"Yes, sir. I'm dreadful sorry this happened, Sir Morton."

Forcing a smile, Morton dismissed the youth, then sat back down at his desk as Jubal left. Albert stirred, clearing his throat. "This is the most . . ." His voice faded and he shrugged, at a loss for words to describe his feelings. "We could have constables watch the cemetery and arrest whoever comes for the notes, Sir Morton," he suggested.

"They would merely arrest some waif who had been paid tuppence to pick up the notes and take them to another hiding place," Morton replied wearily. "Creevey is as cunning as he is ruthless."

"Cunning and ruthless indeed," Albert agreed. "In drafting what to give Jubal, I'll be very careful to make it appear as complete as before, but I'll leave out anything that might be damaging to the firm."

"Very well, but there is little left to damage."

The head clerk nodded in somber agreement as he left.

Morton resumed poring over the papers on his desk for a few minutes, but it suddenly seemed very futile. He sighed heavily, extinguishing the lamp on his desk, then went downstairs to his carriage.

When he arrived at home, he had never been more grateful for Julia's warm, understanding sympathy and love. She made his home a refuge, and his many troubles seemed less onerous as he discussed them with her. But in addition, he had never been more regretful over the subtle difference in their relationship because of his alienation from his mother.

He yearned for the total harmony with Julia that made his life rich with joy, and he also wanted to make peace with his mother. But in his thoughts, what his mother had done remained a betrayal, one that had extended over decades. Any reconciliation he attempted with her would be false, which she would immediately detect. The present state of affairs was tormenting for both of them, but hypocrisy between them would be worse.

The next morning, while Morton was having breakfast, a workman from the dry dock came to the house for him. By the time Morton reached it, the nightwatchman had been taken to the hospital, and the fire brigade was leaving. There had been little they could do, for the dock and the ship in it had been engulfed by flames when they had arrived. The dock had caved in, and the water was littered with charred wood, a pall of smoke hanging over it.

The owner of the ship, a former sea captain, was a grizzled, middle-aged man named John Cosgrave. "Well, I trust you have ample coverage in fire insurance, Sir Morton," he said.

"Unfortunately, I have none."

"Bloody hell!" the man gasped. He looked at the ruined dock and wreckage, sighing grimly. "Will we have to go to court over this?"

"I'd certainly prefer that we keep our monies between ourselves, rather than share it with lawyers. What value do you place on the ship?"

John started to reply, then thought again. After pondering for a moment, he shrugged. "Eight hundred guineas is as low as I can go, and it's lower than I'd go for most. I think it's a fair price."

"It's more than fair, and I'll see that you get it, Mr. Cosgrave."

"There's no hurry, Sir Morton," John said, turning away. "We both know who did this, may his vile soul burn in hell."

The man left, and the foreman stepped up to Morton. His face pale and drawn with anxiety, Virgil Handley was hesitant about speaking until Morton asked about the nightwatchman, then he nodded eagerly. "He'll be all right, Sir Morton," he said. "He'll be up and about in a day or two." Virgil paused, then cleared his throat. "What shall I have the men do?"

"For now, have them restore order here as much as possible. I'll talk with you later about future plans."

The foreman nodded worriedly, calling to the workmen, and Morton returned to his carriage. Stepping into it, he told the driver to take him back home. As the carriage moved away from the docks and through the streets, Morton numbly tried to think of what he could do. The fire at the dry dock had been a final blow, but he was determined not to accept defeat.

Julia remained as composed as ever while Morton told her what had happened, then she asked what he intended to do. He silently shrugged and shook his head, having no idea. After drinking a cup of coffee, he went back out to his carriage to go to work. Word of the disaster had reached his offices when he arrived, and the atmosphere was more somber than ever.

Morton looked up the amount in his account at the bank, and decided to take a mortgage on either his house or his office building for the sum to pay for the ship. With that settled, he turned to a far more distasteful matter that he had been procrastinating over for weeks. The time was long past when he should have begun laying off employees, and he took the rosters out of his desk drawer to make up a list of those who had to go.

It was the most difficult task he had ever undertaken. He agonized for long minutes over decisions between clerks with more seniority and those with more children, and apprentices whose justification for remaining was similarly difficult to compare. He was still working on the list during early afternoon, when a footstep in the doorway drew his attention. Looking up he was startled to see his mother standing there.

She had a cane, which he had never seen her use before, and he noticed that she suddenly looked even more aged and careworn than she had appeared very recently. As she came into the office, they both assumed an attitude of careful, formal courtesy. He stood up and stepped to the chair beside the desk to seat her. "Good day, Mother," he said. "Please sit down."

"Good day, Morton," she replied, opening her reticule as she stepped toward his desk. "Thank you, but I can't stay. I saw downstairs that you've kept your full staff, even though business is very slow now. That's highly commendable and speaks well of you as an employer."

"I'm pleased that you think so, but it will end shortly. Affairs have now come to a point where I must discharge most of them."

"No, you won't have to," she told him, taking an envelope from her reticule and placing it on the desk. "I visited Julia this morning and heard what happened to your dry dock. There is a cheque for three thousand guineas. It should see to your expenses until business recovers from this slump, with enough left over for a few relatively modest investments."

Morton gazed at the envelope, speechless with astonishment, then he recalled her financial situation. "It was my understanding that your cash reserves had been used up in buying Merino sheep," he said.

She nodded, closing her reticule. "Yes, so I took a mortgage on the station. It's only for two months, which will entail little interest. I'll pay it off in full from the payment for last spring's clip, which I should receive from the broker in London within a month or so."

"I can't allow you to do this, Mother!" Morton exclaimed, appalled. "You can't be sure of how much you'll receive for the wool, and you'll need that money. How will you pay the station expenses?"

"We've never received less than five thousand," she replied, her cane tapping as she stepped back toward the door. "And that was when the market was poor. As for expenses, supplies are the main one, and there is an abundance at the station. Ever since we began receiving them by riverboat, we've kept a two-year quantity of nonperishables on hand. As you know, riverboats on the Darling River aren't entirely dependable."

"But you mustn't do this, Mother!" Morton insisted. "You're risking what you've worked for all of your life, and for a pittance of its value!"

Alexandra stopped in the doorway, tears in her eyes as she gazed at him. "The station is precious to me," she said quietly. "But there are other things that I value far more. Good day, Morton."

As she stepped through the doorway and left, tears also came to Morton's eyes. They were tears of anguish over their estrangement, as well as of shame because he was unable to reach out to her in true, heartfelt forgiveness. Presently, he grimly collected his thoughts and stepped to the door, calling downstairs for his carriage to be brought around.

Before he went to the Bank of Commerce to deposit the cheque, he stopped at the Bank of New South Wales, where the station account had always been kept. Morton talked with the manager, confirming what he had dreaded, and he was nauseated with anxiety when he left.

Just after his mother had drawn up the mortgage, the manager of Creevey's bank had come there to buy it, paying a large premium without quibbling over the amount. If anything happened to prevent her from paying off the mortgage on the day it was due, Creevey would take possession of Tibooburra Station for a tiny fraction of its value. And Morton knew that if there was any way he could, Creevey would prevent her from paying it off.

Chapter Twenty-One

"It's a shameful waste, Jeremy," Fiona said. "It's a waste of more beef than most families have within two or three years."

"Yes, it is," Jeremy replied, dismounting from his panting horse. His saddle girth had loosened while the bull chased him about, and he tightened it. "I dislike shooting bulls at all, and I wish we could at least make full use of it. But we can't dry beef in this weather."

Soft, misty rain was falling, and Fiona nodded in reluctant agreement. Buggie said nothing as he dismounted to skin the bull and cut off choice portions of the meat, his expression indicating that his only thought was happy anticipation of fresh beef for dinner. Jeremy stepped back into his saddle and looked at Fiona as she watched Buggie. At their wedding in Toowoomba, she had been stunningly lovely in her new dress for the occasion, but she seemed even more beautiful and appealing to him now.

Her bright red hair added rich color and life to the

rainy day as drops spilled from the wide brim of her stockman's hat, joining the tiny rivulets trickling down her thick coat made from the skins of woolies. With her lovely features reflecting the regret that she had put into words, her wide green eyes gazed pensively at Buggie. Then she glanced at Jeremy, her expression changing to a sparkling smile that was a silent reference to their private moments and their shared secret knowledge of each other.

Jeremy smiled, his love for her so intense that it was a poignant, bittersweet ache within him. Then he turned to Buggie. "Fiona and I will go and find the rest of the herd," he said.

"Aye, very well," Buggie replied, bending over the bull and slicing the skin with his knife. "I'll catch up with you directly."

Jeremy turned his horse and rode in the direction the other dunnocks had fled, Fiona riding beside him. The animals had crushed the damp spinifex and brushed the moisture off climps of mallee and mulga when they had scattered, leaving trails that were easy to see. After a hundred yards, the trails converged where the dunnocks had started collecting together again, and Jeremy led the way toward a hill a short distance to one side.

At the crest of the hill, Jeremy scanned the terrain ahead. The rain limited his visibility, but he could just make out a brushy ravine some two miles away, where the dunnocks had gone. "They've stopped there," he said, pointing. "It's a sheltered place, with mallee to graze, and far enough away for them to have got over being frightened."

"I'm sure you're right," Fiona remarked. "You always know where dunnocks are, and everything else about the outback." She laughed, shaking her head. "But you were wrong about the weather."

"I was wrong," Jeremy acknowledged, laughing. "But this is unusual. If this much rain fell here every year, it would be completely taken up by sheep and cattle stations. Normally, it's much drier than this."

"I would like it just as much when it's dry," Fiona said, gazing around in deep satisfaction. "It's so wonderful to be far away from the dirt, noise, and crowds of the towns and cities. I love the outback, and you've made me so marvelously happy, Jeremy. I truly wish my poor mother could have had the smallest portion of my happiness, but she had none."

Jeremy made no reply, having found that was best whenever Fiona mentioned her mother. During the past weeks, she had spoken about her mother with increasing frequency. Jeremy had learned that the most effective way to help her come to terms with her sorrow was to allow her to simply talk, rather than to turn her memories into a conversation.

Tears came to her eyes and overflowed on some occasions when she spoke about her mother, and then Jeremy held her, providing silent sympathy and comfort. This time, however, her mind turned to humorous incidents associated with her mother. She talked about amusing mistakes she had made when her mother had been teaching her to cook, plant crops, and do other things.

She talked about her mother only when they were alone, and she broke off as Buggie rode up with the meat wrapped in the skin tied behind his saddle. "Let me have the meat and skin, Buggie," she said. "I'll go prepare dinner while you and Jeremy are driving the dunnocks to the valley."

Buggie dismounted and unfastened the rolled skin from his saddle, then lifted it up behind hers and tied it. During the first days after they had left civilization behind, Jeremy had been reluctant for Fiona to venture off alone. That had clashed with her independent character, and with good reason, because he had found that she was fully capable of avoiding dangers. She and Jeremy exchanged a smile as she rode away, then Buggie swung back up into his saddle and followed Jeremy toward the ravine.

Six cows, four stirks, and three calves were in the ravine, and Jeremy and Buggie snapped their stock whips

386 Aaron Fletcher

as they rode around the animals, driving them toward the valley. Twilight was falling when they reached it and the dunnocks filed through the gate. Rain had turned the billabong into a creek, and the campfire under the overhang at the front of the large bark hut cast a cheerful, welcoming glow through the rain and gathering darkness as Fiona moved about it and prepared dinner.

Jeremy and Buggie released their horses with the others and carried their saddles under the shelter while Fiona dished up the food. She cut the length of roasted tenderloin into thick, succulent slices and piled the plates high with well-seasoned carrots, peas, and fried potatoes. Crisp, delicious simnel bread and steaming billys of tea accompanied the meal, and Fiona had made fritters from dried peaches for dessert.

The roaring fire and hot tea dispelled the damp cold of the winter night as they ate hungrily and talked. It was taking longer than before to gather dunnocks, because water was plentiful and the animals were more scattered. Some seventy had been collected, including calves, and Buggie brought up the subject of what they would do after they sold the herd.

"I'd like to take a look at the land that lies southwest of here and north of the Darling River," Jeremy told him, then turned to Fiona. "Is that agreeable to you, love?"

"As long as it's in the outback, I'll be content," she replied.

Buggie chuckled and nodded in approval at her answer, then shrugged indifferently when he was asked the same question. His plate was scraped clean, and his attention had turned to the fritters that Fiona had made. She passed them out, and the portly, bearded man greedily dug into his, eating the crisp pastry and sweet filling with gusto.

When they finished the meal, they drank the rest of their tea and discussed where to search for dunnocks the next day. Buggie was tactful, having taken it upon himself to divide the hut with canvas so Jeremy and Fiona would have some privacy, and he also knew they needed time alone. After drinking his tea, he went into his cubicle inside the hut, and he was sound asleep in his blanket a few minutes later.

The wailing of dingoes and calls of night birds came out of the darkness, and the rain pattered softly on the shelter as Jeremy and Fiona talked about his search for a place to settle. It had become a shared objective, Fiona joining him in his walkabout, but one of no urgency. They were both happy at their camp in the immensity of the outback, enjoying every moment. The conversation ended when a kiss stirred desire, and they went into the hut to make love and then to hold each other close through the night.

The following day, with the rain still falling, it was late afternoon before they found a small herd and drove it to the valley in the gathering dusk. That night, the rain diminished and then ended. The next morning brought clearing skies and an icily cold and windy day, the winter weather becoming more normal for the arid region.

With the improved visibility, Jeremy was able to see small herds at a distance at times, occasionally eliminating the need to search for them. In addition, wet weather creeks began drying up after the second day. The dunnocks became less scattered, staying closer to available water, and the number penned in the valley began growing more rapidly.

Fiona continued speaking of her mother during conversations when she and Jeremy were alone, and she also brought up the subject of Donley a few times. She talked about how crafty and false he could be, hiding his true nature, which was how he had deceived her mother into marrying him. On one occasion, she described Donley's reaction to her mother's death. "Not a word of sorrow did he utter," she said bitterly. "All he did was grizzle about how much trouble and expense the funeral would be."

As usual when she spoke on the subject, her statements called for no specific reply. Jeremy silently nodded in acknowledgement, reflecting that it had been characteristic of Donley. Fiona continued talking and related instances of the man's cruelty to her mother, then she talked about her brothers and how they had left home as soon as they were old enough.

Presently, Fiona began talking about other things, as she always did. The instances when she spoke about her mother were spread among other discussions, because she had an optimistic, cheerful disposition and disliked dwelling on depressing topics. Jeremy understood her feelings, as well as her need to talk about and come to terms with her grief.

On another occasion when Fiona brought up the subject, she blamed Donley for her mother's premature death. "The doctor told me that Mother had no reason to live," she said. "Small wonder, with a husband like Seton Donley. I never had any money to pay the doctor, but it made no difference to him. Doctor Willis was a very kind, generous man."

The name seemed remotely familiar to Jeremy from long before. He started to ask Fiona about the doctor, but they were waiting on a hill for Buggie, who just then rode out of the trees below the hill. When he came up the slope to them, Jeremy pointed out places for him to check for dunnocks. He left, and Jeremy again started to ask Fiona about the doctor as they rode down the hill, but she resumed talking about her mother.

They headed toward a thicket that Jeremy had chosen for them to search, riding at a slow pace so they could talk. Fiona described the progress of her mother's disease, explaining that the doctor had changed his prognosis. "When I asked him about it," she continued, "he told me that he had based his opinion on another woman with the same kind of cancer. She was his patient when he had a practice in Sydney, a woman named Clara McTavish."

Jeremy reined up sharply, suddenly having a clear mental image of the doctor at the house where he had lived as a boy. "No, the woman's name was Clara Tavish, not McTavish, wasn't it?" he said. "Tell me everything that the doctor said about her, Fiona."

Fiona was startled, her horse moving on for a few paces. She stopped it and turned back, thinking. "Yes, I believe the name was Tavish," she mused. "Well, he said that she kept her strength longer than my mother because she had reason to do so. She had several children, one of them small, and she needed to make arrangements for the child's care. He also said that she went back to her home in Scotland to save her children the grief of seeing her die. That's all I remember, Jeremy. Why do you want to know?"

"Clara Tavish was my mother," he said quietly.

"Your mother?" Fiona echoed in astonishment. "If you had ever mentioned her name, Jeremy, I'm sure I would have recalled what Dr. Willis said. Then she didn't abandon you at all, did she? She was dying, and she . . ."

Fiona's voice faded, and she shrugged helplessly, gazing at Jeremy in shock and concern. He numbly lifted his reins and rode on toward the thicket, Fiona following him. The horses broke into a canter, bursting through the brush and making enough noise to frighten any dunnocks that might be there. Jeremy was unconscious of that, heading toward the thicket without thinking and only because that was where he had been going.

His mind reeled with the knowledge that he had committed a grievous wrong against his mother as well as against the Kerrick family. At the thicket, he turned away without glancing into it. There were other places he had intended to search, but he had forgotten where they were. He rode toward a hill, Fiona following him.

At the crest of the hill, Jeremy stopped and looked out over the terrain without seeing it as he struggled to overcome his confusion. Fiona reined up and sat on her horse a few yards away. A few minutes later, when Buggie rode up the hill, she beckoned him. They talked quietly for a moment and then fell silent, watching Jeremy and waiting.

His guilt was agonizing as he thought about his mother

and his inability to make amends. He recalled his grandmother and how warmly affectionate she had been to
him, and he was remorseful over his injustice to her and
the other Kerricks. However, while his mother had been
dead for over a decade, he could still explain his actions
to the Kerricks.

When he sat up and turned to Fiona and Buggie, she
knew what he intended to do. "Do you want to take the
dunnocks to Bourke before going to Tibooburra Station?" she asked. "Or shall we turn them loose?"

"We may as well take those we have now to Bourke,"
he replied, lifting his reins and turning his horse. "After
so many years, a week or two won't make any difference.
Let's go and start getting organized to leave."

Fiona and Buggie turned their horses and rode back
toward the valley with Jeremy. He still felt confused to
an extent, but one thing was clear to him. In deciding to
go to Tibooburra Station, he had acknowledged within
himself that he was a member of the Kerrick family. In
his mind, the name had become his surname, not merely
a means of referring to him.

With that shift in attitude, the sense of rootlessness
that he had felt all of his life disappeared. As a boy, he
had been conscious of having a mother and siblings with
a different surname than his, but now he was aware that
he had origins, blood relatives, and a family. It was as
though he had found his heritage mentally and emotionally, if not physically.

It occurred to Jeremy that the opposite had happened
to Jarboe Charlie. Jarboe had completed his walkabout
and reached the place of his heritage, but for a time, he
had remained at a distance from it in an emotional and
mental sense. Jeremy wondered how great a distance still
lay between him and his physical heritage, and how long
he would continue on his walkabout until he finally found
the place where he belonged.

When they reached the wide cattle track leading to
Bourke, Jeremy began talking with Fiona and Buggie

about the various means of traveling to Tibooburra Station. However, after they had driven the herd down the track to where he could see the Darling River, one option was eliminated. Even though no rain had fallen for several days, the river was flooded, and Jeremy knew that no riverboats would be traveling downstream to Wilcannia.

Then, one evening a few days later, a conversation that Jeremy had with a swagman eliminated going to Tibooburra Station at all. A ragged, wizened man in his sixties, he came up the track just as Fiona finished preparing dinner. Jeremy invited him to share the meal and the camp, and he accepted with a wide, eager grin, saying his name was Obadiah Tuttle.

While introducing himself and the others, Jeremy acknowledged his relationship to the Kerrick family. The swagman became even more cordial, reflecting the fact that he was dependent upon the generosity of station owners. "Just call me Obie," he said, eyeing his plate happily as Fiona filled it with smoked ham, potatoes, and vegetables. "I opined you weren't an ordinary drover, Mr. Kerrick. With tucker like this, you couldn't be. I was proper sorry to hear about Mr. David and Mr. Jonathan Kerrick. They were fair dinkum outback men, and you can be sure they won't soon be forgotten."

"What happened to them?" Jeremy asked.

Obie expressed surprise that Jeremy was unaware that the men were dead, then he explained as everyone began eating. Typical of a swagman's story, it had many unlikely embellishments that Jeremy ignored, gleaning the essential facts. "And then," Obie continued through a mouthful of food, "Mistress Catherine went crank. I mean no offense, Mr. Kerrick, and I'm only telling what happened. She kept seeing flocks of white cockatoos flying through the house and such as that, and everybody on the station was in mortal fear of their lives to go near her. All except Mistress Alexandra, of course, who fears naught that walks, crawls, flies, or swims. So she trussed up Mistress Catherine with rope and took her to Sydney, and they're still there."

Obie took another bite of food, expressing his condolences again, then changed the subject. He had heard that Jeremy and Buggie had crossed the Great Divide with a herd of dunnocks, and now he brought it up, wanting to know more about the journey. Buggie obliged him, embellishing the story in a fashion that would do credit to any swagman.

Along with his intense regret over the deaths in the family, Jeremy disliked the prospect of going to Sydney, because he had no desire ever to see his father again. When they lay down in their blankets around the fire, he quietly discussed it with Fiona. From the first, she had looked forward with keen anticipation to meeting the Kerrick family, and she readily accepted the change in plans. She pointed out that Morton might have mellowed over the years, and Jeremy should reserve judgment about him.

The most direct route to Sydney was by way of a track from Bourke to Bathurst, but Jeremy had never seen it. The next day, while driving the dunnocks on down the track, he talked with a traveler who had been down the Bathurst track, and he said it was a good one. He had heard about the journey Buggie and Jeremy had made to Brisbane, and he congratulated Jeremy for performing a public service by opening a route across the mountains.

The fact that the journey across the Great Divide was well known in the area was again evident to Jeremy three days later, at the mustering grounds on the outskirts of Bourke. The stockyard buyers knew about it, and they discussed it with Jeremy while looking at the dunnocks. As he had expected, the uncertainty of when the animals could be shipped out by riverboat made the offers for them very low. The best offer, forty guineas, was made by the same man who had bought the first herd, and Jeremy accepted it.

The buyer also made an offer for some of the horses, but Jeremy declined to sell them. Even though five pack horses were far more than they needed for the trip to Sydney, he preferred to keep the ones he had rather than buy others when they returned to the outback. After the herd was delivered to the stockyard, the rest of the day was spent in replenishing supplies and having horses shod, then they left at dawn the next morning.

Creeks were swollen and billabongs were overflowing from heavy rains, but several days had passed since the last one, and the track was in good condition. The horses were well rested after the slow journey with the herd, and the cold, clear weather made them spirited. They easily maintained a fast canter for hours, but Jeremy limited the distance they traveled each day to fifty or sixty miles out of consideration for Buggie's age.

At sunset on most days, they camped beside the track in a place that was sheltered from the wind. On some occasions, they met a station owner who was headed home after visiting neighbors or seeing to business affairs, and the grazier insisted that they spend the night at his station. The hospitality was unstinting, children vacating a room at the house for Jeremy and Fiona, and the owner providing a bunk in the barracks for Buggie.

While in Brisbane, Jeremy had heard comments about the depressed state of commerce, and the graziers talked gloomily about the same subject. In addition to wool, most of them sold sheepskins and tallow, but the market for those commodities had completely faded away. Without exception, the graziers were anxiously awaiting word on how much their clip from the previous spring had brought at the brokerage houses in London.

Also without exception, there was lengthy conversation about the Kerrick family and the giant Tibooburra Station. At one station, where the owner had a niece who was a maid in Sydney, Jeremy heard more recent news of his grandmother. In a letter to her family, the maid had stated that Alexandra Kerrick was living in a house once owned by her father on Wentworth Street in the Whitlam district of Sydney.

Bathurst came into view one morning at a junction where the track was joined by several others. Two were the routes to Wilcannia and Menindee on the Darling

River, while others led to the north and south. The tracks combined into a wide, well-traveled road leading into the town.

Situated astride the upper reaches of the Macquarie River, the town had spread out into the surrounding area during the years since Jeremy had passed through it with Jarboe Charlie. The road fed into a busy street in the business district on the north side of the town. The cobblestone street was muddy, and workers in the businesses that lined it were cleaning up and salvaging goods in the aftermath of a recent flood by the river.

The eastern end of the street turned into the road that wound through the foothills and then up into the steep slopes of the Blue Mountains. At sunset, they stopped to camp near the place where Jeremy had camped with Jarboe Charlie years before. The following day, where the eastern foothills of the mountains fell away into the Emu Plains, the Nepean River was swollen, its muddy waters only a few feet below the wooden bridge.

Considering how much everything else had changed, Jeremy was surprised to see that the thick forest beside the river where he had met Jarboe Charlie had remained untouched through the years. A railroad adjacent to the road led to Parramatta, and Jeremy and Fiona had to help Buggie control the frightened, plunging pack horses as a train roared past.

When they reached Parramatta, they stopped for the night at the Drover's Inn to clean up and sort out their belongings. Fiona brushed and aired her dress and Jeremy's suit that they had bought in Toowoomba for their wedding, and carefully folded them away again. Then she put out clean dungaree clothes for herself and the men while they packed up all of the supplies and camping equipment for when they left Sydney. The following day, they rode away from the inn as an early morning train was rumbling into the town.

Sydney had changed so much that at first it was totally unfamiliar to Jeremy. His feeling of being an absolute stranger was accentuated by the curious glances of passers-by at the hats and thick sheepskin coats that he and the others wore, and at their powerful, shaggy horses. The city and the outback were separated by a distance greater than miles.

Then, while leading the way down a teeming street that crossed a hill, he glimpsed the harbor. The sight of the ships at anchor and the smells carried by the cold, gusty wind off the bay brought back his boyhood in a flood of memories. He began seeing buildings and streets that were familiar, but they all now seemed very small and congested.

He found his way to the Whitlam district, then to Wentworth Street. A grocer's delivery wagon was among the traffic on the street, and the driver pointed out where Jeremy's grandmother lived. "She'll be working in the flower beds in the back garden," he added. "Mistress Kerrick spends most of her time in the gardens, regardless of the weather."

Jeremy thanked the man, turning toward the house. He and Fiona rode through the carriage gate, Buggie following them with the pack horses. They went up the drive beside the large, old house, and it opened out into a paved courtyard in front of the stables. When he saw his grandmother kneeling and mulching a flower bed in the garden on the other side of the courtyard, Jeremy was struck by the fact that she appeared so much older than he remembered, more aged than the number of years that had passed would justify.

As she gazed at him, disbelief and a frantic yearning to believe were mingled on her features. Then she grabbed the cane beside her and began pulling herself to her feet. "Jeremy!" she wailed piteously. "Jeremy, is it you? Is it truly you, my dear grandson? Lord God, let it be you!"

Jeremy jumped down from his horse and ran to her as she almost fell. "Yes, it is, Grandmother," he assured her. "Please be careful."

Clinging to him, Alexandra lifted a trembling hand to

his face, her eyes filling with tears of happiness. "My prayers have been answered," she whispered. "After all these years, you've come back to me."

Jeremy hugged and kissed her, stricken with remorse over how he had misjudged her years before. "I've come back to make amends for those years," he told her, then turned to Fiona as she stepped up beside them. "Grandmother, this is my wife, Fiona."

"Please forgive us for being inconsiderate, Mistress Kerrick," Fiona apologized. "In our eagerness to see you, we neglected your feelings. We should have sent a message to forewarn you of our arrival."

"No, no, my dear," Alexandra replied. "The minutes would have seemed like eternities while I waited. Indeed, I would have been overwrought in any event, because God has answered my prayers twofold. Not only do I have my grandson here, but I have a lovely granddaughter as well."

Fiona smiled in response to the warmly affectionate remark, expressing her pleasure at meeting Alexandra. Jeremy watched as his grandmother regained her composure, becoming more the poised, self-assured woman he remembered. He introduced Buggie, then he and Fiona continued talking with her.

After a moment, Alexandra became more the woman Jeremy remembered, taking charge of the situation. "I've questions to ask that would fill books," she said. "Let's get you settled, then I'll send for Deirdre and Morton and his wife. Buggie, would you like a guest room in the house?"

"No, mo'm," he replied. "The stables will be more at home for me."

"As you wish. There is an empty groom's apartment over the stables, and you'll find that it's quite comfortable. Jeremy, I'll take Fiona inside while you're bringing in the baggage. Come along, my dear."

Leaning on her cane, Alexandra linked her arm through Fiona's and led her toward the house. Jeremy and Buggie took the horses to the stables, where a groom and stableboy helped them unload the pack horses. A few minutes later, the supplies and equipment were stored and Buggie was settling in happily, talking with the groom and stableboy. Jeremy gathered up his and Fiona's belongings and carried them to the house.

As he went inside, his grandmother introduced him to the two other women who lived there. Catherine was an attractive woman in her mid-forties, her white hair making her appear somewhat older. Exchanging greetings with her, Jeremy reflected that if there had ever been any basis for Obie Tuttle's story about her emotional instability, she had evidently recovered from it. Her daughter, Eudora, was a pretty, vivacious young woman in her late teens who had recently graduated from Sydenham Academy.

In their large, well-furnished guest room, Fiona took out her wedding dress and Jeremy's suit. Her dress was pale green muslin with white lace on the cuffs, collar, and bodice, complementing her bright red hair and bringing out the sparkling green in her eyes. After they changed clothes and Fiona pinned up her hair with combs, they went back downstairs, Jeremy glowing with pride in her.

Deirdre had arrived, and she rushed to greet them. Now in her mid-thirties, she had a more mature quality in her striking beauty, but her exuberantly affectionate nature was just the same as Jeremy remembered. She and Fiona were friends at first sight, greeting each other warmly.

Moments after everyone filed into the parlor and sat down, Jeremy heard a carriage draw up outside and knew it was his father's. He was ready to respond in kind to an aloof attitude, but when Morton and Julia stepped in, Jeremy saw that his father was very different from what he remembered.

Morton was speechless with delight and wonder for a moment, his pale blue eyes and expression also reflecting diffidence as he took Jeremy's hand in a firm grip. "This is an exceedingly great pleasure that I've longed for over the years, my son," he said, finding his tongue. Then he hesitated and smiled tentatively. "May I call you my son?"

Jeremy was unable to resist the man's humble, sincere warmth, and he smiled. "That would seem appropriate, wouldn't it, Father?" he suggested.

The reply created a stir of amusement among the others, and Morton grinned happily as he enthusiastically agreed. His charming, attractive wife greeted Jeremy, who in turn introduced Fiona to Morton and Julia. Then everyone found seats, and when Jeremy started to apologize for the distress he had caused the family years before, Morton interrupted him.

"No, it's perfectly understandable," Morton said staunchly. "I own to any blame there may be. What you did was perfectly understandable, Jeremy."

"It was, and I lied to your mother," Alexandra put in candidly. "I wrote and told her that you were settled in comfortably at the station. A few months later, I received a letter from her sister. It said that Clara was content and at peace with herself and with God at the end."

This point having troubled Jeremy, he thanked her, greatly relieved. He asked about his half-sisters and half-brother, and Alexandra explained that Agnes and Daphne were happily married and living in England. When she spoke about Benjamin, however, she said only that he was in good health and spirits, then added that she would explain further at another time.

Her glance at the maid who was opening bottles of port and sherry revealed that Benjamin's whereabouts was a closely held secret, and Jeremy nodded, puzzled and curious. The conversation continued over glasses of wine, Jeremy describing what had happened after he fled from Sydney years before. The destruction of the jail at Eureka was a story that Fiona and Buggie had never tired of hearing, and everyone laughed heartily when he related it. They listened in fascination while he told them about his journey into the far outback with Jarboe Charlie and then his life with the Aranda tribe. Then Jeremy talked about what he had done more recently.

The news had spread to Sydney about two men having found a path through the mountains between Toowoomba and Brisbane, taking a herd of cattle across the Great Divide, but the identity of those who had done it was unknown. Amid the exclamations of surprise and pleasure, Jeremy began telling them about the journey. The hours of the afternoon passed until, in the early evening, the housekeeper stepped in and announced that dinner was served.

The conversation continued through the meal, then everyone returned to the parlor. With the discussion moving on to other things, Jeremy detected that the family was having financial difficulties. No direct mention was made of it, but it became clear through hints in what was said. It surprised Jeremy, because he had thought the family was wealthy.

What surprised him even more was a cool attitude between his father and grandmother. The only evidence was that they always spoke to others, never to one another, which made it difficult to detect. Once he noticed it, however, it seemed glaring to Jeremy, because it clashed with the otherwise cheerful, convivial atmosphere of the gathering.

A man named Creevey was mentioned in disparaging terms, and Jeremy asked about him. Morton replied, briefly explaining that Creevey was a businessman with great wealth but no principles. Then he began talking about other things. That was sufficient for Jeremy to conclude that there had been trouble with the man, resulting in the financial difficulties.

Late in the evening, Morton reluctantly took out his watch and glanced at it, then asked if he and his wife could entertain Jeremy and Fiona the next day. "Perhaps I could come here to get you after breakfast," he suggested. "Then, while Fiona and Julia are visiting at the house, I could show you my business enterprises and introduce you to my friends."

Jeremy glanced at Fiona, who nodded in ready agreement, then turned back to his father. "Yes, we'd like that very much," he said. "I need to buy a few things in the city tomorrow, so if you don't object, I'll spend the morning and part of the afternoon with you."

Morton smiled and expressed satisfaction. He and Julia rose, made their farewells, and left, then Deirdre left a few minutes later. Catherine and Eudora went to their rooms, and Fiona also went upstairs, leaving Jeremy to talk with his grandmother. Alexandra poured him another glass of port, and they sat on a couch in front of the fireplace.

After he heard a complete explanation about Creevey and then about Benjamin, Jeremy was even more favorably impressed by his father. "Then he's put everything he has at risk in order to protect Benjamin," Jeremy summed up. "That's highly commendable, Grandmother."

"Indeed it is," she agreed. "He will go to the ends of the earth for those who earn his loyalty. On the other hand, ever since he was a boy, those who betray him will never regain his good graces."

The last remark had a wistful note, making Jeremy wonder if she had been thinking of the cool attitude between her and Morton. He mentioned it, remarking that he had noticed they never spoke to each other. "Naturally, I don't wish to pry if it's a private matter," he added.

Alexandra gazed sadly into the fire for a long moment, then slowly nodded. "Yes, it is private," she replied. "I'm not at liberty to speak of it in any detail. However, Morton believes that I betrayed him."

Tears had come to her eyes, and Jeremy quickly changed the subject, commenting on his deep satisfaction when he had seen that she was in good health. Alexandra blinked away her tears and shrugged doubtfully. "I must use that now," she said, pointing to the cane. "When I was a girl, a horse fell on me and injured my leg. It healed, and I thought no more about it until recently, when it began bothering me."

"Many people use canes, Grandmother."

"Yes, but I've felt myself growing old more rapidly of late," she replied. "That may stop now, though, through you. I miss the outback, and you brought it to me, Jeremy. When you arrived today, I could feel the outback wind on my face. I still do, because I've never met anyone who is as much a man of the outback. It's in your very blood and bones."

Jeremy smiled, telling her that it was where both he and Fiona preferred to be. As they continued talking, he recalled his boyhood memories about her wise, blue eyes. They had seemed to probe gently, fathoming his thoughts and feelings, and he again had that impression while talking with her.

She looked very tired, and when Jeremy suggested that it was time for her to rest, Alexandra reluctantly agreed and picked up her cane. He helped her to her feet, and she leaned on his arm as they left the parlor and went up the stairs. In the hallway, they exchanged a hug and kiss, then Jeremy stepped into his room and Alexandra went down the hall to hers.

Fiona was in bed but still awake, too excited to sleep. Jeremy went to bed and held her close, also wakeful. His wish to unite himself with the Kerrick family had been more than fulfilled by his warm, joyous reception. For the first time, Fiona also had the feeling of being a member of a closely knit, loving family. They lay and talked about the hours of conversation and other events of the day until they finally fell asleep.

Shortly after breakfast the next morning, Morton arrived in his carriage. He chatted with Jeremy and Fiona cheerfully as the carriage moved through the streets to the Wooloo district and the large, Victorian house that Jeremy remembered from his boyhood. Julia came out to greet Fiona, and as they went into the house, the carriage moved back down the drive.

At his offices, Morton glowed with pride and introduced Jeremy to the employees as his son. Jeremy talked with the staff for a time, then he and Morton went back out to the carriage to go to the ropewalk. While crossing the city, Morton pointed out Creevey's gaudy, oversize carriage on the street. Glimpsing the huge man inside, Jeremy commented that Alexandra had told him all about Creevey. Morton explained that he had almost gone bankrupt, but now his business affairs were slowly recovering to an extent.

They spent over an hour at the ropewalk, Morton introducing Jeremy to the employees and showing him around. Then they went to the dry dock, which was being repaired after the disastrous fire. It was midday when they left there, and they stopped at a coffeehouse. After tiffin, they went to the Merchants Exchange, where Morton introduced Jeremy to several friends.

One was a man in his thirties named James Haslett, whom Morton introduced as the general manager of Broken Hill Associates. After greeting Jeremy, James told Morton that he was still trying without success to resolve a difficult problem that had confronted him for many weeks.

"It's getting those supplies to Broken Hill," he continued. "They're waiting at Adelaide, but the Darling River is unsafe for riverboats. It won't be all that long until the crew runs out of supplies, but according to the rumors flying about, the situation is worse than that. The stock is falling in value, and the shareholders are questioning my competence."

"It'll go back up," Morton assured him. "That's as sound an investment as one could have. Talk to the shareholders and explain the problem."

"I have," James replied, shrugging morosely, "but I believe the silent partners are exerting pressure. Those I've talked with understand what's involved, but the pressure continues, and these rumors make it worse. The fact is, my position with the company is in jeopardy, Sir Morton."

Morton stroked his chin, pondering. "This seems very

strange," he mused. "How much of the stock is held by silent partners?"

"Upwards of ten percentum, I'd say. However, it keeps changing. Now that the value of the stock is falling, several of the smaller shareholders are selling out to an anonymous buyer. Why do you ask?"

"This may be Creevey trying to take control of the company," Morton told him somberly. "Not long ago, he asked me to cooperate with him, and he said that he had a lucrative undertaking at hand. This began with the sinking of the ship that carried the first supplies, and he's been known to resort to scuttling ships. Now you have rumors creating panic, the stock falling in value, and shareholders selling out to an anonymous buyer."

"By God, you may be right, Sir Morton," James growled angrily. "Damn that man's eyes. I hadn't thought about it, but this has every sign of his hand in it. I'd like to put a pistol to his head."

"Don't lose your temper," Morton warned him. "Above all, you must keep your wits about you. If you do, you may be able to foil him."

James nodded glumly, agreeing with the advice. Morton continued talking with him for a time, sympathizing and offering to help in any way he could. Then he and Jeremy made their farewells and left.

They returned to Kings Cross and went upstairs to Morton's office, discussing more cheerful subjects. Morton said that he and Julia had made plans to invite all of the family for dinner the following evening, and Jeremy gladly accepted for himself and Fiona. Then, after talking with Morton for a few more minutes, Jeremy prepared to leave and go shopping for a few things that he and Fiona needed.

During the day, he had become more and more fond of his father. He loved his grandmother, and the disagreement between them troubled him. Wondering if he could find some way to act as peacemaker, he tentatively broached the subject, but Morton firmly declined to discuss it.

"I don't wish to be rude," Morton said, "but that's a private matter, Jeremy. It's entirely between your grandmother and myself."

"And I don't wish to pry," Jeremy told him affably. "I only want to suggest that resentment is to other feelings as Creevey is to other men. It does nothing useful and causes harm. When I was a boy, I once saw you on the street and waited for you. I wanted to ask you to come to my school and watch a cricket game, but you walked past without noticing me."

"Good Lord!" Morton exclaimed remorsefully. "Jeremy, I know that I wronged you greatly when you were a boy, and I wish—"

"It doesn't matter," Jeremy interrupted, smiling. "I've dismissed it, because why should that stand between us now? It's in the past. Jarboe Charlie once told me that people should draw lessons from the past, but those who constantly look behind themselves will get nothing more than a sore neck and a good view of their backside." He laughed, stepping toward the door. "I'll go do my shopping now. I enjoyed our time together today, and I'll look forward to seeing you tomorrow evening."

"Yes, goodbye for now, Jeremy," Morton said.

The reply was said in a distracted tone of voice, and Jeremy nodded to himself in satisfaction as he left the office, pleased that he had at least made his father think about the situation.

For several minutes after Jeremy left, Morton sat and stared at the wall without seeing it. The hours since early in the previous afternoon had been filled with joy and pride in the tall, admirable young man who was his son. His mental image of that young man as a boy, standing on the street in disappointment and with wounded feelings when he had been ignored, was a wrenching torment. The immense loss in missed opportunities to enrich his life by being a father and companion to that boy was anguishing.

He thought about the previous afternoon, when he had

gone to meet Jeremy. His pleasure and anticipation had been drowned in apprehension over the attitude that Jeremy might take toward him. However, with more than enough justification for rage and a thirst for revenge, Jeremy had greeted him warmly. He had set the past aside as though it had never happened.

In comparison, his own sense of betrayal toward his mother seemed utterly petty, and something she had said the previous afternoon came to mind. She had admitted writing a lie to Clara Tavish to set the woman's mind at ease about Jeremy. In order to be kind to another, she had taken upon herself the burden of lying. But she had borne a much greater burden in secret and in silence over the decades in order to protect him.

Tears of sorrow and anger at himself came to Morton's eyes as he realized that he had done precisely what Creevey had wished. He had cooperated with the man, becoming his own worst enemy. In addition to breaking the lifelong bond with his mother, he had placed a barrier between himself and his wife. Wiping his eyes, he stepped to the door and called downstairs for his carriage to be brought around, then he put on his coat and hat.

The sense of betrayal had been a shield against reflection, and the memories of all his mother had done for him tortured Morton as the carriage moved through the streets. The most painful of all was the fact that even after he had alienated himself from her, she had mortgaged Tibooburra Station, her life's work, in order to help him. When the carriage moved up the drive as far as the side of the house, he thumped his cane on the floor for the driver to stop, then he stepped out.

The cold, gusty wind tugged at his coat and hat as he walked on up the drive. His mother was kneeling beside a flower bed and mulching it, bundled in a thick coat and with a shawl wrapped around her head. She looked up when he crossed the paved courtyard toward her, then she picked up her cane and leaned on it, struggling to her feet.

Morton rushed to her, almost blinded by tears over the

last few paces, and threw his arms around her. "Will you forgive me for being such a fool, Mother?" he begged. "Can you forgive me?"

"Of course, if you can forgive me, Morton," she replied, bursting into tears of happiness. "My dearest, dearest, son!"

Morton held her tightly, tears streaming from his eyes in his turmoil of emotions, and she clung to him as she wept in joy.

Chapter Twenty-Two

When Jeremy returned from buying leather to make new packsaddle girths, he saw Morton's carriage and Deirdre's buggy at the house. He presumed it was another of the family gatherings that had occurred spontaneously at times and upon invitation at others during the week since he and Fiona had arrived.

As soon as he went into the parlor, however, Jeremy knew that a serious problem of some nature had arisen. Morton sat on a couch with his mother, Fiona and Deirdre on another. Catherine and Eudora were sitting on chairs, and everyone was gravely silent.

Pulling up a chair, Jeremy asked what was wrong. Alexandra lifted a letter from her lap and told him it was from the wool broker in London. "The market is exceedingly poor, because a number of mills have closed," she continued. "The broker placed most of the wool in storage. I expected to receive several thousand guineas, but it was only five hundred."

Morton frowned remorsefully, explaining further,

"Mother took a mortgage on the station to prevent my going bankrupt," he added. "The full amount is due within less than a month, and Creevey's bank holds the mortgage. Even though the amount is a pittance compared to the value of the station, obtaining a second mortgage is out of the question. It would be a direct challenge to Creevey, and no one in Sydney will risk that."

Jeremy glanced at Fiona, her eyes telling him to offer their money, and he turned back to Morton. "If we pool our money, that might be enough," he suggested. "Fiona and I have about two hundred guineas."

Morton forced a smile, shaking his head. "Thank you, but all of our resources would be far short of the amount needed, which is three thousand guineas." He turned to Alexandra. "The long and the short of the matter is that I've destroyed what you and Father spent your lives building."

"Nonsense, Morton," she replied. "And your father would tell you the same thing. Our family was always our first concern. Whatever happens to the station, the Kerrick family will continue."

Dismal silence fell, Morton sighing remorsefully. Jeremy considered it unlikely that he could resolve the problem if his father had been unable to find a solution, but he pondered ways of obtaining money. The wide difference in the price of cattle between Bourke and Brisbane occurred to him, but it had nothing to do with the situation and he tried to dismiss it.

It refused to go away, and he suddenly thought of another place where livestock was of even greater value. At the same time, a source of livestock occurred to him. "When we talked to James Haslett," he said to Morton, "he didn't mention the value of his supplies for Broken Hill that are being held up at Adelaide. Do you have any idea of their value?"

Morton pondered, then shrugged. "He said once that a shipment that was lost en route cost two thousand guineas. Why do you ask, Jeremy?"

"Miners can eat mutton," Jeremy pointed out, "and a

flock could be driven from Tibooburra Station to Broken Hill without crossing the river. Are there other sorts of foodstuffs available at the station, Grandmother?"

"Yes, tons of them," she replied, sitting up in interest. "We've long kept a very large supply of nonperishables at the station." She turned to Morton. "Who is James Haslett, and what is Jeremy talking about?"

Morton explained, then shook his head doubtfully. "Jeremy has come up with a truly excellent idea, and James would eagerly agree to it. However, we have only twenty-eight days, including today. That simply isn't enough time to deliver sheep and supplies to Broken Hill and then return here with a receipt from the mine superintendent so James can issue a cheque."

"If anyone on earth can do it," Alexandra said firmly, pointing to Jeremy, "my grandson can. Is there enough time, Jeremy?"

"I don't know, Grandmother," he replied. "The station is six hundred miles from here, and I don't know the condition of the track, whether creeks are flooded, and how difficult it would be to cross the Darling River. But I do know that doing something is better than doing nothing."

Everyone agreed in a loud chorus of voices, the others joining in the conversation. Someone mentioned the fact that the sheep and supplies would have to be taken across Wayamba Station to Broken Hill, which Elizabeth Garrity detested, but Alexandra dismissed that problem.

"Elizabeth will permit it if I ask her," She said. "Morton, I know the contents of the warehouses at the station by heart. Let's go and see James Haslett to find out what is needed at Broken Hill."

"Very well," he agreed, standing and helping her to her feet. "At least we know that it would pay off the mortgage. I can collect together five hundred guineas, and you have the same. If we could make a bargain with James for two thousand, then we'd have precisely the amount we need. Jeremy, this involves you more than anyone else, so you come with us, please."

Jeremy followed them out, and everyone else in the room stepped out into the entry in a hubbub of hopeful, excited conversation. After donning hats and coats, they went outside, Alexandra leaning on her cane as Jeremy helped her down the steps and then into Morton's carriage. Morton gave the driver instructions, then he and Jeremy stepped into the carriage.

During the drive to the business district, they discussed details of the journey. West of Bathurst, Jeremy was sure he could obtain fresh horses from stations, and Morton could see to it that horses were provided as far as Bathurst. He said that he had approved loans for the owners of the Nepean Inn at Penrith and the Bellwether Inn at Bathurst to start their businesses, and they would be more than willing to fulfill a request from him.

The carriage turned onto Surrey Street, stopping in front of the Broken Hill Associates offices, and they went inside. James was even more harried by worry than when Jeremy had first met him, but after Morton explained the purpose of the visit, the man became exuberantly excited. He took a list out of his desk and began discussing it with Alexandra.

"I don't have salt pork and bully beef," she said. "Instead, I'll provide mutton. Let's say a flock of five thousand sheep."

James readily accepted the substitution, and they went on down the list. The quantities seemed huge to Jeremy, his grandmother agreeing to furnish hundredweights of salt and tea, a dozen hogsheads of flour, and barrels of rice, dried peas, and beans. There were other substitutions, including treacle instead of sugar, and figs in place of leaf tobacco.

"That will leave ample supplies for the employees at the station," Alexandra said when they finished. "But do bear in mind that due to weather and other conditions, we're not certain of being able to do this."

James nodded in understanding, writing out a revised list, and Morton joined the conversation as they discussed prices. They agreed on two florins each for the sheep, then went on to the other items. James then added up the amounts, which totaled just under two thousand guineas.

"I'll round it off to two thousand," he said, handing the list to Alexandra. "Upon the return of that list with the mine superintendent's signature on it, I'll issue a cheque in that amount. When do you think the sheep and supplies might possibly be delivered to Broken Hill?"

"In about three weeks," Jeremy said, all eyes turning toward him.

"That would be excellent!" James exclaimed. "It would dispose of a problem that's been plaguing me and also save my position with the company. It would also save the company itself from falling into the wrong hands. You were absolutely correct, Sir Morton. I have good reason to believe that Creevey has been behind this all along."

"It's had every indication of his sly, underhanded methods," Morton replied. "It would be prudent to keep our arrangement private. If Creevey learns of it, he'll resort to any means necessary to thwart it."

James agreed emphatically, assuring Morton that he would say nothing to anyone about it outside his offices. Then the conversation ended in farewells, James wishing Jeremy a safe journey, and Jeremy went back outside to the carriage with Alexandra and Morton.

During the drive back to the house, Morton brought up the subject of when Jeremy would leave, expecting him to set out that afternoon. Jeremy told Morton that haste would be unwise, because careful preparations for a journey were as essential as good horses. Alexandra supported Jeremy on the issue and raised the discussion to a more general level.

"From this point onward," she said, "Jeremy is the boss cockie. The responsibility is his, so he should make the decisions."

Morton agreed, Jeremy quickly adding that he would welcome all advice, then the discussion on when he would leave continued. After talking it over and thinking about it, Jeremy decided to spend the next day in preparations and leave early in the morning on the following day.

When they reached the house, the others expressed delight over the agreement with James. Everyone began discussing what had to be done, then a heated disagreement developed. Morton mentioned to Alexandra that she needed to write a note to be delivered to Elizabeth Garrity, and Alexandra told him that in order for the sheep and supplies to cross Wayamba Station, she would have to accompany Jeremy and talk with Elizabeth in person.

A thunderstruck silence was followed by a bedlam of protests from Morton, Deirdre, Catherine, and Eudora, all of them pointing out Alexandra's age and the grueling hardships of a race against time into the outback during winter. Alexandra insisted that the only way she could be certain of obtaining Elizabeth's permission was by talking with her in person.

Then she lifted a hand for silence, ending the argument. "Perhaps you are correct," she said. "The point is, I don't know what she will do unlesss I'm there to persuade her, so I'll leave the decision to the boss cockie. Jeremy, I consider it best that I go with you. May I?"

Jeremy felt extremely awkward, as well as just as reluctant as the others for his grandmother to undertake the journey. Fiona was noncommittal, her expression giving no hint of her opinion, but everyone else shook their heads and frowned at Jeremy in a silent demand that he refuse. However, his grandmother's wise, blue eyes were more compelling than all of the misgivings. "Very well, if you think it best, Grandmother," he replied.

Alexandra smiled radiantly, Morton throwing up his hands in a gesture of despair and the others groaning in dismay. Then the subject was dropped and the conversation moved on to other things. When late afternoon came, Morton left to fetch Julia to the house, and Catherine went to give the cook instructions on how many would be present for dinner.

During dinner and in the parlor after the meal, the conversation about the journey was generally optimistic. However, there was an overtone of uncertainty because of the severe time limit, and reservations over Alexandra's going. At the end of the evening, when Jeremy and Fiona were alone in their room, he expressed his uneasiness about taking his grandmother with him. Fiona was more sanguine, commenting that Alexandra might surprise everyone by how well she endured the hardships of the journey.

The weather had turned worse the next morning, the sky covered by dark clouds and blustery wind sweeping ahead of a storm off the coast. After breakfast, Jeremy went out to the stables to look through his supplies and equipment stored there. Picking out items that he and Alexandra would need on the journey, he placed them at one side.

Morton arrived at midmorning and came into the stables, and he gave Jeremy messages to be delivered to the innkeepers at Penrith and Bathurst. "Those notes will assure you of getting horses there," he said. "And I have some bad news. Either Creevey has an informant in James Haslett's offices, or James has an employee with a loose tongue. Our agreement with him is being discussed at the Merchants Exchange and elsewhere in the city."

"Then we can expect trouble from Creevey," Jeremy summed up.

"I'd say that's a certainty."

Jeremy nodded, replying that he would stay alert for any sign of trouble. The discussion turned to the weather as the wind continued to increase. Jeremy intended to take the train to Penrith, and he commented hopefully that the weather might be better west of the Blue Mountains. Morton agreed and talked with Jeremy a few minutes longer, then he left.

When he had finished selecting supplies and equipment, he tied them into a bundle under a canvas cover, Buggie helping him. Buggie saddled a horse, and Jeremy loaded the bundle onto a pack horse, together with his saddle and a sidesaddle. They led the horses out of the stables, Jeremy giving Buggie the messages to deliver to the innkeepers.

"Leave the saddles in the stable harness room at the Nepean Inn," he said, "then take the supplies to the Bellwether Inn at Bathurst and wait there. We'll be there tomorrow afternoon."

Buggie nodded, stepping into his saddle. As the stock-man rode away, Jeremy went into the house and upstairs to his room to pick out the swag he would need. Thinking of what Morton had said about Creevey, Jeremy took out his pistol and placed it at one side to clean and oil it carefully.

When the afternoon came, Jeremy had one remaining thing to do, one that made him feel foolish for even contemplating it. However, he had developed a burning hatred for Creevey, and he felt compelled to make at least a gesture of some nature against the man. Jeremy saddled a horse and rode into the business district of the city, looking for Creevey.

The storm had moved closer to the coast, with low, thick clouds that made the day very dark. The cold, gusty wind tumbled bits of debris down streets that were almost deserted, as most people remained indoors. After riding about until late afternoon, Jeremy saw Creevey's large, ornate carriage at the curb in front of the Merchants Exchange. He turned in at an alley down the street from it, then dismounted and tethered his horse.

The wind moaned around the buildings as Jeremy stood at the mouth of the alley and watched people entering and leaving the Merchants Exchange. Creevey came out, and his driver climbed down from the box to open the carriage door. Jeremy unfastened his shirt and pulled out the bone talisman on the thong around his neck, then he gripped the thong and broke the fastening.

The huge man started to clamber into the carriage, which shifted from his enormous weight. Jeremy lifted the talisman and pointed it at him, then dropped it and stamped his foot on it. Creevey evidently lost his balance on the step at the side of the carriage. He leaned back, windmilling his arms, and the driver sprang behind him to catch him.

The driver pushed on Creevey's broad back, struggling to keep him from falling. The hulking man caught the edge of the doorway and pulled himself into the carriage. The driver closed the door, then climbed up to the box. As the carriage moved away, Jeremy smiled wryly. The evident results of what he had done—absolutely nothing—were what he had expected.

Jeremy glanced at the ground as he turned away, then stopped and looked more closely. Only the thong was on the ground, not a single fragment of bone. Thinking about it, Jeremy concluded that the old, desiccated bone must have shattered into dust, which the wind had scattered. He dismissed the incident with a shrug, stepping toward his horse.

An hour before dawn the next morning, the storm had made landfall and rain was pouring down when Jeremy and Alexandra boarded the train for Penrith. As it moved away from the station, the lights on the platform silhouetted the family standing in the drenching rain and waving. Jeremy and Alexandra waved to them through the compartment window, then sat back on their seats facing one another when the station fell behind.

The storm made Jeremy more keenly aware of the difficulties that lay ahead, increasing his uneasy feeling that he had doomed himself to failure by taking his grandmother with him. Even if he had gone by himself, he knew that the outcome would have been far less than a certainty. Wearing Fiona's sheepskin coat and stockman's hat, Alexandra looked very old and infirm in the flickering light of the small lamp in the compartment.

The first glimmer of dawn penetrated the thick darkness and driving rain while the train was stopped at Parramatta. Then the bleak, dreary day opened out all around as the train plunged down the railroad into the

Nepean valley. At Penrith, Jeremy gathered up their swag, and Alexandra leaned on her cane as she followed him out of the train station.

They made their way through the town to the Nepean Inn, the muddy streets virtually deserted in the downpour. Alexandra went into the inn to find the owner, and Jeremy stepped into the stable. He carried the saddles out of the harness room and was tying the swag onto the back of them when Alexandra came into the stable with the innkeeper.

The man greeted Jeremy with the outgoing manner of a professional host, then pointed to the stalls at one side of the stable. "These are the horses that I keep for the use of my customers, Mr. Kerrick," he said. "Take whichever ones you wish, because they're all good, sound animals."

"Yes, I can see that," Jeremy replied. "I'll do my best to bring the same ones back here when I return."

"Don't go to any bother over it," the innkeeper said, turning back to the door. "I wouldn't be in business here but for Sir Morton's help, and two horses is very little in return for that."

As the innkeeper left, Jeremy carried the sidesaddle toward an older horse, but Alexandra pointed to a young, feisty gelding. "I'll take that one," she said. "You'll find that I'm an experienced rider, Jeremy."

Feeling some misgivings, Jeremy girthed the sidesaddle on the gelding and then saddled a similar horse for himself. Then, when they led the horses outside, he saw that his grandmother had reason to be confident. The horses were reluctant to go out into the cold rain, becoming unruly and prancing about, but she restrained hers as deftly as he did his.

In the rain and wind outside the stable, she flung her cane away. "Now I can't allow myself the luxury of being old and weak," she said in grim determination. "Give me a hand up, Jeremy."

He lifted her up onto the horse and stepped into his saddle, then led the way down the street. It became a road, the town falling behind. The main road came into view ahead, the forest where Jeremy had met Jarboe Charlie on the other side of it. As he turned onto the road toward Bathurst, Jeremy glanced back at his grandmother. He saw that for some reason, she was gazing reflectively at the forest beside the road.

Pounding across the Emu Plains and into the foothills at a fast canter, Jeremy picked a path around the deepest puddles on the road. He glanced back from time to time, and his grandmother showed no sign of lagging. She rode a few yards behind him and followed the path that he chose on the wide road, the pelting rain streaming off her hat and sheepskin coat.

The rain and wind continued as the hours passed, the road winding into the mountains, and Jeremy's hopes that the weather would be better on the other side faded. In the high passes at the crest of the mountains, the wind was a howling gale, lashing rain mixed with snow and sleet from one direction, then another. However, it became evident to him that Alexandra had more endurance and strength that he had thought. The single time he asked if she wanted to rest, she had firmly declined and motioned him on.

When they reached Bathurst, he was starting to tire himself, and the horses were almost exhausted. In the western outskirts of the town, where the Bellwether Inn was set back from the road, Buggie was waiting in the stable doorway. "You've been riding like the wind," he commented cheerfully. "You're here hours ahead of when I expected to see you."

"Yes, we've made good time so far," Jeremy agreed, lifting Alexandra down from her saddle. "Is the innkeeper about?"

"No, his house is near the river, and he went to move his family to higher ground," Buggie replied. "But he left word that you're to have anything you want." He turned to a stableboy. "Go to the kitchen and fetch some tucker and tea. Tell the cook who it's for, and look lively."

The boy ran out, and Alexandra limped to a bale of

hay and sat down on it. Jeremy studied her worriedly as he and Buggie unsaddled the horses and put them in stalls. She was very weary, her face pale and lined with fatigue. Buggie brought the supplies and packsaddle out of the harness room, and Jeremy chose three young, spirited horses from the stalls.

After the horses were saddled, the stableboy carried in a tray laid out with tin plates of mutton stew, damper, and pannikins of tea. While he and Alexandra were eating, Jeremy noted with satisfaction that the hot food and tea appeared to restore her energy to an extent. He asked Buggie if he knew the condition of the tracks to the west from talking with travelers who had passed since the rain had started.

Buggie shook his head, replying that only local traffic had been passing from the west. "A party of five or six men with pack horses passed just at daybreak this morning," he added. "But they were coming from the east."

"Were they from Bathurst?"

"No, their horses were nigh onto being whacked, so they had come from at least as far as Penrith. They must have traveled through the night, so they were heading somewhere post haste, weren't they?"

Jeremy agreed and began discussing the weather with Buggie, speculating on when the rain might end. Privately, he wondered suspiciously why travelers who had ridden through the night had failed to stop at the inn long enough for refreshments. It seemed at least possible that the men had been dispatched by Creevey and would be waiting in ambush down the track.

When he and Alexandra finished eating, they led the horses out of the stable and mounted up. Buggie waved and wished them good fortune as they rode away, Alexandra leading the pack horse. At first the road was a mass of churned mud from local traffic, but when it began breaking up into tracks leading in different directions, Jeremy was able to pick out the imprints made in the mud by individual animals and vehicles.

Among them, he saw hoofprints made several hours

before by a group of horses. The men had ridden up the track leading northwest toward Wilcannia, the same one that he and Alexandra turned onto. As they rode up it, Jeremy scanned ahead through the rain and unfastened a button on his sheepskin coat so he could reach the pistol at his waist more easily.

A mile up the track, the riders had turned onto another track that branched off in a more westerly direction. Reining up, Jeremy studied the hoofprints, and Alexandra stopped her horse beside his. "Elizabeth Garrity had that track made," she said, "to have her supplies delivered and her clip hauled away by drays. The men whom Buggie talked about went that way, so you can button your coat and keep your pistol from getting wet in the rain."

Jeremy smiled. Alexandra missed nothing that happened around her. As they rode on up the track, however, he left the button unfastened and remained watchful. He was less suspicious of those particular men, but he was sure that trouble originating with Creevey would come sooner or later.

The rain limited visibility to a few yards, the track unfolding ahead and leading over gently rolling terrain. At first there were farms, with fences flanking the track, then runs for grazing livestock. Then sheep stations spread back from both sides of the track, becoming progressively larger and the tracks to the home paddocks farther apart.

When the light began fading into dusk, they turned onto the next track leading back to a home paddock. They reached it just at nightfall, and even the warm, generous hospitality that Jeremy had experienced at stations seemed tepid compared to the frenzy of excitement with which his grandmother was received. The station owners were a couple in their forties named Elmer and Henrietta Finch, and they eagerly brought Alexandra and Jeremy into the house, sending a son to unsaddle and stable the horses.

In common with most stations, the house was modest

and functional, with bedrooms set off from a large, central room that was used for cooking, dining, and social gatherings. It was also cheerful and inviting, a fire roaring in the fireplace. Elmer helped Alexandra and Jeremy off with their coats while Henrietta bustled about and prepared pannikins of hot buttered rum.

Alexandra told the couple that she and Jeremy were attending to an important matter involving Tibooburra Station, and time was crucial. "If we may," she added, "we'd like to have dinner and a place to sleep."

"Of course you can," Elmer assured her emphatically, Henrietta echoing his reply. "We're most grateful that you and Mr. Kerrick stopped here, and everything we have is yours, Mistress Kerrick."

He seated them with their hot drinks at the long, homemade table near the fireplace, then he and the children helped Henrietta as she set about heating up leftovers from dinner. The boy who had attended to the horses returned, and a dozen stockmen and jackaroos filed in after him. They quietly took seats on benches against the wall beside the door and listened while Alexandra and Jeremy conversed with the Finches.

The hot buttered rum dispelled Jeremy's chill, and the hearty meal of pork roast and vegetables was delicious. He enjoyed talking with the earnest, good-natured Finches, who were reverently attentive whenever his grandmother spoke. Through various comments, Jeremy learned that Henrietta had inherited the station from her parents, and when she was a girl, his grandmother had once spent the night there. Over the decades, that visit had remained a fresh topic of conversation among the family.

After they had talked for a time, Henrietta regretfully ended the conversation, pointing out that Alexandra and Jeremy needed to rest. In his room for the night, Jeremy took out a calendar stick he had made to avoid the confusion over the date that could develop on a long journey. The slender stick had twenty-eight notches on it, two with diagonal cuts across them. Jeremy marked off a third notch with his knife, then went to bed.

The next morning, he saw that his grandmother had a resilient, dogged strength about her. Even though he was out of bed well before dawn, she was up before him and everyone else. She was stoking the fire and heating water to make tea when he stepped out of his room, and as she greeted him, she looked well rested and more energetic than she had the previous morning.

A short time later, the Finches were up and about, preparing breakfast. After eating their frumenty and drinking their tea, two of the sons left to saddle the horses. Jeremy and Alexandra donned their coats and went out, the family following them, and found the stockmen and jackaroos gathered on the verandah. In a hubbub of farewells, Jeremy and his grandmother rode away as the murky dawn began penetrating the clouds and rain.

The rain finally stopped near midday, though the sky remained covered by thick clouds. Late in the day, the horses were unable to go faster than a trot. Hours of slogging through mud had almost exhausted them, and Jeremy knew it would take longer than a night for them to recover. In contrast, Alexandra appeared to be finding more reserves of strength. Jeremy noticed that she seemed more alert, sitting straighter in her saddle.

At dusk, they turned in at a station owned by a middle-aged couple named Maynard and Sarah Poller, who welcomed Alexandra with the same excited delight as the Finches had. During conversation over dinner, Jeremy mentioned the condition of his horses, and Maynard readily agreed to provide fresh ones. Then he added that Jeremy's horses would have time to rest, because a flood to the west had stopped all traffic on the track.

"It's at Gundaroo Creek," he explained, "just west of Gundaroo village. A swagman told one of my stockmen that nothing has passed there for days, and nothing will be passing for a good many more."

"Yes, I know it well," Alexandra said wryly. "Heavy

rain in the valley that Gundaroo Creek drains will often make it run a banker."

Maynard assured her that more than overflowing, the creek had flooded the entire valley. The reason for a hint of satisfaction in his and Sarah's attitude was revealed when he suggested that Jeremy and Alexandra stay at the station until the flood subsided. They declined, but he persisted until they agreed to return if they were unable to get past the flood.

The following morning, amid the farewells, Maynard reminded them of their promise. They returned to the track and rode up it at a fast canter on the fresh horses, apprehensive about the flood. At midmorning on the bleak, cloudy day, Gundaroo came into view ahead. Located on a knoll, it was a small community that had developed over the years as a marshaling point for itinerant shearers and the teamsters who transported clips to Sydney.

Its population of some twenty adults and half that many children had been temporarily tripled. A line of wagons was parked beside the track, and the drivers were camped with swagmen and with riders who had been stopped by the flood. Jeremy and Alexandra slowed to a walk, riding past the vehicles, people, and cluster of buildings. Then they reined up at the brow of the knoll and looked down at the wide valley that lay behind.

The flood was well short of covering the entire valley, which was some two miles across, but the point was academic for travelers. The track disappeared into a sheet of muddy water about a mile wide, with trees and brush jutting up here and there from its roiling surface.

Alexandra sighed, shaking her head worriedly. "It's stopped everyone else, hasn't it, Jeremy?" she said quietly. "That includes the swagmen, because there isn't a way around it. This valley reaches many miles to the north and south, and all of it will be like this. What can we do?"

"We can try to find a way to get to the other side," he replied, smiling at her. "But we won't find it sitting here, Grandmother."

Alexandra smiled and nodded, and they rode on down the slope toward the water. A hundred yards from the edge, Jeremy led the way off the track into the brush and trees, turning northward up the valley.

At a long, gradual curve in the valley, Gundaroo and its surroundings disappeared behind. An hour passed, then another as they rode up the wide valley, Jeremy studying the trees jutting up from the water, and judging the swiftness of the current from bits of debris floating past. He saw places where he would attempt a crossing by himself, but he wanted one that would pose the least possible risk to his grandmother.

Finally, during the afternoon, he reined up. "I believe we can get across here, Grandmother," he told her. "But it will be dicey."

She gazed out over the water for a moment, then shrugged. "From the way the brush is floating past, the current here isn't as fast as in most places. That's the only difference I see. What am I failing to see, Jeremy?"

"There are paperbark trees that aren't too far apart. Jarboe Charlie taught me that they have shallow roots and wash out of the ground during floods. This valley has flooded many times, so wherever paperbarks are still standing, they're on somewhat higher ground."

"You are truly a man of the outback," Alexandra said emphatically, smiling warmly. "I've seen many paperbarks that were uprooted in floods and some that weren't, but I never drew the right conclusion."

"That doesn't eliminate the danger, though, Grandmother. At best, we'll get wet and cold. At worse, we and our horses will be drowned."

"You're the boss cockie, Jeremy," she pointed out. "I'm in favor of trying to cross here, but the decision is up to you."

Jeremy studied the zigzag path he had picked out between the paperbark trees, weighing the risk to his grandmother against how much he knew Tibooburra Station meant to her. "Well, we don't have days to wait here," he said, "so we'll try it. Follow exactly in the path I take, and if that pack horse gets troublesome, turn it loose. We can get another horse and supplies."

Alexandra nodded, following him as he rode into the water. The first paperpark was twenty yards away through submerged brush. The water barely reached above his horse's belly before the ground sloped back up to the tree, then he passed it and turned toward the next one.

The water was deeper, pouring into his boots and rising higher on his legs with its freezing cold that penetrated to his bones. Then, when he turned toward another paperpark, the ground fell away sharply. His horse lost its footing and lifted its head as it began swimming, the icy water swirling up around the saddle and rising to Jeremy's waist.

The horse found the ground with its hooves, struggling through the water toward the tree, and Jeremy looked back. His grandmother's skill with horses was again evident, because she was staying well balanced on the saddle to assist her horse as it swam, and she kept the halter rope on the pack horse short so it would have to stay precisely behind her. Jeremy waited until she reached the tree, then he turned toward another one.

At a distance of several hundred yards from the edge, the swishing roar of the enormous volume of water was deafening, and the flood seemed to stretch to the horizon. The frigid water and the exertion of swimming had sapped the horses' energy rapidly, and Jeremy shivered from the icy chill as his horse sank lower in the water. When he reached the last paperbark tree before the wide space across the creek channel, he waited for Alexandra.

She rode up beside him, her lips blue as she shook with violent shivers, and Jeremy looked at the first paperbark on the other side of the channel. He had chosen one downstream to avoid making the horses swim straight across the swift current, and now it seemed to be a very long distance away. He lifted his reins and urged his horse forward.

The horse began swimming again as it lost its footing

and sank into the water. When he reached the center of the channel, Jeremy turned and looked back at his grandmother. The water was above her waist, with only the horses' heads visible in front and behind her, and she seemed very small and lost in the vast expanse of muddy water.

Eddies tugged at his horse, veering it away from the tree, and Jeremy turned it back with the reins. Then, a few yards from the tree, a powerful eddy that welled up from the murky depths seized the horse and almost swept it out into the main current again. Jeremy jerked the reins and the horse churned its legs, struggling through the eddy.

As soon as the horse touched the bottom with its hoofs, Jeremy stopped in the deep water and looked back, waiting to make certain that Alexandra's horse overcame the swirl in the current. She and the horses approached, then struck the eddy. Her horse floundered, almost spilling her off the saddle as it began swinging back out into the main current.

Jeremy wheeled his horse back around into the deep water. As it began swimming, he leaned over its head and grabbed the bridle on Alexandra's horse, then heaved his weight back and dragged it toward the tree as he jerked his reins. The horses plunged about, bumping together and lurching toward the tree, and touched the bottom with their hooves.

The horses climbed out of the deep water, panting heavily and trembling with cold. Alexandra tried to smile and speak a word of thanks, but her lips were stiff and she was shaking uncontrollably with chills. Jeremy let the horses rest for a moment, then turned toward the next tree.

The west side of the valley sloped upward sharply, and the water rapidly became shallow. When the horses stumbled out of it, they stood with their heads drooping wearily. Alexandra slumped on her saddle, grimly clinging to it and shaking with cold. Jeremy dismounted to warm up by moving about, and the circulation returned to his numb legs with a burning, prickling sensation as he led the horses up the hill toward a stand of eucalypts.

At the grove, Jeremy lifted Alexandra down from her saddle and seated her against a tree. Turning back to the horses, he hastily dragged the load off the pack horse and took out the rum he had put with the supplies. He gave Alexandra sips of the powerful liquor, and the color rushed back to her face. After taking a drink himself, he put the bottle aside and dug under the tree for dry, decayed bark to use for tinder.

Traveling farther that day was out of the question, and after kindling a fire, Jeremy assembled a bark shelter to contain the heat and placed the supplies beside it. He unsaddled and hobbled the horses, then carried the billys to a brook a few yards away to fill them. When he returned, Alexandra had hung her sheepskin coat on the shelter to dry and was taking off her boots to dry them beside the fire. With a ruggedly strong, resilient constitution that continued to surprise him, she had shrugged off the ordeal of crossing the floodwaters and appeared almost normal.

"You're a truly remarkable man, Jeremy," she said as he placed the billys in the edge of the fire. "What you did today was extraordinary."

Jeremy laughed, taking off his sheepskin coat and hanging it on the shelter. "You're the remarkable one, Grandmother. The journey should be taking a toll on you, but you appear to be gaining strength from it."

"I was wasting away in Sydney, Jeremy. Part of the reason was my pining for the outback, and part was my uselessness there. Now I have a purpose and I'm back in the land I love. Both of those things have come about through you."

Studying her as they continued talking, Jeremy realized that she looked subtly different than before. Instead of aged, she appeared ageless. Behind the facade of lines on her face was the beautiful, fascinating woman of past years, with a vibrant personality and an indomitable will. It was very evident to him that his grandfather had been an extremely fortunate man.

Their clothes began drying in the warmth of the shelter, and when the billys boiled, Alexandra sprinkled tea into them. The shared danger of crossing the flood was an additional bond between them, drawing them closer and making their conversation reflective and personal. Alexandra talked about her early years at Tibooburra Station and then her success in obtaining title to the land. Jeremy told her about his walkabout in search for his heritage, and his conviction that he would eventually find the place where he would have a sense of belonging.

When he finished, he wondered if she would try to persuade him to give up his search and take charge of Tibooburra Station. He knew that she was dissatisfied with having a manager there until an heir in this generation or the next would assume the responsibility for the station. Even though he dreaded the prospect of disappointing her, he was determined to find his own place in life rather than fit himself into that of another.

For a moment, he was certain that she was going to bring it up. Her eyes gazed into his, seeming to probe ever so gently and lovingly into his thoughts. Then she smiled and began talking about an entirely different subject. "When your grandfather died," she said, "a good portion of my life died with him. And after you arrived in Sydney, I became even more remorseful that he was gone. I shall always regret that he missed knowing you as a man, Jeremy. It would have been such a joy for him."

"I wish I could have known him, Grandmother," Jeremy replied, unloading his pistol. "It would have been a great pleasure."

Alexandra fell silent for a moment, watching Jeremy as he dried the pistol and bullets. Then she mentioned the riders that Buggie had talked about. "They were probably stockmen en route to a station," she added. "Even so, I was relieved when they turned onto another track."

"They still headed west, Grandmother," Jeremy

pointed out. "As you say, they probably mean us no harm, but we can't dismiss them entirely. In fact, we can't dismiss any possibility, because meeting up with trouble from Creevey is a certainty. It only remains to be seen what form the trouble will take, and when and where it will happen."

Chapter Twenty-Three

"We realize that there's a risk involved, Mr. Spinney," Alexandra said. "However, we absolutely must get across the river. The ferry isn't operating, and the owner has even taken in the cable."

"Yes, I know, Mistress Kerrick," Albert Spinney replied. "But I'm sure you don't understand the full extent of the danger. A barge is much more difficult to control than a boat, particularly in floodwaters."

Jeremy listened while his grandmother continued talking with the local manager for the steamboat company. A tall, thin man with a cordial manner, he was distressed. While he disliked refusing a request from Alexandra, he was reluctant to allow her and Jeremy to use his company's barge.

Others had gathered around, listening to the conversation. The crowd grew as people wandered down the street lined with businesses that was the end of the track from Sydney, and the main street of Wilcannia. At the waterfront, the street was cluttered with boats that had been dragged back to safety from the swollen river. Only a few remained at the piers that were almost inundated. The only boat that was large enough to transport horses was a riverboat barge.

It was very large, some thirty feet long and ten wide. Jeremy studied it, noting the low gunwale that would make loading horses into it easy. A long sweep shaped like a huge oar was stowed against one gunwale and was the means of moving and steering the barge. Jeremy knew that controlling the large, heavy vessel on the flooded river would be difficult.

That was what Albert Spinney kept repeating to Alexandra, unwilling for her to be placed in danger. Jeremy saw that she was gradually wearing Albert down, and he joined the conversation. "The barge would end up at a distance downstream," he remarked, "because I would have no way of getting it back up here. Would that represent a problem, Mr. Spinney?"

"No, no," Albert replied. "When the next steamboat arrives, I'd simply ask the captain to tow it back up to the waterfront."

"Then I see no reason why we shouldn't use it," Jeremy told him. "My grandmother and I are accustomed to dealing with floodwaters."

"Indeed we are," Alexandra put in quickly. "This would be no more dangerous than other things we've done, and it would be an invaluable assistance if you would allow us to use the barge, Mr. Spinney."

The man hesitated, wavering in indecision, then grudgingly relented. "Very well, Mistress Kerrick," he said somberly. "But I do so with a heavy heart and earnest hopes that you come to no harm."

Alexandra thanked Albert gratefully, and Jeremy led the horses as the three of them went to the barge. It was moored at the near end of a pier, a few feet from the edge of the water. The crowd followed them, the event breaking the monotony of the winter day at the isolated river town.

Albert talked to Jeremy, giving him instructions on

steering the barge. "I'm inexperienced myself," he admitted, "but I've heard boatmen speak about it at length. You should steer downstream at a moderate angle. If you cut across the current, the barge will broach. On the other hand, if you go downstream too sharply, it will gain too much speed."

Jeremy thanked him for the advice and led the horses into the water. Men from the crowd waded in and helped him coax and drag the horses into the barge, the animals disliking the unsteady footing in the vessel as it shifted in the waves and currents. When the horses were tethered firmly in the center of the barge, Alexandra stepped down from the pier into the bow, and Jeremy lifted the long sweep into place at the stern.

The men untied the ropes and tossed them into the barge, then pushed it away from the pier. As it glided ponderously out into the river, a chorus of shouts rose from the crowd, the people calling out in farewell and wishing Jeremy and Alexandra good fortune. The water near the bank was almost slack, with very little current in it. Jeremy pushed on the sweep, turning the bow at an angle toward the opposite bank.

At first it appeared that Albert had overstated the difficulties, as the barge drifted smoothly through the water. Then it met the swifter current farther out in the river. The water on the upstream side began boiling over the gunwale, and the barge staggered on the point of broaching and threatening to swamp. Jeremy quickly eased the pressure on the sweep and swung the bow around at a deeper angle downstream.

The barge struck a powerful eddy and started to spin, the sweep slamming into Jeremy and almost knocking him overboard. Bracing himself, he struggled with the sweep, heaving his weight against it and then pulling back to counter the erratic effects of the eddy. The horses stamped and snorted in fright when the violent shifts in direction threw them against each other.

When the barge came out of the eddy, it was shooting straight downstream, and Jeremy turned the bow back toward the bank at an angle. Just as he heaved a sigh of relief, the barge swept into another swirling eddy. Jeremy almost lost control, and the ponderous vessel veered wildly as the stern started to swing downstream. Pushing and then pulling on the sweep with all of his strength, he fought the eddy and got the barge through it.

After he struggled through yet another eddy, the barge passed the center of the river and met a smooth, much faster current. Jeremy turned the bow at a deeper angle downstream when the barge started to broach in the swift current, then looked ahead for a place to steer the barge into the bank. The swollen river was high on the bank, with partially submerged trees and brush jutting up from the muddy water.

Jeremy picked out a clump of brush in the water that would cushion the landing, but the barge met slack water again as it approached the bank. He turned the bow at a sharper angle toward the bank, choosing a different place where saplings and brush rose out of the water. Then, at the last moment, he realized that the barge had gained too much speed while in the fast current, and it was skimming swiftly through the slack water.

An instant after he shouted at Alexandra to brace herself, a shower of shredded foliage exploded into the air as the long, heavy barge ripped through the saplings and brush, then slammed into the bank with a jarring crash. The impact knocked the horses to their knees, and Jeremy kept his balance by hanging onto the sweep. Alexandra recovered instantly, leaping nimbly out of the barge with a mooring rope and tying it to a tree.

The horses stumbled to their feet as Jeremy stowed the sweep, and Alexandra secured the barge with a second rope. Jeremy untied the horses and examined their legs, leading them and following his grandmother up to the top of the bank. "No harm was done to the horses," he said wryly, "but it was due to good fortune, certainly not to how I handled the barge."

"You got us across the river safely, which is all that matters," Alexandra told him firmly. "This is where we must separate. I will speak directly to Elizabeth while you head north. You should be able to find a flock at Tibooburra Station by tomorrow, Jeremy. The stockman attending it will have ample supplies, but you'll need to take rations for tonight with you."

Turning to the pack horse, Jeremy untied the ropes on the bundle of supplies. As he took out his billy and a few rations, he noticed how lithely his grandmother was moving about. Over the past few days, her limp had diminished, and now it was gone entirely. He smiled, mentioning it. "When you jumped out of the barge to moor it to a tree," he added, "you were hopping about like a young girl, Grandmother."

"As I told you, being old and weak is a luxury I must forgo now," she replied, laughing. "There is too much that must be done."

Jeremy laughed, but he wondered if she would return to Sydney and begin fading away again when they finished. Even worse, he feared that despair would crush the spirit that sustained her vitality if they failed. With only nineteen notches left on his calendar stick and much remaining to be done, the outcome was still very much in question.

When they were ready to leave and go their separate ways, Jeremy tried to think of something appropriate to say. Nothing came to mind, and his grandmother was also silent. He kissed her and lifted her up to her saddle, then handed her the halter rope on the pack horse. She rode away toward the southwest and Wayamba Station as he stepped into his saddle and rode northward.

Across the river from Wilcannia, he found the track that was the boundary between Wayamba and Tibooburra Stations. He rode down it at a fast canter, the dark, windy day slowly passing. During late afternoon, he reached a low, long mountain that his grandmother had told him about. Completely devoid of vegetation, it was called Barren Mountain. At the center of it was the main track into Tibooburra Station, leading straight north through a stand of boxwood, across the mountain, and then on northward.

When he reached the crest of Barren Mountain and gazed ahead, the giant sheep station opened out before him in staggering dimensions, a seemingly endless ocean of mallee and mulga, woodlands, and broad savannahs of lush spinifex. At that moment, he had a strange feeling unlike any he had ever experienced. In a way and against all logic, it was as though he had been there many times before. However, it was different from a sense of familiarity, with subtle overtones he was unable to identify.

The feeling lingered after he camped at dusk, troubling him because he was unable to identify it. That night he dreamed while he slept, which was unusual for him, and he was unable to remember what he had dreamed when he woke. While he was preparing to leave, a noise in the eucalypt under which he had camped drew his attention. Looking up, he saw a red goshawk fly away, having roosted in the tree through the night.

At mid-morning, he turned off the track when he saw a flock in a valley a mile away, a stockman and a jackaroo attending the sheep. The stockman was a bearded, heavy-set man in his mid-fifties named Isaac Logan, who nodded in dry humor when Jeremy introduced himself. "Aye, you'll be Sir Morton's son," he remarked. "Some years ago, there was a fair dinkum ruckus in searching for you, wasn't there? What do you want me to do, Mr. Jeremy?"

"I have a message for the station manager from Mistress Kerrick," Jeremy told him, taking out both the note and the list that James Haslett had prepared. They were wrapped in oilskin, which he opened to make certain which was the message, then he handed it over. "The manager is to load a quantity of supplies into wagons and send them toward Broken Hill. In the meantime, you and I are to drive this flock toward the same destination. The wagons should catch up with us on Wayamba Station within a week or so."

"Aye, about that," Isaac agreed, turning and handing the message to the jackaroo. "You heard Mr. Jeremy.

Look alive, lad." As the youth pocketed the message and rode toward the track at a gallop, Isaac turned back to Jeremy. "If you'd stay with the sheep, I'll fetch my swag."

Jeremy nodded, and Isaac rode toward a bark hut and fold on the hill overlooking the valley. The stockman returned a short time later, leading a pack horse laden with supplies and equipment. Whistling to the dogs, he rode around the flock to the side opposite the track. He cracked his stock whip, and the sheep began moving toward the track.

Some six thousand sheep were in the flock, but Jeremy knew that too much precious time would be lost in separating the number that James Haslett had agreed to buy. The extra ones also provided a reserve for any that might stray, but Jeremy soon saw it was unlikely that any would. Isaac was a superbly skilled stockman, needing little help to keep the sheep moving at a fast walk. At dusk, the strange feeling that Jeremy had been experiencing faded when they crossed over the boundary into Wayamba Station.

Jeremy helped Isaac set up a temporary fold of rope and poles for the sheep, then they camped beside the fold. Following rather than questioning even the most unusual instructions appeared to be the practice at Tibooburra Station, because Isaac was only remotely curious as to why the sheep and supplies were being taken to Broken Hill. While talking with the man over dinner, Jeremy learned that Isaac had worked at the station for over thirty years, and he had two sons who were also stockmen at the station.

Other flocks came into view the following day, the stockmen with them peering curiously at the sheep moving through Wayamba Station. Isaac took a path well away from them, because the flocking instincts of the sheep would draw them together. The sheep grazed while moving at a steady pace, but it seemed very slow to Jeremy. At the end of the day, when he marked out another notch on his calendar stick, sixteen were left.

The jackaroo caught up with them two days later, having followed the wide trail of the sheep. He told Jeremy that immediately upon receiving the message, the station manager had started men loading the supplies into wagons. That night, Jeremy wondered if his grandmother had been delayed, because he had thought that she might have joined them by then. If she had experienced trouble, he hoped it had been in finding Elizabeth Garrity, not in persuading the woman to allow the sheep and supplies to cross the station.

The following afternoon, Jeremy saw his grandmother approaching from a mile away with a half-dozen stockmen. Then, riding toward them, he saw that another of the riders was also a woman, but wearing stockman's clothes. She was the legendary Elizabeth Garrity, whose fiery temper and iron rule over Wayamba Station were the grist for countless swagmen's tales.

When he reined up and their horses stopped, panting from miles at a fast pace, Jeremy saw the basis for the tales. Elizabeth was a slender woman in her forties, her darkly tanned features set in grim lines, and she had a forbidding air of constant, bristling readiness to deal with trouble. She and all of the stockmen were armed, with rifles in saddle boots.

The coiled stock whip in her hand was dark from years of use, and she motioned toward the flock with it as she turned impatiently to the stockmen, who had stopped behind her. "Do you think you're here to view the bloody scenery, then?" she demanded. "Go and see if you can give a hand and move that flock faster! If we're to feed the slimy gullets of the scurvy dag worms at Broken Hill, then let's do it and be done with it!"

As the stockmen rode away toward the flock, Alexandra introduced Jeremy to Elizabeth. For a brief moment, Elizabeth made no reply to his greeting, her blue eyes cold and analytical as she studied him. Then her reserve faded. She leaned over and reached out to shake hands with him, and the grip of her slender hand was as firm as that of a man.

"I'm pleased to meet you, Jeremy," she said, her tone

making it more a statement of fact than a greeting. "Alexandra has praised you incessantly, and I can see it was more fact than boast." She turned to his grandmother, another side of her character coming to the fore in her smile that reflected their warm, close friendship. "I'll trade you a hundred thousand head of prime ewes and wethers for him, Alexandra," she offered jokingly.

"He's his own man, not mine," Alexandra replied, laughing. "The only one with claims on him is his lovely wife, Fiona. And those are ties of velvet, because a more well-matched couple never lived."

"Then they're fortunate indeed," Elizabeth remarked. She gathered her reins, turning her horse. "I'll take a look around down to the south of here and join you at the camp tonight."

The woman rode away, and Alexandra turned toward the flock with Jeremy, telling him that Elizabeth and the stockmen had been patrolling the eastern paddocks of the station. "Some intruders are apparently prowling about," she continued. "There was a ferry on the east side of the river at the end of the track Elizabeth had made, and now it's missing. A stockman found a drowned horse with a saddle on it down the river, and others have seen hoofprints of riders that weren't made by anyone from the station."

"So several riders crossed the river, and had more trouble doing it than you and I did," Jeremy mused. "Perhaps they are the men Buggie saw in Bathurst, because that's the track they turned onto. It could be a forewarning of trouble from Creevey, or it could have nothing to do with us."

"Yes, I told Elizabeth about Creevey, but she's inclined to believe that it's a group of fossickers," Alexandra said. "Ever since the discovery at Broken Hill, this entire region has drawn them. Over the years, she has chased any number of them off the station."

"That's undoubtedly been difficult," Jeremy commented, glancing around at the patches of forest in the brushy, rolling terrain. "An army could hide here if they were careful not to make smoke with campfires."

Alexandra agreed as they slowed their horses to a walk, following the flock. The conversation turned to other things, Jeremy telling her that the wagons with the supplies were on their way, but he continued thinking about the unknown riders in the area. He wanted to believe they were prospectors, but he feared that they had been sent by Creevey.

The stockmen who had joined Isaac had recommended going farther to the east, where the terrain was easier for sheep to cross, and the flock angled toward the river. During late afternoon, it came into view in the distance. Thin veils of mist drifted from it, settling in the shallow valleys and making the patches of forest darker as Isaac and the other stockmen turned the sheep straight to the south again.

Elizabeth returned at dusk, shortly after the sheep were in the fold for the night. Jeremy unsaddled and hobbled his and the women's horses while they kindled a fire a few yards from where the stockmen were making their camp and preparing to cook. The mist from the river had thickened into dense fog that made the chill of the evening clammy and penetrating, and it created bright, glowing halos over the campfires blazing up in the darkness.

During dinner, Jeremy learned that Elizabeth was complacent about the poor wool market in England. Wayamba Station was virtually self-sufficient, with enough supplies to last for years. In addition, she viewed the station as an end in itself rather than a means of profit, and her objective was to maintain it just as it was from year to year. That and other subjects were discussed, but most of the conversation consisted of reminiscing between the two women, with frequent, affectionate mention of Sheila Garrity.

The next morning, a breeze rose and shredded the fog into drifting clouds that passed over the camp, and the stockmen were indistinct shadows through the haze as they moved about. After the quick breakfast, Jeremy saddled the horses. Elizabeth rode away again, searching for signs of the intruders on the station, and Jeremy and Alexandra followed the sheep when the stockmen resumed driving them southward.

The fog lingered through the morning, limiting visibility to a mile or two. When it lifted near midday, Jeremy saw the wagons in the distance behind the flock and pointed them out to Alexandra. They turned and rode back as the line of eight wagons came into view at the crests and disappeared into the valleys in the rolling terrain. With four horses hitched to each one, and jackaroos herding spare horses behind them, the wagons were bouncing along at a fast pace to catch up with the flock.

Two stockmen were leading the wagons, and they rode ahead at a gallop to meet Alexandra and Jeremy. He saw that they were middle-aged men, one with a thick beard and the other a half-Aborigine. They reined up and greeted Alexandra, their attitude that of old friends as well as employees. She introduced them to Jeremy, telling him that the bearded man was Ruel Blake and the other one was Eulie Bodenham.

The two men exchanged greetings with Jeremy, Ruel commenting on the search for him of years before. "Everyone at the home paddock was pleased to hear that you'd turned up, Mr. Jeremy," he said. "And we all knew that you would be over the moon about it, Mistress Kerrick."

"I certainly am," she replied. "I was beside myself with delight when he arrived at the house in Sydney, and I still am. Are all of the supplies I listed in my message in the wagons, Ruel?"

He nodded, assuring her that each item had been carefully checked. She asked about the condition of the wagons, and Ruel expressed confidence that they would reach Broken Hill without needing any repairs. He estimated that the wagons would catch up with the flock during early afternoon, then the two stockmen rode back toward the wagons. Jeremy and Alexandra returned to the flock, discussing the situation in deep satisfaction.

Jeremy happily pointed out that the time remaining before the mortgage fell due was probably sufficient. "Broken Hill isn't far away now," he said. "Unless some disaster occurs, I might be able to get back to Sydney with the receipt from the mine superintendent with a day to spare."

The disaster occurred shortly after dawn the next morning, while the fog was breaking up into clouds and everyone was moving about in preparation to leave. A bank of fog had just drifted past the camp, leaving it in full view from a thick stand of eucalypts two hundred yards away. The morning stillness that lay over the surrounding landscape was suddenly shattered by the reverberating blast of rapid gunfire from the trees.

The camp erupted into instant pandemonium. A deafening clamor of bleating erupted from the sheep as they burst out of the fold and began fleeing in a thunder of hoofbeats. Horses squealed and plunged in panic, struggling with their hobbles and trying to run. Men shouted in alarm as they leaped away from the animals and instinctively dived for cover.

When the first shots rang out, Jeremy's thoughts remained clear and unconfused, assessing the situation. He realized that the shots had been aimed at the sheep, with devastating effect. Any safety margin of time was gone, because finding the scattered sheep would be difficult. The race against time up the track had largely come to nothing, and Tibooburra Station was now in grave jeopardy.

As these thoughts flashed through his mind, furious, white-hot rage exploded within him. He reacted instantly, while the volley of gunshots was still ringing out and the sheep were trampling down the fold. Grabbing his pistol, he dashed through the camp toward the trees.

Everything seemed to move in slow motion, his path full of obstacles. He brushed past plunging horses, shouldered through men scrambling for cover, and leaped between parked wagons. Finally out of the camp, he zigzagged around clumps of brush, pumping his legs and straining for more speed.

When he was close enough to see five or six men among the trees, puffs of gunpowder smoke were still blossoming from their weapons as they fired into the fleeing sheep. In the hazy, early dawn light, the men failed to notice him running toward them. He slowed, taking quick aim and firing rapidly at one of the men. On the third shot, the man reeled back and fell.

The men ducked behind trees and began firing at Jeremy. Bullets clipped through clumps of brush on one side and then the other as he dodged around the dense foliage and continued running toward the trees. Then the shattering boom of a large-caliber rifle rang out behind him, and he glanced over his shoulder.

Elizabeth was racing through the brush behind him, reloading her rifle. Now she was the Elizabeth Garrity of swagmen's tales, her eyes wide and gleaming and her face twisted in a frenzy of rage. Hatless and with her hair flying about wildly, she shouldered her rifle and fired again.

The men began firing at her as well, bullets shredding bits of foliage all around her and Jeremy. Looking ahead, he saw a long depression parallel to the trees, where another bank of fog was drifting toward the brushy clearing between the camp and the trees. Jeremy fired the last bullet in his pistol, then slowed for Elizabeth to catch up with him.

Approaching the depression, he veered toward her and grabbed her arm, then pulled her down beside him in the ditch. She fell heavily, looking at him in surprise, then anger for stopping her. "If we get much closer to them in the open, they won't be able to miss us," he pointed out. "Also, when the men at the camp get their wits about them and start shooting, they might hit us if we're in the center of the field."

As though to punctuate his last remark, a rifle boomed

at the camp, the bullet tearing through the brush over their heads and then slamming into one of the trees. Other rifles at the camp began firing, and bullets whined past overhead. Elizabeth smiled wryly, pushing her hair back. "I let my temper get the better of my judgment," she admitted, "but we've done what was necessary. Those swine thought they would be riding away before anyone fired back, but now they're pinned down. They must have been sent by that man your grandmother told me about."

"I'm sure of it," Jeremy replied, pointing to the fog moving toward the clearing. "We can each go to one end of this ditch, then that fog will conceal us so we can get into the trees on either side."

"Very well. When we move up to the trees in the fog, let's bear in mind that we must be careful not to shoot at each other."

Jeremy agreed emphatically, turning and crawling along the depression as Elizabeth went in the other direction. The stockmen at the camp were moving out into the brush, creating a staccato thunder as they fired rapidly. At the end of the depression, Jeremy opened the ammunition pouch on his pistol belt and reloaded his pistol while he crept closer to the trees, cautiously lifting his head and peering through the brush.

The men in the thicket were firing rapidly at the stockmen, keeping them at a distance and evidently intending to escape under cover of the approaching fog. Horses were tethered behind the stand of trees, and Jeremy glimpsed one of the men crawling toward them. The leading edge of the fog made visibility poor and it was a long shot for a pistol, but Jeremy took careful aim. Just then, Elizabeth fired from the other side of the trees, and the man tumbled over on the ground as the bullet struck him.

The stockmen stopped shooting, the fog blocking their view as it covered the clearing and thicket. Jeremy stood up and held his pistol ready, slowly stepping through the brush and into the trees. He could hear the men moving about, but the fog muffled noises and made them seem to come from all directions. The tree trunks were dark shadows through the murk as he stepped toward the horses, knowing the men would be going to them.

A man suddenly emerged from the fog, lifting a rifle, and Jeremy squeezed his trigger. Just as the man pitched back into the fog and fell, another man a few feet away fired. The pistol made a red glow in the fog, and the bullet droned past Jeremy's ear. Then the characteristic, shattering roar of Elizabeth's large caliber rifle rang out, and the second man uttered a cry of surprise and pain as he fell heavily to the ground.

Cocking his pistol again, Jeremy continued moving quietly toward the horses, then Elizabeth called out, "Where are you, Jeremy?"

"Here!" he replied.

Just as he answered, there was a thudding patter of hoofbeats as a horse raced away at a gallop. "Bloody hell and bedamned!" Elizabeth snarled in disgust. "One of the scurvy, misbegotten swine got away. I could have sent him to his just reward, but I thought it might be you, Jeremy."

He stepped toward the sound of her voice, the fog thinning out, and found her near the horses. "I believe we shot five altogether," he said.

"That's what I counted," she agreed. "We'd best let the others know that it's all over." She turned toward the clearing, shouting, "Harry!"

"Aye, Mistress Garrity?" a man called back.

"Come on, and let's get this tidied up here!"

The fog continued drifting away, leaving wisps of mist in the air as the others came into the thicket. It was a large group, some twenty stockmen and jackaroos having accompanied the wagons. Alexandra stepped rapidly through the trees, looking at Jeremy and then at Elizabeth, then relaxing visibly when she saw that they were unharmed. Five bodies were scattered through the trees, the stockmen and jackaroos peering at them.

"We should have sorted ourselves out faster, Mr. Jeremy," Isaac Logan grumbled remorsefully, others agreeing with him. "We were too slow by far and of no help whatsoever to you."

"Don't berate yourself, Isaac," Elizabeth told him. "Jeremy was out of the camp and at them while I was still wondering what was happening. He's as hard to take by surprise as old Pat Garrity was, and I didn't think I'd ever say that about anyone. Harry, you and another man load these carcasses on those horses there and go fling them into the river. Alexandra, I'd give you a flock to replace the one that scattered, but I don't have one within miles of here. It'll be quicker to mob yours together again."

Alexandra nodded in resignation, and everyone else began moving back toward the camp as the two stockmen led the horses toward the bodies. Jeremy stepped rapidly through the trees toward the clearing, wanting to put the stench of gunpowder smoke and the scene in the thicket completely behind him. His anger gone, the attackers were no longer enemies, but only pathetic creatures who had been doing the bidding of a remorselessly evil man.

After the wounded sheep that were scattered about had been put out of pain, Alexandra and the jackaroos who were attending to the spare horses remained at the camp, and everyone else saddled horses and rode out to search for the flock. It had spread in an ever-widening fan, the sheep running for miles. In his anxiety over the delay, Jeremy took no notice of how the search had been organized until the first sheep were being found. Then he realized that the employees from Tibooburra Station had automatically looked to him for instructions, and he had unthinkingly taken charge.

By the time the sheep had become exhausted and stopped running, the flock had spread out over miles. Elizabeth and her stockmen went in one direction, while Jeremy led the way in another and pointed out places to search. At the end of the day, over two thousand of the sheep had been found and driven back to the camp. Much of the conversation over dinner was about Jeremy's ability to find sheep, but he could think only of the fact that only ten more notches remained on his calendar stick.

With the search resuming at dawn the next morning, over three thousand more sheep were found by the afternoon, the remainder abandoned to become woolies. The horses were harnessed to the wagons and the flock was driven on to the south, covering several more miles before nightfall. The following morning, after they set out again, Jeremy sent a stockman riding ahead to inform the mine superintendent that the sheep and supplies were en route.

Two days later, the end of the journey came into view. While it was more than a welcome sight to Jeremy, the tall wooden fence appearing suddenly and stretching across the surrounding wilderness was also very incongruous, one of the most unusual spectacles he had ever seen. Alexandra remained behind with Elizabeth and her stockmen, who glowered with dissatisfaction, for they detested the mining operation. In contrast, the men just inside a gap they had opened in the fence whooped and danced about in unrestrained joy.

As he rode through the opening, Jeremy was greeted as a hero for bringing the foodstuffs, and the men raised a deafening cheer. One whose businesslike manner set him apart pushed through the crowd and introduced himself as Miles Brodie, the superintendent. A short distance from the fence, a sprawling industrial complex covered several acres. Back from an ore processing plant flanked by large barracks, warehouses, and other buildings, a low, notched mountain rose, deep gouges cut into its sides by steam shovels.

The sheep flowed through the opening, the men eagerly helping the stockmen guide them to a fenced pasture. The wagons followed the flock through the fence and crossed the complex to the warehouses, where other men began unloading them. Miles assigned foremen to count the sheep and inventory the supplies, then talked with Jeremy while they waited.

"This is a godsend, Mr. Kerrick," he said, "because I've been able to obtain only meager amounts of foodstuffs from the small stations south of here. I know there are mountains of supplies at Wayamba Station, but trouble is all that my predecessors and I have ever got from there."

"I won't listen to criticism of Wayamba Station or the Garrity family, Mr. Brodie," Jeremy told him firmly. "They were here first, and this mining operation intruded upon them. They don't like it any more than you would like for someone to graze sheep among your buildings here."

The man reluctantly agreed, then quickly changed the subject. A short time later, the foremen returned from counting the sheep and inventorying the supplies. The superintendent signed the list, and Jeremy rode back through the opening in the fence, the wagons and stockmen following him.

Alexandra had assembled a pack of supplies for his journey, and the stockmen loaded it onto a horse while he said goodbye to Elizabeth and her men. Then, after making his farewells with the employees from Tibooburra Station, he took the reins on his horses and led them as he and Alexandra stepped to one side to talk. With only eight days remaining, Jeremy expressed doubts about reaching Sydney before the mortgage fell due.

"In fact, it's less than eight days," he added. "On the last day, I must be there before three o'clock, when the bank closes for business. Even with no mishaps or delays at all, that's hardly enough time."

"If anyone on earth can do it, you will," Alexandra replied. "You'll save a few hours if you can take the train from Penrith, and it'll be safer. If that hireling who escaped reaches Sydney before you, Creevey will know he underestimated you. He'll send others to waylay you, and they'll probably wait for you on the road near the end of the journey."

"That's true," Jeremy agreed. "I'll try to reach Penrith at a time when I can take the train, but it doesn't operate often enough to make that very likely. I'll probably have to use the road, but I'll be watchful."

"There is an alternative to the road through Parramatta," Alexandra told him. "Just on the east side of the bridge across the Nepean River is a forest. A road leads from that forest to the south, down the Nepean. You could go that way and then take a connecting road east to Sydney."

"Yes, I know that forest well," Jeremy said, "but I didn't know a road was there. You've traveled on it, Grandmother?"

"Once, a very long time ago," she replied reflectively. "I'm sure it's still there, because things of that sort seem to endure forever. It would please me greatly to know it had been of useful service to the family."

The obscure remarks were personal musings rather than comments to him, and Jeremy disregarded them. The conversation continued, Jeremy acutely aware that each minute was precious, but he was reluctant to leave her and end their time together. In a profoundly meaningful way, his journey with her had been identical to the one with Jarboe Charlie. An odyssey within himself as well as across the land, it had been a keenly enjoyable process of enriching his life through ever deepening love for an older companion.

Alexandra ended the conversation, saying she had a request to make. "Will you bring word of the outcome to me at Tibooburra Station?" she asked. "Would you do that for me, Jeremy?"

"Yes, of course, Grandmother."

She smiled, thanking him warmly. Jeremy kissed her, then turned to his horses. He gathered the reins and the halter rope on his pack horse, stepping into his saddle. Alexandra and the others waved as they called out in farewell. Waving to them, Jeremy rode away at a fast canter.

The sky remained cloudy, but no rain came to hamper Jeremy during his ride back to the north. When he reached the barge, however, he found that the lack of rain had also been a disadvantage. The level of the river had fallen, and a third of the heavy barge was resting on the bank.

The barge lay between the shore and several half-submerged trees in the river. After attaching a rope to the stern, Jeremy undressed and swam out into the swift, icy water to loop the rope around a tree. He hastily dressed again, shivering with cold, then yoked the end of the rope to the saddles on his horses. Using a long pole as a lever, he prized at the bow of the barge while his horses pulled on the rope.

Precious hours fled as the horses strained at the rope and Jeremy threw his weight against the pole, shifting the huge vessel an inch at a time. When more of it was afloat, it gradually became easier to move, until finally the last three feet of the bow slid into the water. Jeremy led his horses onto the barge and tethered them, then he pushed the vessel away from the bank and jumped into the stern, setting the sweep in place.

He experienced less difficulty with eddies than before, encountering only one that almost spun the barge around and made the horses stamp nervously. Approaching the other bank, he looked for a place where the barge would catch and hold long enough for him to get to the bow and moor it before it slipped back out into the current. He chose a thick stand of partially submerged saplings and brush, and guided the barge toward it.

The bow of the barge ripped through the foliage, crushing it, and bumped into the bank. The horses staggered, the broken saplings holding the barge as Jeremy scrambled to the bow. Grabbing a rope, he leaped out and tied it to a tree just as the barge began slipping back into the water. He used a second rope to moor it securely, then he led the horses out of it.

Broken ground covered by tangled, scrubby growth stretched back from the river. Jeremy picked a path through it instead of going upstream, not wanting to meet people and be delayed by conversation. Presently, he came to a narrow road leading past scattered houses and small farms. He followed the road, working his way around the southern outskirts of Wilcannia, then turned onto the track a short distance east of the town.

When he came to the first large sheep station during late afternoon, his horses were exhausted. He was almost equally weary, but he declined the insistent offer of meals and a bed for the night, explaining that time was vital. At nightfall, he was back on the track with fresh horses, letting them pick their way through the darkness at a walking pace.

He slept for a few minutes at a time in the saddle, waking whenever one of the horses took a faltering step over a rock or rut in the thick darkness of the moonless night. Late in the night, he stopped to cook a quick meal and to let the horses graze for a short time. When he marked out another notch on his calendar stick, four were left.

Dawn brought another bleak, cloudy day to life. With the end of winter near, several days had passed since the last rain in the region, and the track was dry. Numb with fatigue, Jeremy kept the horses at a fast canter. When he turned in at another station at the end of the day to ask for fresh horses, he had covered well over a hundred miles since daybreak.

After riding through another night, Jeremy contemplated stopping at a station on down the track for a few hours' rest. However, he came upon a swagman who had been bitten by an adder, and taking the man to a station on the pack horse used up several hours. Later in the day, one of the horses threw a shoe. To avoid injuring the horse's hoof, Jeremy had to slow to a walk until he could obtain fresh horses from the next station.

The following afternoon, the horses splashed through Gundaroo Creek, where driftwood was lodged high in trees for over a mile around the stream. The small community east of the creek was busy with preparations for the spring arrival of the itinerant shearers who made the rounds of stations in the area. Near dusk, Jeremy turned in at Poller Station, where he and his grandmother had stopped for the night.

The owners were alarmed by his appearance, his eyes red and his face lined with fatigue. "You're whacked, Mr. Kerrick," Maynard Poller said, his wife agreeing emphatically. "You need to have some tucker, then sog in for the night. If you don't lie down, you're going to fall down."

"No, I can't stay," Jeremy replied. "I'm grateful for your kindness, but every hour is of the greatest importance to me. If you can let me have fresh horses, I must be on my way as soon as possible."

Maynard sighed in resignation and nodded reluctantly, and he went out to have fresh horses saddled. Sarah Poller quickly prepared soup and strong tea for Jeremy, asking how he and his grandmother had crossed Gundaroo Creek during the flood. As he briefly explained, the incident seemed a long time in the past to Jeremy. Shortly after he finished the soup and tea, the saddled horses were waiting outside. He thanked the couple for their help, then rode back toward the track in the gathering darkness.

Twice during the night, Jeremy woke in the saddle to find that the horses had stopped to graze, and he turned them down the track again. When daylight came, he increased the pace from a fast canter to a gallop on the smoother, level stretches of track. The horses were exhausted by midafternoon, and he stopped at a station for a hasty meal and fresh mounts. He returned to the track and slowed to a walk once again when darkness fell.

Hours before dawn on the last day, he arrived at the Bellwether Inn. After the sleepy stableboy helped him saddle horses from the stalls, Jeremy rode through the dark, quiet streets of Bathurst and then carefully picked his way through the junctions with other roads in the foothills, not trusting his sense of distance and direction in his daze of fatigue. Then stretches in the road became steeper as it climbed into the mountains.

The icy grip of winter was still harsh at the higher

altitude, and Jeremy's grinding weariness made the chill more intense as he huddled in his sheepskin coat. When dawn came, he had just reached the crest of the mountains. The horses began cantering, the hours seeming to fly like minutes as he started down the eastern slopes.

It was early in the forenoon when he was crossing the Emu Plains, with possibly enough time to reach Penrith before the midday train left. He rode at a steady gallop, weaving around slower traffic. The horses pounded across the Nepean River bridge, and he turned down the short road to Penrith. Then he slowed and sagged with disappointment when the train station came into view, and he saw there was no train at the platform.

Along with his regret over missing the train, apprehension swept aside the fatigue that made his thoughts sluggish. He knew that if it was as late as one o'clock, he would be unable to reach Sydney before three. As the panting, weary horses ambled on down the street to the Nepean Inn, Jeremy saw Buggie sitting on a bench in front of the stable.

Buggie leaped up, shouting exuberantly in greeting, then he sobered and shook his head sympathetically when he took in Jeremy's appearance. "Aye, that was a very toilsome journey, wasn't it?" he observed.

"I've had easier ones," Jeremy acknowledged wryly, dismounting. "How long ago did the train leave, Buggie?"

"There hasn't been a train here since day before yesterday," Buggie told him. "For some reason that no one can fathom, part of the track was pulled up at Parramatta, and it hasn't been repaired yet."

Jeremy knew the reason, thinking of his grandmother's warning. Creevey's hirelings had stopped the trains and would be waiting in ambush somewhere on the road to Sydney. "Do you know the time?" he asked.

"Aye, it's within a minute or two of noon," Buggie replied. "I've been going to the common room in the inn now and again to look at the clock, and it was a few minutes before twelve a bit ago. I'll take care of those supplies, and you can ride on, Jeremy. I brought some of our horses over from Sydney, and they're inside. Your gelding is among them."

Jeremy nodded in satisfaction. His gelding was a strong, fast horse. He led the horses into the stable, Buggie going in ahead of him to take the gelding out of its stall. After hastily transferring his saddle to his horse, Jeremy led it out of the stable and rode back down the street.

When he reached the main road, he crossed it to the thick forest beside the river, looking for the road his grandmother had told him about. As he guided his horse between the edge of the forest and a fence that enclosed a large, sloping pasture off to his left, he found the road. Barely more than a trail, it led past the forest and on down the river.

Just as he began riding down the road, Jeremy noticed a man some four hundred yards away, in the pasture. Curiously, he was sitting in brush beside a stand of trees and holding something to his face. Jeremy's angle of view changed as he moved on down the road, allowing him to see the man more clearly. Then he saw that the brush concealed the man from the main road, and he was watching the traffic on it through a nautical telescope.

A second man emerged from the trees, pointing toward Jeremy, and the one with the telescope swung it around. He leaped to his feet, looking more closely through the telescope, then both men darted into the trees. Jeremy lifted his reins, nudging his horse with his heels. As it began galloping, four riders burst out of the trees, racing toward the road.

The road weaved through trees, and Jeremy caught glimpses of the men. The pasture fence delayed them, two dismounting to knock down a section of it, and Jeremy was several hundred yards ahead by the time they were pounding down the road after him. They began closing the distance, however, because they beat their horses mercilessly to run faster.

When the distance narrowed to three hundred yards,

they fired pistols at Jeremy each time he came into view. The shots were wild, their aim poor on the running horses, and the bullets struck the ground and trees several yards from him. He knew that his gelding would eventually outrun their horses, but the men continued whipping the horses viciously, and the bullets gradually began hitting foliage that was closer to him.

He noticed that many shots were low, clipping bark from trees at the level of his saddle, then he realized that the men were deliberately trying to hit his horse. Raging anger exploded within him at their savage cruelty, and he decided to fight rather than attempting to outrun them. As he rounded a curve to a long, straight stretch, he nudged his horse with his heels. The gelding surged into a headlong run, its hoofs pounding furiously.

When he was some thirty yards from the next curve, the men charged around the curve behind him. Their pistols roared, bullets digging up spouts of dirt, shredding foliage, and hissing through the air all around Jeremy. His horse raced around the curve, the gunfire died away, and he pulled back on the reins. When the horse slid to a stop, he leaped down from the saddle and quickly tethered the horse to a sapling beside the road.

Taking out his pistol, Jeremy cocked it and stepped back to the curve. He paused at the point of the curve, out of the men's view, and listened to the hoofbeats. When they were about fifty yards away, he stepped on around the curve and lifted his pistol, aiming and firing.

The men, brutally thrashing their horses, were taken completely by surprise. Two of them managed to fire their pistols, and a bullet tugged at Jeremy's hat brim, but he ignored it as he continued firing. The second shot peeled a man from his saddle, and the impact of the third bullet stopped another man in mid-air as his horse ran on. The other two dived from their horses and took cover in the brush at the sides of the road.

The four horses ran past Jeremy as he returned to his horse. A short distance ahead, they slowed to a walk, panting breathlessly. As he passed them, he leaned down and gathered up their reins. A mile down the road, he came to a pasture where horses and cattle were grazing. He opened the gate and released the horses in the pasture, then rode on.

Narrow roads branched off at intervals, leading back from the river into pastures and farms. When he estimated that he was due west of Sydney, Jeremy came to a somewhat wider road and turned onto it. It led through Camden Park, where vineyards, orchards, crop fields, and thousands of acres in pasture stretched back from a huge, brick Georgian mansion.

The road joined a wide main road leading into the southwestern edge of Sydney. The traffic became thicker through the outskirts and into the center of the city, making the last miles seem very long to Jeremy. Seething with impatience, he weaved through the vehicles, his horse trotting for a few paces and then slowing to a walk once again in the congestion. At last, Kings Cross came into view ahead.

An apprentice was watching at a window, and his eyes became wide in excitement and delight when he saw Jeremy. The youth turned away from the window, shouting, and his reaction was shared by Morton and James Haslett as they met Jeremy at the door. Their voices ran together in a babble of words, asking if he had the receipt from the mine superintendent. Jeremy took it out and removed it from the oilskin, handing it to James.

The office staff gathered around, watching excitedly as James unfolded the receipt and examined it. Morton turned back to Jeremy, his jubilation fading. "That must have been a dreadful journey, son," he remarked in concern. "You look as though you haven't rested for days."

"The deeds to Tibooburra Station in my hand and a good night's sleep will put me right," Jeremy said. "What time is it?"

Morton took out his watch and opened it. "Just onto half past two, which is ample time but none to spare. Is the receipt in order, James?"

"Perfectly in order," James replied, pocketing it and

handing over a cheque. "That's the sum we agreed upon, and I trust you have the remainder at hand. I would enjoy seeing this transaction completed, so I'd like to accompany you to the Bank of Securities and Trust, if you don't mind."

Morton nodded, taking out another cheque and placing the two together with a smile of deep satisfaction. "I'm going to take the greatest pleasure in it myself, and you're more than welcome to come along. We'll walk, because it's only a few streets away, and the traffic is very heavy today."

The office staff helped the men on with their coats and handed them their hats and canes, then Jeremy followed them out. They walked down the street, Morton asking about his mother and then the journey, and Jeremy briefly related what had happened. James remarked that Creevey had spared no expense or effort in his scheme to seize Tibooburra Station.

"And yet he failed,", James added. "That will prove to everyone that he isn't invincible, and I'd like to see his face when he finds out."

"So would I, but we're not likely to," Morton remarked.

"Yes, that's true," James agreed. "He hasn't been to the Merchants Exchange or his other usual places for weeks, has he?"

"Where is he?" Jeremy asked.

Morton shrugged, shaking his head. "At his house, I presume, Jeremy. I understand he's still in the city, but I haven't seen him since shortly after you and Mother left on your journey." He pointed with his cane, laughing. "There's Nevin Moule, the bank manager, and I've seen him far more often than I care to. Now it appears he'd rather not see us."

James laughed heartily, agreeing, and Jeremy looked at the man Morton had pointed out. Bareheaded and without a greatcoat, he was standing at the entrance of a large bank building. He was evidently watching the street until time to close, much as the apprentice had watched the street, but for the opposite reason. A small, thin man, he had closely set eyes and sharply pointed features that were drawn into a scowl as he stepped back into the building.

A moment later, they reached the building, and Jeremy followed Morton and James inside. The first thing that Jeremy noticed was an unpleasant odor; then he was struck by the silence in the lofty counting room. While there were no customers, cashiers were at their barred windows at the rear of the room and other employees were at desks behind a counter at one side, but they were all very quiet as they moved about.

Morton and James froze, coming to a standstill so suddenly that Jeremy almost ran into them. Jeremy then saw Creevey, the man's huge bulk overflowing a chair across the room from the counter. He was the source of the odor and the reason for the tense quiet, as the employees tried to act as though they neither smelled nor noticed anything unusual.

The man appeared to have contracted a hideous, virulent disease. Swollen, crimson patches splotched his face, and some had erupted into raw sores. The face powder meant to conceal the open lesions had made them more repulsive, forming into scabs with the thick fluid oozing from them. He was wearing linen gloves, his hands evidently covered with the festering ulcers, because the linen was saturated with crusty yellow fluid. The pungent, fetid stench of putrefaction that wafted from him was nauseating.

He was motionless except for his eyes, which gleamed with savage hatred as he glared at Jeremy and the other two men. Morton and James were frozen in shock for a moment, gazing at Creevey, then Morton stepped toward the counter as he took out the cheques. He placed them on the counter, beckoning the bank manager. "Here you are, Moule. These cheques are to retire the mortgage on Tibooburra Station, in full and as due."

The man reluctantly stepped to the counter, scowling in discontent. He examined the cheques carefully, then turned to Creevey. "Everything seems to be in order, Mr. Creevey," he said apologetically.

The huge man made no reply, remaining completely motionless, but his tiny eyes burned in fury. A moment passed while Moule shuffled his feet uneasily and avoided Creevey's gaze. Then Morton rapped the counter impatiently. "Well, fetch out the mortgage and the deeds to the property, Moule!" he snapped. "I've more to do than stand about here!"

The bank manager stepped to the end of the room, going through a doorway into a private office, then he returned with a folder containing the deeds and mortgage papers. Morton took the papers and studied them, handing the deeds to Jeremy. Unfolding them, Jeremy examined them.

One was a large, old parchment document with official seals. It was a freehold land grant, and it had been signed by Governor Darling rather than by a land commissioner. The second was a deed of purchase for the tract west of the original boundary to the Darling River. Jeremy folded them and put them carefully into his pocket. Morton finished examining the mortgage papers and pocketed them, pushing the cheques toward Moule.

A loud crash behind Jeremy shook the room, and he spun around as Morton and the others turned to look. Creevey had toppled off his chair and was sprawled on his side, a huge, shapeless mass of flesh. Moule exclaimed in dismay, racing across the room toward Creevey. "Fetch a doctor!" he shouted to the employees. "A doctor! Quickly! Quickly!"

Two of the employees ran out, Moule wringing his hands anxiously and bending over Creevey, but Jeremy saw that it was pointless to bring a doctor. The man's eyes were open, but they showed a dull, lifeless glaze. Morton and James looked at Creevey in astonishment, exchanging quiet comments about the fact that the man had suddenly fallen over dead.

The putrid stench had become thick in the air, and Morton grimaced in disgust, motioning toward the door.

"We've seen to our business," he said. "Let's be on our way and leave this to Moule."

They left the building and went back up the street toward Kings Cross, discussing the strange event they had witnessed. Morton was less concerned about the reasons for it than he was with the results. "I don't rejoice over anyone's death," he mused, "but Sydney will be a far better place without him. Compared to him, a pestilence here would have been a benefit."

"Indeed it would have," James agreed. "Now we can go about our affairs without fear of some scheme he might be undertaking. It will be difficult for some to recover their losses, particularly you, Sir Morton."

"I'll recover them soon enough," Morton assured him. "The general business climate appears to be improving, so my prospects are favorable." He smiled, turning to Jeremy. "Benjamin and Beverly will be able to return to Sydney now. Just as soon as we get to my offices, I'll send you home in my carriage so you can rest. Then I'll write a letter to Benjamin and have it dispatched on the first vessel leaving for Auckland. He and Beverly should be here within the next few days."

Jeremy smiled happily, commenting that he would look forward to seeing his half-brother again. "I'm sure that not having to hide and be secretive any more will be a great relief to them," he added, "and they'll be able to get married now. Concerning Creevey, I wonder what sort of illness he had? I've never heard of any sort of disease like that."

"Neither have I," Morton replied, shrugging. "But rather than a disease, it could very well have been a long-standing morbid condition that finally ran its course. One doesn't have to be a physician to look at a man like that and know that he certainly isn't healthy."

Jeremy nodded in agreement, but the explanation seemed inadequate to him. He thought about the bone amulet, wondering if it could have possibly been responsible for Creevey's hideous condition and death. Even in the bright light of day, when the supernatural seemed most fanciful, he felt much less skeptical about it than before.

Chapter Twenty-Four

"Where will you go after you've been to Tibooburra Station?" Benjamin Tavish asked. "To hunt for more wild cattle?"

Jeremy shook his head, tugging on his saddle girth until it was snug. "No, before we came to Sydney, Fiona and I agreed to take a look at the western part of Queensland, so we'll go there. We've ample money for a time, so we've no need to hunt for dunnocks unless the notion strikes us."

"What I really want to know," Benjamin said, "is when you and Fiona might return for a visit. Beverly and I have barely become acquainted with you. We'd like to think that we could look forward to the opportunity of spending far more time with you and Fiona."

Jeremy hesitated, searching for words. The subject had come up in other conversations with Benjamin during the past days, and Jeremy had found it a difficult one to discuss with his half-brother in all of its ramifications. Benjamin regarded the outback as simply a place, and definitely not one that would suit him. He was unable to understand how anyone could be intensely drawn to it, viewing it as a way of life and a state of being.

"We can't promise when we'll be back," Jeremy told him, "but we will. When we do come back, we'll be able to spend more time together."

Benjamin nodded, dissatisfied with the answer, but accepting it. They were in the stables, where Jeremy was saddling his and Fiona's horses in preparation to leave. At the rear of the stables, Buggie was chatting with the groom and stableboy, while Fiona talked with Beverly, Catherine, and Eudora in the courtyard out in front of the stables.

During the past few days, Benjamin had seemed more truly an older brother to Jeremy than when he had been a boy, and he had become very fond of Benjamin and his beautiful wife. Sudden, immense wealth had been thrust upon them, because Beverly was Creevey's only heir. Their first priority had been to make restitution to those whom Creevey had harmed, and Benjamin was still unraveling the tangled skein of the man's affairs.

Benjamin brought up a subject that had given Jeremy sharply mixed feelings when he had returned from Broken Hill. "Well before the baby is due, you'll want to be at a town where there's a good doctor," he advised. "When our baby was born, Beverly and I had hardly any warning at all."

"Yes, Fiona and I have discussed that," Jeremy replied. "Naturally, I'm delighted about having a child, but there's always a danger to the mother. Fiona disregards that, but I can't. As a result, I'm more concerned about her safety and being near a doctor than she is."

"All women seem to be that way," Benjamin remarked, a note of wonder in his voice. "They have an extra measure of courage, and were it left up to men to give birth, there would be very few people in the world." He laughed, shaking his head. "Beverly has more courage than I do in other ways as well. In Auckland, when it came time for us to tell the minister our real names and ask him to marry us, I couldn't face him."

"Beverly had to do it?" Jeremy asked, laughing.

"In a manner of speaking, yes. She had a private talk with the minister's wife, who told her husband. He proved to be very understanding, and we had a quiet, quick wedding without having the banns posted."

They laughed again, Jeremy lifting Fiona's saddle onto her horse. Benjamin turned and looked outside as a carriage came up the drive into the courtyard. "Well, here's Sir Morton and Lady Kerrick to see you and Fiona off, Jeremy," he observed. "You know, no one suffered as much financial loss from Creevey's scheming as Sir Morton did, yet the man has refused to accept a farthing. I persisted in trying to persuade him until he became quite sharp with me on the subject, but it was to no avail."

"He's a proud man," Jeremy said. "Also, he has his own place in life, and he prefers to attend to his affairs himself and in his own way."

"That's true," Benjamin agreed. "You seem much like him in that respect. When you find your place in life, I daresay you'll be much the same."

Girthing the saddle on the horse, Jeremy smiled in reply. He had grown to have deep respect and affection for his father, and he liked to think that they had qualities in common. A hubbub of conversation rose outside as Morton and Julia stepped out of their carriage. A moment later, Morton left Julia talking with the other women and came into the stables.

He handed Jeremy an oilskin package, greeting him and Benjamin. "That's mail for Tibooburra Station," he explained. "A ship with mail from England docked last night. I had an apprentice pick up the mail for the station, because you'll get it there much more quickly than the postal office. One of the letters appears to be from the wool broker."

"Perhaps it's good news about a credit to the station account," Jeremy suggested, stepping to his horse to put the package in his dilly bag behind his saddle. "If so, it'll be more than a bit late for when Grandmother needed it most, but good news all the same."

Morton laughed and nodded in agreement. "Yes, and I believe that's what it is, Jeremy. All the news about business affairs in England is very good, so the wool market is probably opening up more now." He turned to Benjamin. "I talked with the man who bought that house on Grace Street from me, and he's willing to sell it. He'll want more than the amount he paid me for it, but he said that he'd sell it for the right price."

"Excellent!" Benjamin exclaimed in delight. "That's excellent, Sir Morton. Beverly and I want to live in that house so much. As I said, I didn't want to approach the man myself, because I don't know him, and I'm very grateful that you did. He won't change his mind, will he?"

Morton assured Benjamin that the man would sell the house, Jeremy listening to them as he put the package in his dilly bag. On several occasions, Jeremy had heard Benjamin and Beverly mention that they wanted that particular house, which seemed curious to him. It was adjacent to a house that they already owned, because Beverly had inherited it from Creevey.

Gathering up the reins on the horses, Jeremy beckoned Buggie and then led the horses outside, Morton and Benjamin walking out with him. "You won't get very far today, Jeremy," Morton commented. "It's well into the forenoon, and the days are still short."

"Yes, we're going only as far as Penrith today," Jeremy replied. "And we're in no particular hurry. After that journey to Broken Hill, I want to make a leisurely one that I can enjoy."

Morton laughed and nodded, then sobered. "Son, if I tried to thank you for what you did on that journey," he said, "I'd detain you for weeks and still not fully express my gratitude. I'll simply say that I'll be eternally grateful for what you did, as well as for the fact that I have a son like you. And please do come back and visit us when you can."

Jeremy was unable to think of an appropriate reply, so he merely nodded. That was adequate, because Morton smiled, his eyes bright with emotion. They joined the women in the courtyard, and a momentary silence fell. Then Jeremy and Fiona began making their farewells with everyone.

The city had become oppressive for Jeremy, fueling his restless yearning to return to the outback, and he knew that Fiona felt the same. However, leaving those he had come to love saddened him, and Fiona had tears in her eyes when he lifted her up to her saddle. He mounted himself then they exchanged waves with everyone as they rode out of the courtyard, Buggie following with the pack horse and spare horses.

Instead of going out Parramatta Road and through what amounted to an extension of the city, Jeremy chose the rural route his grandmother had told him about. The busy streets were quickly left behind, and small farms and pastures flanked the road leading away from the edge of the city.

Along with the city, the sadness of leave-taking was left behind, and for some reason, life seemed particularly enjoyable to Jeremy and filled with promise. The breeze was crisp, but the day was bright and sunny, with a feel of spring in the air. The people at the farms were tidying up from the winter rains and working on plows, and a few wildflowers were budding on the verges of the road. The sky teemed with flocks of parrots, pigeons, doves, and other birds that brought the day alive with their chatter.

There was little traffic, and when they turned onto the road through Camden Park, they were the only travelers. Fiona was curious about the fact that the route crossed the property instead of skirting around it, and Jeremy speculated that the owners had permitted a right of way to develop as a convenience to people in the area. "It's a huge estate," he pointed out. "A road around it would be miles longer than one across it."

Fiona nodded, the three of them exchanging a wave with a gardener who was repairing the trellises in the vineyards behind the mansion. Back from the vineyards and adjacent orchards, the road led past sheep pens and a fenced pasture where thoroughbred Merino sheep grazed, then rolling, grassy hills opened out. Scattered flocks of sheep were patches of white against the hazy green of new, early spring growth on the hills. The distant stockmen exchanged waves with Jeremy, Fiona, and Buggie.

At the boundary of Camden Park, buildings on adjacent properties were set far back on each side, and the grasslands changed to brushy, open forest. The river came into view, lined with tall trees, then the road joined the one leading north toward Penrith. At the pasture where Jeremy had left the four horses, he pointed them out. They were grazing peacefully among the cows and other horses, now without their saddles and bridles.

Jeremy talked with Fiona and Buggie in amusement about the undoubtedly surprised delight of the pasture owner upon coming into possession of four more horses, together with riding equipment. Then, a short distance up the road, the laughter faded. The day after returning to Sydney, Jeremy had reported the attack to the authorities, and constables had found two bodies in the brush beside the road. In his resentment over having been forced to kill, the curve in the road seemed haunted by death to Jeremy.

Fiona noticed spots of raw wood on trees where bullets had ripped away bark, and the evidence of facts that Jeremy had glossed over made her fall silent in dismay at the mortal peril he had undergone. However, with the particularly high spirits that had infused him ever since setting out on the journey, Jeremy shook off his gloomy feelings. Then he talked and joked with Fiona until she was cheerful once again, her beautiful face wreathed in the radiant smile that was such a source of joy in his life.

When they reached the end of the road, the sun was behind the Blue Mountains and birds were roosting for the night in the thick forest beside the river. They camped at the place where Jeremy had met Jarboe Charlie, kindling a fire in the same circle of stones. It blazed up brightly, driving back the gathering darkness and the chill of the early spring evening as they sat around it, the billys boiling and food cooking in pans.

Fiona stirred the pans, talking about the deep layer of old ashes in the circle of stones. "A great amount of firewood has been burned here at some time or other," she said. "Either your friend camped here for a very long time, Jeremy, or other people have camped here."

"Other people camped here," Jeremy told her. "Jarboe Charlie said that he found these stones in place here, and they had been here many years."

"Is this where you got that bottle you used as a water bottle?" Buggie asked. "The one that got broken?"

Jeremy nodded, pointing out the place beside the fire where Jarboe Charlie had dug the bottle out of the forest debris. The discussion turned to speculation about who might have camped there before, then to other things. Fiona dished up the food as they continued talking, and the delicious flavors of the succulent lamb chops, potatoes, and vegetables were enhanced by the slight taste of smoke from being cooked over an open fire.

When they lay down beside the fire in their blankets, Jeremy's happiness was so intense that it kept him awake for a time. His beloved Fiona was at his side, her head pillowed on his shoulder, and they would have a child before the next winter came. He looked forward with great anticipation to seeing his grandmother again and giving her the deeds to Tibooburra Station. In addition, he felt a supreme contentment he was unable to define, and he attributed it to the combination of all the other things.

Well before dawn the next morning, they made their way out of the forest in the darkness and rode across the Nepean River bridge. When daylight came, they were past the foothills and riding up the steep slopes into the mountains. The frigid cold of winter lingered at the heights, and they huddled in their sheepskin coats as they crossed the crest of the mountain range and started down the other side. At dusk, they camped beside the track west of Bathurst, on the threshold of the outback.

The following day, they were back in the land they loved, the immense sweep of the outback reaching to the horizon on every side. They stopped at the stations that had helped Jeremy and his grandmother, and spent the night when they arrived late in the day. For each one, Jeremy had bought presents consisting of cigars for the men, yards of muslin and lace for the women, and toys and sweets for the children. The people accepted the gifts with delight, protesting that they had expected nothing in return.

The weather was unsettled, with occasional cloudy and rainy days, but the drenching rains driven by bitterly cold winds had ended for another year. Spring was arriving in the outback. The sunny days brought out shoots of new growth on the broad expanses of savannah, and animals were more active. Emus scampered across the track ahead of the horses, the brush teemed with small animals. Red kangaroos, wallabies, and blue racers bounded about on the hills. The raucous cries of parrots, the insane laughter of kookaburras, and the calls of other birds made a constant background of noise. At Gundaroo, the first of the itinerant shearers had arrived.

During conversations at stations, Jeremy learned that the story of his and his grandmother's swift journey had joined the annals of the outback as related by swagmen, the facts greatly improved upon. He also heard that the Darling River was still flooded, and west of Gundaroo, he spoke with travelers who had recently left Wilcannia and who confirmed the flooding. None knew if the ferry was operating, which raised the prospect of a delay.

They arrived in Wilcannia during mid-afternoon on a crisp, sunny day, the breeze off the river stirring dust along the street. Riding down the street, Jeremy exchanged waves with people who had been among the crowd around the barge on the day he and his grandmother had crossed the river. When the waterfront came into view, he was relieved to see that the ferry cable was in place across the river, and the large, raft-like ferry was waiting at its slip downstream from the piers.

The ferry operator, a portly, amiable man in his fifties, had also been one of those in the crowd around the barge. He greeted Jeremy jovially and lifted his cap to Fiona, introducing himself as Jake Ruddell. After pocketing the fee that Jeremy handed over, he opened the gate at the end of the ferry for them to lead the horses aboard. "I knew you would make it across safe and sound in that barge, Mr. Kerrick," he said. "However, you'll find this trip a great deal less harriating."

"I'm sure I will," Jeremy agreed, laughing. "When I come back, I'll go see Mr. Spinney and thank him properly for the use of the barge."

"Aye, he'll enjoy talking with you again," Jake replied. "When the barge was found back on this side of the river, we all opined that you had been in too much of a hurry to tarry for a chin wag. It won't be long until the barge is up here at the piers again, and riverboats are blowing their horns every so often for me to lower my cable so they can pass."

Jeremy nodded. The river was still flooded, but its level was much lower than before. When the horses were tethered, Jake put a rudder in place at the end of the ferry and cast off. It moved away from the slip, the pressure of the current against its side and the rudder driving it along the cable, which rumbled through large rollers at the upstream side of the ferry.

Jake changed the angle of the rudder, adjusting the speed of the ferry, and commented in satisfaction on the high water level. "When it gets low during summer," he explained, "the current is so slow that it takes me much longer to get across. By then, though, it's low enough to cross on a horse, and few people use the ferry. My busy time is when the clip from Tibooburra Station is brought across and loaded onto a riverboat."

"It isn't as busy as when the clip from Wayamba station was also brought here, though, is it?" Jeremy remarked.

"No, it isn't," Jake replied. "The profits from this ferry aren't what they were, but the man who owns it also owns piers and boats. He makes ample money, even if he isn't overly generous with wages."

Jeremy smiled at Jake's tone of wry amusement as the man continued to talk about the river. He said that even when it was shallow during summer, it was the same color as at present, always so muddy that it was referred to as the only river in the world that flowed upside down.

The ferry approached the other bank, Jake slowing it with the rudder, and it eased up to its slip. He lifted the rudder out of its posts and carried it to the other end while Jeremy and the others led the horses off the ferry. They mounted and rode up the bank from the landing, exchanging waves with Jake as the ferry started back across the river.

At the top of the bank, they set out down the track leading to the west, and Fiona commented on the long distance to the main track into Tibooburra Station. Jeremy explained that the track had been made on the original land grant, then years later, the land west of the station to the Darling River had been purchased. "Wayamba Station did the same," he added. "In addition to providing more land to graze sheep, that eliminated the possibility that other stations might be established on the west side of the river and perhaps encroach upon Tibooburra and Wayamba Stations."

"I can understand how that would be a possibility," Fiona said. "This land that was purchased is large enough for several stations. I've always heard that these two stations are huge, but their actual size beggars description."

Jeremy agreed, pointing out that his trip across Wayamba Station with the sheep and wagons had taken several days. They continued talking as they rode on down the track away from the river. When it and the town fell over the horizon behind them, the surroundings again had the distinctive feel of the deep outback, of limitless lonely spaces on each side. The track unfolded ahead through the vast, unchanging landscape of brushy hills, grasslands, and scattered stands of eucalypts and other trees.

They camped at sunset in a grove of gaunt, shaggy gum trees and continued on down the track early the next morning. The sun rose, its luxuriously comfortable warmth dispelling the chill of the night and bringing another spring day alive with the bustle of animals and birds. When they reached the boxwood thicket at the base of Barren Mountain, they turned onto the track leading over the mountain and northward through Tibooburra Station.

At the crest of the mountain, they reined up, the immense sheep station reaching over the far horizon in three directions. In its enormous size, it had varying weather patterns scattered across it. Showers were falling on the distant northwestern paddocks, broken clouds cast moving shadows over the landscape in other parts, and the south and east sections basked in bright sunshine. Jeremy once again experienced a strange sensation similar to a sense of familiarity, and Fiona gasped in awe as she gazed around.

Buggie was equally impressed, his protruding eyes huge as he shook his head in admiration. "I've never seen sheep graze this good in any other part of the outback," he commented. "And it's sufficient for hundreds of thousands of sheep. This is more like a region than a sheep station."

"It is," Fiona agreed in wonder. "Now I fully realize what your grandmother had at risk, Jeremy, and I don't know how she endured the uncertainty."

"Yes, and she's still enduring that uncertainty," Jeremy observed. "When I last talked with her, she seemed confident that I would reach Sydney in time. I can't be sure, though, because it's difficult to tell what she's thinking. In any event, now she'll know the outcome."

Fiona smiled and nodded, lifting her reins, and they rode on across the mountain and down the broad track through the station. In readiness for shearing, flocks were closer to the track than when Jeremy had been to the station the first time. He occasionally glimpsed them in the far distance as the track followed the rolling contours of the terrain, leading over hills covered with thick mallee and mulga, then through broad valleys where the breeze made waves in the tall, lush spinifex.

The valley where Jeremy had met Isaac Logan came into view, and the stockman was there with another flock. Seeing them, Isaac left his jackaroo with the sheep and rode toward the track at a headlong run. He reined up, lifting his hat to Fiona and exchanging a nod with Buggie as Jeremy introduced them, then he quickly asked if Jeremy had reached Sydney in time.

The bearded stockman whooped exuberantly at the answer. "That's fair dinkum good news indeed, Mr. Jeremy," he said happily. "Mistress Kerrick was certain you would, and none of us doubted it. All the same, it's a great pleasure to hear you say it."

Jeremy nodded in understanding. "Yes, I'm sure it is. It's a matter of surpassing importance to everyone here, not only my grandmother."

"It's that, and more," Isaac assured him. "Many of us have spent most of our lives here, and we have a great fondness for Mistress Kerrick and the rest of the family. When anything untoward happens to the station or to the family, it's a calamity of the worst sort for all of us. With your permission, I'll send my jackaroo to let others in the nearby paddocks know."

"That's a very good idea, Isaac," Jeremy replied. "Will we reach the home paddock before nightfall?"

Isaac laughed heartily and shook his head as he began naming off the paddocks in the south-central section of the station. He told Jeremy that they were in Gidgee Paddock, with Boar Paddock, Bingara Paddock, and others to the north. "The last one before the home paddock," Isaac continued, "is Dingo Paddock. It was once called Bushranger Paddock, and I was there on the day many years ago when Mistress Kerrick renamed it. You'll know you're in Dingo Paddock when you pass a long valley that stretches off to the west of the track, with a knoll in the center of the valley. If you keep your horses moving smartly, you'll reach the home paddock by midday tomorrow."

"We'll be on our way, then," Jeremy said. "I'll look forward to talking with you again soon, Isaac."

The stockman echoed the remark, lifting his hat to Fiona, and rode back toward his flock as Jeremy and the others continued on down the track. Jeremy increased the pace to a fast canter, which interfered with conversation, and they rode in silence. His thoughts turning inward, he tried without success to analyze the unusual feeling that the station created within him.

It was simply there, similar to knowing the place, and defied more precise characterization. In addition, he found it difficult to examine any subtlety of feelings because of his keen anticipation of seeing his grandmother again and the intense, general sense of well-being that had possessed him ever since setting out on the journey. He tried to ignore the feeling, but it remained as a background to his thoughts.

The sky became cloudy, the showers to the northwest moving toward the track. By late afternoon, the breeze had freshened and had a damp feel, foretelling rain. When they stopped for the night, Jeremy and Buggie built a bark hut, and the first drops fell while they were eating dinner. It was a light, gentle rain, pattering softly on the hut.

When they lay down in their blankets, Buggie quickly fell asleep and Jeremy talked quietly with Fiona, trying to describe the peculiar impression that the station created on him. "It's probably because you heard talk about the station as a boy," she suggested. "Very dim memories from childhood can make things associated with those memories seem familiar."

Her explanation missed the point that the feeling was only similar to a sense of familiarity, but Jeremy knew that his description of it had been very confusing at best.

He acknowledged what Fiona had said, and she settled herself comfortably with her head on his shoulder to go to sleep. Moments later, her breathing was slow and regular, and Jeremy listened to the quiet rustle of the rain on the hut as he fell asleep.

During the dark, early hours of the morning, he woke from a dream that remained clear and fresh in his mind. His vague recollection of his dream on the first night he had slept on the station suddenly became a similarly sharp memory, because the dreams had been the same. Each had been a rapidly flowing series of vignettes of his life, images of events from his boyhood up to the present. The only difference between them was that the dream from which he had just awakened had included the most recent incidents.

Jeremy thought about the dreams, then dismissed them as the aimless wandering of his mind while he slept. A glow of intense pleasure swelled within him as he reflected on the fact that he would reach the home paddock and see his grandmother again that day, and it joined the deep contentment that he had experienced all during the journey. He lay and listened to the rain on the hut, waiting until time to get up.

When he judged that dawn was near, he sat up and stoked the fire under the overhang in front of the hut. As it blazed up, Fiona stirred, then Buggie stopped snoring with a snort and got up from his blanket. Fiona heated the leftovers for breakfast as Jeremy and Buggie put on their oilskins and went to saddle the horses. At dawn, Jeremy heard a noise in the tree above the hut. He looked up, seeing a red goshawk flying away.

The track was very wet when they set out, the horses splashing through puddles, but the rain had diminished to sprinkles. Some two hours later, Jeremy knew they were in Dingo Paddock when he saw the long valley that Isaac had described on the west side of the track. A steep hill rose from the valley, a sheep fold on it. At the side of the track overlooking the valley were fire-blackened stones set in circles where people had camped.

The rain turned into a misty drizzle and then stopped altogether, the sky remaining cloudy. Near midday, the trees and brush opened out at the foot of a long, gentle incline covered with spinifex. Jeremy looked ahead eagerly, having a strong, intuitive conviction that the home paddock was in the grasslands on the other side of the slope.

Another red goshawk, or perhaps even the same one, swooped overhead and flew low along the track ahead. It soared back up into the sky and turned westward, its wings a blur. A moment later, it was a speck against the clouds, then it disappeared. From behind, Buggie commented that the goshawk must have dived toward prey and missed. Jeremy nodded in agreement, even though he had seen no snake or other small animal on the track.

They rode up the slope, where the goshawk had skimmed the track. At the crest, they abruptly stopped when they saw the home paddock. Fiona and Buggie exclaimed in awe, but Jeremy was silent with shock. His mind reeled in a violent flux of emotion and sudden understanding.

The home paddock was as different from the others as was the station itself from other stations. The land fell away into a vast valley with a tree-lined creek at its center. The station house was on a hill in front of the creek, and at one side of the hill were the shearing shed and its pens, the warehouses, barracks, cookhouse, and other structures in the complex of station buildings. On the other side, gardens, fruit orchards, and cottages for married stockmen spread along the creek, with an Aborigine village farther down the stream.

The most arresting feature was the station house. Appearing suddenly in the deep outback, it was almost overwhelming in its visual impact. It was a three-story mansion of stone set in landscaped gardens, and aside from the entrance portico supported by columns, it was unadorned by architectural details. Its huge size and straight, simple lines gave it an aura of authority and power. Like a great, majestic stone keep on the hill, the house dominated the surrounding miles of landscape.

Gazing at the home paddock, Jeremy relived the dream that had pervaded his sleep at the station. It was as though each event of his life had led him inevitably to this place at this moment. The sense of well-being he had felt during the journey had arisen from deep within, because at some remote level, he had known all along where he was going. His feeling of familiarity was in fact one of homecoming. This was his heritage. Here was the place where he belonged. His walkabout had ended.

"It's magnificent, Jeremy," Fiona said reverently. "It's so different from other home paddocks, with their bungalows and sheds standing about here and there. But more than its appearance, it's so..." Her voice faded as words failed her, and she sighed in awe. "Coming upon it so far out here in the outback, it's so wonderful. Let's stay here for a time, Jeremy."

Jeremy was silent for a moment, struggling to adjust to the turmoil of wonder and joy gripping him, then he turned to Fiona. "No, let's stay here forever, love. Let's spend the rest of our lives here."

"This is the place you've searched for?" Fiona cried in delight. "It was Tibooburra Station all along, but you didn't know it?"

Jeremy shrugged, gazing at the house again. "In a way, I suppose I knew it, but didn't fully realize it," he replied. "I think my grandmother knew, and that's why she wanted me to come here."

"Well, whether or not you knew it," Buggie put in jovially, "I'm more than pleased. I'm ready to prop up my feet and rest these old bones, and this is more grand than any place I've ever seen."

"You'll always have a home here, Buggie," Jeremy assured him. "You'll have a home where you can do whatever you wish."

His bulging eyes glowing with happiness, the old man grinned and nodded. Jeremy and Fiona exchanged a joyful smile, then they rode on down the track. Someone at the home paddock noticed them and began ringing the station bell, announcing the arrival of travelers.

As the clear, melodious notes of the bell carried across the distance, natural forces seemed to combine in a display of splendor to make the moment more memorable. A rift opened in the clouds and a vast, shimmering rainbow appeared across the valley, tinting the shafts of sunlight with rich, vibrant iridescence. Like sunbeams through stained glass, they gave the valley the aspect of an immense cathedral, the house its altar.

A woman stepped out of the house, and Jeremy immediately recognized his grandmother from far away as she came down the walk through the lawn to the brow of the hill. Alexandra waved, and Jeremy and Fiona waved in response, their horses cantering down the track. Then Jeremy noticed thick smoke billowing up from among the huts in the Aborigine village.

A moment later, over the hoofbeats of the horses, Jeremy heard the deep rising and falling notes of didgeridoos, the clatter of rhythm sticks, and voices harmonizing in a chant at the village. It was against all reason and logic, but somehow he knew that the Aborigines had been watching and waiting. The moment they had anticipated had come, and they had begun their corroboree to mark the arrival of the new owners of Tibooburra Station.

Evelyn Rogers
Dark of the Moon

Somewhere in the lush grasslands of the Texas hill country, three brothers and a sister fight to hold their family together, struggle to keep their ranch solvent, while they await the return of the one person who can shed light on the secrets of the past.

Matt acknowledges a reality lovely widow Juliana Rains refuses to admit: Some drives are too fierce, too powerful, to deny. Like Matt's need to prove himself to his father and brothers. Like his burning desire for revenge against the low-down snake who is trying to destroy his family. Like his love for the genteel widow whose sweet lips and delicious curves make him uncontrollable.

RENEGADE MOON
ELAINE BARBIERI

Somewhere in the lush grasslands of the Texas hill country, three brothers and a sister fight to hold their family together, struggle to keep their ranch solvent, while they await the return of the one person who can shed light on the secrets of the past.

No sooner has he rescued spitfire Glory Townsend from deadly quicksand than Quince finds himself trapped in a quagmire of emotions far more difficult to escape. Every time he looks into her flashing green eyes he feels himself sinking deeper. Maybe it is time to stop struggling and admit that only her love can save him.

The Cowboys DREW

LEIGH GREENWOOD

The freedom of the range, the bawling of the longhorns, the lonesome night watch beneath a vast, starry sky—they get into a woman's blood until she knows there is nothing better than the life of a cowgirl . . . except the love of a good man.

As the main attraction for the Wild West show, sharpshooter Drew Townsend has faced her share of audiences. Yet when Cole Benton steps into the ring and challenges her to a shooting contest, she feels as weak-kneed as a newborn calf. It can't be stage fright—she'll hit every target with deadly accuracy—can it be love? Despite her wild attraction to the mysteriously handsome Texan, Drew refuses to believe in romance and all its trappings. But when the cowboy wraps his strong arms around her, she knows that she has truly hit her target—and won herself true love.

___4714-4 $5.99 US/$6.99 CAN

Dorchester Publishing Co., Inc.
P.O. Box 6640
Wayne, PA 19087-8640

Please add $1.75 for shipping and handling for the first book and $.50 for each book thereafter. NY, NYC, and PA residents, please add appropriate sales tax. No cash, stamps, or C.O.D.s. All orders shipped within 6 weeks via postal service book rate.
Canadian orders require $2.00 extra postage and must be paid in U.S. dollars through a U.S. banking facility.

Name_____
Address_____
City_____ State _____ Zip _____
I have enclosed $ _____ in payment for the checked book(s).
Payment <u>must</u> accompany all orders. ☐ Please send a free catalog.

ATTENTION
— BOOK LOVERS! —